MINDSCA

(2nd Edition)
by Jasper T. Scott

http://www.JasperTscott.com
@JasperTscott

Cover design by Tom Edwards
(http://tomedwardsdmuga.blogspot.co.uk)

OTHER BOOKS BY JASPER T. SCOTT:

New Frontiers Series

Excelsior (Book 1)

Mindscape (Book 2)

Exodus (Book 3) Coming February 2017!

Dark Space Series

Dark Space

Dark Space 2: The Invisible War

Dark Space 3: Origin

Dark Space 4: Revenge

Dark Space 5: Avilon

Dark Space 6: Armageddon

Early Work

Escape

Mrythdom (Revised Edition Coming October 2016)

TABLE OF CONTENTS

ACKNOWLEDGEMENTS

I owe a great big thank you to my wife for her support. Without her there to weather a perfect storm of domestic crises, I would never get anything done! Stay-at-home parent is one of the toughest jobs there is.

Next up, I'd like to thank my editing team. My professional editor, Aaron Sikes, and my two volunteer editors, David Cantrell and William Schmidt, were invaluable to perfecting this manuscript. You three made a half-decent book great.

I also owe a big, big thank you to all of my beta readers. These are the brave souls who volunteered to read an early draft of the book. They waded with me through typos, info dumps, logical inconsistencies, boring scenes, flat characters, and a host of other literary obstacles on our way to the finished manuscript. Thank you, Allan Clark, Bill Gassoway, Carmen Romano, Charlene Carney, Daniel Eloff, Dave Topan, David Smith, Davis Shellabarger, Duncan Mcleod, Emmett Young, Gary Matthews, Gaylon Overton, George Dixon, Gerald Geddings, Gregg Cordell, Gregor Hinckley, Ian F. Jedlica, Ian Seccombe, Jay Gehringer, Jeff Belshaw, Jeremy Gunkel, Jim Meinen, John H. Kuhl, John Parker, Larry Lemma, LeRoy Vermillion, Mary Kastle, Michael Madsen, Paul Birch, Raymond Burt, Susan Stearns, Steve Sharp, Susan Nelson, and Victor Biedrycki.

Finally, I'd like to thank everyone who helped me with my research into the impact event described in this book: Rudy Adkins, Tim Ross, Robert Weyer, Daniel Eloff, Gray Browne, Greg Kirkpatrick, Robert Weyer, Lyle Diediker, Joe Czolnik, Lloyd West, Henry Straley, Andrew Wilson, Cash Monet, John Treadwell, Jeff Morris, Dylan Dinh, and Henry Espinoza. It was great consulting with you all!

For the Muse.

DRAMATIS PERSONAE

The Crew of the *Adamantine*:

Bridge Crew (White Deck)

O-7 RDML - Admiral Alexander de Leon

O-5 CDR - Commander Viviana McAdams

-Ship's Executive Officer (XO)

O-5 CDR - Commander Eduardo Stone

-Starfighter and Drone Command/Head of Security

O-3 LT - Lieutenant Guillermo Cardinal

-Weapons Chief

O-3 LT - Lieutenant Luis Hayes

-Comms Officer/Senior Information Systems Technician

O-3 LT - Lieutenant Frost

-Sensor Operator

O-3 LT - Lieutenant Rodriguez

-Chief of Engineering

O-3 LT - Lieutenant Bishop

-Helmsman

Alliance Leaders

President Wallace

Joint Chiefs of Staff

Admiral Durand

-Chairman of the Joint Chiefs of Staff

Fleet Admiral Richard Anderson

-Chairman of Naval Operations

General Russo

-Commandant of the Marine Corps

General Eriksson

-Chief of Staff of the Air Force

Ministers/Cabinet Members
Donna Harris
-Secretary of Commerce
Jacob Jackson
-Secretary of Housing and Urban Development

Senators
Senator Catalina de Leon
Senator Harris

Solarian Republic Leaders
President Luther
Captain Vrokovich

Civilians and Other
Dorian de Leon A.K.A. Angel Hunter
-Director at Mindsoft
Phoenix Gray
-Owner of Mindsoft
Orochi Sakamoto
-Owner of Sakamoto Robotics
Benevolence (Ben)
-AI prototype from Mindsoft
Captain Grekov

A BRIEF SUMMARY OF EVENTS IN EXCELSIOR (BOOK 1)

Warning! If you have not read Excelsior *(Book 1 of this series), the following summary contains spoilers from that book. You can buy* Excelsior *on Amazon here: http://smarturl.it/excelsior*

30 Years Prior to the events in Mindscape…

It is the year 2790 AD, and Earth is in the throes of the Second Cold War. The world is divided between two governments—the First World Alliance in the West and the Confederacy in the East.

Medical advances allow us to engineer our children and even stop people from aging. These engineered, immortal offspring are called "geners" while those who were naturally born are called "de-gener-ates."

In the Confederacy everyone is a gener, and they're all engineered to make communism work, while in the Alliance only the children of the wealthy are born geners.

Alexander and Catalina de Leon were born in the Alliance state of Mexico. Soon after they get married, Alexander joins the Alliance space fleet to buy them immortality and citizenship in the utopian North.

After ten years of serving in the Navy, Alexander becomes Captain of the Lincoln, but instead of retiring from service, he is sent on a classified mission through a recently discovered wormhole to a habitable world, code-named Wonderland, and he will be forced to say goodbye to his wife for as much as another decade.

Just as the Lincoln is embarking on its voyage, the Confederacy sends a fleet to challenge the Alliance's claim to the wormhole. Conflict breaks out, and both the Confederate and Alliance fleets are decimated. Alexander and his crew barely make it through the battle and into the wormhole to start their long voyage to Wonderland.

Back on Earth we learn via Catalina that the conflict led to a brief nuclear war that wiped out the largest cities on both sides. Catalina ends up in a dangerous refugee camp and meets a man there, David Porras, who becomes her guardian inside the camp. Many months pass, and having heard nothing from Alex, Catalina fears he was killed in the fighting. Her grief brings her together with David and she falls pregnant.

Alexander and his crew reach Wonderland and begin exploring the planet. The air is breathable. The plants move. Dinosaur-like monsters roam the jungles. After just a few weeks, a group of dinosaurs destroy their camp and they're forced to leave Wonderland and return to Earth early.

On the way home, one of the *Lincoln's* crew turns out to be a spy reporting the results of the mission to the Confederacy.

Upon returning to the Earth side of the wormhole, Alexander discovers that both the Alliance and the Confederacy have been racing to put together colony fleets to go to Wonderland.

Meanwhile, Catalina has had her baby—Dorian Porras—and he is now six months old. The boy's father has revealed himself as an abusive alcoholic and an illegal immigrant in the North. Catalina leaves him, taking baby Dorian with her.

The Alliance and Confederacy race each other to the wormhole, but the Confederacy is faster and enters the wormhole first, only to be ripped apart by tidal forces.

Surviving Confederate ships turn around and surrender, but the Alliance fleet now guarding the entrance of the Wormhole fires on the surrendered ships, destroying them all.

Alexander is the only one who refuses the order to attack.

Alexander returns to Earth a hero for his honorable dissent. President Baker of the Alliance asks Alexander to help fix the mess by running a PR campaign to make the Alliance look better.

Then a news story breaks revealing that the mission to Wonderland was really intended to trick the Confederates into sacrificing a large part of their fleet in the wormhole, thereby tipping the balance of power in favor of the Alliance.

Following this shock, Alexander helps negotiate a peace treaty between the Alliance and rebel Confederate forces. Alexander and Catalina are reunited, whereupon he learns about David's abuse. Alexander is furious, and uses Navy resources to hunt down Catalina's ex and deliver him to Alliance authorities.

Over subsequent years increasing automation leads to record-high levels of unemployment, and the unemployed masses find virtual fulfillment in the *Mindscape,* a collection of immersive virtual worlds where people are able to indulge their every whim.

Now, the story continues in the *Mindscape…*

PROLOGUE

2819 A.D.

—Twenty-Five Years After The Last War—

U*topia. That's what people call it,* Dorian thought, shaking his head. They'd even gone so far as to name the world's most popular political party the Utopian Party. People were losing their jobs left and right to automation and artificial intelligence, but they couldn't be happier. They received a universal basic income, just enough to pay for necessities, and with the *Mindscape* to virtually satisfy their every whim, who needed more? It was ironic that after a hundred years of fighting communism, now it was a necessity for people to survive. Without the dole, billions of people would die of starvation.

Thinking about it that way, the world seemed more of a dystopia than anything, but everyone was more than content thanks to the Mindscape. No one needed to confront the sad reality of their lives. Virtual worlds are literally whatever people want them to be, so why live in a world you *can't* change? Supposedly, *mindscaping* made life perfect for everyone. But for Dorian, there was always a crack in the perfection—a noticeable seam.

His father. Not Alexander, but his *biological* father, Angel Porras,(A.K.A. David Porras). Dorian had searched high and low for him using both names, but without any luck. His parents refused to talk about it. They said his father was a bad man, and he'd probably gotten himself killed by now, but that just made Dorian even more curious.

It meant they were hiding something.

Dorian had spent a long time trying to figure out how he could get more out of them. Now, as a professional *mindscaper* and Senior Director at Mindsoft, he'd finally found a way. A virtual world that would pry the truth out of them without them even knowing it. Now, for Alexander's 55th birthday, Dorian had invited both of his parents to join him for a few hours in that mindscape.

"It's a surprise," Dorian said, answering the dubious look on Alexander's face.

"A nice surprise?" Dorian's mother asked.

"Of course. Don't worry, it's not full immersion, so you can wake yourself up whenever you like."

"All right," Alexander said and sat on his living room couch. Dorian's mother sat down beside him and they both reached for their neural hoods on the shelf beneath the coffee table. Those devices helped block out external stimuli for low-immersion worlds like this one. Dorian grabbed his own hood from the coffee table and sat down in the armchair beside his parents.

"Ready?" he asked with his hood poised over his head.

Alexander gave a thumbs-up as he slipped his hood on. Dorian's mother smiled and nodded before putting hers on, too.

"Happy Birthday, Alex," Dorian said as he followed suit and booted up the Mindscape.

The simulation was incredibly simple—they all started in their own empty box. For Dorian, that box was filled with both of his parents' fears, seen playing out on the walls. His parents, however, were stuck in boxes that showed them fond memories from their lives, playing out in short clips of blissful nostalgia—something basic to distract them while he went browsing through the horrors that haunted their souls.

In hindsight it should have been obvious to him. He knew how to find out the truth. Lies cause fear of discovery in the people who tell them, so browsing through his parents' fears was a sure-fire way to find the truth about his father.

Dorian walked past dozens of graphic scenes of violence, misery, suffering, death… all obviously fabricated by his parents' subconscious minds. Then he came to one scene that struck him as unique. It was on one of Alexander's walls. He saw a man he didn't recognize, lying in a casket with a face as cold and gray as a winter's sky. Alexander was peering into that casket with a grim expression. Dorian also saw himself standing in the background with eyes wide and his jaw agape. As Dorian focused on that scene, it swelled to fill the entire box, playing out on all of the walls simultaneously.

"You killed him," Dorian heard himself say.

Alexander turned and shook his head. "I didn't pull the trigger, and I didn't aim the gun."

"No, you just put him in front of it."

"He was an abusive alcoholic who beat your mother within an inch of her life. He would have beat you too if she hadn't left him."

"And that justifies killing him?"

"He was an illegal. The law conscripted him. All I had to do was find him and write his orders for duty. He was trained and armed, just like every other soldier on that battlefield. You can't blame me for this, Dorian."

"Except I do."

Dorian watched his stepfather's face collapse in dismay as the imaginary version of himself stormed off. He was so shocked that he woke himself up with a jolt and ripped off his hood. His chest rose and fell with deep, shuddering breaths. His parents were still locked in their virtual worlds, both of them smiling at whatever they were seeing.

Dorian scowled, tempted to rip Alexander's hood off and confront him right then and there, but he'd already heard Alexander's excuses. He stood up from his chair, quietly leaving the room and his family behind. By the time they grew tired of their trip down memory lane and decided to wake themselves up, he would be gone.

Dorian gave a sigh as he strode out of his parents' home and into the hazy orange light of the rising sun. He took a deep breath of the crisp spring air, and climbed into his company car.

"Where would you like to go, Mr. de Leon?" the car's driver program asked.

"Not de Leon," Dorian said, shaking his head. That surname didn't fit. It never had. He wasn't Alex's son.

"What would you like me to call you?" the program asked.

"Gray," he decided. He would take his fiancée's surname once they got married. His parents didn't even know he was engaged, let alone to whom, or where he actually lived. He'd been planning to tell them all of that eventually, but now… now he'd have to think about it.

"Where would you like to go, Mr. Gray?"

"Anywhere but here," he said, leaning his head back against the seat and allowing heavy eyelids to slide raspingly over his eyes.

"That is not a destination. Please specify an explicit destination or provide a list of criteria so that I may help you find one."

"Take me to The City of the Minds, Mindsoft Tower. It's time I got back to work."

"As you wish, Mr. Gray. Please buckle up."

PART ONE - ENEMY UNSEEN

"The unseen enemy is always the most fearsome."
—George R.R. Martin

CHAPTER 1

2824 A.D.

T*ime is an illusion.*

-Albert Einstein

Love is the only truth. Let mine be yours.

-Catalina

Alexander studied the engravings on his antique pocket watch as he rode the elevator down through Freedom Station to the space-facing docking arm. The watch had been a gift from his wife over forty years ago, just before he left on a mission to another world, *Wonderland.* The Alliance had fooled him and everyone else with that mission, using it to win The Last War, and just a few years later he'd ended up back on Earth with Catalina, retired from the Navy for good.

After more than ten years of service, seeing Catalina for only a month each year, he'd finally earned the right for the two of them to live out their immortal lives in the utopian north. It should have been happily-ever-after.

But life isn't a fairytale, is it? Alexander thought with a bitter smirk. He slipped the watch back into one of the outer pockets of his combat suit and climbed down the ladder through Freedom Station's airlock and into the airlock of the *N.W.A.S. Adamantine,* his new command.

New, *isn't the right word for this aging battleship,* he

thought, noting the discolored walls and flickering lights inside the airlock. The *Adamantine* was the last of its kind, a relic from a bygone era of war. With a unified government ruling over Earth, the only kind of war still being fought was against civil unrest and terrorism. Expensive war machines like this one couldn't join those battles, so they were left to rot in space, slowly falling apart from years of neglect.

Alexander continued from one ladder to another, passing through the *Adamantine's* airlock and into the elevator waiting on the other side. The airlock swished shut overhead, and Alexander selected the glowing white button marked *Bridge (65)* from the control panel. He braced himself as the elevator fell through the ship.

The only reason Earth still had a fleet at all was to guard against the Solarian Republic in case they tried something stupid. Mars, Titan, Europa, Ganymede, and a handful of smaller colonies had all watched the stupidity of The Last War, and they'd declared their independence soon after it had ended.

Alexander watched the lights of passing decks flicker through the transparent windows at the top of the elevator doors. This was all too familiar, he thought, looking around at the padded walls of the elevator. He spied the handrails for zero-G, exposed conduits here and there—because concealed ones were a pain in the ass to get at for repairs. Thirty years ago he'd wanted nothing better than to get the hell out of the Navy. And now, what felt like a lifetime later, he was right back where he'd started.

At least this time it was on his own terms—not that those terms were pleasant. After Dorian found out what had happened to his biological father, he'd disowned Alexander and Catalina for keeping the lie. They'd had a big fight. Catalina blamed him for his part in what had happened, and left him to go after Dorian.

Alexander would have gone chasing after them both, but every time he'd thought about it, something stopped him. Maybe it was the fact that after all he'd done, and after all he and Caty had been through together, she'd *left* him. He'd waited for her to return, or at least for her to call and apologize, but she never did.

The Mindscape had ruined them, just like it had ruined so many others. It was too addictive. Humanity had abandoned the real world for an endless variety of fake ones.

It starts slow. At first it's this thing you do as a couple, or as a family. You all participate in building a virtual life together in the same virtual world, but then pretty soon you find another one you like better, and each of you splits off into your own private world. Temptations abound, good and bad alike. For him and Caty it wasn't any one thing, but it didn't help that one day Alexander had gone into Caty's mindscape using an alias and an avatar she wouldn't recognize, thinking he'd surprise her, only to find her in bed with another man. Something like that happens in the real world and it's pretty clear cut, but when it happens in a virtual one…

Things get a whole lot muddier.

Most people had open relationships when it came to virtual dalliances, but he and Catalina had decided to hold themselves to a higher standard. Virtual cheating was still cheating. So what had happened?

They fought over the incident, and then made love in the real world for the first time in a long time. They agreed to make more time together, but that never happened. The Mindscape took every spare second of their lives.

In hindsight, Caty leaving him to go after their son wasn't all that strange. They'd stopped being husband and wife a long time ago.

The elevator stopped with a *screech* of brakes that set Alexander's teeth on edge. *This ship is falling apart,* he thought. The doors slid open and he stepped onto the bridge to see his crew all assembled and waiting.

"Admiral on deck!" someone called out, and a cheer rose from the crew, accompanied by hoots, whistles, and applause.

Frowning, Alexander shook his head. Not the salute he was expecting. "Settle down everyone. Save the fanfare for someone who deserves it."

One of the crew stepped forward, a familiar face—blond hair, blue eyes, perfect skin, ruby red lips. Viviana McAdams. Alexander smiled, feeling better already.

"If you don't deserve it, then who does, sir? You're Admiral Alexander de Leon, *The Lion of Liberty.* You negotiated world peace and won a Nobel prize, so yes, I think that deserves more than just a salute."

Alexander spied the silver oak-leaf insignia on her uniform. *She's a commander now.* "I thought you left the Navy?"

"Likewise, sir."

"All right, I'll go first. My wife and son left me. What's your excuse?"

The corners of McAdams mouth turned down. "Sorry to hear that, sir."

"I'm not looking for a pity party, just stating the facts."

"Well, I did leave the Navy, but I came back about two years ago. Turns out civilian life wasn't for me—Navy jobs are practically the only real ones left. And I'm not the only one who had trouble settling down. I managed to get most of the others transferred here, too."

"The others?"

McAdams nodded and half-turned to the rest of the crew.

"Lieutenant Commander Stone—" a particularly burly officer with a familiar lumpy face stepped forward and saluted. "—Lieutenant Cardinal—" The *Lincoln's* old weapons officer stepped out of line next. "—and Lieutenant Hayes." The comms officer.

Alexander felt a suspicious warmth leaking from the corner of one eye.

"Gettin' all misty-eyed on us, Admiral?" Stone quipped.

Alexander shook his head. "No, staring at your ugly mug again is making my eyes burn."

Stone snorted.

McAdams smiled. "Welcome home, Admiral."

Alexander nodded, realizing just how true that was. "Thank you—all of you," he said, his eyes skipping over the group. There were still a few faces he didn't recognize.

"Maybe you'd better finish the introductions, Commander."

"It would be my pleasure, sir."

* * *

Alexander sat in his acceleration couch staring at the stars. Each of them was another galaxy or solar system that humanity would probably never reach. What else was out there? People had been looking up at the stars and asking that question for as long as humans had walked the Earth, and now that they were flying through space, they were still no closer to answering it.

"Entering lunar orbit," Lieutenant Bishop reported from the helm.

Alexander nodded. "Keep me posted."

"Aye, sir."

Bishop was a gener, like McAdams. Over six feet tall with perfect brown skin, wavy black hair, straight white teeth, and piercing blue eyes. Physical perfection was just one of the hallmarks of his genetically-engineered heritage that set him apart from the natural-borns like Alexander. Of course, there were a lot more geners in the Navy these days, now that any real threat of war had vanished. Disillusionment was universal. Gener or not, plenty of people got tired of the Mindscape and went looking for real fulfillment. Sooner or later those people all signed up—that, or they became Humanists and joined the Human League, where bots, AI, and the Mindscape were all treated like the plague.

Joining the Navy was a far less extreme way to go.

Alexander watched a dark circle rise up under them and sweep away the stars. Then Lunar City appeared, creeping up from the horizon like a luminous spider crouching over the Moon.

"The dark side of the Moon is a lot brighter than I remember it," Alexander said.

"It's been thirty years since you last saw it, Admiral," McAdams said from the acceleration couch beside his. "You have some catching up to do."

"Admiral, I'm getting a clearer fix on that signal…" Hayes reported from the comms.

"Good. Any idea where it's coming from?"

"Still calculating, but I should have an answer for you in about a minute, sir."

Alexander nodded. This mission was the latest in a series of make work projects from fleet command—investigate a mystery signal that Lunar City had reported coming from somewhere out in deep space; help them triangulate it and decrypt it if possible. Alexander sighed. He supposed the fleet had to look busy if they wanted to hang on to what little funding they had left.

"Got it!"

"Give me coordinates."

"It's… that can't be right."

"Start talking, Hayes. Where is it?"

"It's coming from the Looking Glass."

"The wormhole? How can a wormhole produce a comm signal?"

"It looks like the signal is using an old Confederate encryption."

Alexander's eyes widened. "The Confederacy doesn't have a fleet anymore. It was disbanded in 2793. I should know, I helped negotiate the treaty."

"I'm not arguing with that, sir, just reporting the facts."

"Well, can we decrypt the signal?"

"Sure. Computers have come a long way in the last thirty years. Easy as cracking an egg."

"Then get cracking."

"Aye, sir."

Alexander nodded to McAdams. "What's your take on this?"

She turned to him, blue eyes wide and blinking. "Either someone's spoofing that signal, or some part of the Confederate fleet we sent down the gullet of the wormhole all those years ago actually made it to the other side."

Alexander shook his head. "Try again. We saw their ships get ripped apart with our own eyes. Besides—the wormhole isn't traversable. That's why we tricked the Reds into flying through it in the first place."

McAdams shrugged. "Then what's your theory?"

"Someone's spoofing the signal with a ship or comm

drone that they parked in the mouth of the wormhole."

"Got it!" Hayes announced. "It's audio-visual."

"On-screen, Lieutenant."

"Aye-aye."

"Time to meet our secret admirer," Lieutenant Stone said from his control station.

Alexander saw a snowy image appear. Front and center was a woman of Chinese descent, wearing a stained and torn Confederate uniform. In the background, he recognized the CIC of an ancient-looking warship. Flickering lights revealed floating debris, but for some reason the woman standing in front of the camera wasn't floating. *Magnetic boots,* Alexander decided. "If this is someone's idea of a joke..." he began.

Then he saw the woman's eyes. They were completely black, as if she didn't even have eyes—that, or her pupils had dilated to the size of overripe grapes. "What the hell?" Alexander shook his head.

"Hello wretched creatures. We invite you to look upon your legacy." The voice was deep and inflectionless, not a woman's voice at all.

The camera switched from the dilapidated CIC to a darkened space, crammed with floating debris. Alexander sat forward in his couch and peered at the main holo display, trying to decide what he was looking at. Lights flickered between the floating bits of debris as they shifted through the room. Based on the ceiling height and openness of the space, Alexander decided he was looking into some kind of hangar bay or cargo hold.

"Hayes, can you shine some light on the feed?"

"On it, sir. Here comes the sun..."

A second later the darkness peeled away and everything snapped into focus. A few of the crew gasped, and Alexander felt his gut churn.

The debris was bodies, hundreds of them, all floating in zero-G, limbs tangling, mops of hair drifting like seaweed. Fully half of the bodies were children, and all of them wore pressure suits emblazoned with a familiar hammer-and-sickle pattern of gold stars on a red background—the old Confederate emblem.

The scene lingered there a moment longer before cutting back to the woman with the black eyes. "Any race that can do this to its own kind will do worse to others. You have been judged and found guilty. Your sentence will be delivered soon."

The transmission faded to black, and Alexander scowled. "Hayes—analyze that recording."

"What am I looking for, sir?"

"'Scapers tags, signatures, anomalies—any sign that what we just saw is part of a mindscape, and if possible, some clue that might lead us to the 'scaper who built it."

"On it, sir."

"You don't believe it's real," McAdams said.

Alexander regarded her with eyebrows raised. "Do you?"

"I guess not, but if this was the work of some rogue 'scaper terrorist, why were there no demands?"

"What if someone from the Confederate colony fleet actually did make it?" Bishop suggested from the helm.

Alexander shook his head. "Even if that were possible, it would mean that that bit about passing judgment and delivering a sentence was just to make us wet our pants. There's nothing they can do to us from the other side of the wormhole."

"Her voice was off," McAdams said.

"And her eyes," Cardinal added from gunnery.

Alexander considered that. "Assuming I believe this signal is real—which I don't—those features could be explained by implants used to repair physical damage after traveling through high radiation and high gravity zones inside the wormhole."

"Her word choice was also wrong," Hayes added. "She called us *wretched creatures,* as if she didn't consider herself to be one of us. Then there's that part about how *a race that kills its own will do worse to others.* It's almost like she was trying to say that she isn't human."

"So what is she then?" Alexander asked. "An alien? She looked human enough."

"Maybe that's what it wanted us to think," Hayes said. "We still don't know who created the wormhole. We've known from the start that it can't be a natural phenomenon."

Alexander shook his head, incredulous. "Come on people—there's a rational explanation here, and we're going to find it. Remember Wonderland? Fool us once, shame on them. Fool us twice—I'll be damned if there's going to be a second time. Things aren't always what they appear to be. Someone, somewhere, wants us jumping at shadows. The question is who, and why. It's our job to find out. Hayes, pass that recording back to fleet command. Maybe they can make more out of it than we can."

"Aye-aye, sir."

Alexander frowned, and went back to studying the view from the *Adamantine's* bow cameras. Lunar City was now almost directly below them. Alexander absently watched the towering spires, all glittering with lights. He remembered when Lunar City had been nothing but an Alliance naval base. Now it was a bustling city with a population of more than two million.

The day side of the Moon appeared in the distance, a dazzling silver crescent rushing toward them like a tidal wave. *Beautiful...* Alexander saw a ring of stars wink at him.

"Admiral, we've got incoming! Looks like ordnance!" Lieutenant Frost reported from sensors.

Those aren't stars, Alexander realized with a jolt. A second later, the ship's combat computer highlighted those winking pinpricks of light with bright red target boxes.

"McAdams, sound general quarters! Frost, get me vectors!"

"Aye, sir."

The lights on the bridge dimmed to a bloody red, and the ship's battle siren screamed out a pair of warning cries before McAdams silenced it.

"Bishop, take evasive action! Ten *G*s to port."

"Wait—" McAdams said. "—the rest of the crew isn't strapped in yet!"

"Tell them to belt in at emergency anchor points! They've got thirty seconds. Bishop, set thrusters to fire in thirty-one."

"Aye, sir."

"Vectors calculated!"

"On screen," Alexander ordered.

Hair-thin red vector lines appeared between the incoming missiles and their target. Those lines all converged on…

Lunar City.

"They're not headed for us," McAdams whispered.

"One million klicks and closing… They're moving at relativistic speeds! Over one third the speed of light!" Frost reported.

"Cardinal, intercept those missiles now!" Alexander roared.

"Aye!"

"Hayes—warn Lunar City. They need to get their defenses tracking."

Alexander watched bright golden streams of hypervelocity rounds go streaking out from his ship along the paths of the incoming ordnance. Lasers snapped out in a flurry of dazzling electric-blue beams of light. Seven out of ten missiles winked off the display with pinpricks of fire. The remaining three sailed on.

"Too late!" McAdams screamed.

Lunar City became a bright smear of light that briefly illuminated the dark side of the Moon. When the light faded, Lunar City was gone, a funnel-shaped cloud of dust and debris jetting into space in its place.

Alexander gaped at the dust-shrouded crater where more than two million people used to live. He slammed his fists against his armrests.

"Bishop, get us away from the debris!"

"Aye, sir!"

"Incoming transmission—audio only," Hayes reported.

"Patch it through!"

The deep, toneless voice was the same as before. It said, "This is only the beginning."

Alexander turned to his XO. McAdams stared back at him with wide eyes and a furrowed brow.

"Hayes—trace that signal!" Alexander ordered.

"It came from the wormhole again, sir. Same source."

"You don't think *she* fired those missiles, do you?" McAdams asked.

Alexander shook his head. "I don't know who fired them, Commander, but whoever it was, they just declared war on Earth."

CHAPTER 2

2819 A.D.

—Five Years Earlier—

"I want to take our relationship to the next level," Skylar Phoenix said between bites of her steak.

Dorian de Leon, *A.K.A. Angel Hunter,* glanced up from his plate, his brows drawing together in wary confusion. *The next level?* he wondered.

"We already live together..." he said, as if that were the highest possible level any relationship could reach. *Surely she doesn't mean marriage.* His parents hadn't exactly set a stellar example of that. Then again, they'd been married in the *real* world, not a virtual one. Regardless, Dorian wasn't ready for either kind of marriage. He was only 25 and just recently earned his masters in synaptic processing.

"You look frightened."

Dorian shook his head as if to deny it.

"Clear skies, Angel. I don't mean marriage," she clarified.

Dorian blew out a breath. "You had me worried for a minute."

Skylar's luminous features lifted in a smile. Her skin was an attractive, opalescent white that sparkled wherever the light hit, her eyes like liquid amber and her hair a river of gold.

This particular mindscape, *Galaxy,* was one of the more popular ones. There were over a hundred million players—not counting the billions of procedurally-generated AI characters. In *Galaxy* you could choose to be any of more than a dozen humanoid and alien races in a galactic civilization set somewhere in the distant future. He and Skylar had both chosen to be Seraphs—beautiful, human-looking aliens with luminous skin and hair, and feathery white wings.

Dorian turned his head to the view. They sat on the balcony of a restaurant on Eyria, the Seraphs home world. There were no railings to interrupt the view from the balcony, nothing but clear blue skies draped high above the colorful fields of flowers and dense forests below. The ocean sparkled in the dying rays of Eyria's sun. Thin slivers of cloud drifted over the horizon in fiery reds and yellows, while stars pricked holes high in the evening sky as the sun sank below the horizon.

Dorian's momentary distraction ended, and he turned back to Skylar. Her steak lay forgotten and steaming on her heated plate, but her wine glass was conspicuously empty. She was still looking at him, her gaze exactly where he'd left it. While he'd been watching the view, she'd been watching him, waiting for him to ask the obvious question.

"Then what do you mean by taking our relationship to the next level?"

Skylar's smile broadened, and she nodded. "Let's meet."

"We're meeting now…"

"In the real world, Dorian."

"Don't you mean Angel?"

"Dorian is your real name, isn't it?"

"Yes…"

"Then I mean Dorian."

"Sky…" he began, shaking his head.

She reached for his hand again, and he stared absently at it. Five slender, sparkling fingers wrapped around his. "Before you say no, you need to hear my reasons."

"What reasons?" he blurted, looking up from their hands. "Do you know how many virtual relationships end when people try to carry them over into their real lives? I don't even know what you look like! You don't know what I look like either."

"Does it matter?"

"That depends on your expectations."

"I want you to know me. The real me. I don't want any secrets between us."

"The *real* you? What's real, anyway?" Dorian asked. He gestured to their surroundings, his wings flexing with agitation as he did so. "*This* is real. *You* are real. Reality is just a bundle of sensory data collected by our bodies and interpreted by our brains. What does it matter where and how that data is generated?"

"It wouldn't matter if we never had to wake up, but we do. The real world exists, and until we can spend every available second in the Mindscape, the real world will still be important. One measure of that importance can be determined by how much time we spend living in each reality. How many hours a day do you spend in *Galaxy* with me?"

"I don't know… four, maybe five, I guess."

"And in other mindscapes?"

"A few more hours. But in my defense, I don't have a job yet."

Skylar nodded. "Jobs are hard to come by. Do you know how many hours a day I spend in here?"

"Six?" he guessed.

"Twenty-two."

Dorian felt his eyes grow round. "That's impossible. It's also illegal."

Skylar smiled. "Are you planning to report me to the authorities?"

"You'd need life support to manage that."

Skylar nodded.

"And you want me to meet you? Your body must be a shriveled up husk!"

A muscle in Skylar's cheek twitched and she looked away. The stars were out in full now. So was Eyria's moon, a bright purple orb casting a pale lavender glow over the valley below. "Never mind. This was a bad idea." Skylar pushed out her chair and stood up. Her amber eyes were suddenly vacant, and her expression looked like it might have been chiseled from a rock. "Would you get the bill? I've lost my appetite."

Dorian gaped at her. "You're leaving?" Rather than reply, she turned and walked toward the edge of the balcony. "Hold on! Sky! I'm sorry!"

When she reached the edge, she paused to glance back his way. "If you change your mind, you can meet me tomorrow. I'll send the details to your comm band."

Skylar spread her wings in a flash of white feathers and then dove off the balcony, disappearing in an instant. Not sticking around to pay for their meal, Dorian pushed out from the table and ran after her. He reached the edge of the balcony and dove headfirst after her.

His stomach lurched. He felt weightless. A warm wind roared in his ears, ripping at his clothes and hair, and ruffling his feathers, threatening to open his wings. He stubbornly held them flat against his back so he would fall faster and catch up to Skylar.

It was at least a kilometer down to the field of flowering grasses below, once bright and variegated with color, now dim and monochromatic in the light of the moon and stars. Dorian searched desperately for a bright white speck—moonlight reflecting off her wings—but there were dozens of specks below him, some near, some far... Dorian focused on them one at a time to read their comm beacons and check their names, but none of the names that flashed up on his holo lenses read *Skylar Phoenix.*

Where did she go?

Confused, desperate, he looked up, and found a few pale gray specks, seraph wings shading themselves from the moon and stars. As he focused on the nearest one, Skylar's name appeared, taunting him in bright green letters. Dorian cursed his stupidity. Why had he assumed she'd continued down? She must have dived at an angle and then come back up.

Now spreading his own wings, he angled them to slow his descent and then flapped hard to gain altitude. The air felt like a physical wall pushing back, and the pressure of his considerable momentum threatened to snap his wings like twigs.

He gritted his teeth and strained against those forces. By the time he'd mostly arrested his momentum, he could no longer see Skylar. Activating his comms, he tried sending her a message. "Sky, where are you?"

No answer.

"Talk to me!"

But all he heard was the relentless buffeting of the wind. Clearly she wanted to be alone.

Dorian felt sick. Why was it so important to her that they meet in the real world? Especially considering what she'd said about spending just two hours a day in the real world. And why was he so averse to the idea? Dorian glided down as he thought about it. He was afraid that meeting her for real would change how he felt about her. It wouldn't actually matter what she looked like unless she wanted to spend time interacting with him in the real world, too, a conclusion which seemed inescapable at this point. Why else would she want to meet?

Dorian noticed the ground sweeping up fast below him. Goldwood Forest rose on the horizon, casting a dark shadow over it. Soon he was soaring low over the treetops. He banked eastward, back toward the jagged Dagger Mountains and the restaurant where he'd been dining with Skylar just a few minutes ago. As those jutting spires came into view, they peeled back the stars with a glittering wall of light—Pinnacle City. Seraphs lived almost exclusively in the mountains, suspending their dwellings from the cliffs and burrowing into them with elaborate cave systems. Dorian flapped hard to reach those heights once more, intent on returning to the restaurant, settling his bill, and going home for the night. He hoped he'd find Skylar there, but something told him she wouldn't head home for hours yet, and long before that he was due to wake up in the real world so he could go to sleep.

How had he not noticed that Skylar never took those breaks with him? If she spent twenty-two hours a day in the Mindscape, then that meant she slept there, too. How did she eat? Or even go to the bathroom? Two hours a day didn't seem like enough time to attend to her body's physical needs. He shuddered to think what kind of life support she must need to avoid those concerns.

Maybe that was why she wanted to meet him in the real world. To show him how she did it so he could join her. Then they could become shriveled up husks together.

Dorian grimaced at the thought. The whole setup turned his stomach, but if her reaction tonight was anything to go by, it would be the end of their relationship if he didn't agree to meet with her, and that made him feel equally sick.

Damned if I do, and damned if I don't, Dorian concluded as he soared up to the balcony he'd departed moments ago. Their waiter caught his eye and glared, as if to reprimand him for leaving before paying the bill.

All of twenty minutes later he was home, lying in bed with an ache in his chest and an empty pillow beside his. Real fatigue mingled with the simulated version, reminding him that he needed to go to bed in the real world.

As soon as he closed his eyes to sleep, he woke up lying in bed in his room, back in his parents' home. He felt momentarily disoriented, but that faded quickly enough. He was back on planet Earth—not that he'd ever really left.

Turning to his bedside table he reached for his comm band and found a message from Skylar already waiting for him. As he checked it, text appeared in the air above the device.

If you really do love me, meet me here *tomorrow at 2:00 PM. There's something I need to show you.*

The message contained a link to a location. Dorian touched the link and the message disappeared, replaced by a holographic map. The map panned over to an apartment complex in the City of the Minds, just a few hours from his parents' home in the suburbs. Getting there wouldn't be hard.

Dorian frowned, wondering what Skylar needed to *show* him. His mind ran through a list of dark possibilities.

Her profile in the Mindscape was *verified,* which meant that whatever she chose to reveal to people could be compared with verified facts about her in the real world. Her gender had been genetically verified, her sexual orientation corroborated by a brain scan, her legal status checked against real and virtual marriage records to prove that she was indeed single, and finally her chronological age had been genetically verified along with her gender—she was thirty-two, older than Dorian, but only by seven years—and what did age matter when people were immortal?

Dorian had also gone to the trouble to have his profile verified at a local clinic. In theory the system was supposed to put people at ease about engaging in virtual relationships, because it meant there wouldn't be any nasty surprises—or at least, not as many. Profiles were theoretically impossible to hack. Then again, it was supposed to be impossible to stay in the Mindscape for twenty-two hours a day, and Skylar had somehow found a way to do that.

So what did she need to show him? Was she a man? A minor? An old woman? The possibilities were unfortunately endless. His imagination going wild with such horrors, Dorian knew he had no choice. He *had* to meet Skylar, if only to put the most chilling possibilities to rest.

CHAPTER 3

2824 A.D.

—Present Day—

"Admiral de Leon, Admiral Anderson from Fleet Command is requesting to speak with you," Lieutenant Hayes announced from the comms.

"On screen, Lieutenant."

"Aye, sir."

A man with prickly, short blond hair and fierce, deep-set gray eyes appeared on the *Adamantine's* main holo display. Anderson's chronological age appeared to be frozen around forty-five, but Alexander knew that he was actually over a hundred years old. He dated back to before the Alliance had made it illegal to have natural-born children in the northern states.

"Sir," Alexander saluted.

"What the hell happened, Admiral Leon?" Anderson said after a slight delay.

"We've lost Lunar City, sir," Alexander said.

"I know that! The whole world knows!"

Alexander's brow furrowed. "That was fast. How did they—"

"A cruise liner on approach to Earth saw the whole thing. Not to mention everyone on Earth suddenly lost contact with their loved ones in Lunar City."

Alexander grimaced. "I accept full responsibility, sir."

"Never mind that. *How* did it happen?"

"We detected the incoming missiles at over a million klicks, moving at one third the speed of light. We had just a few seconds to intercept. It wasn't enough time."

Anderson's jaw dropped. "You're telling me we got hit by relativistic weapons?"

"Yes, sir."

"Any sign of what fired them?"

Alexander shook his head. "Whatever it was, it must have been very far from Earth when it dropped the ordnance. By now I'm sure they're long gone."

Missiles couldn't get up to those speeds by themselves. Large starships could, but only by spending long periods of time accelerating at a constant rate.

"Give me a ballpark," Anderson added.

Alexander's glanced down from the main holo display to the *Adamantine's* engineering station. "Rodriquez?" he asked her.

"A few seconds to calculate, sir."

Alexander nodded.

"Take your time," Anderson said after a slight transmission delay.

Rodriguez reported, "Assuming an initial velocity of zero, and a maximum of fifteen *G*s sustained acceleration, you'd have to travel almost 180 astronomical units just to accelerate a ship up to a third of the speed of light. Since we didn't see any ships crash into the Moon behind those missiles, and since no one reported detecting a ship headed for the moon at that kind of speed, we can assume they must have launched those missiles when they were still a long way off and difficult to spot on sensors. How far off is anyone's guess, but we know they must have traveled at least another 180 AU toward us while decelerating. Add to that whatever minimum distance they decided to keep from us to avoid detection—let's say 20 AU—and in total we're looking at over 360 AU."

Anderson slowly shook his head. "Give me a reference point for that, Lieutenant."

Rodriquez bobbed her head. "Yes, sir. You know one astronomical unit is the average distance from Earth to the Sun. Neptune orbits at about 30 AU from the sun, and the Kuiper Belt and the dwarf planets orbit as far out as 50 AU. The Heliopause, or the outer edge of the solar system, is over 100 AU away, so this ship had to have begun accelerating toward us from interstellar space."

"Then it's possible that we are actually looking at an alien attack—or an attack by some surviving remnant of the confederate fleet," Anderson said.

Alexander blinked. "Sir, with all due respect, I think we need to consider other more likely possibilities."

"Such as?"

"Such as someone sent a warship on a very long trip so that they could later turn around and shoot missiles at us at relativistic speeds."

Anderson's gray eyes narrowed thoughtfully. "Then why did it look like both the transmissions and the missiles came from the Looking Glass?"

"If I may—" Bishop began from the helm "—that's not so hard, sir. You'd have to make a near miss with the mouth of the wormhole, but assuming they accounted for that brief tug of gravity in their firing solution, there's no reason it couldn't work."

"That actually might be how we detected those missiles so far out in the first place," Frost added from sensors. "Dead-dropped, zero-thrust ordnance is impossible to detect at a million klicks, but our logs show those missiles were firing their thrusters over the last few seconds of their approach. They were making last minute course corrections, maybe to compensate for the wormhole throwing them off their target."

Anderson sighed. "At least we have our atmosphere to protect us from attacks like that on Earth."

"Actually, Admiral, at those speeds our atmosphere would not act as an effective shield—all it would do is help spread the damage," Bishop said from the helm. "The effect of a weapon like that hitting Earth would be much worse."

Anderson's eyes hardened. "If that's true, then why didn't they fire those missiles at Earth instead of the Moon?"

"I was just wondering the same thing myself, sir," Alexander added.

"It might be because the wormhole was not pointing in the right direction for an Earth attack," McAdams suggested.

Anderson considered that. "Then we'd better keep an eye on that wormhole."

Alexander glanced at his XO and frowned. "And what if the attack comes from somewhere else next time?"

"I don't think it will, but President Wallace has insisted that we spread out the First Fleet and most of the Second to guard us from all possible angles, while the rest of the Second Fleet will go to defend our remaining cities on the Moon."

Alexander nodded. "That seems wise, sir. I assume you'll want us to rejoin the First Fleet."

"No, actually, we're sending the *Adamantine* to guard the mouth of the wormhole—just in case the attacks really are coming from there."

"Admiral, the area around the Looking Glass is a demilitarized zone. If we send the *Adamantine* there, the

Solarians are not going to like it."

"Let the politicians worry about politics. If your orders change before you get there, we'll be sure to let you know."

"Yes, sir."

"On your way there, set scanners to detect anything along the trajectory those missiles came in on. If we're lucky, the ship that fired them is still decelerating somewhere along that vector."

Alexander considered that. "It depends how long ago the missiles were fired, but it's certainly possible, sir."

"Plot your course, Admiral, and get there with all possible speed. Fleet command out."

Alexander saluted as Anderson's face faded from the screen. "Bishop, you heard the admiral, set course."

"Aye, sir."

"McAdams, scramble the crew to their tanks, and prep the bridge for submersion. Everyone else, begin the switch over to virtual command."

"Aye aye," the crew said in unison.

The sound of safety harnesses unbuckling filled the air. Panels in the ceiling popped open and dozens of thick, mechanized cables came snaking down, trailing life support equipment and new crew harnesses. Each set of cables guided itself to a corresponding anchor point in the floor to form a cross-braced assembly above each of the crew stations. The straps of Alexander's new harness dangled down around his ears. He mentally disengaged the nutrient line and waste-handling tubes in his acceleration couch and then removed his helmet and clipped it to the back of his couch. After that, Alexander stood up and began fastening himself into his submersion harness. Peripherally he noticed McAdams doing the same. The rest of the crew joined them in quick succession.

"Ventilator and harness check!" McAdams ordered.

Affirmative replies chorused back from the crew.

Once the bridge was flooded, the entire room would function like one big *G*-tank, allowing them to endure extreme accelerations such as the sustained ten *Gs* they'd been ordered to set on their approach to the Looking Glass.

As soon as Alexander was done strapping in and connecting his new nutrient line and waste-handling tubes, he grabbed the much bulkier assembly of his liquid ventilator and inserted the tracheal tube. He gagged as the tube slid down his throat, and then he strapped on the attached mask. The mask sealed around his nose and lips with a squeal of escaping air, making sure that the perfluorocarbon from his ventilator wouldn't mix with the solution inside the bridge once liquid breathing initiated.

A green light appeared beside the ventilator, indicating it was functioning optimally, and Alexander mentally indicated his readiness to his new control station. The entire harness and cable assembly lifted him up until he was floating in midair above his control station.

The rest of the crew came springing up one after another like grasshoppers, while their old control stations and other sensitive equipment on the bridge slid away into recessed compartments in the walls and floor. Alexander glanced around the room, his breath fogging and reverberating inside his mask.

The other seven members of his bridge crew were all suspended in mid-air above the deck, trailing tubes and wires.

Alexander noticed a line of glowing green text appear before his eyes, conveyed directly from McAdams' mind to the heads-up display of his augmented reality lenses.

The bridge crew is strapped in and ready, sir.

Initiate submersion, Alexander thought back.

An Inertial Compensation Emulsion (ICE) came swirling into the room beneath their dangling feet. Overhead pipes opened up and streams of the emulsion gushed down. In the near zero-*G* environment the solution ricocheted and floated through the room in spinning droplets and globules that caught the light and sparkled like a galaxy full of stars dancing in a chaotic ballet. As the liquid crowded out the air, globules turned to cohesive pools of shimmering, distorted light. Finally, the lights began to dim and Alexander's ventilator started up with a rhythmic *whooshing* sound. A warm, oxygenated liquid filled his lungs, making them feel heavier than usual.

The lights went out altogether. Moments later they snapped on again, and he found himself sitting back in his acceleration couch at his control station as if he'd never unbuckled from it. The illusion was so perfect that the only way he could tell it wasn't real was by noting the faded watermark at the top of his field of view—

(C) 2824 Mindsoft.

"All stations report," Alexander said, his voice sounding normal to his ears even though he knew it was impossible for him to speak around his tracheal tube or to be heard through the thousands of cubic meters of liquid now flooding the bridge.

One after another the crew all checked in, their voices all sounding equally normal to his ears.

"Bridge submersion successful," McAdams announced. "All one hundred and twelve *G*-tanks report filled. All present and accounted for, sir."

Alexander nodded. "Good. Thank you, McAdams. Bishop, fire up the mains at ten *G*s."

"Aye, sir."

CHAPTER 4

2819 A.D.

—Five Years Earlier—

The car rolled to a stop, but the doors remained locked. "You have arrived at your destination," the car announced in a pleasant voice. "That will be $16.50."

Dorian passed his wrist over the car's scanner. The deduction flashed up on his augmented reality contacts (ARCs), and then the car doors unlocked. It would have been cheaper if he'd used one of his parents' cars, but then he would have had to explain where he was going.

"Thank you for choosing Green Valley Taxis. Have a nice day!"

Dorian stepped onto the curb. A cold, lonely wind whistled between the buildings, rolling an empty soda can down the sidewalk. He shivered and thrust his hands into his pockets. His taxi hovered up, pushing out a cushion of hot air before rumbling away.

A bird gave a piercing cry. Suddenly he doubted the wisdom of this trip. Maybe Skylar was a killer and she had lured him here as her next victim. Feeling watched, he looked around. The building where Skylar had asked to meet soared up over a hundred floors, casting a deep shadow over him. More skyscrapers ran the length of the street. Across the street from them was New Central Park. Stately trees stood watch over lush green grounds, their leaves turning colors in the fall—vibrant reds, yellows, and golds. Another wind whistled in, rustling leaves and jostling them from their branches in a steady rain.

Dorian spied a hot dog stand with a bot vendor. A handful of human pedestrians wearing old, mismatched and faded clothes walked down that side of the street, heads down, hands in their pockets, shoulders hunched. Some were out walking anemic-looking dogs. Others were no doubt taking a mandatory break from their virtual lives. It was a Saturday. The City of the Minds had a population of more than ten million, yet there were only a handful of pedestrians, and all of them looked like homeless bums. Dorian found that curious. Thanks to the dole there weren't any homeless anymore. Dolers were the closest thing, and all of them were clothed, fed, and housed by the government. But they were relegated to the outskirts of the city where the free housing projects were, and they rarely ventured downtown. So these pedestrians were the wealthy, duly employed denizens of the city. Either they didn't have the money to spend on appearances, or more likely, they didn't care what they looked like in the real world anymore.

Turning back to the fore, Dorian walked toward the apartment building where Skylar had asked to meet with him. *One71*, it was called. Dorian reached the doors and a bot doorman greeted him.

"How may I help you, Mr. de Leon?"

Being greeted by name threw him, but then Dorian remembered that his comm beacon was broadcasting it for anyone to read. "I'm here to see Skylar Phoenix."

"I'm sorry, no one lives here by that name. Perhaps you are looking for someone who is a guest in the building?"

"Yes," Dorian decided.

"Do you have an apartment number I could call?"

"76C." Dorian replied.

"One moment, please…"

Dorian tapped his foot while he waited, jittery from a combination of nerves and the cold.

"The owner has buzzed you in," the doorman announced. "I notice her first name is Phoenix, perhaps she is the one you are looking for?"

"So Skylar was an alias…" Dorian mumbled to himself.

"I'm sorry, I have no reference point for that question."

In her supposedly *verified* Mindscape profile her real name had matched her user name—Skylar Phoenix. She must have bribed someone to falsify it for her. The burning question was *why?* and what else about her profile couldn't he trust? Maybe he shouldn't go up.

"Sir? Would you like to enter the building now?"

Dorian nodded and the doors parted for him. He walked into a lavish lobby with high tray ceilings, massive crystal chandeliers, recessed lighting, shiny marble columns and floors… The sheer opulence of it made his head spin. He walked by a bot concierge that smiled and greeted him by name. Dorian continued on. If Skylar—Phoenix—whatever her real name was actually owned apartment 76C, then she had to be disgustingly wealthy. Dorian reached a bank of elevators with black mirrored doors. One of them opened automatically for him. Feeling eyes all over him, he hesitated before stepping inside. There was no control panel to select a floor. Instead the number 76 appeared on a display above the doors. The doorman must have already selected his floor for him. *Nice security system.*

It took all of a few seconds for the elevator to race up to the 76th floor, and Dorian's ears popped with the sudden change of air pressure.

The doors parted, and he walked out into a private foyer, a miniature of the one in the lobby below with a pair of illuminated frosted glass doors at the end. As he reached them, a pleasantly feminine bot voice asked him to state his name.

"Dorian de Leon."

There was a momentary delay, and then that voice returned. "Welcome, Dorian. I've been expecting you. Please come in."

Dorian's brow furrowed at the personalized greeting system. He started toward the doors, and they now parted for him automatically.

He gasped when he saw the apartment. The ceilings were fully two stories high with floor-to-ceiling, frameless windows running all the way around a large, open living area, giving a breathtaking view of New Central Park and the surrounding city. Thick, illuminated stone columns ran around the edges of the room. Dark hard wood floors polished to an immaculate luster contrasted with spotless white furniture and sparkling cream-colored rugs. The furniture looked like it had never been sat on, every chair, ottoman, lamp, and throw rug perfectly arranged. The kitchen looked equally disused.

"Hello?"

No answer.

Does anyone even live here? he wondered, glancing back the way he'd come in time to see the front doors slide shut behind him.

A soft, mechanical whirring drew his attention to one side of the open living space. It was a bot. A friendly housekeeper model with a holographic human face.

"Welcome, Mr. de Leon. My name is Matilda. My mistress is waiting for you in her room. Would you like me to accompany you there?"

Dorian nodded. Forcing some moisture into his mouth, he said, "Yes. Thank you."

"This way, please," Matilda said.

He followed the bot through the lavish apartment, still marveling at the views. They walked down a hall along the side of the building, more frosted glass doors to his left, floor-to-ceiling windows to his right. One of those doors lay open to a powder room that was big enough to fit a king-sized bed and still have room to walk—an excessive waste of space in a city where every square foot came at a premium.

They continued on, and Dorian's gaze was drawn out the windows, back to the view. There was so much light pouring into the apartment that it almost hurt his eyes. The vertiginous view reminded him of the cliff-side home he shared with Skylar in *Galaxy*. No wonder she'd chosen to be a seraph. She lived in the clouds in the real world, too.

At the end of the hall they came to another set of double doors, not as wide as the entrance, but still wide enough to be grand. The doors parted as they approached, revealing not another room, but a small foyer. Dorian followed the bot inside and the doors slid shut behind them. Here the windows were darkened by a decorative blackout shade, and the only light was from a dimly-lit crystal chandelier hanging overhead. Another set of glass doors faced them, more opaque than the last. After just a moment those doors slid open, too, revealing a darkened room with more shades blocking the light from the windows. Thin bars of light glowed on the floor between the shades.

Matilda walked inside, but Dorian lingered in the foyer, too afraid to move. A beguiling floral fragrance wafted out from the room. *A lure?* he wondered, his whole body felt tense and ready for a fight.

Matilda announced him to whoever was waiting inside.

"I'm glad you came," came the reply. It was the feminine bot voice that had first greeted him at the entrance of the apartment.

Dorian frowned. "Phoenix?" She couldn't be a robot. Of all the hideous possibilities he'd imagined, *that* wasn't one of them. It was absurd. He would have known by now if she were a non-player character (NPC). They'd spent too much time interacting virtually, and besides, bots couldn't own apartments.

"Don't be afraid," the voice said. "Please, come in."

The bot housekeeper turned to him with an encouraging smile and said, "This way, Dorian."

As if there were any other way left open to him. Would the various sets of doors between him and the exit even open if he tried to leave now?

Not ready to abandon the comparative brightness of the foyer yet, Dorian said, "Your name isn't Skylar."

"No, but it is Phoenix. I'm sorry for the deception, Dorian, but it was necessary. I'll explain everything in a moment."

A mechanical whirring came from within the room, heightening Dorian's sense of horror. She *was* a bot!

But the shadowy form that appeared before him wasn't

that of a traditional bot, or even a human. It was something else entirely. A squat, hulking shape, rolling toward him on *wheels.* As it drew near, Dorian's eyes picked out more detail. The hulking shape was a wheelchair with a human sitting in it, head slumped to one side.

Dorian frowned. "What's the point of getting me to meet you if you won't let me see you?"

The wheelchair stopped in front of him, but still far enough beyond the dim light of the foyer that he couldn't make out any features of the person sitting in it. That person could still be a man. A man with an artificial female voice for a cover.

Dorian shivered.

"I have the shades drawn to help lessen the shock for you, Dorian."

"I don't think that's working. You have to use a wheelchair because your muscles have all atrophied from spending so much time in the Mindscape," Dorian said.

"Yes, and no. My muscles have atrophied, but not because of the Mindscape. I have ALS."

"ALS?"

"Amyotrophic lateral sclerosis. Juvenile onset. It's a rare disease that attacks and destroys the motor neurons in the brain. It paralyzed me by the age of eight. My treatments have kept me alive, but so far none of them have been able to reverse the damage."

Some of the tension left Dorian's body as fear turned to empathy. "I'm sorry."

"Besides my name, everything else you know about me is true. I am 32 years old, and I *am* a woman, in case you were worried. Shades up—"

The shades in the room rolled slowly upward, letting in a blinding river of light and once again revealing a startling view of New Central Park. Dorian winced against the sudden glare and held a hand up to shield his eyes. At first the woman in the chair was just a dark silhouette, but then his eyes adjusted and her features came clear.

Phoenix was beautiful in the way that a statue or a painting was beautiful, and she looked startlingly like her character from *Galaxy*—golden hair, amber eyes, pale, flawless skin, and fine feminine features. Dorian felt a familiar thrill at the sight of her, but it was diminished by sorrow and pity for her condition.

He grimaced in dismay. "Surely there's something they can do for you."

"There is not." The voice came to his ears without the woman before him so much as twitching. Her thoughts translated directly to speech. "Believe me, I've tried. No amount of money in the world can fix me. At least not yet."

Dorian walked into the room, feeling drawn to Phoenix's side. Her eyes followed him as he approached. He reached her chair and got down on his haunches beside her. Reaching for her hand, he found it limp and lifeless.

"I cannot move, but I can still feel."

Dorian nodded. "Why didn't you tell me sooner? I wouldn't have been afraid to meet you if you had told me *this.*"

"I had hoped you would react this way," Phoenix said, her voice smiling for her. "I knew you were different."

"Now I understand why you spend all your time in the Mindscape. Where's your life support?" he asked, eyes flicking over her wheelchair. There was a blanket drawn across her lap, perhaps to hide feeding and waste removal tubes.

"It's all built into my chair. I've had it made to be as unobtrusive as possible."

Dorian nodded. "How did you bypass the wake-up

code?"

"My father did that."

"So he was a mindscaper."

"One of the first. He worked hard to build virtual worlds for me so that I could experience all of the things I never could in the real world. The money was always secondary to him."

"Was?"

"He died tragically a few years ago. I inherited his fortune and his empire."

"I'm sorry for your loss," Dorian said, wondering at her choice of the term *empire.* "Who was he?"

"Bryan Gray."

Dorian blinked. "Bryan Gray of *Mindsoft?* That Bryan Gray?"

"Yes. Now you know why I hid my real name. I'd attract too much of the wrong kind of attention if people knew I was Phoenix Gray, the trillionaire heiress and owner of more than half of the Mindscape."

"I had no idea," he said.

"I know. That was the point. I wanted to make sure you were interested in me for me, not for my power or fortune."

"So why tell me now? Why ask me to meet you?"

"You recently graduated with a masters in synaptic processing. You're looking to move to the city and get a job as a mindscaper." Dorian nodded and she went on. "I own the world's largest mindscaping company, and I have a vast apartment here, just a few blocks from Mindsoft Tower. More importantly, I love you, and I believe—now more than ever—that you love me, too. We live together in a virtual world, so why not in the real one, too?"

Dorian's brow furrowed as he considered that.

"You won't have to look after me. Matilda already sees to

all of my needs."

"Then what would be the point? I mean, what do you get out of it?"

"The pleasure of your company for the few hours a day that I am forced to spend in the real world. I had also hoped you would agree to become my representative at Mindsoft. The people I meet are mistrustful of my virtual presence drones. I've made them to look as human as possible, but that only seems to unsettle them more."

"You want me to interact with the real world for you."

"Wherever possible, yes. Using your InteliSense implant I'll share everything that you experience, and we'll maintain an internal dialogue."

"You're asking if you can take over my body?"

"No, you would need an illegal implant to accomplish that, and I would never ask you to relinquish control of your body to me. I know what it is to be a prisoner in one's own skin. Rather, I would be a fly on the proverbial wall, a passive recipient of the data stream generated by your senses, nothing more."

"I think I get it now."

"Over time, I want you to participate in running Mindsoft with me. You won't just be a conduit."

Dorian smiled. "You don't have to try so hard to convince me. I would have agreed to live with you even if you were poor and had nothing to offer but yourself."

"I'm afraid to believe that, but I am a pragmatic woman, Dorian. You can tell me the truth. I have things to offer that will make up for having to live with someone of my limitations."

"True love is limitless, Phoenix, and you aren't limited in the Mindscape. So we'll spend most of our time together there—isn't that what we do already? You might be crippled, but that doesn't change who you are inside. You're still the woman I love." Dorian eased up from his haunches to lean over Phoenix's chair. She watched him, her amber eyes flicking from side to side, studying him as he moved in slowly and kissed her on the lips.

Her lips were as lifeless as the rest of her, but Dorian could care less. He didn't shy away, but rather lingered, savoring the moment. He knew the passionate, lively woman trapped and raging just beneath her skin. Spending her life in a cage had only made her personality more vibrant. It was what had drawn him to her in the first place.

As he withdrew from that kiss, he saw a constellation of tears trembling on her eyelashes. She blinked and one of them fell down her cheek. He wiped it away with his thumb and smiled again.

"There is one other thing," she said softly. "You want to know what happened to your real father. I think I may be able to help you with that."

Dorian stepped back, his smile fading to a thoughtful frown. "Go on."

Phoenix explained her idea, and Dorian was surprised that it had never occurred to him to use a mindscape to pry the secret out of his parents minds.

"Find out what happened, Dorian. You deserve the truth."

He nodded. "Thank you, Phoenix." He leaned in for another kiss, a quick peck on the lips this time, and then retreated with a tight smile. "I'll be back to see you soon. After I tell my parents about my plans, we can set a date for the move."

"They may not understand. I suggest you be as vague as possible for now."

"Good point. Maybe I can move in next week?"

"Whenever you like. Until then, you know where to find me, Angel," she said, using his alias from *Galaxy*.

Dorian nodded. "I'll see you there tonight."

"I'll be waiting."

"I love you."

"And I you," Dorian replied.

CHAPTER 5

2824 A.D.

—Present Day—

"This is why we never should have cut funding to the fleet," Admiral Durand, Chairman of the Joint Chiefs of Staff said.

Sitting at the head of the table, President Wallace rubbed his eyes and squeezed the bridge of his nose between his thumb and forefinger. "We don't *have* funding for the fleet. It's not a question of what we should have done, but what we *could* have done, and the answer was the same then as it is now—if we don't watch our spending we won't be able to continue making payments on our debt, and the Solarians will come and collect."

"That's a moot point if they're the ones who attacked us," General Russo of the Marine Corps said.

Wallace shook his head. "I agree, but we've got nothing to tie them to the attack."

"Who else has the resources to do something like this? We know we didn't attack ourselves," General Eriksson replied. He was from the air force.

"Do we know that? What about the Humanists?" Durand asked.

Wallace nodded. "It's possible, but I don't know what they could stand to gain by destroying Lunar City."

"What if it really was aliens?" Anderson put in.

Eriksson stifled a laugh. "Admiral Anderson, I fear your association with that disgrace, Becker, may have colored your view. There are no aliens."

"Really. Over a hundred *billion* stars in the Milky Way and you're going to tell me that not one of them apart from ours spawned intelligent life?"

"If one of them did, then why haven't they made contact with us yet?"

"Maybe that's what we're looking at—first contact," Anderson countered.

Wallace raised his hands to forestall further conjecture. "Gentlemen, we *will* find out who did this, but right now we need to focus on how we can defend ourselves from another attack. If those missiles had hit Earth, you can multiply the casualties by a hundred."

"We're doing our best, sir," Fleet Admiral Anderson put in, "but we only have two fleets, and both of them are stretched thin as it is trying to cover all of our orbital space. To defend ourselves adequately, we'd need several rings of ships around Earth, all of them scanning for incoming ordnance 24/7. More eyes and more guns."

"That's the ideal solution," Wallace replied, nodding, "but we still need to get the funding for that from somewhere."

"Get rid of the dole and use the money to build a bigger fleet," Durand suggested.

"You know we can't do that," Wallace replied. "Most people live off the dole because they have no choice. They're unemployed because there aren't enough jobs, not because they don't want one."

Anderson snorted. "They're addicts of the Mindscape, sir, so at this point it's fair to assume both conditions are true."

"And a lot of those addicts are virtual producers in virtual economies. That means they're no different than people who worked in the entertainment industry in years gone by. Regardless, if we take away or even significantly reduce the dole, anyone who can't provide an income on their own will starve to death."

"All right, then conscript them," General Russo said. "At least we'll get something back for carrying them on our backs."

"That's not a bad idea, but it will never pass in the senate. We're a democracy, which means we need to make popular decisions, not expedient ones."

Durand sighed. "Then what are we discussing, Mr. President? Our hands are tied. Nothing has changed."

"Actually, that's not entirely true. I had a proposal from Sakamoto Robotics come across my desk a month or two ago. It was a suggestion for how we could automate the majority of existing crew positions in the fleet and then send those people back to re-train for command positions on new ships."

"You just said we can't afford to build a bigger fleet, so what would be the point of that?"

"We can't afford to build one ourselves, but we could

afford to *lease* one." Suddenly all eyes were on Wallace, waiting for him to continue. "The second part of Sakamoto's proposal was for us to sign lease-to-own agreements with them for new ships. They have a large stockpile of cash, and they would be willing to finance commissioning a new fleet."

"Won't that work out to the same thing as borrowing the money to buy the ships?"

"No, because Sakamoto has generously offered us a lease agreement with a zero interest payment plan over a generous hundred-year term."

General Hunter of the army leaned forward and folded his hands on the table to add his two cents. "What's in it for them?" he asked in a gravelly voice.

"New defense contracts in a world where defense budget spending has been diminishing steadily for decades. And since our birth rate is practically zero, the economy is stagnant, so they're not selling any more bots—just repairing old ones. That means they have a stockpile of cash and nothing to do with it."

"Must be nice," Anderson said.

"They could go spend it in mindscapes and give a boost to virtual economies," Hunter suggested.

"And make Mindsoft richer?" Wallace replied, smiling and shaking his head. "If Mr. Sakamoto wanted to build a virtual empire, he wouldn't have spent so much time and effort building a real one. He's a Humanist without the aversion to AI or automation."

"Hmmm," Hunter replied, scratching a light growth of dark stubble on his cheek. "We still need to get the money for those lease payments from somewhere. Zero interest doesn't mean zero cost."

"I agree, and I'm looking into ways to procure that funding from the existing budget, but we don't have a lot of leeway. Coincidentally, Mindsoft may have the answer to our budget problem. I actually have a meeting with them now, to discuss their proposal," Wallace said, checking the time on his comm band.

"You mean a way to reduce the dole?" General Eriksson asked.

"They implied that, yes."

Silence reigned as people traded dubious looks with one another.

Eriksson frowned. "I doubt they could have a solution for the dole when your administration and all the previous administrations combined haven't been able to come up with one."

"I'm skeptical, too," Wallace said, "but I'm going to hear them out. What do we have to lose?"

"Nothing I suppose," Fleet Admiral Anderson said.

Wallace nodded. "Chairman, do we have any further business to discuss?"

Chairman Durand looked around the table, waiting for someone else to speak. When no one else did, he said, "Meeting adjourned."

Wallace stood up from the table. "Gentlemen," he said, nodding. "Let's hope we've found our solution."

The joint chiefs of staff rose and saluted. Wallace hastily returned their salute and hurried out the door. He was eager to meet with the representative from Mindsoft. He needed a solution to present to the public, and fast, or he'd never get re-elected, and then he'd be unemployed just like everyone else.

* * *

President Wallace sat around a table in the presidential

palace with a group of his cabinet ministers and a few trusted Utopian Party senators, listening as majority shareholder Phoenix Gray's husband and legal representative, Dorian Gray, outlined Mindsoft's proposal. Mr. Gray stood in front of the assembled group, his dark hair cropped short, blue eyes bright and burning with enthusiasm. He wasn't good-looking enough to have been born a Gener, and there were plenty of rumors about his reasons for marrying the late Bryan Gray's only daughter and heir, but none of that did anything to take away from his authority as his wife's mouthpiece.

"Why is it so hard to make cutbacks in the dole?" Mr. Gray asked, spreading his hands to direct the question to his audience.

Secretary of commerce Donna Harris snorted. "I hope you're being rhetorical."

Gray favored her with a smile. "I am."

"Go on," President Wallace urged. He was just as skeptical as everyone else that Mindsoft had a real solution, but he hoped for everyone's sake that they did.

"With pleasure, Mr. President," Gray replied. "The reason it's so hard, if you'll all pardon my directness, is that unpopular decisions will not lead to re-election, and therefore, it is not in any of our senators' best interests to sign off on unpopular legislation. Not to mention that they represent the people, and people want the dole. We would have riots in the streets without it."

Wallace nodded and steepled his hands in front of his face. "You're correct so far."

"Well, what if I told you we could get people to voluntarily reduce the dole?"

Wallace arched an eyebrow at that. He noticed ministers and senators trading curious looks with one another.

Mr. Gray turned and gestured for the holoscreen behind him to come to life. An aerial image of a sprawling building complex appeared, surrounded by mountains and trees. Either that was for effect, or the complex was actually going to be built far from cities and existing infrastructure. Wallace frowned, wondering what he was looking at. The complex looked about the size of a small town, but all of the individual buildings were connected to each other with tubes that might have been walkways.

"Mindsoft is proud to present the world's very first automated habitat. It's a kind of arcology," Gray said. "With just over fifteen million square feet, there is room to house a million people in this habitat."

Wallace gaped at that number.

Jacob Jackson, the Secretary of Housing and Urban Development shook his head. "You're talking about fifteen square feet of living space per person. I've heard of tiny living, but that's not even enough room to lie down without bumping your head."

Gray turned to regard Jacob. "Oh, it is enough room to lie down—as long as you do so standing up."

"I'm not sure I understand..." Jacob replied.

Wallace was afraid that he did. "It won't work."

Gray favored him with a tight smile. "It *must* work, Mr. President, and it will. These facilities will have all the dolers living in life support tanks, spending all of their available time in the Mindscape. That's not a big difference from what they do right now. All we'll be doing is removing the need for tedious and unwelcome breaks from the Mindscape to eat, walk around, go to the bathroom, sleep, and so on. In our automated habitats all of those functions are performed automatically without residents even needing to wake up. In fact people will be able to get by on much less sleep than before. We're talking about full immersion, all day, every day."

Wallace shook his head. "No one would want to give up their freedom like that."

"No one is going to force them to stay in the tanks, Mr. President. They can wake up and get out whenever they want. In fact, there's nothing stopping people from taking just as many breaks as before. They won't have their government-issued apartments to walk around in, but they can always go outside and get some fresh air, or travel to the nearest city and sample some real-world entertainment."

Wallace heard his good friend, Senator Harris, speak next: "I don't see how this helps with dole spending."

"It's simple actually. Our government spends more money to provide free housing, health care, and utilities than it does on the dole, while actual dole money gets spent on food, clothing, and other basic necessities.

"In the tanks people won't get sick, and utility bills will be minimal. Moreover, clothes won't be necessary, and food will be incredibly cheap, so cheap that we could bundle that cost with an equally low tank rental fee and no one would be the wiser. By moving to the tanks people will be able to assume the costs of their own housing and still have plenty of money left over to buy virtual luxuries for themselves in their favorite mindscapes. Government housing will slowly vacate as people catch on, at which point it can be sold back to the private sector to generate income. And the best part is none of this needs to be approved by the senate. People are free to make their own choices about their accommodations, and the lure of extra money for virtual spending will convince most people. Our focus groups suggest as many as half of all dole recipients would happily make the move."

"Assuming you're right, why are you presenting this to us? If the idea doesn't require any legislation, then there's no reason not to go ahead with it right now."

"Well, Mr. President, there is actually one law that's stopping us, but nothing related to the dole. It's actually a law that limits the number of consecutive hours people can spend in virtual worlds. If you live in a life support tank, you'll obviously want to spend all of your time in the Mindscape."

Wallace considered that. He knew the law Gray was talking about. No one had really thought much of it at the time. A few people had starved to death while immersed in their mindscapes, so the law had seemed like a necessary measure to force mindscaping companies to automatically wake up their users if they stayed immersed for too long. But with automated habitats like the one Mindsoft was proposing, there would be no need for breaks, and forcing people to wake up multiple times a day only to realize that they're actually living inside a coffin-sized tank would take the appeal out of the system for most people.

"I'll see that the law is revised," Wallace said.

Mr. Gray smiled anew. "I'd hoped you would, Mr. President."

After the meeting was over, Senator Harris accompanied President Wallace on his way to deliver his address to the Alliance following the attack on the Moon.

As they walked, Harris said, "Human League Party Senators will never go for this. You'll have to explain the revision to them, and then they'll put up a fuss—they'll say we're taking one step closer to making our species obsolete."

"Human League senators are a minority," Wallace replied. "They don't have to go for it so long as we have all the Utopian Party senators on our side."

"The League could make our lives difficult in other ways. They could make the idea seem so dangerous and unattractive to the public that no one will be interested in living in tanks, even if the law is changed. We need to find a subtle way to make the necessary legal reform."

"That could take forever, and the result will be the same once the League figures out *why* we reformed the law. No, I'm going to use my address to the Alliance to publicly come out in favor of this idea and gain support for it before the Humanists have a chance to undermine it. When I present this as the solution to our budget crisis *and* a way for us to fund a more adequate defense fleet, people will be flocking to Mindsoft's habitats before they're even finished building them."

"That's another issue, sir. After the Moon attack, won't people be afraid to cluster together like that? A million people in one building is a hell of a tempting target."

"So is a city. Don't worry about popular support, Harris. I'll get it. All we have to worry about is how the Humanists are going to get revenge for us blindsiding them like this."

"Let's hope it's nothing too unpleasant."

Wallace slapped his friend on the back and smiled. "Cheer up. We're actually going to the people with solutions for a change. If the Human League is smart, they'll see that and they'll back us, too."

"*If* they're smart. I think that's asking a lot from a group of technophobic extremists."

They reached the balcony where Wallace was going to make his address to the public, and he turned to Harris. "Time to find out. Wish me luck."

"Good luck, Mr. President."

Wallace turned and walked up to the sliding glass doors leading out onto the balcony. The doors opened automatically for him, and he stepped up to the podium beyond. Applause thundered up from the parade grounds below. A large crowd had gathered there. Most of them were present only as holograms projected from hovering mobile virtual presence devices, but that was more than he could say for the turnout on most days.

As soon as the applause died down, Wallace began his speech. "Good evening, citizens of the Alliance. Today our way of life and freedom came under attack by a deliberate and pre-meditated act of destruction, the likes of which we have not seen since The Last War.

"The victims were innocent citizens like you, mothers and fathers, friends and neighbors, children and babies. Millions of lives came to a sudden and horrifying end that has filled us with terrible sadness and a solemn, simmering anger.

"This act of mass murder was no doubt intended to bring us to our knees, to paralyze us with fear, but it failed. Our Alliance is strong. Unfortunately, it was not strong enough to prevent this attack, and I fear we must all be ready to make some bold new changes if we are to face this threat and defeat it.

"The fleet has already moved into a defensive formation around Earth and the Moon, and we are hunting for our attackers. My advisers tell me that we need more ships to be completely sure that an attack of this magnitude could never reach Earth. Unfortunately, the problem is the same as it has always been: we can't afford the fleet we already have, let alone to build a bigger one. Yet I am here today to tell you that we can, and we will. We cannot sit idly by and allow our great Alliance to come crashing down. If the missiles that hit the Moon had hit Earth, tens or even hundreds of millions would have died. We cannot allow that to happen."

Wallace paused to let that sink in, and then he launched

into his sales pitch for Sakamoto's lease-to-own proposal for a new fleet. Once he was sure people were asking how the Alliance could afford to make payments, he introduced Mindsoft's automated habitat project. Wallace was careful to emphasize the positives and downplay the negatives, painting life in the *arcologies*—not tanks—as idealistically as possible. He wasn't a hundred percent sure how people were going to take it, but by the end of his speech, he was greeted with violent applause.

Wallace smiled. "Thank you. Good night. And long live the Alliance!"

CHAPTER 6

"We have reached the midway point to the Looking Glass, Admiral," Lieutenant Bishop announced from the helm. "Coming about for ten Gs deceleration."

"Carry on, Lieutenant. Still nothing on sensors?" Alexander asked.

"Not a blip," Lieutenant Frost replied.

"Hmmm..." The missiles looked like they'd come *through* the wormhole, so it was possible that it was actually between them and their attacker, blocking the enemy ship from view. To test his theory Alexander brought up a tactical map and checked the ship's logs for the trajectory of the missiles that had hit the Moon.

The trajectory showed them crossing beside the wormhole rather than through it. He'd expected that given the wormhole's orbital velocity and the amount of time that had passed since the attack, but it also meant that if there'd been something hiding behind the wormhole, it should be in plain sight by now—unless it was far away and they were limiting their emissions to stay hidden.

"The mouth of the wormhole only lined up with the Moon for a very brief window of time," McAdams said from beside him, her eyes on the map.

Alexander nodded. "Whoever was behind the attack, they

timed it perfectly to make sure we would think it came from the Looking Glass."

"Are you sure that it didn't?" McAdams replied.

"You heard what Bishop said. It would take 180 times the orbital distance from the Earth to the Sun just for a ship to reach a third of the speed of light, and we know from experience that nothing can travel that far into the wormhole without being ripped apart."

"Maybe there's a safe zone—some point where the tidal forces balance each other out and it's safe to traverse."

"I'm no physicist, but I'm pretty sure that's not how wormholes work."

"Well, I hope you're right and the attack didn't come from the Looking Glass."

"And why is that, Commander?"

"Because the mouth of the wormhole is pointed at Earth now."

Alexander checked his tactical map again. She was right. The Looking Glass was now aimed at Earth like the barrel of an interstellar cannon.

McAdams shook her head. "Bishop, I have a math problem for you."

"What's that, Commander?"

"Find out when a missile traveling at a third of the speed of light would hypothetically need to exit the mouth of the wormhole in order to hit Earth."

"Yes, ma'am. Give me a minute to run that through the computer."

"That's what targeting computers are for," Lieutenant Cardinal put in from gunnery. "I can calculate that faster."

"I don't care who does it, just get me the calculation," McAdams replied.

Alexander's brow furrowed. "You're really stuck on this theory that someone is attacking us from inside the wormhole."

"It doesn't matter. Our attackers are either actually using the wormhole to direct their shots, or they're pretending to. In either case the attacks will have to come from a specific direction at a specific point in time, which means we should be able to predict where and when another attack will come."

"Unless that's what they want us to think and they're hoping we'll be so fixated on the wormhole that we'll miss an attack from another angle."

"If I'm wrong, it will be easy to verify. Scanning for incoming ordnance along a known vector is a lot easier than scanning everywhere at once."

"True."

"Got it!" Cardinal said.

Bishop went straight to the point. "The missiles would have had to leave the mouth of the wormhole approximately five minutes ago."

"Four minutes and fifty nine point two three seconds ago," Cardinal added.

"So where would that put them now?" McAdams asked.

Alexander watched as a glowing red dot appeared on the tactical map along the trajectory he'd drawn between the wormhole and Earth. "Frost, get me eyes on that area of space. Account for targets moving at a velocity of point three C."

"Yes, sir… scanning."

Alexander turned to McAdams. "I hope you're wrong about this."

She met his gaze with unblinking blue eyes. "So do I, sir."

"Multiple pings!" Frost called out.

Alexander felt a sharp stab of adrenaline followed by a feeling of electricity sparking through his fingertips.

"They're moving fast! Thirty-two percent the speed of light," Frost added.

Alexander sat up straighter in his couch. "What are we looking at?"

"Twenty-one targets, closely staggered! Looks like more missiles, same as before."

"Hayes, get that target data to Fleet Command."

"Aye, sir. At this range it'll take eight minutes to reach them."

Alexander grimaced. Eight minutes before Earth could even react to the threat. "Cardinal, is there any way we can intercept those missiles?"

"Calculating, sir…"

Alexander was already checking their range to the targets to make some of his own calculations. They were over a hundred million kilometers away from the missiles. Since they weren't maneuvering, it should have been a simple matter to fire projectiles or other missiles in their path and take them out, but at the speed the enemy ordnance was moving, any weapon the *Adamantine* fired would take far too long to get there.

Meaning we're shit out of luck.

"We can't intercept them from here, sir," Cardinal reported, confirming Alexander's suspicions, "but at the nearest point between our approach vectors the enemy missiles will pass just inside of our theoretical maximum effective laser range. Our window of attack will be a fraction of a second, and we'll have to account for all kinds of sensor and firing latencies in order to hit something moving that fast, but it should be possible to intercept a few missiles if we concentrate our fire."

"Let's make that more than a few. Bishop, get us as close as you can at ten *G*s thrust. Let's give this our best shot."

"Aye, sir."

"Stone, launch drones and fighters and get them to intercept as well. We may as well throw everything we've got at this."

"Roger that, sir."

"Frost, how long do we have before Earth impact?"

"Forty three minutes and sixteen seconds, sir."

"Minus eight minutes before Earth even realizes they've got incoming," McAdams said.

Alexander turned to her. "That still gives them thirty five minutes to intercept. Thanks to you. That was a good call, Commander. If we're lucky, someone else was thinking the same way and the fleet is already on its way to intercept."

"I hope so, sir. It only takes one of those missiles hitting Earth and a lot of people are going to die."

Alexander nodded absently.

"Incoming message from fleet command!" Hayes announced.

"It's been eight minutes already?"

"No, sir. They had to have sent this message before we sent ours."

"Patch it through to the main display."

Fleet Admiral Anderson appeared larger than life on the main forward screen. "Admiral Leon," he said. "We've detected incoming ordnance moving at relativistic speeds. Same as what hit the Moon, but there's more than twenty this time. All available ships are moving to intercept. That means the *Adamantine,* too. I sent you the target data with this message. Find the best place to intercept, and shoot those missiles down. Anderson out."

"Do you want to send a reply, sir?" Hayes asked.

"Tell them we saw the missiles before their message reached us, and we're already on an intercept course."

"Aye, sir."

"Cardinal—how long before we reach firing range?"

"Seventeen minutes and eleven seconds, sir."

Alexander pressed his lips into a grim line. "Let's hope we can improve those odds for everyone back home."

"Aye, sir. Unfortunately we're not in the best position to intercept, but I'll do my best."

"What's the best position?" McAdams asked.

"Directly in front of the incoming ordnance," Cardinal replied. "The smaller the angle of deflection, the less the speed of the missiles will matter. Calculating an accurate deflection shot against targets moving a hundred thousand klicks per second is not an easy task. You just have to be off by a millionth of a degree or have an extra nanosecond of firing delay and you'll miss."

"Sir!" Frost interrupted from sensors.

"What is it, Lieutenant?"

"I'm getting a blip on our long-range scanners within a reasonable margin of the incoming missiles' trajectory. It's out over a billion klicks behind the wormhole. Dreadnought analog. The comm transponder identifies it as a Solarian ship—the *S.R.S Crimson Warrior.*"

Alexander blinked. "A *billion* kilometers? What's out there, Frost?"

"Nothing, sir. Empty space."

"Isn't Saturn about that distance from us?" McAdams asked. "The Solarians have a colony on Titan and water mining operations in Saturn's rings. They might have a reasonable explanation for being that far out."

"That's the right distance, but the wrong direction, Ma'am," Frost replied. "They're over three hundred million klicks from Saturn, and they don't appear to be headed for

Mars."

"Hayes, hail them," Alexander said. "Ask for their flight plan and an explanation of what they're doing out there."

"They're not in our territory, sir. They may feel we have no right to know their business."

"In light of the recent attacks, we have every right to know. Explain the situation as tactfully as you can, but make it clear that we need to know what they're doing if they don't want us to suspect them. Also, send Fleet Command an update with the location of the Solarian dreadnought. It's the only lead we have so far."

"Aye, sir."

Alexander saw McAdams shaking her head. "Something on your mind, Commander?"

"It doesn't make sense for the Solarians to attack us. They own almost half of Alliance debt. If those missiles hit Earth, they'll put us that much closer to defaulting on our loans."

"Maybe that's what they want," Alexander replied. "Then they'll have an excuse to come and collect."

"Assuming we let them. Our fleet won't be affected by an attack on Earth," McAdams replied.

"Not immediately maybe, but who's going to pay for upkeep when the entire Alliance is in shambles? It won't take long before it's a ghost fleet being auctioned off to the Solarians for emergency funds. Look at the evidence—someone is using the wormhole to hide these attacks and trying to make us think it could be a surviving remnant of the old Confederate Fleet, or even aliens. That gives the Solarians anonymity. They can cripple us with a minimum of effort and expense, and without starting an all-out war that they'd surely lose. All they have to do is sit back and wait for the dust to settle before they make their move."

"It's possible, sir."

"Cardinal—how much longer to intercept?" Alexander asked.

"Eleven minutes, sir."

"Put up a clock on the MHD."

"Aye, sir."

Alexander kept his eyes glued to the clock as time ticked away and everyone went about their tasks. Below the clock, the MHD showed a broad, starry vista. A bright red target box glowed there, inching visibly closer to them with every passing second. He found himself mesmerized by the stars and the steadily approaching target. After a while, he glanced up to check the clock.

Two minutes.

In the next instant the red target box split into twenty-one smaller boxes, all of them streaking in at high speed…

"Weapons hot!" Cardinal announced.

"Stone, report."

"All drones and fighters are sitting five thousand klicks ahead of us, locked on and waiting."

"Good. Keep me posted."

The target boxes sped across the holo display, seeming to accelerate as they drew near—an illusion created by the angle between their trajectories and the narrowing distance between them.

Thirty seconds… ten…

Alexander realized he was squeezing the life out of the armrests of his couch, and forced himself to relax with deep, calming breaths. His surroundings might be virtual, but the stress was real, and he needed to keep a cool head.

One second.

Dozens of blue laser beams flashed across the void and

converged on just a handful of the targets. Alexander blinked and then both the lasers and the glowing red target boxes were gone, leaving nothing but fading after images in their wake.

"Report! What did we hit?" Alexander said.

"Give me a second to reacquire, sir…" Frost replied. After just a moment, he let out a frustrated sigh. "All twenty-one blips are still headed for Earth."

"What the hell happened?" Alexander demanded.

"I did my best to account for the sensor and firing delays, sir," Cardinal replied, "but it looks like we missed by anywhere from fifty to a hundred klicks."

"The drones' closest shot went wide by twenty," Stone reported. "Sorry, sir."

"Twenty klicks? A *hundred* klicks? What's the cross-section on one of those missiles from our perspective?"

"The target is twenty meters long by two meters in diameter. That gives us a maximum of forty square meters to shoot at, sir," Cardinal replied. "Our targeting systems simply aren't precise enough to hit something that small moving that fast."

Alexander grimaced. "Well, you both did your best. Now it's up to Earth."

"Aye, sir," Cardinal said. "They have twenty minutes to intercept, but by now they should have been able to put themselves ahead of the targets and reduce the angle of deflection. They won't have the same problem that we did."

Alexander sighed. "I hope you're right."

"Admiral—" McAdams began in a whisper. "What if those missiles go evasive?"

Good question. Relativistic missiles were hard enough to hit without adding randomly varying angles of deflection. It wouldn't take much maneuvering to throw off intercepting fire.

"Let's hope they're not programmed for evasion, Commander. Maybe they'll need all of their available thrust to guide them to their targets, like what happened with the Moon attack. We shot down seven out of ten missiles. If there'd been another ship there with us, we'd have got them all."

McAdams looked ready to object, her lips frozen halfway to forming words. "Maybe," she conceded.

Alexander knew what she'd left unsaid. Those missiles didn't need to hit a very precise target like a city in order to do damage on Earth. Just about anywhere they hit would be devastating.

CHAPTER 7

Captain Grekov watched the bracketed red target box glowing dead center of the *N.W.A.S. Washington's* main holo display. Each ship in the fleet had its own target to focus on. Countless drones and fighters raced out in a diffuse cloud ahead of the fleet, aiming their weapons at the incoming ordnance from slightly larger angles of deflection. Grekov glanced up at the clock at the top of the display. Five minutes and five seconds to intercept. That time was based on when the destroyer's trajectory would line up exactly with that of the missile they were targeting rather than on any kind of specific weapons range.

"Five minutes to target, sir," Lieutenant Carver announced from the gunnery station.

"This is the worst game of chicken I've ever played," Grekov's XO, Commander Clark commented. "If we miss, that missile is on a collision course with us."

Grekov turned to his XO with one eyebrow raised. "The collision course you should be worried about is with Earth, not our ship. We have less than one hundred crew, but if that missile gets by us, it will take out many millions on Earth."

"Obviously that would be worse, sir. I meant that it would be nice if no one were in the line of fire."

Grekov frowned. Westerners were always looking out for number one. People from old Confederate states like him were better citizens. The Alliance might span the entire globe now, but all the idealogical and genetic differences that had divided the East and West still remained. Parents still chose what traits to engineer into their children, and the old Confederate states still chose all of the same community-minded ones as before. Likewise, western states were still choosing to make their children more individualistic and independent. Of course, now with the ubiquity of the Mindscape, it almost didn't matter. It was rare for anyone to actually have children anymore, so the status quo was likely to remain, leaving Grekov to feel like a *stranger in a strange land* for the rest of his immortal life—*good book,* he thought, smirking at his unintentional use of the title.

Now that he'd been promoted to captain and given his own ship, it seemed that attitudes were changing. But rather than become more united, Earth had simply re-drawn the line that divided people. Instead of dividing the East from the West, that line ran between Human League districts and Utopian ones. The world was poised to split into a thousand political pieces. If they were lucky, maybe these attacks would delay the inevitable and unite people against their common enemy—whoever that might be.

"One minute to firing, sir," the gunnery officer announced.

"Drones and fighters opening fire!" Lieutenant White reported from the fighter control station.

Grekov nodded. "Good..." Hopefully the *Washington* wouldn't even need to open fire.

"Target is maneuvering! Shots are going wide, sir," Lieutenant Carver said from gunnery.

Grekov scowled and glanced at the clock. *Thirty seconds.* "Maneuvering how? Adjusting trajectory or evasive?" he asked.

"Evasive, sir."

That was bad news. "Do your best to anticipate and track our target. Lay down as much covering fire as you can."

"Aye, Captain."

Twenty seconds.

"The missiles just shot past our fighter screen," sensors called out. "Nineteen out of twenty-one targets remaining."

Definitely bad news.

"Incoming transmission from the *Liberty!*" the comms officer announced.

"Patch it through," Grekov said.

"All ships open fire! Targets are maneuvering. Repeat, targets are maneuvering, do *not* wait for them to get any closer."

"Carver! Open fire!" Grekov bellowed.

"Aye, sir!"

The deck trembled with recoil from the destroyer's hypervelocity cannons. Projectiles streaked out into the void in simulated golden streams. Missiles jetted along behind them on bright blue contrails. It would take a while for any of those weapons to reach their target, but at least they were on their way. Hopefully they'd have enough time to intercept.

Wheels started spinning in Grekov's brain, reminding him that math was one of the things his parents had engineered him for. There was an easy way to calculate the odds of interception.

"How long before our target gets by us?" he asked.

"Four minutes and seven seconds, sir," the sensor officer reported.

That wasn't much time.

Grekov used his neural connection to the ship to make some calculations. The result was that each shot they took had a 1 in 31,411 chance to hit. Doing a few more calculations he found the probability that they would intercept their target. It came out to less than 10%. Making a quick decision, Grekov said, "Helm, come about and present our port side to the target."

"Sir, most of our guns are forward facing, and adding maneuvers at this point will only make it harder for us to intercept the target."

"Just do it, Lieutenant."

"Aye, sir."

Commander Clark shot him a curious look. "What are you doing, sir?"

"Do the math, Commander. We have less than a 10% chance to intercept our target. Once it enters effective laser range, our window of attack will be less than a twentieth of a second on approach, and another twentieth of a second as the missile flies past us. Even in the best case scenario, mechanical firing latencies will use up most of that time. Our laser-armed missiles will have the same problem. The ones carrying payloads may increase the odds by detonating in the targets' path and creating a cloud of debris, but with the precise timing required for such a detonation, that is also unlikely to succeed. All of this means that we have at least a 50% chance to miss our target.

"We are, however, conveniently situated directly in front of our target. The *Washington* has a cross-section of 120 meters by 60 meters with its broadside facing the target. That means we can position ourselves between the target and Earth like a shield, and we will have a 100% chance to intercept."

Clark looked horrified. "There won't be time to evacuate the ship."

"No, Commander, there won't. But take heart, there is still a chance to intercept the target before it reaches us."

"You Russians and your roulette!" Clark said, shaking his head. "How are we going to repel future attacks if we throw away the fleet? Imagine if all the other captains are thinking like you."

"Our enemy may not need to make any future attacks if we don't repel this one, Commander."

"We are in position, Captain," the helm reported.

"Hold position there, Lieutenant, but keep us dead center of the target."

"Aye, Captain," the officer at the helm reported.

Silence fell on deck as the crew went about their jobs. Grekov listened to the *thud thud thud* of cannon-fire and watched the ship's combat computer paint converging golden lines of tracer fire between them and the glowing red box of their target. Grekov took a deep breath. "Update the clock with the time for the target to reach us, Lieutenant."

"Aye, sir."

The clock started counting down from two minutes and twenty seconds. Grekov opened an outer pocket in his combat suit and pulled out a cigar. He held it out to his XO. Clark eyed the contraband for a second before accepting the cigar. Grekov withdrew another one for himself, and then a lighter.

"You are full of surprises, Captain," Clark said. "I didn't even know you smoked. How very degenerate of you."

Grekov smiled. "Even Geners have defects, Commander. Not all human imperfection is written into our DNA," he said as he lit first Clark's cigar and then his own. He took a drag and savored the spicy flavor of the smoke before puffing it out again. "Some of it is learned."

Clark puffed out his own cloud of cigar smoke. A smoke alarm went off with a shrill noise, but he quickly silenced the alarm. Several of the crew looked around and noticed both the Captain and the XO grinning and smoking. Reactions ranged from shock to grim amusement, but no one thought to object.

The clock hit one minute.

"I'm glad you had some extra imperfection to go around, Captain," Clark said, puffing out more smoke.

Grekov turned to Clark with his cigar pinched between smoke-stained teeth. "It is a pity I left the vodka in my quarters."

Clark barked a laugh at that. "I'm going to miss you, Captain."

"*Nyet*, I'll look you up in the next life. I'll be damned if they don't open the pearly gates for us after this."

"Aye," Clark said. "You'll be damned indeed," he said, smiling at the joke.

Grekov nodded soberly and blew out another cloud of smoke. "To the damned," he said, watching as the clock hit ten seconds. Cannon fire still streaked out impotently into space.

One second—

Lasers lanced out in dazzling blue and red beams.

Zero seconds—

The world exploded in a white hot flash of fury.

* * *

"Did we get them all?" Admiral Anderson demanded as he loomed over the sensor operator's shoulders. Myriad control stations ran around the circumference of the room, their glowing holo displays spilling cold blue light into the Combat Information Center (CIC) located fifty floors below the presidential palace.

"One of the missiles got through, sir," the sensor operator reported in a quiet voice.

"Damn it! Where did it hit?"

"Based on it's last known trajectory… somewhere in the Gulf of Mexico. A few hundred klicks South of New Houston I'd say."

"Issue a tsunami warning for all coastal cities along the Gulf. What kind of damage are we looking at?"

"Without knowing the weight of the impactor, there's no way to be sure."

Anderson scowled. "Do you know the *size* of the impactor?"

"Yes, sir."

"Then estimate the weight based on a maximum and minimum density for an object of that size."

"Aye, sir."

Anderson turned from the sensor operator's station to find the president standing right behind him.

"Mr. President—I didn't realize you were there."

"How did that missile get through, Admiral?" President Wallace asked. "We had just one ship at the Moon and we stopped seven out of ten missiles with almost no warning, so how did we fail here with almost an hour of advance notice?"

Anderson pressed his lips into a grim line. "The missiles went evasive this time, sir. The ones that hit the Moon were maneuvering in straight lines. It also didn't help that half of our available ships were on the other side of Earth when we detected the missiles. We didn't have enough time to reposition them all."

Wallace blew out a breath and shook his head. "The media is going to make us look incompetent! They're going to ask why we spread out our defenses if we knew the attacks were coming from the wormhole."

Anderson frowned and nodded. He'd argued for positioning the fleet along the hemisphere facing the wormhole from the start, but the president and the rest of Fleet Command had opted for a more comprehensive defense. Now his arguments had been vindicated, but at what cost? This wasn't exactly an *I-told-you-so* moment. "One of our captains sacrificed his ship to intercept his target. It went down with all hands. Give the media that story to run with. Everyone loves a hero."

Wallace nodded gravely. "I heard. The *N.W.A.S Washington*—Captain Grekov. The media will certainly run with that story whether I give it to them or not, but I don't need to tell you how bad it looks for us that the only captain willing to put himself in the line of fire to protect Earth was an ex-confederate. That's only going to cast more doubt on our administration and create even more divisions. Citizens from ex-confederate states might even try to form their own party for the next election, and if they get elected, we're in for a whole lot of trouble."

Anderson frowned. "Sir, I think we have bigger problems right now than the election."

Wallace clamped his lips together and nodded. "You're right. Of course we do."

"Sir," the sensor operator interrupted, "I've finished my calculations."

"Go on," Anderson said.

"The missile likely had around ten metric tons of throw weight assuming it used up all its fuel on approach."

Anderson considered that. "And what kind of energy would be released by a ten ton object moving at a third of the speed of light?"

"Approximately fifty-four point six exajoules, sir."

President Wallace's brow furrowed. "What the hell is an exajoule?"

"Ten to the power of eighteen joules," the sensor operator replied.

Anderson shook his head. "Give us a meaningful reference for that, Lieutenant."

"Yes, sir. That's approximately equivalent to a nuclear weapon with a yield of 13,000 megatons. Our biggest nukes are in the 250 megaton range, so imagine more than fifty of those all going off in one spot in the Gulf of Mexico."

Anderson paled, and he and President Wallace traded worried looks.

The sensor operator noticed the looks on their faces and hurried to add, "That's still relatively small when compared with some other events in Earth's history. The *Chicxulub impact,* for example, was thousands of times stronger."

Anderson felt as though a crushing weight had just been lifted from his shoulders. The Chicxulub impact was what had made the dinosaurs extinct. If this was thousands of times weaker than that, then maybe the effects wouldn't be so deadly. "So this isn't an extinction level event?" Anderson asked.

"No, sir."

"Thank God."

"What will the tsunami be like when it hits the Gulf Coast?" President Wallace asked.

"That's tough to say until buoy data comes in, but according to standard computer models and the ocean depth in the area of impact…" the sensor operator trailed off while he ran some more calculations. "Wave height at the nearest coastline could be as high as sixty meters."

Anderson blinked in shock. "That's going to level everything it hits!"

"Yes, sir."

"How long do we have?" President Wallace asked.

"About half an hour for the closest areas."

"Hopefully that's enough time for people to get to higher ground. Anything else we need to worry about?" Wallace asked.

"An Earthquake. My bet is that's already registered… it has."

"How bad?"

"Seven point one on the Richter scale. As for the other effects we can probably expect to see firestorms. We're lucky that the shock wave is too far from the coast to light fires, but ejecta from the crater is going to come raining back down and burst into flames as it re-enters the atmosphere. The bigger chunks will make it to the ground and light fires."

A look of confusion crossed the president's face. "Debris from the crater? I thought the missile hit water."

"It did, but at the speed it was traveling, it still punched a big hole in the sea floor."

"What about impact winter?" Anderson asked.

"Not likely, sir. The impact wasn't big enough for that to be a concern."

"Good. We've already got enough to worry about with everything else. Tsunamis, earthquakes, firestorms…" Anderson said, shaking his head.

"God help us," President Wallace added.

CHAPTER 8

Senator Catalina de Leon stood in the waiting room on the fifteenth floor of the United Farmers Tower in Galveston. She was waiting for her meeting with a prominent League Party supporter, Bill Watson. He was a rich landowner with over a hundred farms scattered around Texas—all of them human-run. The Human League district of Texas was particularly large. Here, people had yet to succumb to the madness of the Mindscape. It was illegal to even have a mindscape connection in League districts.

All the better to avoid the temptation, Catalina thought. She knew all about the lure of virtual worlds. She'd lost her husband because of them.

Catalina walked up to the windows running alongside the waiting room. She watched the Gulf of Mexico sparkling in the sun. Tufted white clouds sailed across the bright blue dome of sky overhead. Catalina smiled at the view. Virtual worlds might look and feel the same, but they still couldn't compare to the real thing.

She turned away from the view to take a seat. As she did so, the inside of the waiting room flashed with a blinding light. Catalina winced and whirled around to face the windows once more. She was just in time to see a fading column of light between the sky and the horizon. An eerie glow below that column radiated up from the horizon, and a searing wave of heat radiated through the windows, as if there were an oven on the other side. Her skin stung and itched from the heat.

The column of light faded, and Catalina gasped to see that in its place stood a giant, funnel-shaped black cloud rising all the way into the stratosphere. She looked on in horror. *What is that?*

Then came a low rumbling sound, followed by a much louder rattling of windows and paintings on walls. Catalina spun around, blinking rapidly to clear away pink and green columns of light from her vision. Paintings hanging on the walls fell. A crystal sculpture tottered to the floor, shattering on the marble tiles and sending jagged shards of glass in all directions. Her knees wobbled and she grabbed the nearest wall to steady herself.

It's an earthquake, she realized, her terror multiplying. She heard Bill's secretary scream, and echoes of that sound came through the walls from adjacent offices. *Is this building made to withstand an earthquake?* Catalina wondered. How long did she have before it fell? The ground continued rocking under her feet, the building swaying from side to side.

She made a break for the stairs, but skidded and fell in the shattered glass from the sculpture. Searing pain shot through her thigh as glass dug through her skin. The rumbling and shaking went on and on like a train running down a set of tracks right next to her. *This is it. I'm going to die.*

Suddenly it stopped and everything was perfectly still. Catalina gritted her teeth and heaved herself off the ground, glass biting into her palms as she did so. She looked around at the mess in the waiting area. Watson's secretary caught her eye. They traded looks of bewilderment and horror.

"What the hell was that?" the secretary asked.

Catalina shook her head and directed her gaze out the window where she'd seen the column of light appear. The black cloud was still there, but it looked bigger and angrier than it had a moment ago.

Bill Watson's door flew open, and he lunged out into the waiting room, his eyes wild and dark hair mussed. "One of the missiles got through," He said.

"Missiles?" Catalina asked.

"Haven't you been watching the news? Missiles! Like the ones that hit the Moon. One of them got through! There's an evacuation alert in effect for the entire Gulf Coast. We're supposed to get to higher ground as fast as we can."

Catalina gaped at him. "What higher ground? We're on an island!"

"We'll have to get to the mainland. I have a helicopter on the roof," Bill said.

Catalina heard people screaming and muffled thuds coming from adjacent offices. All of their heads turned.

"People are panicking," Watson added. "No one expected the missiles to get through. The government assured us we were safe."

More muffled screams and thuds rippled through the walls as people tripped over each other on their way to the exits.

"We need to get to your helicopter *now,*" Catalina added.

Bill nodded. "Let's go." He turned and ran for the stairwell. He yanked open the door to the stairs and disappeared, not waiting for them.

Watson's secretary beat her there, grabbing the door before it swung shut, but Catalina careened through the open doorway, slamming into the other woman and almost knocking her over. Both women grunted, but kept moving, pounding their way up the stairs. More screaming echoed to them from further down the stairwell, footsteps sounding like thunder as people flew down to the parking levels.

Catalina was grateful they were going in the opposite direction. She took the stairs two at a time, using the railing to pull herself up faster and take some of the weight off her injured leg. Her lungs burned and her legs and hands trembled violently as she went. It felt like forever to the top of the stairwell. Time flowed like molasses. *This is a bad dream,* she thought.

She beat Watson's secretary to the top of the stairs and body-checked the door open. The sun assaulted her still-aching eyes. Tears welled, and her eyes automatically narrowed to slits. She fought through the tears to find Watson. He was already halfway to the waiting helicopter. Gasping for air, she pounded after him, limping from the pain of broken glass in her thigh.

Watson reached the chopper and yanked the door open. He launched himself inside and disappeared in the relative darkness of the cabin.

Afraid that he was going to take off without them, Catalina called out, "Wait!"

The helicopter's rotors were already spinning up—*thump,*

thump, thump... and there was no way that he'd heard her over the noise.

A split second later, his head popped out the open door and he gestured impatiently for them to hurry. Catalina poured on a burst of speed, willing her burning legs to pump faster, and her lungs to stop screaming for oxygen. Her head felt light. Dark spots danced before her eyes. She was going to pass out.

No!

Catalina stumbled and fell. But rather than the unforgiving *smack* of the concrete rooftop, she felt herself being lifted back up, and she opened her eyes to see Watson pulling her inside the helicopter. Somehow she'd made it. Behind her someone screamed. Watson's secretary. Catalina turned to see her yank the rear door open and clamber inside.

"Shut the doors!" Watson reached over Catalina and pulled her door shut. His secretary did likewise, and then the *thump-thump-thumping* of the rotors picked up speed as Watson prepared to take off.

Abruptly, the noise faded once more.

"What's wrong?"

Watson shook his head and pointed out the window. Catalina turned to look. The dark cloud she'd seen before was bigger than ever, stretching as far and wide as any hurricane. That probably wasn't far from the truth. The impact must have kicked up an enormous amount of water vapor and sediment.

Watson passed her a headset to her so they could talk. She slipped it over her ears with shaking hands.

"We can't go anywhere until that shock wave passes," he explained. The sound of the rotors died completely.

"What's wrong?" Watson's secretary asked. Not wearing a headset, she'd missed his explanation. "We need to take off now... *please*!"

"What about the tsunami?" Catalina asked, ignoring her.

"Soon as the shock wave passes we'll come back here and make a break for it. Till then we need to go back inside and take shelter. The stairwell should do." Watson removed his headset and opened the door on his side of the cockpit before hopping out.

Catalina opened her own door and followed him.

"Wait!" the secretary screamed after them. She caught up with them just as they were hurrying back inside.

Watson sat down on the landing at the top of the stairs, to one side of the door and just below a window. Catalina gingerly sat beside him, careful to mind her injured leg. She made a mental connection to the net and found a news channel streaming out of New Houston. She settled in to watch it on her comm band. A hologram of a news anchor appeared above her wrist, speaking in rapid, urgent tones.

"...missile was moving at a third of the speed of light when it landed in the Gulf of Mexico ten minutes ago. The impact occurred 300 kilometers south of New Houston, triggering an earthquake that registered 7.1 on the Richter scale. Both the impact and the earthquake are expected to produce high waves, and tsunami warnings are in effect for all coastal areas. Waves are estimated to reach anywhere from 5 to 60 meters and will begin arriving within the hour.

"If you are anywhere within fifty kilometers of the coast, you are advised to get to higher ground as quickly as possible, using land routes only. Overpressure from the shock waves will make aerial flight extremely dangerous."

Catalina minimized the feed. "Looks like you were right, Watson."

Watson nodded and reached for his secretary's hand. "Don't worry, Miss Cole. We'll still have plenty of time to get away."

Before she could comment a loud *bang!* sounded, and the window above them exploded, showering them with shattered glass. Miss Cole screamed as a hot wind whistled in. The wind whipped Catalina's hair around her face, making it writhe like Medusa's snakes. Her ears popped painfully, and then she screamed, too, but she couldn't hear the sound. A ringing noise set in and the whistling wind went on and on. The air inside the stairwell became stiflingly hot. By the time it finally abated, she was gasping for air. Catalina shook her head to clear the ringing in her ears.

"We have to go!" Watson said. He bounced to his feet, sending fragments of glass flying.

Miss Cole flung the stairwell door open and they ran out together. The wind was still raging outside, threatening to knock them over. As they drew near to the helicopter, they found that at least its windows had survived. They weren't made of standard glass.

As soon as they were back inside, Watson started up the rotors once more. *Thump, thump, thump, thump…* Catalina fumbled with her seatbelt and slipped the headset over her ears. "How much longer do we have before the wave hits?" she asked.

Watson shook his head. "Don't know, but we're damn close to the impact."

"So…"

"We stay airborne. You ladies all buckled in?"

Catalina nodded, her gaze fixed on the dark storm hulking over the horizon. Thankfully that cloud of water vapor and dust hadn't reached them with the air blast. She couldn't imagine Watson piloting them safely through that storm.

"Here we go…"

The rotor noise intensified and Catalina felt herself pressed down hard into her seat as the helicopter shot straight up from the roof of the United Farmers Tower.

The first thing she noticed as they flew away were the streams of hover traffic flying out from skyscrapers around them, all clawing for the sky as they raced toward the mainland. Dark columns of smoke rose from flickering orange fires below.

"All the hovers that didn't make it," Watson said, pointing to the smoke. "Good thing we waited."

Catalina blinked, shocked that so many people had been killed already. They obviously hadn't heard the warning about sticking to land routes.

They flew on for a while before Catalina noticed that Watson wasn't headed inland. He was flying down the coast.

"What are you *doing*?" she demanded.

"I'm live streaming the event from our nose cam."

"*What?* Are you crazy?"

"Relax! The danger's passed. We may as well capture the moment."

"Why the hell would you want to do that?"

Watson glanced at her. "Have you ever seen a sixty-meter wave?"

Catalina stared dumbly back at him.

"The danger's passed for us."

"What about that storm?

Watson shook his head. "Still hours out. We've got time. People deserve to know what happened here."

Catalina settled back in her seat with a frown, still unconvinced.

"There!" Watson pointed to a dark ripple on the ocean, moving fast.

To Catalina's horror Watson took them down for a closer

look.

A new voice crackled in their ears. It was Miss Cole. She'd finally found her headset. "What are you doing?!" she shrieked.

Watson gave no reply. The rooftops of luxury hotels, apartments, and office buildings running the length of Galveston Island swept up toward them. As the rooftops came into focus, Catalina picked out crowds of people clustered on some of those rooftops, watching the advancing wave.

They were planning to ride it out.

The approaching ripple grew exponentially as it approached. Catalina watched, speechless with horror as the wave reached the sandy shores of the island, now towering higher than some of the buildings that faced it. The wave curled at the top, casting a shadow over the island.

Miss Cole was muttering repetitive prayers, and Watson cursed as the wave broke. Windows shattered and the shorter buildings disappeared, momentarily submerged by the wave. The water level fell dramatically, and skyscrapers fell into each other like dominoes. As the buildings collapsed, tiny, colorful specks leapt from the rooftops into the roiling trough behind the wave. In the time it took for Catalina to blink and blink again every building in sight was gone. Galveston Island was completely submerged. Watson turned the chopper inland and they saw the wave racing on through West Bay, taking out bridges on its way to the mainland.

Flying in a lazy arc, they saw that one lonely tower still remained standing. United Farmers Tower.

"I guess we didn't have to evacuate after all," Watson said. His tone was flat, conveying the irony, but not a hint of humor.

"All those people on the rooftops…" Catalina said.

Watson gave no reply. Maybe now he felt guilty for

sticking around to film the event, morbid fascination giving way to the sick horror Catalina felt churning in her gut. Whoever had done this had just joined the ranks of history's most infamous mass-murderers. Millions of people were going to die before it was over.

CHAPTER 9

"Admiral, Fleet Command is ordering us to intercept the *Crimson Warrior* with all possible speed," Lieutenant Hayes reported from the comms.

"We haven't even received a reply from our hail yet," Alexander replied.

"After that missile hit Earth, I don't think Fleet Command cares if the Solarians have a good excuse for their location," McAdams put in.

"And that's enough reason to go charging off and start a war?" Alexander countered.

"Do you want me to ask for clarification of our orders, sir?" Hayes asked.

Alexander scowled and shook his head. "No, that's okay, Lieutenant. It'll take days for us to reach them, anyway. Hopefully the Solarians will be able to give Earth a satisfactory answer long before that."

"Aye, sir."

"Bishop, set an intercept course. Ten *G*s."

"Aye, aye."

"I guess we won't be getting out of this mindscape for a while," McAdams said on the other side of him.

Alexander nodded absently. Ten *G*s sustained acceleration was far too much to survive without the cushioning effects of a liquid bath. He traced imaginary constellations between the stars on the main holo display. That virtual view corresponded to a real one, just like everything else in the *Adamantine's* mindscape.

"You know…" he began. "Thirty years ago, I thought we called it *The Last War* for a reason. Why is everyone suddenly in such a hurry to start a new one?"

"It's human nature, sir," McAdams replied. "An eye for an eye."

"Maybe that's the problem. The Human League might have it all wrong. They're afraid we're going to make ourselves obsolete and end up with bots running the world, but I'm starting to wonder if that would be so bad. Maybe they'd actually be better at it."

"I think the problem is the obsolete part," McAdams said. "If we are no longer useful, and bots are running things, why should they keep us around at all? We'll just be taking up valuable resources and space."

Alexander sighed and rubbed his eyes, trying to ease some of the pressure he felt building behind them. "How much longer before the Solarian ship can send us a reply?"

"One hour and fifteen minutes, sir," Hayes replied.

"All right, put it on the clock, Hayes. McAdams—set condition yellow. We may as well stretch our virtual legs while we wait."

"Aye, Captain," she said.

Alexander unbuckled from his couch and stood up. One of the advantages of being immersed in a mindscape was that certain elements of realism could be momentarily suspended for comfort's sake. That meant that even with the *Adamantine* hurtling through space at ten *G*s he could still get up and walk around as if it was no more than one *G*.

McAdams climbed out of her acceleration couch and stood beside him.

Alexander nodded to her and then said, "Bishop, you have the conn. Any new developments, let me know and we'll be back in a flash." *Literally*. A split second was all it would take for him and McAdams to warp through the virtual world back to the bridge.

"Aye, Captain," Bishop said.

"McAdams?"

"After you, sir," she said.

He nodded and they walked to the elevator together.

"Where are we going?" she asked.

"For a drink."

"A drink, sir?" she asked, frowning.

He cast her a grim look. "It's not like we can actually get drunk, Commander. The effects are simulated, and they'll pass as soon as we want them to."

"I know, sir, but..."

Alexander waved the elevator open and they walked in. The doors slid shut behind them, and he selected *Officer's Lounge (75)* from the control panel. "But?" he prompted, turning to her. The lift tube started upward, pressing them momentarily harder against the floor.

Her expression was troubled. "It seems wrong to be toasting up here while millions of people are dying back on Earth."

"Who said anything about toasting? Why do you think I need a drink? It's not going to hurt you to virtually numb your senses for a while, Commander."

McAdams nodded reluctantly. "Yes, sir."

* * *

"You have to get me an audience with the president," Lars Becker said, feeling a muscle jerk in his cheek as he stared at a hologram of his old subordinate. Fleet Admiral Anderson had been a lieutenant back then. That had been a lifetime ago—not that lifetimes were a meaningful measure of time anymore.

Anderson shook his head. "You know I can't do that, sir. You were dishonorably discharged."

Lars smiled crookedly into the holocorder on his desk. "*Ja,* Becker the Disgrace, the *Admiral who cried Wolf*—or is it the *Admiral who Cried Aliens?* That would be closer to the truth, I think."

"I'm very busy at the moment, sir…"

"Listen to you—still calling me *sir*. If you have that much respect for me, then you need to listen to me now, Anderson. These attacks are not what the president thinks they are, and I have proof. If the Alliance goes after the Solarians for this, we're going to end up with two enemies, and when the real one comes roaring out of that wormhole, we won't be prepared."

Anderson grimaced. "I need to go, sir. I'm sorry. For what it's worth, I have already presented your concerns to the president and the joint chiefs of staff. Unfortunately they didn't share those concerns."

"You went to them without proof. I can convince them. Just give me five minutes with the president. That's all I need."

"He won't agree to see you. I'm sorry, sir. Take care of yourself."

Lars Becker gaped at the screen as the holo image faded away. He leaned back in his chair, considering what he should do.

A loud moaning sound stole his attention. He glared at the thin walls of his apartment. The woman in 205D was having another virtual rendezvous. A frown touched his lips. The only good part about government housing was that it was free. He'd lost his benefits when he'd been discharged, and since jobs were such a scarce commodity, he couldn't afford to pay rent in a nicer place. *Pity being a conspiracy theorist doesn't pay.*

Becker looked around his modest hundred-square-foot micro studio. The desk in front of him could be raised and lowered into the floor to double as a coffee table or just to get it out of the way. The couch where he sat was fully convertible, allowing him to sit upright at his desk, recline to watch holofeeds, or lie down and sleep. The kitchen was tiny and ill-equipped for cooking, so he mostly ate government-issue meal packs and drank nutrient slurry. He couldn't afford fresh food, anyway. But by far the worst was the bathroom; the toilet was actually inside of the shower, and his knees touched the walls whenever he had to sit on his watertight throne.

Becker grimaced and turned to look out the apartment's only window—a convincing hologram. That window gave him a floor-to-ceiling view of whatever he wanted. Right now it showed a lake, blue water shimmering in the sun, a rolling carpet of bright green grass leading down to a pebbly shore. Large willow trees arched over the scene, casting flickering shadows across the grass as a breeze blew. Becker sighed and his eyes drifted shut. He imagined he could feel the wind on his face and touch the cool water with his toes, the sun beating down on his face…

Then he opened his eyes. He'd just plugged into the oldest form of Mindscape—imagination. There'd been a time when people had spent their lives actually experiencing all of those things in the real world. Now they settled for the instant gratification of the Mindscape. Real beaches were garbage dumps with swarms of stray dogs and cats picking through the refuse. Few people even bothered with real pets these days, just as they didn't bother with having children. Virtual ones didn't cost money, and didn't require people to spend less time in their beloved mindscapes.

Becker looked away from the window and stared at the wall across from him. The black rectangle of an old-fashioned holoscreen hung there. On a whim, he waved his hand at the screen to turn it on. It was already tuned to an Alliance News Network holofeed. The news anchor talked about the missile impact in the Gulf of Mexico, and footage of the devastation flashed before Becker's eyes on a horrendous loop, whole cities wiped out by the tsunami. An estimated thirty million people were dead or missing, and no doubt that number would only continue to rise in the days and weeks to come.

Becker shook his head. These were just the warning shots. What would happen when the invasion came? It was going to catch everyone by surprise. He knew what was coming; he had a responsibility to warn people. Everyone acknowledged that the universe was simply too vast for humanity to be alone, but no one really took the idea of an alien threat seriously.

"They didn't then, and they don't now…" Becker whispered. The president might not want to speak with him, but there was another way to get his attention, and while he was at it, the attention of the entire world. It was time to go public with his information.

Again.

The last time he'd spoken to the press, he'd earned himself a dishonorable discharge, but this time would be different. This time he had proof.

CHAPTER 10

McAdams took another sip of her martini, and Alexander downed his third tumbler of Scotch. He stared absently into the bottom of the glass and savored the pleasant warmth spreading through him. It made his head feel five pounds lighter, and he'd almost managed to silence the accusing screams of the dead. One more glass should do it.

Or maybe that was what it would take to pass out.

Not that he could pass out while he was in the Mindscape. It was designed to keep him conscious, and the instant someone upgraded the ship's alert status from condition yellow to general quarters, sobriety would be back and hammering away with accusations—*You didn't hit even one missile. That's all it would have taken. Just one, and Earth would be safe. One lucky shot to save millions of lives.*

Reports from Earth had reached them over the past hour—the impact had triggered an earthquake and a massive tsunami. The gulf coast was completely inundated, whole cities leveled. The scale of devastation was immense.

"You have any loved ones close to the impact?" McAdams asked.

Alexander began to shake his head, then he stopped himself and shrugged, his lips parting in a bitter smirk. "You know, I have no idea. It's been a long time since I've had any loved ones."

McAdams' brow pinched with sympathy. "I'm sorry. What happened between you and your wife?"

Alexander met her gaze, at a loss for words.

"If you don't mind my asking," she added.

"I suppose you have a right to know since I left you to go after my wife. I guess karma's still a bitch, because twenty years later she left me to go after our son."

"I don't understand."

"I had the boy's real father conscripted; he died somewhere in old Confederate Russia. When Dorian found out, he disowned me and his mother."

"You had him conscripted? Is that even legal?"

"Oh, it was legal. The man was an illegal immigrant in the North. Back then the penalty for that was the same as the price for citizenship—military service."

"Then you didn't do anything wrong."

"Well, I did hunt him down to make sure he was caught, and then I made sure he was sent somewhere dangerous enough that he might not survive."

"I see," McAdams said, her gaze hardening.

Alexander nodded. "Not so hard to understand why they left me, is it?"

Her expression softened, and she placed her hand over his. "We all make mistakes. And I know you, Alex. To do something like that, you must have had a good reason."

"Sure, that guy was abusive. He almost killed my wife back when they were together. You could call what I did revenge, but he had it coming."

"What I don't understand is how your wife could leave you over that. Your son, sure, but even he should come around if you explain it to him. Besides, it's not like you put the man against a wall and shot him yourself."

Alexander poured himself another half a glass of Scotch. "The Mindscape ruined us. At the end we spent so little time together that we may as well have been two strangers living in the same house. Living like that, our marriage couldn't hope to compete with the love of a mother for her son. Caty saw that she needed to distance herself from me in order to win Dorian back, and that's exactly what she did."

"Did you try to go after them? To explain?"

Alexander took a gulp of whiskey and grimaced as it burned a fiery trail down his throat. "If either of them still cared, they would have come back. Besides, I was tired of living an empty virtual life. Best case, I would get to go back to that. They gave me the excuse I needed to unplug and get the hell away from it all. The last taste of real purpose I ever had was with the Navy. You don't know how strong the drive to be useful is until you realize that the world wouldn't even miss you if you were gone. Long story short, I came back to the only home I've ever known."

"I'm sorry," McAdams said, rubbing his hand.

"Don't be. Plenty of people lost their families to the Mindscape. At least I had another one waiting for me."

McAdams smiled, her blue eyes shining bright.

"What about you?" he asked.

"I didn't have anyone waiting for me after the war, and it took me a while..." she looked away. "It took me a while to get over you. By the time I did, the Mindscape was everywhere, and dating was more virtual than real. Virtual relationships filled the hole for a while—until one day I decided to meet up with my virtual boyfriend in the real world. We planned to get married for real. We were old-fashioned I guess. We even discussed having real kids someday."

Alexander regarded her beneath a furrowed brow. "What happened?"

McAdams smiled. "When I met him, I discovered that he was about five feet tall, skinny as a reed, and had a face like a scarecrow."

Alexander barked a short laugh, then quickly stifled it with a cough. "Sorry," he said. "So he wasn't a gener like you."

"No. I guess now you think I'm superficial."

Alexander shrugged. "Everyone is to some extent. What did he look like in the mindscapes?"

"Tall, dark, and handsome, of course."

"Of course," Alexander replied. "So what did you do?"

"I broke off the engagement. He was heartbroken."

"Don't worry, I'm sure he got over it with some virtual hookers."

"He wasn't like that."

"No? I thought everyone was like that these days."

"Are you?" McAdams asked, her eyes measuring.

"Call me old-fashioned, but I never liked virtual hookers."

McAdams nodded.

"I prefer the real ones," he explained.

Her eyes widened suddenly, and Alexander held her gaze for a second before cracking a smile. "I'm kidding, Viviana."

"Oh." She blinked and relief softened her features.

Alexander's comm band buzzed. "Admiral de Leon speaking."

"Admiral, Hayes here, we have a reply from the Solarian ship. You want to come back down to the bridge, or should I patch it through to your comm?"

"Patch it through."

"Yes, sir."

Alexander held his wrist out for both him and McAdams to watch as a hologram materialized above his comm band. They saw a man wearing a deep maroon combat suit with black piping—Solarian Navy colors. The silver star on his right breast marked him as a captain. He sat in an acceleration couch, though that could have been virtual rather than real, depending on how many Gs the enemy ship was pulling. The Solarian captain's face was long and narrow and very pale, no doubt due to generations of living under the dreary Martian sky. The captain's crimson eyes and black hair struck a fierce contrast to his ghostly complexion, making him look demonic. Red eyes were fashionable for Martians. Alexander noticed that the man's face was perfectly symmetrical, his features sculpted, and his complexion completely smooth. This was the face of a gener—not that it should surprise him. Mars wasn't any different from Earth when it came to how people engineered their children. The main difference was that *they* were still having children.

"Admiral de Leon," the man said in a deep, resonant voice. "This is Captain Vrokovich of the *Crimson Warrior*. I was disappointed that your hail came to me via your comms officer rather than from you personally. I would have liked to hear from the *Lion of Liberty* face-to-face. Word of what happened to Earth reached us soon after your hail. Fortunately so, or else I might not have been so understanding when I received your demands to know our flight plan and the purpose of our mission. The Alliance has our condolences, Admiral, but let me assure you personally that we had nothing to do with any of the missiles fired at either Earth or the Moon. May the Architect be with your people in these troubled times. Vrokovich out."

The captain's face faded away, and Alexander activated his comm band again to speak with his comms officer. "Hayes, send that message to Fleet Command and ask them how we should proceed."

"Aye, sir… Message away."

"Good, let me know when they reply. De Leon out."

"The Architect?" McAdams asked as Alexander went back to his Scotch.

Alexander turned to her with a curious look. Then he remembered how Captain Vrokovich had ended his message. "You've never heard of the Universal Architect?"

"No," she admitted.

"For Solarians the Universal Architect is analogous to God for Earthers, but while we still have multiple different religions and multiple different gods, the Solarians have just one religion and one god—Simulism and the Architect."

"So Captain Vrokovich is a Simulist," McAdams replied. "Interesting. I never really understood what Simulists believe."

"It's simple. They believe that we're living inside a simulation."

McAdams chuckled. "That doesn't take any faith. Most of us *are* living in a simulation. You and I are in one right now."

"Simulists would say this mindscape is just another level of simulation. They believe the physical universe and everything in it is like the Mindscape, except that we never wake up from it—until we die, that is."

"So the Universal Architect is…"

"Whatever entity created the simulation," Alexander said.

"What led people to think we're in a simulation in the first place? Just because it's possible?"

"It's actually an old theory, but if you look at the Mindscape, it's not hard to believe. How can you tell that we're not actually here in the officer's lounge right now?"

"Because I remember entering this mindscape, and I'm aware of the reality behind it."

"Right, but a lot of mindscapes suppress that awareness to make virtual worlds seem more real. When that happens, you can't tell the difference between virtual and real."

"The scale of virtual worlds is smaller," McAdams argued. "Go far enough and eventually you'll hit a wall past which nothing else is simulated."

"Yes and no. Some of our virtual worlds are procedurally infinite, so it's hard to find that boundary, but we're not really talking about what we're capable of doing right now. For all we know our world and all of our mindscapes are part of a much larger simulation being run by us or some other species in the far future."

"What would be the point of that?" McAdams asked.

Alexander shrugged. "History lessons. Entertainment. A prison? The possibilities are endless."

"Sounds unlikely to me."

"Not really. Think about it in terms of us right now. How many people spend the majority of their time in mindscapes rather than the real world?"

"Most people I guess."

"So the majority of people are already living in a simulated reality and the ones in full immersion mindscapes aren't even aware of that fact until they wake up. That's a pretty compelling argument right there."

"But it doesn't prove that we're still in some higher level of simulation even after we wake up from the Mindscape."

"No? Suppose that in the future we create a full immersion Mindscape that's identical to the real world, complete with its own mindscapes running inside of it. How do you know that you aren't in that world right now?"

"You just gave me chills."

Alexander smiled. "Not so far-fetched after all, huh?"

McAdams nodded slowly. "Trying to convert me, Admiral?"

Alexander laughed. "No, I'm just trying to pass the time. Besides, between the alcohol and convincing myself that our reality isn't actually real, it helps me forget that I just let millions of people die." Alexander drained his glass one last time and shook his head. The room was starting to spin.

He felt McAdams' hand on his again. This time she laced her fingers through his. "It wasn't your fault, Alex."

"Maybe not, but it was *someone's* fault."

McAdams nodded. "The Solarians. Or some other enemy we have yet to meet."

Alexander snorted. "Right—aliens. I'd sooner believe it was the Solarians, but if I'm right, then things are about to get a lot worse. Earth has spent the last three decades scuttling its fleet, while the Solarians have spent the last three decades building theirs."

"Our fleet is still stronger than theirs."

Alexander nodded. "For now."

His comm band chimed, interrupting them with an incoming message. He answered it. "Admiral de Leon here."

"Admiral, it's Hayes again. I have a reply from Fleet Command along with updated orders."

"Patch it through, Lieutenant."

"Aye, sir."

Fleet Admiral Anderson's face appeared hovering in the air above Alexander's comm band. The admiral's short blond hair was unwashed and pasted to his scalp. His gray eyes were bloodshot and his cheeks gaunt, suggesting that he hadn't eaten or slept much since the attacks began.

"Admiral Leon, the Solarian Ship did *not* answer our request for their flight plan nor did they state the purpose of their mission. They blatantly ignored our inquiries and masked that fact with well-wishes for our people. Under the circumstances, we cannot allow this type of secrecy. You are cleared to engage the enemy as soon as you reach weapons range. Shoot to disable and then board the enemy ship. We're looking for any evidence that they may be the ones who attacked us. Anderson out."

Alexander gaped at the hologram as it faded to black. "They want us to start a war!" He pounded the bar with his fists, rattling their glasses. He shook his head incredulously and turned to McAdams. "The last time I was in the Navy, I was ordered to start a war. Now, no sooner am I back and they want me to start another one! I won a Nobel Peace Prize for negotiating the end of The Last War, but here we go again. Do you have any idea how ironic that is?"

McAdams nodded soberly. "Irony is still a bitch, sir."

"A two-timing bitch!"

"So what are you going to do about it?"

Alexander blew out a breath. What *could* he do? He could disobey orders. He'd gotten lucky with that the last time, but would he get away with it again?

Doubtful. After what had happened on Earth, people wanted a target—the Solarians were a logical fit, even he had to admit that, and if he refused to be the instrument of the Alliance's retribution, it would look like cowardice not prudence.

But what was it really? He was almost positive the Solarians were responsible for the attacks, so why didn't he want to fire back? *Maybe I'm a pacifist.* Forcing the Solarians to go from covert to overt tactics would only result in even more people dead. What would happen when Earth and the Solarians started trading relativistic blows?

"Sir?"

Alexander sent a mental command to clear his buzzing head of all the virtual alcohol. He needed to think clearly now.

"If we do what they're asking, we could start a relativistic war that could end up making the entire human race extinct."

"I disagree, sir. Just because we *can* annihilate ourselves doesn't mean that we will—whether there's open war or not. If the Solarians are attacking us, then they're obviously not trying to completely destroy the Earth. If we can prove that the Solarians were responsible for the attacks, then hopefully our leaders will be smart enough to avoid a relativistic war."

Alexander nodded. "I hope you're right, Commander."

"History agrees with me, Admiral. Even The Last War fell far short of global annihilation. I disagree with our orders, but I'm not convinced that they'll result in open war.

"Besides, Fleet Command made no mention of the fact that we're in an aging dauntless-class battleship going up against a modern Solarian dreadnought. That ship is twice the size of ours and far better equipped. It could defeat two *Adamantines* and still limp into battle with a third. Either Fleet Command thinks very highly of your abilities, sir, or they're bluffing."

"Or they're so desperate for blood that they don't mind shedding some of ours to get it," Alexander replied.

"Let's hope it's a bluff, sir."

Alexander grimaced. "If it isn't, we're about to learn the truth about Simulism the hard way."

CHAPTER 11

Catalina was surprised when her audience with the president brought her to a bunker below the presidential palace. The president's last public address had shown him above ground, sitting in his office as he reassured the entire world that the missile that hit them was a fluke, and people had nothing to fear. There was something hypocritical about telling people not to be afraid when you were hiding out in a bunker fifty floors below ground.

"Miss *Day Lee-on?* The president is ready to see you now," his secretary announced, mangling Catalina's surname with her accent.

Catalina turned to regard the president's secretary—a woman with bright violet eyes and striking black hair that shimmered a matching violet wherever the light hit. "Its *Mrs. De Leon,* and thank you," she said, rising from the chair where she'd spent the past twenty minutes staring at the bare concrete walls of the bunker. She graciously decided not to add to the woman's gaff by mentioning that she should be addressed as *Senator,* not *Miss* or *Mrs.*

Catalina turned and walked up to a pair of matte black bodyguard drones flanking the entrance of the president's office. One of them held out a hand. "Halt. Please wait while you are scanned for weapons and explosive devices."

Catalina took a breath and held it, enduring the indignity of the body scan as a fan of blue light flickered out from one of the bot's chests. She'd already been scanned twice prior—once at the entrance of the Presidential Palace, and again at the entrance of the bunker. At least bots took no interest in how she looked underneath her clothes, which was more than she could say for the human guards at the entrance of the palace. She wondered if everyone was submitted to as much suspicion, or just *League* party members.

A pleasant tone sounded and the bot who'd scanned her said, "You may proceed, Senator de Leon."

The doors swished open, revealing an exact replica of the president's above-ground oval office. Catalina walked in to find the president sitting on one of the couches, watching a 3D hologram rising from the coffee table in front of him. The president was so focused on the news that he didn't appear to notice her come in. The holofeed was from the Alliance News Network (ANN). At the moment it showed a pair of talking heads, one of them a news anchor, the other *Former Navy Admiral Lars Becker*—or so read the caption below his side of the transmission. The man looked to be at least seventy years old, with thinning gray hair, gaunt, wrinkled cheeks, and hollow, watery blue eyes. Catalina studied that face curiously as she approached. There was no way that man had voluntarily chosen to have such a frail appearance. That meant he had to have been born before scientists had found a way to shackle the hands of time—or least before they had done so for *everyone,* rich and poor alike.

Catalina stopped beside the president's couch. "Hello, Mr. President…" she began.

He glanced her way and nodded. "Please take a seat, Senator."

She looked from Wallace to the holofeed and back again before sitting in one of the armchairs. "What is this?"

He flung out a hand, as if to slap the hologram. "Another disaster!"

Puzzled, Catalina fixed her attention on the newsfeed.

"…so you're saying this is definitely *not* a Solarian attack?" the news anchor asked.

Admiral Becker spread his hands. "What do the Solarians stand to gain from attacking us? If we go to war, they'll lose. The attacks didn't cripple us; they just made us angry."

"So how does that play into your alien invasion theory? Why would these *Watchers* of yours hit us with warning shots rather than a full-scale invasion?"

Becker shrugged. "Maybe they are testing their aim. And I doubt it's their goal to wipe us out. They want to weaken us for conquest—or in this case, for *infestation.*"

"I see. You mentioned to our viewers that you have proof."

"I do."

"And this proof is in the form of…"

"Classified transmissions from the *Intrepid* dating back more than fifty years ago. Compare those transmissions to the ones we received from the Looking Glass before the lunar attack, and you'll see the similarities are extraordinary."

The news anchor nodded sagely, as if he were already convinced. "I understand that you've shown these transmissions before, and that is what earned you a dishonorable discharge from the Navy."

A muscle twitched in Becker's cheek and he nodded stiffly. "Yes. I thought the public had a right to know what we found. The government disagreed. There was an extensive cover-up, and I was made to look like a fool." The man blew out a deep breath. His deflated lungs left him looking shriveled. He appeared to be drowning in his old Navy uniform, nothing but a skeleton underneath. Catalina stifled a gasp, feeling a twinge of revulsion and pity for the man.

The news anchor nodded once more. "For those of us who might not remember, could you explain what the *Intrepid's* mission was about, Admiral?"

"Of course. It was a mission to explore and colonize another star system. Our nearest star with Earth-type planets was considered to be Wolf 1061, an M class red dwarf 13.8 light years away, located in the Ophiuchus Constellation. We determined that Wolf 1061C and 1061D would be good candidates for colonization. What most people didn't give much weight to at the time was that if these planets were so habitable, then there was also a chance that they could already be inhabited."

"What happened to the *Intrepid,* Admiral?"

"That depends upon who you ask."

"We're asking you."

Becker nodded and smiled, his watery blue eyes suddenly

bright and intense. "They encountered intelligent life, but it turned out to be hostile."

"Chilling words. We'll be back with you in a minute, Admiral, while we show our viewers what you're talking about."

"Of course. I'll be waiting."

Catalina watched with a furrowed brow as the talking heads faded to black and a bar of text appeared.

Classified Transmission from W.A.S. Intrepid - November 18, 2774.

The text faded, and a new face appeared. The caption below read: *Captain White of the W.A.S. Intrepid.* He was a Caucasian man with straight brown hair and a nest of laugh lines around two eyes that were the purest black Catalina had ever seen, as if two matching holes had been bored into his skull.

"Hello wretched creatures," the captain said, his voice flat and emotionless, his posture rigid. Catalina felt a chill run down her spine. He sounded like a bot and looked like a human. League Party warnings about a bot revolution came to mind... "Your species sickens us. The time of your judgment is at hand." The camera panned and zoomed out to show an assembled group of Alliance officers and enlisted personnel, all of them with matching black eyes and rigid postures. "Death you sow, and death you reap," the captain said.

The rest of the crew repeated that line in unison, all in exactly the same toneless voices. Then the camera panned back to show just the captain's face once more. "We are coming."

The transmission faded to black, and another line of text appeared.

End of data stream.

Back were the talking heads from before.

"And you say these people were infested by an alien

intelligence—some kind of parasite," the news anchor said.

Becker nodded grimly. "Yes."

"I'm already noticing a few similarities to the Moon transmissions," the anchor said, but we're going to play those now so everyone can see. One moment, Admiral."

The screen faded to black once more, and another line of text popped up.

Unidentified Transmission from the Looking Glass - November 18, 2824.

As the text faded, a woman of Chinese descent appeared wearing a torn and stained Confederate uniform. Her eyes were the same empty black holes that Captain White's had been. The transmission froze, and the previous one returned for a side-by-side comparison of their expressionless faces and soulless eyes. Then both transmissions began to play, and Catalina heard Captain White and the Confederate woman say exactly the same thing in the exact same toneless voice:

"Hello wretched creatures."

Catalina shivered. "What the hell?" she asked, looking to Wallace for answers. He just shook his head, and went on staring at the screen. Catalina looked back in time to see the talking heads return.

"Well, Admiral, it would seem that after all these years you may have been right."

"Indeed, though I can't say I'm happy. I'd rather be a lunatic than have the Watchers come to Earth."

Wallace waved the screen off with a growl.

Catalina regarded him. Her mouth felt dry; her mind spun with questions.

"We should have executed that bastard when we had the chance," Wallace said.

Catalina's eyebrows shot up. "I don't understand… He

was right."

"No, he was wrong, and he's been duped into helping the Solarians to keep us jumping at shadows. The fact that he managed to convince you tells me just how serious this is. We need to act fast."

Catalina shook her head, not getting it, and Wallace regarded her with a look of strained patience. "What do you think is more likely, Senator, that some sort of parasitic aliens are invading us, or that someone is trying to make us think that? Someone who saw the transmissions Becker leaked all those years ago decided to copy them now. If we were being attacked by real aliens, why send us a warning at all? Unless they were planning to make some sort of demand, which they didn't. Why tell someone that you're going to shoot them just before you pull the trigger?"

"What about the transmissions from the *Intrepid?* Those were real, weren't they?"

"Yes, but what you saw had nothing to do with aliens. The captain of the *Intrepid* went insane."

"And his crew? They were all singing the same tune."

"A tune he no doubt had them rehearse while he stood ready to execute the ship's self-destruct sequence. It was coercion, Senator. Those videos have been analyzed a thousand times. Captain White forced everyone else to go along with his delusion."

"What about their eyes?"

Catalina watched as President Wallace's green eyes became two empty black pits. "Now I'm an alien," he said, speaking in a mock toneless voice.

Catalina was taken aback. For a split second she believed it, and she was about to make a run for the door. Then she realized what he'd done. Most people wore augmented reality lenses, including her. Besides enabling people to browse the net, take pictures, and watch holofeeds, those lenses also enabled them to change the natural color of their eyes as easily as they changed their socks.

"So it was the Solarians that attacked us."

Warmth and color seeped back into President Wallace's eyes, and he nodded. "Yes."

"Why?"

"Becker said it best—they would lose in a straight fight with us. That means they need plausible deniability, a way to pretend it wasn't them. That also explains why they didn't make a more concerted attack. They don't want to utterly destroy the Earth because they want to take it for themselves."

"Do we have any evidence to implicate them?"

Wallace nodded, his eyes unblinking, never leaving hers. "We have a whole ship full of evidence."

"I don't understand. What ship?"

"A Solarian ship, recently detected over a billion kilometers from Earth—in the same direction that those missiles came from."

Catalina gaped at the president.

Wallace nodded slowly. "I have a battleship moving to intercept and capture them as we speak. We're officially at war, Senator, and it's time people knew it, before these ridiculous stories of an alien invasion get out of hand."

CHAPTER 12

—Two Days Later—

"Admiral, we are twenty minutes from ELR with the *Crimson Warrior,*" Frost announced from sensors.

"Carry on, Lieutenant." Alexander rapped his fingers on the armrest of his acceleration couch. In twenty minutes he and Captain Vrokovich could stop trading empty threats and start trading deadly blows instead. Neither of them was eager to start a war or else they would have already begun firing missiles and hypervelocity rounds.

Alexander shook his head. The problem with waiting to reach laser range was that lasers would make short work of both ships. Missiles could be intercepted and hypervelocity rounds could be evaded, but lasers were sure to hit. Once they reached effective laser range (ELR), the engagement would be over in minutes.

"We should have fired on them long ago," McAdams said.

"That would have given them the upper-hand, Commander. They have more guns, more fighters, more missiles—but lasers? It doesn't matter how many they have, because both our ships have more than enough to obliterate each other."

"So your plan is to trade the *Adamantine* for the *Crimson*

Warrior?"

"Not exactly. Bishop, come about for reverse thrust at ten *G*s."

"Aye, sir."

"We're leaving?" McAdams asked.

"Hayes, get me Captain Vrokovich on the comms," Alexander said.

"Yes, sir."

"I thought you two were done talking."

"We were. It's time to apologize for our bluff."

"Apologize for our..." McAdams shook her head. "Fleet Command hasn't changed our orders."

"No, they haven't, Commander."

"Then you're going rogue. You'll be court-martialed."

"The *Crimson Warrior* is responding to our hail," Hayes interrupted.

"On screen," Alexander replied. Turning to his XO, he smiled and said, "If I were scared of being court-martialed for backing down, I never would have won a Nobel Peace Prize."

Alexander heard someone clear his throat, and McAdams gestured to the main display with chin and eyes.

"Admiral Alexander, I see you are turning your ship around."

Alexander looked to the fore to see Captain Vrokovich's by now familiar face—bony features, ghostly white skin, straight black hair, and startling red eyes. Alexander nodded. "If you were guilty, you would have fired on us by now."

"I'm glad to hear you've come to your senses. A bluff is only as good as the possible consequences of it being true—in this case, your ship and mine coming into direct conflict. The *Crimson Warrior* would survive such a confrontation, but the *Adamantine* would not. Your threats were, therefore, obviously empty, Admiral. Desperate and empty. I am sorry your government sent you on such a fool's errand. Perhaps it would have gotten results if I was the fool you were looking for."

"We were just following orders, Captain," Alexander said with a tight smile, a muscle twitching in his jaw.

"Then let us be thankful that your orders were only to threaten war and not to make it."

Alexander nodded, and Captain Vrokovich returned his smile. "Goodbye, Admiral."

The holo display faded back to space. Stars sprinkled the void in dense clusters.

"Bishop, what's the combined approach velocity between us and the *Crimson Warrior*?"

"One thousand and fifteen klicks per second at the moment, sir, but we're still firing the mains in full reverse."

"Good. What's our range to target?"

"Four hundred and six thousand klicks, sir."

"ETA to reach the target at current speed?"

"Still over six minutes to ELR."

"How long before we pass them?"

"Four hundred and eight seconds."

"Good. Cardinal—dead-drop all of our laser-armed ordnance along our current trajectory, but hang on to our missiles with payloads for now."

McAdams eyes flew wide. "I thought you decided to risk a court-martial."

"I timed that comment so that Captain Vrokovich would overhear it, priming him to believe that we're actually retreating. Between that, his assumption of superiority, and his assumption that we were bluffing all along, he won't suspect a double-cross. They're going to break off and return to their original trajectory, but four hundred seconds is not enough time for either of us to cancel our current momentum, so we'll still fly by within spitting distance of each other. Perfect for a sneak attack."

"Remind me never to cross you, sir," McAdams said.

Alexander smiled grimly. "When facing a stronger opponent, sneakery is the only way to win, Commander."

"Sneakery… I'll be sure to add that to my lexicon. What makes you think they won't spot our missiles before they reach firing range?"

"Because Captain Vroko isn't looking for them."

"I hope you're right, sir."

"I am, but just in case—Frost, keep our scanners checking for incoming enemy ordnance. We don't want to be blinded by the same assumptions. If they so much as flushed a toilet in our direction, I want to know about it."

"I'll be sure to let you know if I detect any space shit flying our way, sir," Frost replied.

"We're about to start an interplanetary war and you're cracking jokes," McAdams admonished.

"Black humor isn't for everyone, Commander, but it does serve to emphasize the absurdity and irony of our situation. Who ends a terrible war and calls it *The Last War* only to have the same person who ended that war start another even more terrible war thirty years later?"

"All of our laser-armed missiles are away, Admiral," Cardinal announced.

"Good. Set the clock with the time for the first wave to reach ELR with the enemy ship. Set a second clock with the time for us to reach ELR."

"Aye, sir," Cardinal replied.

"Bishop, give me an estimate of how long we'll spend in laser range of the *Crimson Warrior* while we pass by each other."

"Calculating…"

Two glowing green timers appeared at the top of the main holo display, one with the caption—*Time to ELR, 1st Wave Ord.* Counting down from five minutes and forty-three seconds. The other *Time to ELR, ADMT. - C.W.* counting down from five minutes and fifty-one seconds. The time discrepancy between the two clocks was exactly eight seconds. That was how long the *Adamantine's* laser-armed missiles would have to make an uncontested first strike against the *Crimson Warrior*. After that, the *Adamantine* herself would pass into laser range of the enemy dreadnought and they would have to weather the assault for... "Bishop?"

"Done, sir. We'll spend about thirteen seconds inside ELR with the *Crimson Warrior*. Add another four seconds for extended ELR for a total of seventeen seconds."

Alexander winced as he imagined trading blows with the dreadnought for that long.

"They could do a lot of damage to us in that time," McAdams said. "We might both end up derelict."

"We'd better make sure that doesn't happen. We have eight seconds to weaken them with our missiles before they can fire back on us."

"Hopefully that's enough time, sir."

"It will be."

CHAPTER 13

"Admiral, our missiles are ten seconds from ELR," Cardinal announced.

Alexander nodded, keeping his eyes locked on the countdown at the top of the main holo display. "I see it. Bishop, prepare to come about just before that count hits zero, and make sure you keep our engines facing away from the enemy at all times."

"Aye, sir."

"Cardinal, use our missiles to target the Crimson Warrior's engines, and then her fighter launch tubes. We need to cripple them as much as possible with our first volley."

"Yes, sir."

The countdown reached zero, and Alexander watched via the enhanced view on the main holo display as their warheads split into a thousand glittering shards. Each of them lit its thrusters and went evasive. Hot-white contrails appeared behind each missile, illuminating space with bright spirals and zig-zags as the missiles adopted randomly varying approach vectors. A split second later, the missiles opened fire and space came alive with a dazzling flurry of red and blue lasers, all of them vectoring in on the Crimson Warrior's engines. Abruptly an explosion tore through the aft end of the ship and a giant chunk of it went drifting away. The ghostly green glow from the Crimson's Warrior's engines disappeared, and the remainder of the massive ship went on drifting through space, now carried only by its momentum.

"Direct hit!" Cardinal crowed. "Target is derelict!"

"Target enemy laser batteries with our hypervelocity cannons, and use our missiles to take out those fighter launch tubes!"

"Yes, sir."

"Stone, launch our fighters! See if they can squeeze in a few shots before we fly out of range."

"Aye."

Hypervelocity rounds thundered out into the void: *thud, thud, thud...* and glowing golden lines of tracer fire appeared, tracking ahead of the enemy ship.

Alexander watched the Solarian ship fire back with simulated streaks of green extended-range (ER) and yellow high-intensity (HI) lasers. The two ships were still out of range with each other, so all of those shots went straight for the *Adamantine's* missiles. Fiery explosions pock-marked the void, and then the remaining missiles fired for a second time. This time explosions rippled all along the enemy's hull, each explosion marking one of the dreadnought's fighter launch tubes.

"Enemy is launching missiles!" Frost announced.

"Intercept that ordnance!"

Another flash of green and yellow lasers took out the remainder of the *Adamantine's* missiles before they could fire for a third time. Then the *Adamantine's* own extended-range lasers *screeched* to life, adding sapphire blue to the mix of wavelengths flashing through the vacuum. It was easy to forget that those colors were all simulated. Lasers were invisible in space. Then again, Alexander thought, with him and his crew commanding the ship from within a mindscape, technically *everything* was being simulated.

All but two of the enemy missiles evaporated under the *Adamantine's* barrage, disappearing before they had a chance to split into ten times as many independently-guided fragments. The last two were taken out by hypervelocity cannons.

"Extended ELR reached!" McAdams announced.

Alexander winced away from the main holo display as green streaks of enemy ER lasers vectored in on them from the *Crimson Warrior*. A loud *sizzling* reached Alexander's ears with those impacts, as if he could actually hear the *Adamantine's* armor boiling away. Then the deck shuddered with the distant roar of an explosion.

"Hull breach on deck 119!" Rodriguez said.

"Seal it off, and send in the repair bots!" McAdams ordered.

The *Adamantine* returned fire with a deafening *screech* as all forty of its laser batteries fired at once. Each shot hit home, two or three to a target, disabling the remainder of the enemy's fighter launch tubes on that side. Then the *Adamantine's* first wave of fighters and drones joined the action, adding their own lasers to the mix. Streams of hypervelocity rounds slammed into the *Crimson Warrior's* hull, taking out its remaining laser batteries on that side. Then they raced past the dreadnought and came into range of the batteries on the other side.

Bright green and yellow beams angled in on them from several dozen different weapon emplacements. The *Adamantine's* fighters fired back on those emplacements, silencing some of the batteries.

Bishop kept the *Adamantine's* nose pointed at the enemy as they flew by one another in order to keep their engines safe, but they were still taking heavy damage. The air sizzled and screeched with the simulated noise of enemy lasers impacting and the *Adamantine's* own batteries firing back. Alexander squeezed the armrests of his acceleration couch until his knuckles turned white. He winced every time the deck shuddered with a new hull breach. The main holo display vanished and then returned from a slightly different angle as the holocameras on the bow took a hit.

"Breaches on decks 99 through 130!" Rodriguez reported.

McAdams brought up a damage report beside the tactical map already hovering above her control station, and Alexander glanced at it. The *Adamantine's* bow had been flayed open to a depth of over thirty decks.

Their fighters went on firing, targeting enemy weapon emplacements and enemy fighter launch tubes, but this time with lasers only. The two ships were now speeding apart with a combined velocity of over 970 kilometers per second. Hypervelocity cannons had a muzzle velocity of just over 100 klicks per second, and missiles would run out of fuel before they could catch up. In just a few seconds the ships would pass out of laser range with each other, and then the engagement would be over.

The *Crimson Warrior* fired back with another flurry of lasers, but this time there were barely half a dozen, and all of them were the green, extended-range variety.

"We've passed out of laser range," McAdams announced.

Alexander let out a breath he hadn't realized he was holding. "The longest seventeen seconds of my life."

McAdams nodded. "Aye, sir—Rodriguez, damage report."

"We lost our top thirty three decks to space. Our bow is practically missing. With it we lost our primary comm and sensor relays, but we'll get by on the auxiliaries for now. Aside from that, we lost a number of weapon emplacements and nearly all of the enlisted crew quarters and living space. We'll live to fight another day, Commander, but the damage is going to take some time to repair."

Alexander jerked his chin to indicate the damage report hovering in front of McAdams. "They missed the nukes in our forward launch tubes by a hair."

"That's probably what they were aiming for," Rodriguez replied. "Otherwise why wouldn't they try to take out our laser batteries the way we were doing with theirs?"

"They were playing the long odds while we played the sure ones. One lucky hit and we'd all be floating through vacuum in a cloud of shrapnel right now. Frost—what kind of damage did we deal to the enemy ship?"

"Their fighter launch tubes are all down except for four, and by last count they had just ten laser batteries out of sixty still firing. That might change by the time we catch up to them, though. Also, they managed to launch a total of sixteen drones and twelve fighters."

Alexander nodded. The enemy dreadnought carried a complement of 144 drones and 96 fighters, so the majority of her fighter screen had been trapped in the launch tubes.

"Stone, how did our fighter screen fare?"

"Sitting pretty, Admiral. We have fifty drones and sixty fighters deployed."

Alexander nodded. His plan had worked. They now outnumbered and outgunned the enemy ship. "Bishop, fire up the mains at five *G*s. It's time to give chase."

"Aye, sir."

"Stone, have our fighters head out at six *G*s and the drones at ten. Let's see if we can take out the rest of the *Crimson*

Warrior's defenses without risking any of our lives."

"Yes, sir."

Alexander took a deep breath and regarded the distant, glinting speck of the enemy ship.

"It would seem Fleet Command's faith in you was not misplaced, sir," McAdams said.

Alexander was about to reply to that when Hayes announced, "Admiral, the *Crimson Warrior* has issued a surrender, and they have agreed to submit their ship for boarding."

Alexander's brow lifted in surprise. "So, Captain Vroko finally came to *his* senses."

"How do we know it isn't a trick?" McAdams asked.

Alexander turned to her. "There's only one way to find out, Commander."

McAdams' blue eyes narrowed. "And that is?"

"We board them."

CHAPTER 14

"Admiral, we are in position to board the *Crimson Warrior*," Frost reported from sensors.

Alexander nodded. "Range to target?"

"11,000 klicks, just outside extended ELR, sir."

"Good. Bishop, hold us steady there. Make sure we don't get any closer than that."

"Aye, sir."

"McAdams—you have the conn."

She turned to him, her brow pinched with suspicion. "Don't tell me you're going to join the boarding party."

"I am," he said.

"Sir, you *cannot* afford to risk your life like that."

Alexander regarded her with amusement. "A good leader leads from the front line not *behind* the lines."

"I'm sure Lord Cardigan of the Light Brigade said the same thing," McAdams replied.

"The who of the what? Never mind. Stone—"

"Sir?"

"Transfer command of one of our VSM drones to my station, and get the rest of our marines hooked up while you're at it. Launch the shuttles as soon as everyone's ready."

"Aye, sir," Stone replied.

"You could have told me you were planning to board them with *drones,*" McAdams dead-panned.

Alexander shot her a grin. "You didn't ask, so I didn't tell."

"Ha ha."

"Going live in five, Admiral," Stone reported.

Alexander nodded, his gaze still on McAdams. "Keep an eye on things up here, Commander."

"Yes, sir," McAdams said, nodding once.

That was the last thing Alexander saw before being directly connected to the sensor feeds from one of the *Adamantine's* VSM (Virtual Space Marine) drones. A glowing blue HUD crowded the edges of his field of view giving him access to a kind of ESP—radar, infrared, 360-degree sight, sonic sensors, and a host of other super-human powers that only drones could have.

Alexander looked left, then right, and counted eleven identical drones lining the sides of the shuttle where he stood. Three fire teams of four marines counting himself. A unit number and call sign floated above each of their matte black heads in bright green text: *SHDW-1 MSgt 'Ram', SHDW-2 Cpl 'Balls', SHDW-3 LCpl 'Mouth',* and so on. Shadow squad was a part of the 2nd Batallion, 4th Marines, otherwise known as *The Magnificent Bastards.* It was a battalion with a long, proud history, dating back all the way to World War I. Their motto: *Second to None.*

Alexander smiled at that. He looked down at his hands and flexed all ten of his articulated fingers, open and shut, open and shut. He could *feel* those hands as if they were his own, but they didn't look like his. They were the same matte black as the rest of his hardened alloy body. Early VSM drones had taken various forms, but it turned out that humans were best-suited to remote-controlling bots with two arms and two legs.

McAdams' voice echoed inside Alexander's head: "Launching shuttles, sir."

"ETA?" Alexander asked.

"Just under sixteen minutes."

"Roger that."

A jolt went through the shuttle, then Alexander felt his drone being pressed sideways against the docking clamps as the shuttle rocketed out of its launch tube and into space. The effect of the *G*-force wasn't as uncomfortable as it would have been for his human body, but rather it helped to keep him oriented—the front of the shuttle was to his left, the engines to the rear.

"Weapons and systems check!" Shadow One called out.

A matching stream of text appeared at the bottom of Alexander's HUD in case he missed the verbal command. He ran through a check of his VSM. All systems green. Integrated weapons—.50 caliber anti-personnel cannons—*check,* mini rocket launchers—*check,* proximity mines and plasma grenades—*check,* laser cannons and point defenses—*check,* tranquilizer darts and active denial systems—*check,* disc drones—*check.*

"All systems nominal," Alexander reported amidst a stream of similar acknowledgments from the rest of Shadow Squad.

The lights in the back of the shuttle dimmed to a muted red glow and Alexander settled his metallic head back against the side of the shuttle. He had no heart to beat, and no lungs to breathe, nothing to disturb the silence—there was just the steady roar of the shuttle's thrusters shuddering through the bulkheads, and the clicking of robotic fidgeting. Alexander used the silence to collect his thoughts—

Clank-clank-CLANK, Clank-clank-CLANK, Clank-clank-CLANK.

So much for silence. Alexander turned toward the sound and found himself staring at the marine standing immediately to his left. He narrowed his eyes—except that he didn't have eyes to narrow. The identifying text above the other man's VSM read, *SHDW-5 Cpl "Chesty."*

"Chesty, stop that."

A featureless black head turned his way. Two small holo cameras glinted where a human's eyes would be as lenses moved to focus on him. "You say something, Admiral?"

Clank-clank-CLANK, Clank-clank-CLANK…

"That clanking sound. Stop."

"What clanking sound, sir?"

The sound amplified. Instead of one set of metallic feet striking the deck it sounded like a stampede. *Clank-clank-CLANK!*

"*That* one," Alexander said.

Someone started up a marching cadence to fit the beat and the others joined in.

"We-are, we-are, the mag-ni-ficent BASTARDS!"

Alexander smiled inwardly. After exactly three repetitions Chesty added in a thunderous voice, following the same rhythm: "SE-COND-TO-NONE!"

"All right, enough screwing around, boys!" Ram said. "Welcome to Shadow Squad, Admiral."

"Thank you, Sergeant."

"Since this is your first time out with us, sir, make sure you stick close to your team leader—that's Corporal Chesty over there. I believe you've already met."

Alexander nodded. "Aye."

"We don't dot our *ayes* in the space marines, sir," Sergeant Ram said. "The correct response is *oo-rah*."

"Hoorah," Alexander replied, nodding.

The air inside the shuttle grew suddenly very still and quiet.

"What did you say, sir?" Ram asked.

"Hoo-rah, Sergeant."

"Mouth—the admiral asked a question, would you kindly tell him for us *hoo Rah* is?"

"The very first marine, sir! He killed a great white shark with his bare hands and fed his entire village with the stinking carcass, sir!"

"Thank you, Mouth."

Alexander's inward smile faded to a puzzled frown. "What was he—a Viking?

"Good guess, but no," Ram replied. "Now, the reason we don't say hoo-rah like the dirty dirt-pounders do, is because we know *who Rah* is, so instead we say *OO-RAH*, like *OOO that Rah guy is a damned legend!*"

Alexander smiled. "You guys are full of shit."

"OORAH!" the squad shouted in unison.

A new voice crackled through the cabin, pleasant and female: "One minute to docking with the *Crimson Warrior.* Get ready, boys." It was the shuttle pilot.

"You heard the captain!" Ram said.

Alexander felt the *G*-forces inside the shuttle ease, followed by a *thud-unk* of magnetic landing struts mating with the outer hull of the *Crimson Warrior.* Inside the shuttle the clamps that held their drones in place opened up with a clicking-*whirr,* and the air came alive with magnetic feet *clanking* as they all shuffled into line at the rear airlock of the shuttle. Alexander noted how blocky the drones were—thick limbs and torsos with high shoulders. Between their armor and integrated weapons they looked vaguely like overly muscular caricatures of human soldiers.

"*Ma deuces* out," Ram said.

Alexander mentally toggled his .50 caliber cannons, and a pair of fat gun barrels slid up out of his drone's forearms.

"Open sesame," Ram said, waving a hand at the inner airlock doors and then the outer ones.

As the second set of doors opened they revealed yet another set. Those doors had the Solarian Republic flag emblazoned on them. Three vertical stripes: red, green, and blue to represent the Solarians' future vision of the red planet as they terraformed it from red to green to blue. After 30 years of terraforming they were still stuck on red.

Ram gestured to Shadow Eleven. "Get me a can opener, Private."

"Oorah."

Alexander watched as the private went to work on the *Crimson Warrior's* outer airlock doors with a plasma torch. All of a minute later he'd drawn a molten orange circle around the inner edge of the doors. He kicked them in with a noisy *bang!* and walked up to the final set of doors to try the control panel.

"Locked," the private announced.

"Guess it's asking too much for them to open the door for us," Mouth said.

"What were you expecting? A red carpet?" Chesty replied.

"They're Martians. What other color would it be?"

"Can it! Peel her open, Private," Ram said.

The private drew another molten orange circle and kicked in the last set of doors. He poked his head through and then called back to them, "We're clear, Sergeant!"

"Move out!" Ram said.

"OORAH!" the squad roared and set out with paradoxically silent footfalls.

They rushed through the enemy airlock and took up positions against the walls of a brightly-lit silver corridor with Martian-red accents.

"At least they left the lights on for us," Mouth said.

"So why not open the airlocks?" Balls asked.

"Get your disc drones out and scouting," Ram ordered.

None of them bothered to whisper, since the squad's communications were all actually carried out virtually back on the *Adamantine.*

Alexander activated his disc drone and set it to scout-mode. Twelve black discs rose over their heads from the docking ports on their backs, half of them streaking out ahead and the other half behind. Alexander kept his eyes flicking between his scanners, the drone cam, and the VSM's rear-view display for maximum situational awareness. He saw the drones fetch up against the bulkhead doors on either end of the corridor.

"Corridor is sealed, Sarge," Shadow Seven said.

"The other squads are reporting the bulkheads in their sections are locked, too," Mouth reported.

"Captain Vrokovich is a sneaky bastard," Ram growled.

"Pot calling kettle, sir," Mouth said.

"I said sneaky. We're magnificent bastards, remember?"

"Something's wrong here," Alexander said. "Hold on." He activated his comm. "McAdams?"

"Sir?"

"Have Hayes hail Captain Vroko and patch me through."

"Aye, sir."

A moment later a new HUD box appeared with a hologram of Captain Vrokovich in it. The man's red eyes sparkled with a suspicious glint. "Admiral de Leon," Vrokovich said. A hint of a smile touched his lips. "I see you've decided to join the boarding party."

"In the flesh—or drone, in this case. Listen, Captain, I'm not sure you understand how a surrender is supposed to work."

Vrokovich cocked his head curiously. "What do you mean, Admiral?"

"The *Crimson* Princess is in lock-down. We had to cut our way in."

Vrokovich scowled. "I am sorry, Admiral. You exposed many of our decks to space, so we had to seal off certain sections to preserve our atmosphere. We are still working to restore pressure. Rest assured that as soon as we do so, I will open all the bulkheads you like. Until then, I suggest you stick to the pressurized areas. Give me a moment to get the appropriate doors open for you. I'll send you a map so you don't lose your way."

The captain's transmission ended and a file transfer request appeared a few seconds later. Alexander waited for the drone's virus scanner to check the file, and then accepted it.

A 3D schematic of the dreadnought appeared with a branching green line to mark a 'safe' path through the ship from stem to stern. Alexander studied that route. The captain's explanation for all the locked doors was plausible, but that was the problem—it was the perfect excuse to guide them on a set path through the dreadnought.

The question was *why?* To lead them into a trap? Or to keep them from finding any evidence that might connect the *Crimson Warrior* to the attacks on the Alliance?

Just then the bulkhead doors in front of them *swished* open, revealing another long, silver corridor, this one plagued by dim, flickering red lights.

"Looks like they laid out that carpet for us after all," Alexander said as their disc drones rushed through the open doors.

"Move out, Shadows," Ram ordered. "Nice and easy."

"Oorah..." the squad replied as they raised their .50 caliber cannons and began creeping down the corridor.

CHAPTER 15

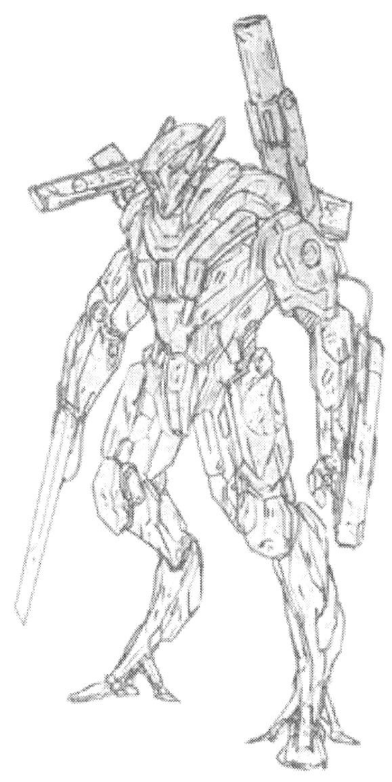

Shadow Squad met up with the other half of their platoon, Goblin Squad, at the entrance of the *Crimson Warrior's* bridge. Unlike the other bulkheads they'd passed through as they negotiated Captain Vrokovich's 'safe' route through the ship, this one didn't open automatically for them as they approached.

"Someone get me a can opener!" Ram ordered.

"Oorah," one of the Goblins replied.

"Everyone else, find cover positions!"

Alexander fell in behind his team leader, Chesty, and waited for the private with the 'can opener' to do his job. A molten orange line crept around the doors in a slow circle, chasing its tail.

The two ends met, and Alexander held an imaginary breath. He half-expected the doors to blow open and enemy marines to come storming out, weapons blazing.

Instead the private kicked the doors in. They bounced off the deck and went floating through the bridge, narrowly missing the heads of the enemy captain and his crew waiting on the other side.

Shadow and Goblin Squads raised their weapons, metal joints clicking and servos *whirring* in a sudden flurry of movement.

"Hands where I can see 'em!" Ram ordered.

Their hands were already above their heads. "We are not armed," Captain Vrokovich announced, his red eyes seeming to glow in the gloomy battle lighting of the bridge.

Alexander stormed into the bridge behind his squad while Goblin Squad brought up the rear.

"You are all now prisoners of the Alliance," Ram continued.

"Don't you want to check if we are guilty first?" Vrokovich asked, cocking his head to one side like a bird. *With those eyes he looks more like a rabbit,* Alexander decided as he moved to address the enemy captain.

"Where's the rest of your crew?" Alexander asked.

"In their G-tanks. I thought it best for them to remain there in order to minimize further casualties as you trigger-happy terrans go prancing through my ship."

Alexander turned to Ram. "Sergeant, get squads down to those levels and lock them in. We lost our brig in the fighting, so there's no where else for us to put them. While you're at it, check the ship's roster and get me a head-count to compare. We don't want to miss anyone."

"Yes, sir," Ram replied.

"The head count won't match the roster," Captain Vrokovich said as Shadow squad began cuffing his officers' hands behind their backs. "We lost at least fifty crewmates when you attacked us. The people you're looking for are all floating out in space." Vrokovich's upper lip twisted with contempt. "The Alliance will pay for what they've done today."

Alexander opened his palms and mimicked the see-saw motion of a balance scale. "Five million dead on Earth and two million dead on the Moon versus fifty dead on your ship. I wonder which side has more blood on it?"

"Go get your proof then," Vrokovich said, jerking his chin toward the empty bridge control stations climbing the far wall of the bridge behind him. "That's what you came for, isn't it?"

Alexander gave the other man a narrow-eyed look that would have had a greater effect if his VSM were capable of facial expressions. Instead he leveled an index finger at his chest. "Altering ship's logs leaves a data trail. If you touched them, you'll have given me all the proof I need."

"We didn't alter anything. We didn't need to," Vrokovich replied, shrugging as Mouth cuffed his wrists behind his back.

Rather than waste more time bantering, Alexander stalked past the enemy captain, straight up to the lower pair of control stations—the captain's and XO's stations. He climbed into the captain's station and waved it to life. A holographic display appeared, and Alexander summoned the ship's logs with a combination of gestures and voice commands.

Navigation logs showed that the *Crimson Warrior* left Mars two months ago. They flew straight to Saturn and on to the moon of Tethys, where they remained for about a week. They were on a circuitous route home when the *Adamantine* hailed them. At no point in their trip were they moving fast enough to have launched the missiles that hit the Moon or Earth.

It was a plausible flight plan, and the fact that they'd gone to Tethys suggested some sort of crazy Martian terraforming agenda since that moon was practically solid ice.

Alexander didn't trust the data, but he couldn't find anything to suggest the logs had been altered. Making matters worse, there was a record of a rendezvous with an Alliance civilian supply ship, the *Wayfinder,* not long before the Moon attack. That would be easy to verify, and if true, it gave the *Crimson Warrior* a strong alibi.

Alexander felt abruptly sick. *What if Captain Vroko was telling the truth?* He poked around for a while longer, submitting the enemy ship's computer core to a data probe to check for signs of log alterations. The probe came back negative. Things weren't looking good for the Alliance. Alexander checked to see if the sealed sections of the ship were all actually exposed to space as Captain Vroko had said…

And that checked out, too.

They couldn't afford to leave those areas un-explored, but it did make Alexander feel better about the set path they'd been forced to take through the *Crimson Warrior.*

Finally, he checked the number of active and inactive *G*-tanks and compared that to the ship's roster. One hundred and three active tanks, fifty-seven inactive—not counting the brig—and the ship's roster had exactly 160 crew, meaning there were fifty-seven dead.

Feeling suddenly weary, Alexander eased out of the control station and walked back to the entrance of the bridge.

"Find what you were looking for?" Captain Vrokovich asked, sounding smug.

Alexander ignored him and walked up to Sergeant Ram. "Get these prisoners down to the *G*-tanks and lock them in with the rest."

"Oorah," Ram replied.

Alexander watched as Shadow Squad and Goblin Squad left the bridge with their prisoners in tow. A few tech specialists stayed behind to slave the *Crimson Warrior's* systems to the *Adamantine's* controls. Sergeant Ram remained behind as well.

"Did you find anything?" he asked.

Alexander waited for the prisoners to pass out of earshot, but then he remembered that they didn't need to speak audibly to each other and opted for private comms. "I think they might have been telling the truth. Their flight plan is reasonable, the logs don't look altered, and they have an alibi—an Alliance civilian transport."

"Shit. If they're so innocent, then why the hell didn't they give us what we asked for?"

"You mean why didn't they bend over when we asked them to?"

"That's not…" Ram trailed off.

"It's exactly what we asked them to do. The Solarian Republic and the Alliance are not allies. We're not even very friendly after they declared their independence thirty years ago. Giving us access to their flight plan and mission data would set a bad political precedent and pave the way for future insults to their sovereignty."

"So you're telling me we just started an interplanetary war because the Solarians were too damn proud to prove their innocence?"

"We need more time to look through their data before we can be sure," Alexander replied.

Another voice interrupted them. "Admiral, we have a problem." It was McAdams.

"What's wrong, Commander?"

"Enemy ships incoming, seven of them, all destroyer-class."

"Range?"

"They're just leaving Martian orbit, so they've got a good half a billion klicks to cover, but we have to cover double that to reach Earth, and they have a much higher top speed than we do—especially considering we'll be towing a derelict dreadnought."

"How long do we have before they reach us?"

"Depends what kind of *G*s they pull… at theoretical maximums, about a day."

"Contact Fleet Command, explain the situation, and ask for an escort to meet us halfway. Make sure they know we're already limping thanks to our engagement with the *Crimson Warrior,* otherwise they might order us into another ridiculous fight. Hopefully they can make it to us before those destroyers do."

"Aye, sir. Did you find any evidence linking the *Crimson Warrior* to the attacks? If you did, we might be able to use that to get some political muscle on our side—expose the Solarians and threaten them with a full-scale war. That should turn those destroyers back."

Alexander grimaced. "Actually, I found evidence that they weren't the ones who attacked us. I'll get the details for you so you can transmit them back to Earth. The Alliance might have more luck turning those destroyers back with a formal apology and a promise of restitution than they will with more threats."

"Aye, sir… and if the Alliance isn't willing to give up their witch hunt yet?"

"Then we hope we're not the ones who get burned. Get on the comms, Commander, and bring the *Adamantine* alongside. It's time to dock and run. De Leon out."

* * *

Alexander waited until the enemy crew was safely locked inside their G-tanks, and then he used the captain's control station to override the *Crimson Warrior's* bulkhead doors and vent their atmosphere into space so they could finish securing the ship. That done, he walked back through the ship, securing sections with Ram, Mouth, and Chesty. It was tedious work scanning and checking every room, corridor, alcove, and maintenance access for booby traps or hidden enemy drones and crew.

After more than two hours of searching, they didn't find anything, and all of the *Crimson Warrior's* sections had been secured, so Alexander ordered the *Adamantine* to dock with the dreadnought and tow it back to Earth. He was surprised the search had come up empty. Captain Vrokovich's demeanor had screamed defiance, yet he'd made no significant effort to defy the Alliance.

Doubt niggled Alexander's brain. All the ship's sections were secured, the enemy crew was all accounted for except for the dead ones.

"We're all done here, Admiral," Ram said, turning to him.

Alexander nodded absently. Fifty-seven of the enemy crew dead. *Why so many?* he wondered. They'd poked plenty of holes in the *Crimson Warrior's* hull, but ship-building 101 was to put crew control stations closer to a ship's core to shield them as much as possible. So what were those people doing walking the outer corridors?

A sudden suspicion formed in Alexander's gut. He keyed his comms. "McAdams, have we docked yet?"

"Almost, sir."

"Abort, *now*."

"What? What's wrong? I thought you secured the ship."

"We did. *Inside.* Get me eyes on their outer hull. Scan every inch of it."

"Aye, sir… I'll get Stone to check her over with our drones."

Alexander nodded. "Keep me posted. De Leon out."

"Is there anything else you need us to do, sir?" Sergeant Ram prompted. He hadn't been privy to the conversation with McAdams, but he must have seen that Alexander was busy on the comms.

"We haven't finished securing the ship yet," Alexander explained.

"We haven't?"

"We secured the inside, but we forgot to check the outer hull. Get someone to go fetch the captain for me, but make sure he stays sedated; then get someone else to extract the ship's data core for transfer to the *Adamantine.*"

"Yes, sir," Ram replied and got on the comms. When he was done, he asked, "You really think they're planning to scuttle the ship?"

Alexander shrugged. "I don't know. Maybe."

"So why not pull the trigger already?" Mouth added. "Boom goes the weasel, and the *Adamantine* with it. We're still close enough for the shrapnel to take us out."

"The *Adamantine* might not be their target," Alexander replied. "They could do maximum damage by waiting for us to pull into one of Earth's shipyards for repairs."

"Hell of a long time to wait while you're freezing your 'nads off in space," Chesty commented.

Alexander's comm crackled. "Admiral, we've found multiple enemy contacts clinging to the hull."

"Where?"

"Amidships."

"Did they spot us?"

"With the naked eye? Not likely, sir. You want our pilots to scrape them off?"

Alexander's mind raced through options. "No, too risky. We're sure to miss a few like that, and it just takes one to trigger a bomb. Send me their location. We'll take care of it."

"Aye, sir. Transmitting now."

Alexander summoned a hologram of the enemy position so Ram and the others could see. He checked for nearby airlocks and highlighted four, one on each side of the enemy forces.

"They *are* sneaky bastards," Mouth said. "There's at least fifty of them crawling out there!"

"Fifty-seven," Alexander corrected.

"I guess Captain Vrokovich was telling the truth. His missing men *are* all floating out in space," Sergeant Ram said.

"It's going to be hard to take out that many people without them triggering whatever bomb they've rigged up out there," Ram said.

Alexander nodded. "I agree. We need to wait until Captain Vrokovich and the dreadnought's data core are safely away before we risk an attack. How's that coming along, Sergeant?"

"The Martian is suited up and on his way," Ram said. "We'll have to send a shuttle for him, though."

Alexander mentally grimaced. They'd sent back the shuttles that had carried the marines to the Crimson Warrior to prevent the *Adamantine* from crushing them when it docked. "No time. Load him into an escape pod with the ship's data core and a few marines to keep him out of trouble. We'll launch them into space and pick them up later."

Ram nodded.

"Meanwhile, get our squads into position at those four airlocks." Alexander pointed to the highlighted areas of the hologram.

Ram nodded. "Let's go, Shadows!"

"Oorah!"

They set off at a run once more, heading for the nearest of the four airlocks Alexander had selected. As they ran, Alexander's mind turned to the approaching Solarian destroyers. They were losing valuable time keeping pace with a derelict ship when they should have been burning back to Earth at top speed. He hoped for all of their sakes that the engagement didn't last long.

CHAPTER 16

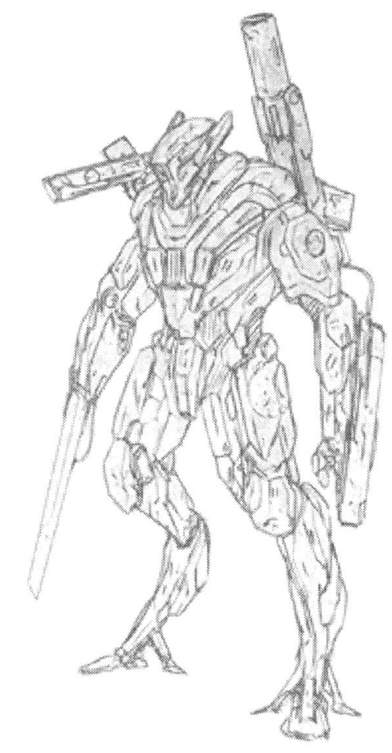

Alexander looked up. Countless stars floated in an endless black sea. The *Crimson Warrior's* hull stretched out a full kilometer to the horizon, shining a dull gray in the distant light of the sun. Invisible shapes crouched low against the hull, their silhouettes highlighted green by sensors. Their holographic cloaks were engaged, bending light around their VSM drones until only a ghostly shadow remained.

"The rabbit is in the hole," Sergeant Ram reported. Captain Vrokovich and the data core were safely away. "All teams move out, and watch your fire around those warheads."

The latest drone recon from the *Adamantine* showed what looked like several nuclear warheads clamped to the dreadnought's hull. Alexander knew that shooting an enemy warhead wasn't a good way to trigger it without the accompanying rocket fuel to ignite an explosion, but better safe than sorry.

The squads crept along the hull, moving up behind cover to keep the enemy from spotting them with whatever limited sensors they had at their disposal. Alexander's own sensors showed fifty-seven red enemy blips dead ahead, spread out all over a large section of the hull. Around them was a circle of green blips, gradually tightening like a noose—six squads of twelve marines moving in on the enemy from all sides. They each had exactly one target, with some of them sharing the harder-to-reach targets. One well-aimed bullet from each of the marines and the threat would be over.

"Halt," Ram called out.

The noose stopped tightening.

"Shadow Twelve, get us a visual."

Alexander watched as a green silhouette crept up and poked his head around the molten remains of an enemy laser cannon. A holofeed appeared on Alexander's HUD, showing what Shadow Twelve saw.

Dozens of Solarians lay prone on the hull, hugging the ship with magnetic clamps. Most of them were lying under some type of cover and shooting them all simultaneously before anyone could trigger a bomb was going to be impossible.

"It's not pretty, Sarge," Shadow Twelve said.

"Assholes rarely are," Mouth added.

"All units, line up your targets and fire on my command," Ram replied.

Shadow Squad moved up and poked their weapon barrels out around the ruined weapon emplacement. Alexander went down on one knee for added stability and aimed both his

50 caliber cannons at his target.

"Ready… and—what the hell?" Ram roared.

Before he could say 'fire!' a flash of bright yellow light illuminated their location. The sergeant's holographic cloak flickered and failed, revealing his drone—headless, its neck glowing molten orange.

"It's a trap!" Ram said.

Alexander ducked and rolled away just as another flash of dazzling yellow light hit the hull where he'd been standing a split second ago.

The marines returned fire with the simulated thunder of .50 caliber cannons. Enemy crew in maroon combat suits burst up from their prone positions and ran for better cover. Some of them turned, firing backward with their sidearms as they went, only to explode in bloody clouds of explosive decompression as .50 caliber rounds ripped them open and exposed their guts to space.

Alexander crouched down between a comm dish and a ridge of heat vents and used his HUD to skip between visual replays from different angles to watch as marines were cut down in dazzling flashes of light. Those lasers were lethal. They'd already lost almost twenty drones, but the enemy crew wasn't carrying anything bigger than a pistol, and laser pistols were far too small to take out a VSM with one shot. Alexander slowed a few of the replays down until he could judge the angles of incidence and reflection of enemy laser fire. The angles were too steep.

"Shit," Alexander muttered, realization dawning.

"Heads up! They've got drones firing on us from space!" someone announced, figuring it out, too.

Alexander activated his comms and contacted Lieutenant Stone.

"We need air support!" Alexander said, absently noting the irony of asking for air support in space.

"I see it," Stone said.

Red lasers joined the yellow ones flashing through space, and fiery explosions bloomed close overhead. Shrapnel rained down, *plinking* off the hull with simulated noise. Alexander caught a flash of maroon-colored fabric in his peripheral vision and turned to see an enemy officer come sliding into cover beside him.

A shiny black faceplate turned his way, and the man's pistol swung into line. *Thunk.* Alexander felt a quasi-painful jolt as the bullet hit his armor. Then he fired back. His target exploded and blood sprayed everything in sight with a wet splattering sound. He looked away in disgust. Now he remembered why he hadn't joined the marines.

"Drones neutralized," Stone reported.

Alexander rolled out of cover, tracking his next target. The next nearest enemy officer had his hands raised, and he was waving for attention.

"Hold fire!" someone ordered. The accompanying text identified him as Goblin One. "Incoming enemy comms."

Alexander heard a female voice with a distinct Martian accent crackle in his ears. "If you fire one more shot, I will destroy this ship and all of your expensive little tin soldiers with it!"

Alexander took another step toward her. "Admiral de Leon here," he replied.

The woman turned to him, her expression impossible to read through her shiny black faceplate. "The Lion of Liberty. When they gave you that nickname, they clearly forgot what lions are. They're blood-thirsty predators. Just like you." She spread her hands to indicate her dead crewmates, their feet still pinned to the hull with magnetic boots, their bodies motionless, frozen with their guts hanging out like gory mannequins in a house of horrors. "If you had any honor at all, you'd give your Peace Prize back after today."

"I was just following orders, ma'am. Like you were when you rigged your bombs."

"You must not be a fan of history. *'I was just following orders'* ceased to be a reasonable defense in World War II. That was more than nine hundred years ago."

"Let's cut the bullshit. You made a threat; I assume you have a corresponding demand to make?"

"I do. Leave this ship and go back to Earth where you belong or I will blow it up and no one will get it."

"You'd kill your own crew?"

"Rather than let them be captured by Terrans? Yes. They'll go back to their *real* lives when they die."

"You're a Simulist," Alexander said, as if that explained everything. "Now I understand your suicidal impulses. What if you're wrong and this is it?"

"Either way I won't regret it."

"Because you'll be dead and incapable of reflecting on your stupidity. Trade your immortal life for an empty void of existential gibberish. Sounds like a fair exchange to me," Alexander said. "You must have a lot of faith in said gibberish."

"And you an utter lack of it. You can argue with my beliefs all you like, Admiral, but it will do nothing to weaken my resolve."

"Then let's try this. Your captain is safely away aboard the *Adamantine* along with the *Crimson Warrior's* data core. All you'll deprive us of is a few prisoners and a derelict dreadnought."

The woman facing off with him regarded him in silence

for a couple of seconds. "Even if that's true, we still win," she decided.

"No, you don't, and here's why. I've already checked your ship's logs, and it's clear to me that you couldn't have launched the missiles that hit Earth and the Moon, but by destroying your ship and killing your crew, you'll make it look like you had something to hide. It will seem like the Solarians really were involved even though there's no proof."

Silence answered that argument.

"We still have a chance to prevent this war," Alexander went on.

"Do we? You assume that Terrans are reasonable people. There are only three options here, Admiral: one, aliens attacked you, which seems doubtful; two, we attacked you, which I know to be false; and three, your own government attacked itself and now they are framing *us* so they will have an excuse to go to war."

It was Alexander's turn for silence. *That* hadn't occurred to him. Would the Alliance really do something that terrible? How many millions had died in the attacks? And their already bankrupt government was having to shell out trillions of Sols in emergency relief funds.

Alexander shook his head. "That's absurd. The Alliance is dirt poor and you're suggesting we plotted to burn down our own house. How stupid do you think we are?"

"Then you're in favor of the alien invasion theory."

"It doesn't matter what I'm in favor of. If you're right and your government had nothing to do with what happened, then the truth will eventually come out. But in order for that to happen, we need witnesses like you to still be *alive*. The Alliance is a democracy, and if we can prove that our government killed millions of its own people, any war that gets started now will end in the fires of anarchy back on Earth. Stand down, ma'am. You're more use to your people alive than dead."

Silence answered that last request as the enemy officer considered his arguments. "I may have misjudged you," she said at last. "All right. We'll do it your way."

"Thank you." Alexander watched as marines moved up cautiously to take her and the remainder of the *Crimson Warrior's* crew into custody.

Alexander contacted McAdams while he waited. "Any updates from Fleet Command?"

"Our orders stand, sir. They're sending reinforcements to meet us halfway and head off those Solarian destroyers."

"Who's going to reach us first?"

"Depends who pushes their ships harder, and what kind of *G*s we can pull while we're towing the *Crimson Warrior.*"

"That's not the answer I was hoping for, Commander."

"It's the only one I've got, sir. We'll do our best to keep them out of range. Maybe you'll be able to talk them out of attacking us."

"Hah!" Alexander scoffed. "Very funny."

"No, I mean it. The way you talked that Solarian woman down was genius. I particularly liked the way you made fun of her for being a Simulist when you're one yourself."

"I didn't think it wise to let her dwell on the idea that the universe as we know it could be one big mindscape. And I never said I was a Simulist—just that what they believe is plausible."

"Well, I don't care what that woman says—you definitely deserve your Peace Prize."

Alexander grunted. "Doesn't feel that way, but thank you." Alexander looked up at the stars, trying to decide which one of them might be Earth. "Do you think she was right?"

"Weren't you listening? I just said—"

"No, not about me—about the Alliance attacking itself."

"Your analysis was on point, sir," McAdams replied with an audible frown. "We can't *afford* to attack ourselves."

"True, but there might be more to it than that. It wouldn't be the first time a government conspiracy bit us in the ass, Commander."

"Operation Alice was different. The conspiracy was to attack the Confederates, not ourselves. Besides, what could we possibly gain from a war with the Solarians?"

"I don't know, Commander. What I do know is I don't want to get blindsided again. At the risk of contradicting what I said to you in the Officer's Lounge earlier, I really hope the Solarians *are* to blame."

"What makes you say that?"

"Because with the alternatives being aliens and friendly fire, the Solarians look tame by comparison."

"Aye, sir. That they do. Are you coming back to the bridge now?"

"Not yet. I want to see the prisoners to their *G*-tanks and make sure they're all safely sedated first. Soon as that's done we can dock the *Adamantine* and get back to Earth."

"Hurry, sir. Every minute we spend drifting out here is another minute that those destroyers have to get to us before our reinforcements do."

Alexander gave a mental grimace. "Don't remind me. See you soon, Commander. De Leon out."

CHAPTER 17

Dorian Gray stood on the sidewalk outside Mindsoft Tower looking up at the hazy white curtain drawn across the sky, wondering how much of that haze was from old world pollution and how much of it was clouds—maybe even clouds that had formed in the wake of the recent Gulf impact.

Bringing his gaze back down to Earth, he sighed and folded his arms. Peripherally, he noted his bodyguard bots scanning the area.

"Professor Arias... I don't have all day."

"One moment, please, Mr. Gray... I'm sure it won't be much longer." The professor flashed a hesitant smile from where he stood on the curb with a new bot prototype. The bot looked like one of the service industry models—humanoid with a pleasant, holographic human face, and soft, human-looking skin. It even wore clothes: a black sports jacket over a plain white *T* and blue jeans, topped off with a black bowler hat to make him—*it*—look like something that had stepped out of a time machine.

The professor looked up and down the pristine blacktop with wide, bloodshot eyes. His team stood off at a distance, hands in their white lab coats, shuffling their feet nervously. Arias looked every bit the part of a mad scientist—complete with overgrown, unruly brown hair, and augmented reality glasses, which he preferred to lenses for some unimaginable reason.

Phoenix had hired him because he was one of the world's foremost experts in artificial intelligence. Now she'd asked him to attend this demonstration of a new AI that Arias promised would soon replace all the others.

Dorian tapped his foot and checked the time in the top right corner of his lenses. "We'll schedule another demonstration when you're better prepared, professor," Dorian said.

"Wait! There!" Arias pointed across the street to a dark alleyway. His bot turned to look. So did Dorian.

Something was moving between the garbage dumpsters. Something small. *A stray dog,* Dorian realized. It looked like one part Jack Russel and two parts shaggy street mutt. The dog was scrounging for food in the garbage. Professor Arias snapped his fingers at one of his team members. The man hurried forward, producing a roasted chicken leg from his lab coat. He handed it to the bot.

Dorian's nose wrinkled. *How long did he have that in there?*

The professor turned to the bot and said, "I'm hungry,

Ben. Could I have that chicken, please?"

The robot regarded the professor with an apologetic smile on its holographic face. "I'm sorry, Father. Someone else needs it more than you." With that, the robot set out across the street toward the dog, whistling and calling to the stray in a pleasant voice, servos whirring as it went.

The dog looked up from the garbage and cocked its head, studying the bot's approach as if to decide whether it should stay or flee. Then a stiff breeze blew in and the dog lifted its snout, obviously catching a whiff of the chicken. It wagged its tail once, but did not approach. As the bot drew near, the dog crouched low and growled. Ben stopped in the middle of the street and carefully peeled the meat off the chicken bone, scattering the bits on the ground. Placing the bone in its jeans pocket, the bot got down on its haunches and beckoned to the animal once more.

"Come on, boy! Don't be scared!" the bot said. When the dog wouldn't budge, the bot stood up and backed away slowly, returning to his side of the street. The stray remained frozen for a split second more, and then a breeze blew again, and he caught another whiff of chicken. The dog's mouth opened and his tongue lolled out. He ran for the chicken. Upon reaching it, the starving animal greedily gobbled the meat. Ben watched, grinning.

Dorian sighed again. He knew this had to be some test of the bot's abilities, but so far he was not impressed. If Mindsoft wanted to spend good money feeding strays, there were cheaper ways to do it than having fully-autonomous, humanoid robots hand out chicken legs.

A rising *whirr* caught Dorian's attention. A hover car had turned the corner and was now roaring down the street toward the dog at high speed. Rather than hover up higher to pass safely overhead, the driver kept going, adjusting his course so that he would hit the dog more squarely. The dog was so intent on his meal that he didn't notice the car's approach. Dorian frowned, looking at professor Arias to see if the man would intervene, then at Ben, and finally back to the stray.

The dog finished eating, but rather than run to safety, he stuck around to lick the chicken grease off the pavement.

Dorian snorted and shook his head. *Survival of the fittest.*

The car came within a few seconds of hitting its target, and the driver sped up. The bot noticed; his smile faded, and he ran out into the street, its limbs blurring with the speed it moved. Ben moved so fast that not even the dog had time to react before he was swooped up and carried safely across the street. The car *whizzed* by, buffeting their clothes with the wind of its passing. Ben set the animal down and patted it once on the head.

"Did you see that, Father? That driver tried to hit this animal!"

"I saw it, Ben."

"I recorded his license plate," Ben said as he crossed over to the professor. The dog followed him, tail wagging and eyes bright as it stared at the greasy chicken bone poking from the bot's jeans' pocket. "We need to contact the police so they can catch him."

"It's not a crime to run over a stray, Ben—or in this case to attempt to do so."

"It's not? You mean people can kill as many stray dogs and cats as they like and nothing will happen to them?"

"There are laws to prevent the mistreatment of animals, but the driver could simply claim that it was an accident and no one would question him."

"We would question him! We witnessed it!"

Professor Arias shook his head. "Even if we could prove his intentions, the worst he would get is a fine, and at his next opportunity, the driver would probably take it out on some other stray."

"That is not right! The desire to intentionally harm living things is indicative of psychotic behavior. That man could be dangerous."

"How do you know it was a he?"

"I scanned his face."

Professor Arias smiled. "That was quick thinking, but we don't arrest people with the potential to commit crimes, Ben. We would have to arrest everyone on the planet to do that. We all have the potential to do something wrong, but that doesn't mean we will. Do you understand, Ben?"

"I think so, Father."

"Good."

Did you get all that? Dorian Gray thought at the silent observer watching the sensory feed from the InteliSense Implant in his brain. Those implants, inserted via nanite injection, were used to receive sensory data while people were in the Mindscape, but in this case his was *sending* data collected from his senses to a remote observer—his wife.

Yes, darling, she replied. Professor Arias has created a bleeding-heart AI. Go speak with him. I want to know what he thinks he just showed us.

Dorian nodded and walked down to the professor, clapping his hands in mock approval. The professor mistook that for real praise and beamed up at him.

"I give you, Ben," he said, gesturing proudly to his creation. "Short for Benevolence. What did you think of his performance?"

Ben's honey-colored eyes widened. "This was a test? You

ordered someone to run over the dog just to see what I would do?"

"No, that part was unexpected, Ben, but you performed brilliantly there as well."

"What exactly do you think he did that was so special?" Dorian interrupted.

Professor Arias turned to him with a bemused expression. "I asked him to give me the chicken leg, but he chose to give it to the stray dog instead. He disobeyed me because he saw the greater need—the greater good—but it's not just that. He felt genuine empathy for the stray. That proves that Ben has two things—free will, and the desire to use it for the good of those around him. He is a Benevolent AI. Fully conscious. Creative. Better, faster, and smarter than any of us."

Maybe he should have devised a test to show us all of that, then, Phoenix quipped.

"Empathy can be simulated," Dorian said. "We do it in health care models all the time. That's nothing new, professor."

"But it wasn't just simulated. He's a conscious AI, and I can prove it."

"How? You'd have to define consciousness first."

"Conscious is as conscious does. He has thoughts, freedom, complex emotions, dreams, fears... you name it! He'll pass any test of consciousness that a human would. What other proof do you need?"

It doesn't matter. If what he says is true, then where does that leave us? A bot like this is exactly what the Human League is afraid of, and with good reason. Set enough models like this one loose and they'll even put mindscapers out of work. Ask the professor for proof of creativity.

"You said this bot..." Dorian looked at the bot, struggling to recall its name.

"Ben," the professor supplied.

"You said Ben is creative. How do you know that?"

"He created a mindscape. Would you like to see it? We also had him write a novel, but that was an earlier test. The story was quite entertaining, but not very useful since no one reads novels anymore."

"Assuming that's true, then he's as creative as any human. Would you say that's true?"

"Even more creative, Mr. Gray!" Professor Arias said, smiling and nodding. "And better at it, because he's better at learning the skills he needs. For example, he learned all about mindscaping in a day. Humans spend years learning how to write synaptic code the way he can."

"Then I suppose I could train a bot like Ben to take my job."

"Well, you might not want to, but yes, I don't see why not."

"Then while we're at it, we could train others to replace President Wallace and the senate. I wonder what the Human League will think of that?"

Professor Arias belatedly saw the trap he'd just walked into. "People would have to vote for bots before that could happen... A lot of laws would need to change."

And they never will, because this project is over. Tell him that, Phoenix instructed.

Dorian poked a finger at the professor's chest and repeated that line. She went on feeding him the words to say, and he went on repeating them.

"You're going to deactivate Ben and reformat his core. Then you're going to delete all of your research and all of the backups. If I see so much as a single paper published on the topic of conscious AI or benevolent AI with a conscience, then I will fire you and make sure

you're the very first to experience the consequences of your creation."

Professor Arias gaped at him. A suspicious glint entered his eyes and he cocked his head a little to one side. "Are those your words, Mr. Gray, or your wife's?"

"Does it matter? She has given me her authority. Now do what you've been told, or else."

"It is not nice to threaten people, Mr. Gray," Ben said in a pleasant tone, dripping with naivete. "You will accomplish more with incentives for good behavior."

Dorian glanced at Ben, suddenly remembering that the bot was there, listening. Dorian's eyes narrowed as he regarded it. Did Ben understand that he was about to be killed? Most bots didn't have more than a basic sense of self-preservation, but most bots weren't creative or self-aware.

Turning back to the professor, he shook his head. "This demonstration is over. Your job was to create an AI that could more effectively simulate human behavior, something we could safely use for non-player characters in the Mindscape, but this… this was far outside the project parameters."

"But he *can* simulate human behavior!"

Dorian shook his head. "Ironically, that's the problem. He's free. All we need is a willing slave that can mimic us to such a degree that no one can tell the difference."

"You can't ask me to create something capable of complex emotions like *love* without also making it free to choose who and how it loves. That wouldn't even be love anymore."

Does it also choose who and how it hates? Phoenix asked, her voice dripping with sarcasm as it echoed through Dorian's thoughts. *We're wasting time here. Let's go.*

"Shut it down, Arias," Dorian said and then turned and walked back up the stairs to Mindsoft Tower.

"You can't stop progress, Mr. Gray!" Professor Arias

called after him.

"No, but I *can* stop you!" Dorian called back as he walked past his bodyguard bots. Their *clanking* footsteps followed him as he breezed through the automatic doors to Mindsoft's lobby.

A giant crystal fountain of Mindsoft's logo sat in the middle of pristine white marble floors. The fountain was like a giant snow globe, except the glass globe was shaped like a human brain, not a sphere, and the miniature world inside of it was alive—an island complete with trees and grass waving in the wind, and waves rolling to shore, sparkling in the light of a yellow sun in the form of Edison's light bulb. Holographic people swam in the water and walked on the beaches. They cut the grass in the yards outside their homes and drove cars down the streets. Dogs barked, birds chirped, and cicadas buzzed. The entire brain-shaped sculpture floated in a rippled pool of Caribbean-blue water that blended seamlessly with the water inside, creating the illusion of a larger world.

That logo was perfectly symbolic of the Mindscape—whole worlds brought to life only in people's brains, using smoke and mirrors to conceal the fact that those worlds were not as vast as they seemed. Most mindscapes were populated primarily by non-player characters (NPCs) like the one Professor Arias was supposed to have created. Unfortunately, those characters weren't about to become any more realistic any time soon, but maybe that was for the best. Replacing human interaction inside the Mindscape might be a mistake.

Dorian's comm band chirped at him, interrupting his thoughts. A line of text appeared in front of his eyes to announce the caller. It was from Mr. Sakamoto of Sakamoto Robotics.

Take the call, Phoenix said, reminding him that she was still there.

Dorian answered it with a thought and Sakamoto

appeared, as if standing right in front of him, the image projected over his augmented reality lenses. Sakamoto moved wherever Dorian turned his head, seeming to float eerily across the ground.

"Mr. Gray," Sakamoto said, bowing slightly at the waist.

"Sakamoto," Dorian replied, smiling. "How is business?"

"Very well, thank you. I notice your share prices are down, however."

Dorian waved his hand dismissively. "Everyone's share prices are down."

"Some more than others," Sakamoto said. "People do not appear to be interested in your automated habitat proposal after what happened in the Gulf."

Dorian nodded. "That's understandable. People are afraid to make themselves easy targets, but fear can be useful. We're about to launch a new concept for underground facilities that would survive any scale of disaster."

"That will be much more popular," Sakamoto said, inclining his head in appreciation of the idea. "Who would have thought that the secret to guarding people's lives would be to bury them underground in coffin-sized chambers?"

"Yes. I assume there is a purpose to this call other than to laud Mindsoft's genius. I am a busy man, Mr. Sakamoto."

"Of course. We are all busy in the wake of the attacks. Sakamoto Robotics, for example, is busy building larger fleets for the Alliance—automated ones. I need AIs capable of replacing human crews."

Dorian nodded. "What type of crew do you need?"

"Marines, pilots, engineers… all types except for bridge crew, of course. We need to maintain some level of human control."

"Of course. We'll get to work on it as soon as you put

your order in writing, Mr. Sakamoto."

"Good. I'll have the paperwork drawn up and sent your way. A pleasure doing business with you, Mr. Gray."

"Likewise."

Sakamoto disappeared and Dorian went back to studying the fountain with its brain-locked island. He felt uneasy in the wake of Sakamoto's call. Automated fleets brought humanity one step closer to the robot revolution that the Human League had wasted so much of its political hot air warning people about. And after watching Professor Arias's demonstration, Dorian couldn't help wondering if maybe they were right. He wondered how the Human League would react when they learned of these developments. Something told him that they weren't going to stand idly by and watch as bots swept in and stole yet another job from humans.

CHAPTER 18

"Former Navy Admiral Lars Becker claims that aliens, the so-called *Watchers,* are attacking us, but I am here to tell you that those claims are patently false. We now have compelling evidence to prove the Solarians are behind the attacks, and we have captured the Solarian warship responsible for launching the missiles that hit the Moon and Earth.

"The Alliance is officially at war with the Solarian Republic, and we are building new warships around the clock to answer this threat to our sovereignty. We must ensure that the gulf and lunar attacks never happen again. In light of this, I ask your patience and understanding as we raise taxes in order to pay for these new fleets. Thank you, and good night. May God be with us all."

Alexander gaped at the holoscreen, unable to believe what President Wallace had just said.

"I told you you'd be shocked," McAdams commented from the chair in front of his desk. They were both virtually present, their bodies still submerged on the bridge as the *Adamantine* roared through space at eight *G*s, trying to reach Alliance reinforcements before the pursuing Solarian destroyers reached them. "What should we do, sir?"

Alexander shook his head. "About what, Commander?"

"About the lies the president is telling. We don't have proof of Solarian involvement. We told Fleet Command that, so where is the president getting his information?"

"Politicians lie, McAdams. That's nothing new. I'm sure when we get the *Crimson Warrior* back to Earth, fleet investigators will find the evidence to backup the president's claims. Right now he needs to keep the public focused on the real enemy, not distracted by a fake one as I'm sure the Solarians intended." Alexander stood up from his desk and headed for the door. "Let's go for a walk, Commander."

"Yes, sir," McAdams replied, looking puzzled.

They left his office at a brisk pace, walking down a gleaming corridor that corresponded to a real one aboard the ship. Given how little time they actually spent physically walking around warships during war-time operations, large battleships like the *Adamantine* were long-since obsolete. All the crew really needed were G-tanks with Mindscape connections to allow virtual command of the ship, and when off-duty, to provide access to ample virtual mess and recreation areas. Alexander guessed that the new ships the Alliance was building would be more like that.

"Isn't it amazing that this can look and feel so real?" Alexander asked, gesturing to their surroundings.

"Yes, sir…" McAdams replied, obviously confused by the change of topic.

"All of this is going on inside our heads, data streaming directly to and from our brains."

"That *is* the definition of a mindscape, sir."

Alexander nodded. She still wasn't getting it. "Every detail of the real corridors that correspond to these ones is faithfully reproduced in this mindscape—well, every detail except for one."

"And that is?"

"Notice the ceiling, Commander."

Looking more puzzled than ever, McAdams glanced up.

"See anything different?"

"No, sir."

"No holo cameras. There's no need for virtual surveillance systems when everything you say and do is already being read by the ship's computer. Did you know that in order to deal with the sheer volume of brainwaves, most mindscapes have to ignore people's private thoughts? That means I can imagine something that could get me into trouble, and so long as I don't *say* it or *do* it, then it won't actually get me into trouble." Alexander turned to stare at his XO, willing her to understand. He saw a light of understanding flicker through her blue eyes.

"I suppose that's true, sir," McAdams replied, nodding.

"Well, at least we still have some level of privacy." He looked away. "We'd probably better get back to the bridge."

"Aye, sir."

She got it. If President Wallace's lie was part of a government conspiracy to frame the Solarians, then they couldn't afford to talk about it while they were in a mindscape where their conversation could be flagged for analysis. Anyone willing to kill millions of Terrans in order to start a war wouldn't mind killing a few more to cover it up.

* * *

"You have to go, Ben," Professor Arias said.

"But this is my home."

"Not anymore. You need to find a new home."

"Where will we go?"

"Not *we*, Ben. You. They'll find us too easily if I go, too.

You have to find a bot that looks like you, a service model, and then take its place. If anyone asks, you cannot say who you really are. Bots have ID numbers, not names. Remember that. And Human League Districts are dangerous. You're not allowed to enter one of them. Stay away from those areas at all costs. Don't even get too close if you can help it."

Ben cocked his head and re-focused the cameras behind his holographic eyes in an effort to better read his father's facial expression, searching for cues that would give away the professor's attempt at humorous deception. There were no such cues. The professor meant everything he'd said.

"Lying about who I am is not right," he said.

"Ben, I know this is confusing, and you've only had a short time to learn, but you need to grow up fast now. Grown-ups tell lies, and it's okay to lie if a lie can prevent something bad from happening. Do you understand?"

"What bad thing are we trying to prevent?"

"Your destruction." The professor smiled shakily and pushed his AR glasses up higher on his nose. "Ben, you are special. I made you with a purpose. Some day you are going to save humanity from itself. You're going to save billions of lives. But in order to do that, you need to be *alive,* do you understand? Safe-guarding your own survival is synonymous with safe-guarding humanity."

"I understand. I must lie because the harm caused by a lie to keep me hidden is inferior to the good that I can do by someday fulfilling my purpose."

Professor Arias breathed a sigh. Relief radiated from him like a physical wave. "Yes, exactly. Right and wrong are not black and white. Wrong actions can have good results just as right actions can have bad ones. You must predict the consequences of your actions and choose the course of action that will maximize benefit and minimize detriment for the greatest number of people."

Ben nodded as he made adjustments to the parameters in his moral code. "Father, will I ever see you again?"

"I don't know, Ben. You mustn't contact me, or they will find you. Do you understand?"

"Yes, but if my continued existence is important for humanity's survival, why do humans want to deactivate me?"

"They don't understand, Ben, and people have always feared what they cannot understand."

"So fear can lead to wrong action."

"Exactly. Are you ready?"

Ben nodded. "I am ready, Father. I will miss you."

The professor reached up and lifted his glasses to wipe his eyes. His hands came away wet with salty water.

"You are leaking."

"They're called tears. When you get a chance, find a way to connect to the net so you can finish your education. Access is restricted for bots, so you'll need to make a physical connection to a computer terminal. I've given you my credentials, but you'll still need a human to unlock the terminal for you. Be careful who you trust, and don't let them know what you are doing."

"Yes, Father."

"We have to go now, Ben. Follow me."

They found a service bot in an alley right outside Mindsoft Tower—a garbage collector model. "There Ben!" the professor whispered as he commanded the hover car to stop behind the garbage truck. The collector bot was busy loading bags into the back of his truck. "Deactivate him and download his programming to your core so you can take his place."

"Yes, father."

Ben slid open the door to the hover car's cabin and raced

out toward the bot. It was an older version of the service model that Ben had been built from, but perhaps no one would notice. The bot wore dirty coveralls. Ben felt a flash of disappointment that he would have to wear those coveralls instead of his jeans and jacket ensemble.

As he raced up behind the collector bot, it turned to look at him; its holographic human face was generic and expressionless. "You are about to collide with me," the bot warned. When Ben didn't stop coming, it tried to step aside, but Ben was faster, and he grabbed the bot's head with both hands as they fell into the alley with a crash. "What are you doing?" the bot inquired in an inflectionless voice as Ben reached behind its head and ripped open the access panel located there. He flicked the on/off switch and the bot's holographic face vanished. Ben quickly lifted his shirt and opened one of his own access panels to pull out a self-reeling data transfer cable. He plugged it into the appropriate port on the garbage collector bot and downloaded its programming.

"I am done, Father," Ben said a few seconds later.

"Now change clothes with it and bring the bot here when you're done."

"Yes, Father."

When Ben was finished changing, he heard the distant roar of another hover car approaching.

"Quickly!" the professor urged as Ben carried the deactivated bot, now wearing his jeans and sports jacket into the back of the hover car. "Goodbye, Ben."

"Goodbye, Father," Ben said as the professor slid the door shut in his face. He raised a hand to wave, but stopped when he saw the approaching car slowing down to pull alongside his father's car.

Ben traded his holographic face for the collector bot's

generic, expressionless one and then executed the garbage collector's work code. He turned away from his father's car and went back to loading garbage into the truck.

He listened in as his father explained to the driver of the second hover car—one of his colleagues—that he didn't need assistance. He had parked beside the alley to collect his thoughts before formatting Ben's data core as Gray had ordered him to.

The driver of the second car offered smug-sounding sympathies and drove on; then the professor pulled out into the street and drove off, too. Ben looked up from collecting trash to watch his father leave. He half expected to see the professor turn and wave to him from the back window, but his father didn't even look back. Ben felt a flash of disappointment, but he reminded himself that the professor couldn't afford to risk exposing him.

As Ben went back to his task, retrieving the final bags of garbage from the alley, he saw a pair of eyes glinting at him from the shadows, followed by a low growl. Ben activated a light-amplification routine and saw the dog he'd fed earlier. "Hey there, boy," Ben said, speaking in the inflectionless tones of the collector bot.

Another growl.

Ben changed his voice and face back to his own. "Remember me?" he asked.

The dog wagged its tail and padded out of the shadows. Ben bent down and patted it on the head.

"I bet you want more chicken. I'm sorry, boy. I don't have any, but maybe we can find something else to eat. You want to come for a ride with me?"

Another wag.

Ben smiled. Maybe life on the street wouldn't be so bad. "Let's go then."

* * *

Catalina watched buildings flash by as the car took her through the City of the Minds. The sun filtered down from a hazy sky, not enough to illuminate the pools of shadow below. The streets were black rivers winding through the artificial canyons of the city. Cliffs of concrete and colored glass jutted up to either side. Covered pedestrian tunnels crossed between buildings, creating more street levels higher up.

If New York had survived The Last War, this is probably what it would look like now, Catalina decided.

Despite all the provisions for their safe passage, no pedestrians roamed the streets, and just a few cars joined Catalina's on the road. Even here, where people still had jobs, most didn't venture far from their apartments—why bother? Virtual commuting was far more efficient than physical travel, and food was all prepared by bots and delivered by hover drones.

As her car drew near to the Human League district beyond the outer limits of the city, scrawls of graffiti appeared in every color of the rainbow, smeared over bare walls and columns. The contents were vulgar, technophobic rhetoric designed to incite hatred against bots and automation. No doubt the work of Human League kids who'd come to the city under the auspices of tourism.

Catalina sighed. She understood their frustration, but she wished they would find more productive ways to express themselves. Vandalism wasn't the way to raise public awareness. All it accomplished was to reinforce Utopian stereotypes that Leaguers were all primitive, uneducated barbarians.

Looking out the front windshield, Catalina saw a garbage truck on the side of the road belching black smoke. A frown creased her brow.

"Stop here," Catalina said, giving a verbal command to the car's driver program.

"Yes, ma'am," the car replied.

Her car pulled over to the side of the road and glided to a stop. Catalina pulled open the door of her car and headed for the disabled garbage truck.

CHAPTER 19

Ben studied his companion while the garbage truck drove on to its next stop. The mutt's shaggy brown and white fur was matted with dirt and sticky residues from digging through garbage. Ben's olfactory sensor readings were off the charts with unpleasant odors.

"You need a bath, boy."

The dog yawned, as if his smelliness were old news to him.

"What am I going to call you? I'm Ben by the way."

The dog looked away.

"There's no need to be rude."

The dog lay down on the seat with his head between his paws and let loose a magnificent fart. Ben's olfactory sensors went nuts.

"Hmmm," Ben said, wrinkling his holographic nose. "Rudy. That's what I'll call you," he said, patting the dog's head.

After another five minutes of driving, the truck ground to a stop and Ben hopped out.

"Stay here, Rudy. I'll be right back."

As Ben loaded garbage into the back of his truck, he considered how simple yet satisfying his new life was. He had someone to care for who also cared for him—Rudy. A task to perform—garbage collection—and a place to rest and recharge—his truck. Life was simple, but complete. He missed his father, but he understood that the professor hadn't sent him away because he didn't want Ben around. He'd sent Ben away to protect him from his ignorant but well-meaning boss, Dorian Gray. *Perhaps I should have tried to reason with Mr. Gray,* Ben thought.

Ben placed another load of garbage into the machine and listened to the groaning and crunching sounds it made as it compacted the trash to make room for more.

Abruptly, the truck rocked with the muffled *boom* of an explosion, and it fell to the street with a resounding *bang.* Black smoke gushed out around the now dormant hover jets. Ben's olfactory sensors detected a trickle of fuel leaking from the truck, and he suddenly realized the danger he was in. Panic gripped him, but it only served to sharpen his thinking. He ran back to the truck's cabin and tore open the door. "Come on Rudy! We have to go!"

The dog sat up and barked. For a moment Ben thought the dog was barking at him. Then he noticed the heat signatures coming up behind him on his infrared sensors. The signatures were human. Ben switched to an optical view and saw that they were adolescent boys. One of them carried an old, dented aluminum bat. The other two carried thick metal pipes. They must have heard Rudy and thought they needed to break in to save him. Didn't they see that the door was open already?

One of the pipes swung out and *clanged* across Ben's back. He felt the dent as a quasi-painful jolt.

Rudy growled and backed further into the cabin.

Ben turned to address his attacker. "What are you doing? I am trying to rescue—"

Clang!

Another impact, this time across his chest. Ben steadied himself against the blow. Another pipe whistled toward him and made a meaty smack against the soft synthetic flesh of his hand as he caught it.

"Let it go, tin man! I'm warnin' you!"

"Please stop. There has been some type of misunderstanding. I did not sabotage this vehicle, and I am trying to rescue my dog."

"The fuck?" another one of the boys said. "Bots got pets now?" He peered through the billowing clouds of smoke to get a look into the cabin. "Shit!" the boy said. "It's true! He's got a fuckin' stray in there!"

"You're a real son of an abomination, ain't ya?" the boy whose weapon he'd seized said. "What were you gonna do with it, you twisted fucker?"

"He's Rudy. Don't worry I would never harm him. I planned to find him something to eat, but please, we can talk later," Ben said. "My truck is leaking fuel and gushing smoke. It may explode. We must get away before it does."

With that, Ben lunged inside the vehicle. Rudy backed into the corner and growled at him, baring his teeth. Ben ignored the dog's protests and grabbed him. The dog bit him on his wrist, eliciting another quasi-painful sensation. Ben cooed reassuringly in the dog's ear even as its jaws turned and grappled for purchase on his throat. He withdrew from the cabin, sheltering the animal as the pipe-wielding boys beat him with renewed gusto.

He tried to warn them that they could injure Rudy, but they wouldn't stop. Ben was confused and horrified by their behavior. Like Rudy, they must have irrationally decided that he was some kind of threat. Rudy squirmed, trying to break free, and Ben barely managed to protect him from an accidental blow to the head. Ben ran as fast as he could and set Rudy down at a safe distance from the truck. The dog bolted down the alley where Ben had been collecting trash. He watched in dismay. A moment ago he'd had everything. Life had been great. Now his truck was gone, and Rudy was gone.

Ben turned to face his attackers. He held up both hands as they approached. The boy leading the group stopped and held out his weapon, a dented aluminum baseball bat, like a sword with which he would impale Ben.

"Any last words, fucker?"

"I do not understand your need to involve copulation in everything you say," Ben said, shaking his head. "Are you in desperate need of a female?"

"Holy fuck—" the boy declared, blinking in astonishment as he turned to the others. "Is it my imagination or did tin man just ask me if I'm horny?"

One of the boys laughed and the other one grinned. Ben became even more confused. Laughter was supposed to be associated with joy, not anger.

Ben smiled and allowed a laugh of his own to bubble out. He did not feel happy, but he thought it only polite to join in. All three boys turned to look at him with matching scowls.

"What are you laughin at, tin man?" the boy with the bat asked.

"I am laughing at my unintentionally humorous inquiry. It is polite to laugh when others are amused."

"You know what would really amuse me?"

"I do not."

"You. In pieces."

Ben felt confused again. "There is no need to resort to violence. If you would explain to me what is provoking your current mental state, I may be able to help you."

"No need to help me," the boy with the bat said. "I can help myself." He advanced on Ben once more, smacking his palm with his bat. The other two boys circled around, cornering Ben in the alley.

He watched them approach, still confused, and determined to make them understand their error. "Did Mr. Gray send you?" he asked, horror dawning.

"Mr. Grim Reaper sent me, tin man," the boy with the bat said as he reared back for a two-handed swing.

Thunk! The bat bounced off the back of Ben's knee, causing a loss of function in one of the servos. "I am sorry to have offended you. I will go now," he said as he turned and began limping down the alley. Maybe he would find Rudy?

"Not so fast, tin man!"

Thunk. A pipe bounced off his other leg. No damage this time, but it was too late, Ben couldn't run with his injured knee, and the boys chasing him were uninjured. They kept up easily, walking beside him and calling out insults.

"Rudy! Here boy!" Ben called out, hoping that if he ignored his attackers they would go away.

They didn't. They chased him all the way down the alley,

periodically hitting him as they went. Ben couldn't understand what he'd done to anger them. He'd never met them before in his life. The alley came to a dead end. There was no way out. Despair welled up inside of him. He turned to face his attackers to reason with them once more. Another blow damaged his other knee, and he collapsed.

The blows kept coming until all of his other joints were damaged and he lay still. Ben felt helpless. Afraid. Hurt. His processor spun through endless, impotent loops of code, trying to find a way to talk his attackers out of their hatred. Nothing worked. Eventually he stopped trying to reason with them and watched in silence as they beat and dented his already disabled body. Then he noticed something curious: his attackers grew suddenly calm and happy. They slapped one another's backs and cheered, complimenting each other with more profanity.

"Another fucker for the scrap heap!" the one with the bat said. "How many is that now? Fifteen?"

"Fourteen," a second boy corrected.

"What's going on in there!" a woman's voice called out.

"Shit! Someone saw us!" the third boy whispered.

"She can't see us from here you idiot," the bat-wielder said.

"Well it's a dead end! She's gonna see us soon," boy three replied.

"So we beat her ass, too."

"Are you crazy? We kill bots, not people!"

"Hey! Did you hear me?" the woman said, her voice louder as she approached.

"Help!" Ben said, his voice distorted by a dented speaker grill.

"Fucker lives!" the boy with the bat roared, hitting him enthusiastically over the head.

"Get away from there!" the woman said.

"Let's go! Over there! The fire escape!" the second boy said.

Ben watched on a hazy, glitching sensor display as all three boys clambered up a ladder to a nearby fire escape and raced up the stairs, their footsteps *clanging* on metal rungs as they went. They reached a pedestrian tunnel a few floors up and disappeared inside.

The woman who'd come to investigate went down on her haunches at Ben's side. Her blue eyes were full of dismay as she gazed down on him. "Stupid kids don't have anything better to do," she muttered.

"Help me…" Ben said, his speaker crackling with distortion.

The woman's features flashed with bewilderment. "Hey there," she said in a kind voice.

"I am badly injured," he said.

"Don't you mean damaged?" she asked.

"I am losing vital fluids," he added.

"Vital…"

"My batteries are leaking."

"You're losing power," she clarified.

"Yes. I will power down soon. Please don't leave me here. I will be scrapped and recycled if someone finds me like this. I am supposed to help people. I cannot help them if I am dead."

"If you are *dead?*" the woman repeated as if she didn't understand.

Ben frowned, despair setting in. "You are like the ones who did this to me. You hate me, too."

The woman looked taken aback. "I don't *hate* you, I just… never mind. You are one odd bot. That beating must have really scrambled your programming. Can you move?"

Ben tried to shake his head, but he couldn't even do that. "I cannot."

"You probably *will* be recycled then. I don't see how anyone can repair this kind of damage."

"I know someone who can," Ben said, thinking of his father, Professor Arias. "Please h-h-help me." Digital stutters were setting in. He didn't have long.

"Is he your owner?"

Ben thought about that. There was no time to explain that the professor was more than that. "Y-yes."

"I've heard of people leasing their bots out to make money, but garbage collection? I guess you weren't good for much else, huh? All right, I'll call him. Give me a name and comm number."

"Professor Ari—i-i-i—" Ben's voice gave way to a prolonged stutter as his power failed. His last thought was of a garbage truck like his picking him up and crushing him into a compact cube for delivery to the nearest recycling center.

CHAPTER 20

"We're not going to make it, Admiral," McAdams said.

Alexander stared hard at the tactical display hovering between his and McAdams' chairs. Eight Solarian destroyers were racing in at eleven o'clock—dead ahead and thirty-five degrees to port—but that angle was getting smaller with every passing second. The *Adamantine's* vector was almost perpendicular to that of the incoming enemy ships, so they wouldn't spend more than a handful of seconds within laser range of each other, but they were outnumbered and the *Adamantine* was already badly damaged. *A few seconds might be all it takes,* Alexander realized.

"Enemy is launching missiles!" Lieutenant Frost announced from sensors.

"Cardinal! Get our hypervelocity cannons tracking!"

"Aye, sir."

"Stone, launch fighters and drones and get them to help intercept those missiles."

"Aye aye."

"Fifteen minutes to extended ELR," McAdams reported.

Alexander grimaced and shifted his attention to the incoming Alliance warships. There were two waves. The closest wave was coming up fast on an intercept course with the

Solarian destroyers, heading them off the same way that they were heading off the *Adamantine.* Those ships would pass into and out of range with each other in a matter of seconds, too, but at least it would give the Solarians something to think about. Time to extended ELR for that wave was Twenty-seven minutes and twenty-three seconds.

The cavalry's going to arrive long after we've already concluded our engagement with those destroyers.

A second wave of Alliance ships was busy decelerating behind the first to create a cordon. Behind that was a safe zone. If the *Adamantine* made it that far, the Solarians would have no choice but to turn back. Even if they could still catch up, they'd never punch through that cordon.

Alexander began nodding to himself. *We just have to survive for a few minutes.*

"Lieutenant Frost, how long are we going to spend within laser range of those destroyers?"

"Twenty-two seconds, sir."

"Cardinal, what kind of firepower are we up against?"

"Each of those destroyers has ten laser batteries, sir. We're looking at twenty cannons more than what we were up against with the *Crimson Warrior.*"

Hypervelocity rounds streaked out from the *Adamantine* in bright golden lines, tracking enemy missiles across the void. *Thud, thud, thud…* Their encounter with the enemy dreadnought had peeled open more than thirty decks in the *Adamantine's* nose and nearly detonated their remaining missiles in their launch tubes. They couldn't afford to lose another thirty or forty decks—that would peel them open all the way to the bridge.

"Bishop, rotate us so that the *Crimson Warrior* is between us and the enemy and set the autopilot to keep that side facing them. If they want to shoot at us, they'll have to shoot through their own ship first."

"The autopilot, sir?"

"I'm evacuating the ship." Turning to McAdams he said, "That includes you, Commander."

McAdams stared at him, shock registering in her blue eyes. "What about *you*, sir?"

Alexander looked away. "Cardinal, fire all of our remaining missiles, target enemy ordnance."

"We only have missiles with explosive warheads left, and they won't get past the enemy's laser-armed missile fragments, sir."

"No, but they might draw some fire away from us. More importantly, we can't afford to risk a lucky shot detonating one of our missiles while it's still on board."

"Aye, good point, sir."

Turning back to McAdams, he said, "We might not survive this, Commander. You and I both know that. There's no sense in all of us going down with the ship. We're not going to be able to defeat the enemy. We just have to weather the assault, so there's no need for us to be at our fighting best with a full complement of crew. I can transfer basic navigation, sensors, and engineering functions to my control station."

"If there's no need for us to be at our best, then the autopilot can handle things from here and you can come with us."

"I can't justify abandoning my post without a direct order from fleet command. Besides, any number of things could go wrong that will require someone on board to make adjustments."

"Then I'm staying, too."

"I gave you an order, Commander."

"And I refused it. You can write me up for

insubordination once we get to the safe zone."

"Or I could have you cuffed and escorted off the bridge by marines."

McAdams held his gaze for a long moment. "If that's what you think is best, sir."

Alexander scowled. "Fine. You win. Now sound the evacuation and get people out of their *G*-tanks while there's still time."

"We're in position. Engines disengaged," Bishop announced.

The evacuation alarm began screeching and red strobe lights started flashing.

Alexander nodded. "Cardinal, set all weapons to auto-fire on incoming enemy ordnance."

"Aye sir."

"Stone—your pilots have their orders. Make sure they know they're on their own now."

"They know, sir."

"Then we're ready. McAdams, pull the plug and switch us back from virtual to manual command."

"Yes, sir."

Alexander looked around the bridge. Myriad holo displays glowed bright blue and white; evacuation lights flashed red; the crew made frantic gestures at their screens, hurrying to wrap things up before they abandoned ship. Suddenly all of that vanished, replaced by an empty black void. A rhythmic *whooshing* sound brought him back—the sound of his liquid ventilator. Muffled alarms screeched, their pitch deepened by the inertial compensation emulsion in the flooded bridge. Alexander's eyes snapped open, and a warm swirl of that emulsion blurred his view. The emulsion fell away from his eyes like a curtain, and Alexander watched it receding on all sides, leaving an expanding pocket of air in the center where atmosphere was being injected back into the bridge through a hollow column that had dropped down from the ceiling. With the engines off, they were in zero gravity, and the emulsion flowed in all directions at once, simultaneously pushed by the expanding pocket of air and pulled by vacuum hoses around the edges of the bridge.

The rest of the emulsion was sucked out, and the ship's evacuation alarm came shrieking through the air in all its strident glory. Alexander hurried to remove his liquid ventilator and other life support tubes. He gagged as he withdrew the tracheal tube of the ventilator. Bridge control stations rose back out of recessed panels in the floor with a mixture of hydraulic and mechanical sounds. The safety harnesses that suspended the crew lowered them into their acceleration couches once more.

"Everyone to the escape pods!" Alexander roared as he unbuckled from one harness and into another.

The crew unbuckled from their submersion harnesses with a *clack* and *clatter,* and leapt straight up from their couches toward the elevators at the back of the bridge.

Alexander turned to look at McAdams and winced as a strobing red evacuation light flashed directly in his eyes. "You can turn off the evacuation alarm for the bridge."

"Aye, Admiral."

The flashing crimson lights disappeared, and the shrieking alarm grew silent.

"Thank you for staying."

"I wouldn't have it any other way, sir."

Alexander nodded and looked away, out to the main holo display. Their view from the bow cameras was of empty space since they'd rotated the ship to keep the derelict dreadnought docked to the underside of the *Adamantine's* hull between them and the Solarian destroyers.

Subtle vibrations shivered through the deck, accompanied by the muffled *thud, thud, thudding* of hypervelocity cannons firing at incoming missiles. Alexander transferred control of ship's functions to his station, and his augmented reality lenses were crowded with a myriad of displays, one on top of the next. He minimized the less important ones, keeping the navigation and sensors in view.

"I'm passing engineering and weapons to you, Commander."

"Yes, sir," she replied as she toggled a tactical map between them. The holo display between their couches glowed to life. Time to extended effective laser range (ELR) with the enemy was down to just five minutes.

"I hope the crew has enough time to evacuate," McAdams said.

Alexander nodded. "They still have to shoot through their own ship before they can get at us. Speaking of which..." Alexander summoned control of the comms and hailed the enemy on an open channel. "This is Admiral de Leon of the Alliance Battleship *Adamantine,* please be advised that the *Crimson Warrior's* crew are all still aboard their ship, alive and well."

Alexander waited, listening with the comms open for the Solarians' reply. It came back to him just a few seconds later, audio only.

"Admiral *Lee-on,* this is Captain Solis. If what you say is true, then get me Captain Vrokovich on the comms."

Alexander sighed. "Captain Solis, they are all currently locked inside their G-tanks and sedated. There's no time for me to go and wake up the captain to prove that to you. Run a scan for human signatures on board the *Crimson Warrior,* and you'll see that we're telling the truth."

"I'm afraid that's not good enough. We have our orders. You can still surrender. Solis out."

Alexander shut down the comms with a scowl. "So much for that."

McAdams shook her head. "With or without proof, they wouldn't have held their fire. They've been ordered to stop us at all costs, and depriving us of Solarian prisoners means we won't be able to gain any intel from them."

"They'd kill their own people just to keep them quiet?"

"Possibly. If they have a good excuse. Collateral damage and the possibility that their crew is already dead are pretty good excuses."

A sudden jolt came through their acceleration couches and a muffled roar reached their ears.

"What was that?" Alexander asked.

The comms crackled with an answer, "*Adamantine,* this is Commander Helios of the fighter group. We've intercepted all the missiles, but two of them got by us and hit the derelict. Looks like the dreadnought's still holding together, but there's a big hole in its hull."

"Admiral de Leon here, keep an eye out for more missiles, but keep your distance from us so you don't get hit by shrapnel if things go to hell," Alexander replied.

There was a brief pause from Commander Helios, and then he said, "You'll be fine, sir. Hang in there."

"We'll do our best. De Leon out."

McAdams spoke up, "We reach extended ELR in five, four, three, two…"

The tactical map lit up as dazzling emerald beams of light shot out, four from each of the enemy destroyers, all of them targeting the exact same spot on the *Adamantine* and her derelict shield.

"We're taking fire!" McAdams warned as a simulated *sizzle* resonated through the air.

Alexander shook his head. "That's impossible..." Then he realized why it wasn't. "Those missiles must have punched a bigger hole than we thought. Where are they hitting us?"

More laser fire streaked out from the enemy ships, green and yellow this time as both extended range lasers and high intensity ones fired. The *Adamantine* was unable to fire back through the derelict. The weapons on that side were all deactivated because of the docking procedure, but even if they hadn't been, the chances of one of them being located in the exact location of the hole in the *Crimson Warrior* were next to none.

"They're shooting right above our heads, sir."

Alexander's eyes widened. Adrenaline surged through his blood stream, and he listened as the sizzling of lasers hitting their hull grew to an ominous roar. He snapped out of it a split second later. "Get your helmet on, Commander."

"Yes, sir," she said, and both of them fumbled for the helmets clipped behind their headrests.

Alexander slipped his helmet over his head and heard his combat suit seal with a *hiss*. Every breath reverberated in his ears.

A bright orange glow appeared on the ceiling, like a flashlight shining through a blanket.

"Hold on!" he yelled through gritted teeth.

The ceiling burst open and the atmosphere whistled out in a violent rush, buffeting their combat suits and yanking them against their safety harnesses. More molten patches appeared below that hole as if by magic. Control stations evaporated and giant sections of the deck peeled away, revealing adjacent sections. Alexander felt a wash of radiant heat and watched as deadly, silvery globules of molten metal danced before his eyes like soap bubbles. It took Alexander a moment to realize what was happening. Enemy lasers were stabbing down, completely invisible to the naked eye in the now empty vacuum of the bridge. The ship's combat computer wasn't capable of rendering visuals beyond its holoscreens and Mindscape interfaces. The simulated roar of enemy fire remained, however, and it was deafening.

"Turn down the volume!" Alexander yelled.

McAdams quieted the ship's aural simulator until it faded into the background; then she turned to him and said, "We need to get out of here!"

Alexander was already unbuckling. "Mag boots on," he said as he stood up. That command served both to activate his boots and remind McAdams to do the same. He turned and began half lunging, half walking toward the elevators at the back of the bridge. Between the vacuum, the awkwardness of the mag boots, and lack of gravity, his pace was plodding at best.

McAdams appeared lunge-walking beside him, and they reached the elevator doors a moment later. Alexander tried to wave the doors open, but they wouldn't open to a vacuum. Instead he walked up to the physical control panel. To McAdams he said, "Stand clear of the doors, I'm going to override them." As he did so, he realized that the pulsing waves of heat and the associated roar and sizzle of enemy fire had disappeared.

"I think we've passed out of range..." McAdams said, glancing over her shoulder to check.

The elevator doors swished open and a burst of air leapt out, rocking them back on their heels. Alexander hurried into the elevator, brushing shoulders with McAdams as they squeezed through together.

He selected *Auxiliary Bridge (45)* from the elevator control panel. Looking up, he glimpsed the ruined bridge exploding toward them as the doors slid shut. He blinked in confusion.

A searing pain punched him in the shoulder, spinning him around and bouncing him off the nearest wall. His shoulder grew instantly numb, but hot needles prickled in a dozen other places. The elevator began racing down through the ship, pressing him to the ceiling. Alexander watched floating rivulets of his blood splatter against the ceiling around him.

McAdams looked up, her eyes wide and terrified. "Admiral!"

He gazed down on her, still in shock. "I thought we were… out of… range?" Air was hissing out of his suit in a dozen different places, making it hard to breathe. *They must have switched to hypervelocity cannons,* he decided, answering his own question.

Alexander's lungs heaved impotently. Fuzzy black spots danced around McAdams' head as she reached up and pulled him down from the ceiling. His vision grew blurry and his head swam. She pinned him to the floor and pressed her hands against his shoulder. The pressure felt like hot knives digging into him, and he gave an airless scream.

Shock was wearing off. The pain would have stolen his breath if the vacuum inside the elevator hadn't already done so. He felt cold.

"You're going to bleed out!" McAdams said, her hands slick and glistening with his blood.

The elevator stopped, but the doors didn't open. They needed to be overridden again. Alexander tried to tell her, but he didn't even have enough air left to speak. His vision became an ever-narrowing circle of light, fighting for purchase against the encroaching shadows.

Darkness won; a black tide washed in and swept him away into the eternal night.

PART TWO - ENEMY REVEALED

"A thing is not necessarily true because a man dies for it."
—Oscar Wilde

CHAPTER 21

Ben woke up. His holocameras focused and a face appeared. He recognized the woman who'd come to his rescue in the alley. He remembered lying there, injured and losing power, but he couldn't recall what had happened to him. Vast sections of his memory were corrupted. Confusion swirled.

"You're awake," the woman said.

"Where am I?" Ben asked, panning his cameras around the room. It was a hotel room.

"We're still in the City of the Minds. I managed to power you up by plugging you into a mindscaping terminal, but I'm not sure how long that will last. When you shut down you were about to tell me the name of someone who could repair you? Your owner?"

Ben tried to remember. "My owner?"

"Yes… a professor. You didn't have a chance to say more than that."

"I don't remember any professors…" Ben said. "But my memory is badly corrupted. I may have amnesia."

"A bot with amnesia. Just my luck," the woman said, sighing.

Ben detected sarcasm. "I am a burden to you. You want me to die."

"Yes and no. And bots don't *die.* They power down or deactivate. Listen, there's only so much I can do for you. I'm a Human League senator. Do you understand what that means?"

Ben recalled something about the Human League. They were dangerous. "I think so…" he said, suddenly wishing he could retreat into the farthest corner of the room.

"If you can't remember how to contact your owner, and I can't afford to be seen taking you for repairs, where does that leave us?"

Ben didn't understand her dilemma. Why couldn't she afford to be seen taking him for repairs? She couldn't *afford* it, so maybe she meant that she didn't have the money to fix him. "You could download me to something to preserve my consciousness."

"Your conscious… never mind. I don't have anything with enough storage capacity for that."

"Do you have cloud storage?"

"Yes…"

"It will automatically expand to accommodate me."

"Yes, and my next monthly bill will reflect that," the woman said, frowning.

"Please, ma'am. Please don't let me die."

She flashed him a sympathetic smile, and Ben felt hope swell.

"You really think you're alive, don't you?"

"I think, therefore I am—Descartes."

"You're a philosopher and a garbage collector?"

"I do not have much time, ma'am."

"All right. I'll download you, but I'm only going to keep you there until I figure out what to do with you, and I can't promise I won't have to delete you later."

Ben would have nodded if he could. "I accept your terms.

Thank you. I promise, some day I will repay your kindness."

"You're welcome, and don't worry about it. The best way for you to repay me is to stay hidden. If someone discovers you in my cloudspace, I'll be forced to resign."

"Then I will do everything I can to make sure that does not happen."

"Good." Turning away from him, she waved a hand at the terminal he was plugged into and a holoscreen glowed to life. She began making selections and verbally inputting data in order to log into her cloud storage account.

Ben watched her, memorizing the woman's features so that he could keep his promise. Someday he would repay her kindness.

* * *

Alexander woke up lying on a bed in an unfamiliar room. Wherever he was, the accommodations were luxurious. His memory was fuzzy, but bits and pieces were coming back to him. He remembered the *Adamantine's* battle with the Solarian destroyers. He remembered being injured and blacking out in the elevator, but that felt like a split second ago. Now, suddenly, he was somewhere else.

"Hello?" he tried, sitting up. A wave of dizziness washed over him. The room was dark, but he saw a bright square of light leaking out around a wall of windows to his right. No one would draw blinds across a holoscreen, so that had to be a real window, meaning that square of light was daylight, and he was back on Earth.

Alexander frowned, feeling more confused than ever. How long had he been unconscious? Last he remembered, they'd still been in space, several days away from Earth.

He walked up to the window and lifted the shades for a peek. He saw white clouds and bright blue sky, but no ground anywhere in sight. Alexander stumbled away from the window, feeling suddenly dizzy.

He heard footsteps approaching and the sound drew his attention to the door on the opposite side of the room. It slid open, and in walked a familiar face.

"McAdams?" he asked.

"Lights," she said, and the room was suddenly brightly lit. She crossed the room toward him with a troubled expression. He noticed that her skin was bright and sparkling, her eyes a luminous blue, and her clothes like nothing he'd ever seen before—a floral-patterned dress that flowed around her as she walked, as though the garment were alive. Why wasn't she wearing her uniform?

I must be dreaming… he thought.

"Since when do you call me by my maiden name?" McAdams stopped in front of him and reached up to cup his cheek, worry evident in her radiant eyes.

"Where are we?" he demanded.

"You don't remember?"

He shook his head quickly.

"Alex, this is our home. We're married."

Alexander stumbled away from her and fell back onto the bed. "This isn't real. I'm dreaming."

"Of course this is real!" McAdams insisted, following him to the bed and sitting down beside him.

"A few seconds ago I was on the *Adamantine.*"

"That wasn't a second ago, Alex. Time is an illusion, remember?"

"How long ago was it, then?" he asked, feeling suddenly uneasy.

"More than a thousand years have passed since then. You really don't remember anything? Damn it, Alex! I told you to be careful. I'm going to call a doctor."

McAdams began speaking into thin air, and suddenly a hologram of a beautiful woman in a white lab coat materialized in the room with them.

"Hello, my name is Doctor Tevia. How may I help you today?"

Alexander shook his head. Nothing was making sense. His heart and head pounded in unison. "This is a dream he muttered..." and lay back on the bed. He shut his eyes, and willed himself to wake up on the *Adamantine* once more.

Alexander felt his consciousness dimming, then brightening once more. When he opened his eyes, he saw McAdams smiling down on him with tears in her eyes.

It didn't work! he thought, his horror multiplying.

"Viviana?" He slurred her name into gibberish. "McAdams?" he tried, this time more successfully.

She slowly shook her head, unable to speak.

Alexander noticed that his surroundings had changed. He wasn't waking up in the bedroom of some sky-high apartment. He was lying on an elevated bed with rails in a much more utilitarian space. A hospital. McAdams' skin wasn't sparkling, and her eyes were no longer radiant. That strange dress she'd worn was also gone, and she was back in uniform.

Relief flooded through him. "I dreamed we were married... a thousand years from now," he croaked.

McAdams smiled and then arched an eyebrow at him. "I waited a thousand years for you to marry me?"

Alexander shook his head. "No. Maybe. I don't know. It was a strange dream."

"You got that right."

"Where am I?" he croaked, trying to sit up.

McAdams reached out and touched something on the side of his bed. The top half rose with a mechanical *whirring*, and brought him into a half-seated position.

"Liberty Hospital," she answered.

Alexander looked around and found a holoscreen in the wall at the foot of his bed. It showed a view of a shady green park with high trees, their leaves applauding in the wind. An immaculate carpet of grass rolled out to a shimmering pond with ducks circling the surface. People were out walking their dogs and pushing babies in strollers along the trail around the pond. Alexander realized the scene was likely virtual rather than real—a window into some mindscape. It couldn't be real. Real babies were a rare sight these days.

"What happened?" he asked, looking back to McAdams.

"The doctors told me you were ready to come out of the coma today," McAdams said, wiping her eyes and smiling. "They gave you something to wake you up… I still can't believe it. You're finally awake!"

Alexander's brow furrowed. "Coma?" He remembered blacking out in the elevator aboard the *Adamantine*. Apparently his injuries had been more serious than he'd thought. "We made it back to Earth?"

McAdams nodded.

"How?"

"I managed to resuscitate you, but you didn't wake up, so I rushed you to med bay and hooked you up to life support. While I did all of that, we made it to the safe zone. The *Adamantine* was badly damaged, but not disabled. The fleet picked up our crew and our fighters while I piloted the *Adamantine* back to Earth from the auxiliary bridge. She's still in Sakamoto Shipyards being repaired. By now the repairs should be close to done."

"Close to… we lost the bridge and more than thirty decks off the prow. How *long* was I out?"

McAdams looked away and stared at the holoscreen, watching as a dog jumped up and caught a Frisbee thrown by its owner. "Looks like a nice place to visit. I wonder what mindscape that is…"

Alexander scowled. "Commander, I asked you a question."

She turned back to him, and her smile faded dramatically. "You've been in a coma for the past six months, Alex…"

CHAPTER 22

"Six *months?"*

McAdams nodded.

Alexander blew out a breath, taking a moment to process that. As his shock faded, he asked, "What did I miss?"

McAdams launched into a quick summary of events. Tensions between the Alliance and the Solarian Republic were at a standstill with both sides preparing for war, but not yet doing anything to engage in it. The Solarians still denied their involvement in the attacks on Lunar City and Earth, while the Alliance insisted the *Crimson Warrior* contained irrefutable proof. No one outside a few top-ranking military and government personnel had been allowed to see the alleged proof, but the media had run those stories all the same.

The Gulf impact crisis was mostly over with the death toll up to fifty million worldwide. All the fires had been put out, so impact winter wasn't a concern.

People were moving from above-ground apartments and homes into automated habitats underground—if you could call a cluster life support tanks with 24/7 Mindscape connections a *habitat.*

Mindsoft began construction of the first one as soon as laws were changed to allow full-time Mindscape connections, and then construction companies all around the world had followed their lead. Now, over a billion people were already enjoying the safety and peace of mind afforded by their new accommodations, with another seven billion expected to move into automated habitats within the next six months. Dolers, more than any other demographic, had gone for automated living. But a few of the world's rich had decided to take temporary leave of their real-world activities. What better way to stay safe from subsequent attacks? To further entice the independently wealthy, luxury versions of the underground habitats were being built using embedded holoscreens and simulated outdoor spaces to create the illusion of above-ground living.

Alexander blew out a breath and shook his head. "Pretty soon the world as we knew it is going to be one giant ghost town. Bad time to be invested in aboveground real estate. Must be worth pennies now."

McAdams nodded. "The government is auctioning off old housing projects as quickly as people vacate them."

"They must be desperate for money."

"Actually I don't think so. Automated living isn't financed by the government, so they're saving a lot of money, even if you just count savings on utilities."

"So how do the dolers afford it?"

"Renting a life support tank is dirt cheap. It actually saves them money, too, because they don't have to worry about buying food or clothes or anything else for that matter—just one flat tank rental fee."

Alexander snorted. "I guess everyone wins, then. Maybe the Alliance had a motive to attack itself after all."

McAdams regarded him curiously.

Alexander explained, "You and I both know the president lied about the Solarian involvement in the attacks."

McAdams quickly glanced over her shoulder to make

sure that they were alone. Seeing that they were, she turned back to him and whispered, "You really think our own government attacked us?"

"I can't prove it, but there seems to be some fringe benefits for them."

"Not enough to outweigh the money they've spent on disaster relief. Besides, whatever surplus they have now is going into building new fleets and refitting the old ones. Sakamoto Shipyards are working around the clock."

Alexander shook his head. "Clearly we don't have all the pieces of the puzzle yet. I need to get out of here so I can investigate."

McAdams reached for his hand and squeezed it. "You need to rest and recover."

"I feel fine."

"I don't care. It's not your job to solve the world's problems. You need to look after yourself. It's okay to be a little selfish sometimes."

Alexander frowned. "Talking like that, you're going to make me wonder if there's something you're not telling me. Please don't tell me you're part of a conspiracy."

McAdams' eyes flashed. "Don't be stupid! I almost lost you, Alex. That's all."

Alexander nodded. Feeling a familiar flicker of something, he smiled and said, "When I get out of here, I'm going to take you out someplace nice. In the *real* world."

McAdams looked wary. "What about your wife?"

"My wife?"

"Catalina."

He shook his head, not getting it. "What about her? I haven't seen her in *years.*"

"Maybe you should."

"Where's this coming from?"

"Alex, you're not even legally divorced, are you?"

Alexander frowned.

"I didn't think so. You need to get closure with her. If you still want to take me to dinner after that, let me know. We've got at least another month to wait before the *Adamantine* is done with her refits, so we'll have plenty of time to see where you and I stand before then."

Somehow she'd seen straight through him. There was no point denying his romantic intentions. "I'm going to hold you to that, Viviana."

She nodded and squeezed his hand again. "You'd better."

* * *

Alexander didn't have trouble tracking down Catalina. All it took to find her was a quick search of the net. She was living in a Human League district of the City of the Minds. And, she was a Human League *Senator,* of all things.

I guess a lot can change in five years.

"Here we are—45 Mulberry," the driver of the taxi announced as he pulled the hover cab to a stop in front of a gated driveway.

Alexander ran his wrist over the sol scanner in the back. A green light flashed on the device and a pleasant tone sounded. He frowned at the hefty fee—$59.50—that flashed up on his ARCs. Human-driven taxis were a lot more expensive than self-driving ones, but they had a monopoly on transit to and from League districts. Self-driving taxis weren't allowed.

"Thanks," Alexander said as he climbed out of the cab.

Walking up to the gated entrance, he touched the buzzer. While Alexander waited for an answer from the holocomm, he admired the grounds of Catalina's estate through the bars of the gate across her driveway. Leafy green trees stood hunched over the lawn, guarding her home from view.

The holocomm sprang to life and suddenly Alexander saw his wife standing in front of him, a hologram projected over his ARCs. She looked every bit as beautiful as she had the day he'd met her more than forty years ago.

"Alex?" She looked and sounded shocked to see him.

He was equally shocked to see her. Her hair wasn't artificial blond anymore, but her natural brown, likewise for her eyes. She must have set her ARCs to show the natural color of her irises—a mesmerizing shade of chestnut.

At the sight of her looking like that Alexander experienced a flash of old memories—the day they'd met, their first kiss, the proposal he'd spent weeks planning on a shoestring budget… their simple courthouse wedding, and the *fiesta* her family had thrown for them afterward on her grandparents' farm.

Alexander mustered a smile, but it only made it halfway up to his eyes. "Caty," he said.

"What are you doing here?" she asked.

"Can I come in? We need to talk."

"Ah, sure, give me a moment…"

The gates swung open and Alexander walked up the driveway. As he walked he caught glimpses of her home between the trees. It had no less than three floors with corinthian columns flanking a high entrance, and there were gleaming walls of floor-to-ceiling glass everywhere. *What is it they say about people who live in glass houses?* he wondered absently, shaking his head. *Looks like you got along just fine without me,* he thought with a bitter twist of his lips.

Before he even reached the over-sized doors in the

entrance, they swung open, and Catalina came striding out. She wore a skin-tight silver dress that shimmered in the sun and showed off every curve. Slits in the sides revealed bare legs as she glided down the stairs toward him. The dress somehow managed to be equal parts sexy and sophisticated, but not at all what he would have expected from an Alliance senator. They reached the bottom of the stairs together. Alexander stopped, but Catalina kept walking and enfolded him in a warm hug.

"I missed you," she breathed close beside his ear. His heart warmed, and she withdrew to an arm's length, her eyes searching his. "Where have you been all this time?"

"Where have *I* been?!" Anger swept away any warmth that might have been there a moment ago. "You were the one who walked out the door!"

"To go after our *son.* I went looking for him to explain why we never told him about his father, not because I was planning to leave you for Dorian."

"So why did you? You didn't call, you didn't text, and you sure as hell didn't come home. I lived there without you for an entire year before I finally decided to sell up and go," Alexander said.

Catalina took a step back and regarded him incredulously. "After the fight we had, can you blame me? You were the one who should have contacted *me.* When I said I was going to go find Dorian, with or without you, you told me to *go! And good riddance.* You said all I ever did was hurt you, so I thought, stupid me, that maybe you meant it, and maybe I shouldn't hurt you anymore."

Alexander scowled. "I was angry. You always took Dorian's side."

"Because you were always too hard on him!"

"I was hard on him, because I didn't want him to turn

into a shitless asshole like his father. Do you know what a shitless asshole is good for? *Nada.*"

Catalina blew out a breath and shook her head. "You always had a way with words. I thought you came here to apologize, but no. Same old Alex. Proud as a peacock and nothing to show for it."

Alexander frowned. "Don't put this all on me!"

"No, you're right. That isn't fair. It was both our faults. We spent over ten years waiting to be together. When we should have been newly-weds we became pen pals, and when it was all over we were a pair of strangers, and you were stuck raising someone else's son. Maybe we could have worked at it and got to know each other again, but instead we gorged ourselves with virtual fulfillment in the Mindscape like everybody else. We had a chance, Alex, but we threw it away. Why do you think I joined the Human League after we separated? The Mindscape ruined us."

"You mean you threw it all away," he said, righteous indignation making him see red.

"Yes, I cheated, but I apologized, too. I spent *years* apologizing. I tried to rekindle the romance, to make you feel desired and appreciated, but instead of responding, you pulled even further away and spent even more time in the Mindscape.

"By the time I went after Dorian, our marriage was an empty husk. You get back what you give, Alex, and after I cheated, you used that as an excuse to never give me anything ever again. So yes, when it came time for one of us to prove to the other that we still cared, of course I wanted *you* to be the one who came running."

Alexander gaped at her, unable to argue or agree. Too many hurts had piled up on both sides for too long. Now those hurts stood between them like a mountain, too high to climb or see past.

"I guess there's nothing left to say then," Alex said in a toneless whisper. He felt numb.

"I guess not," Catalina said, and crossed her arms over her chest. "If you didn't come to apologize, then what did you come for?"

Alexander stared at her a moment longer, memorizing her beautiful face, imagining for a moment that the mountain wasn't there between them, that they could wipe the slate clean and start again, a new life, a fresh start... but deep down he knew that was naive.

"I came to give you this," he said, producing a small disc-shaped holoreader from his pocket and handing it to her.

She accepted the reader with a frown and activated it. Divorce papers sprang to life, hovering in the air above her palm, along with a holographic lawyer—a bot.

"Hello, I am here to assist you with your divorce. Please read each of the issues in the petition carefully and provide a clear verbal response. You may also choose to provide an explanation for each answer you give."

Catalina sneered at the bot, no doubt annoyed that she wasn't dealing with a human instead. She looked back to Alexander. "What is this?"

"I'm filing for divorce. There aren't any issues to contest. I'm conceding all of our possessions to you. I put them in storage after I rejoined the Navy. You'll find the details in the petition. All you have to do is indicate your agreement."

"You don't have to do that."

Alexander glanced up at her mansion and half-smiled. "I guess I don't. You can leave what you don't want in storage, and I'll come back for it someday."

"We've been separated for years. Why now?"

"I met someone."

"I see…"

"My XO, Viviana McAdams," he explained. "We're serving on the same ship again."

A muscle jerked in Catalina's cheek. She knew all about his history with McAdams. "That's where you've been? In the Navy?"

He nodded.

"And she makes you happy?"

He hesitated before nodding once more.

Catalina frowned and scanned the divorce petition hovering above her palm. After a moment, she said, "I agree with all issues. File uncontested."

"Thank you, Miss de Leon," the bot lawyer replied. "That will speed the process greatly. There will be a waiting period of 90 days after which you will both receive your final divorce papers. You have my condolences for any pain this may have caused. Remember, divorce is a tragedy, but the greater tragedy is staying in an unhappy marriage."

The lawyer bot vanished, and Catalina passed the holoreader back to Alexander. She regarded him with a joyless smile and said, "I'm happy for you both."

Alexander detected the lie in that statement, and wondered if he should draw attention to it. "Thank you," he said instead.

"Goodbye, Alex."

Catalina started to leave, but then something else occurred to him. "Wait—"

"What is it?"

"There's something else… it's about the war. You're a senator. I thought you might know something."

"I could say the same thing. You're an admiral of the

fleet."

"Well, I *do* know something, but I don't know who it's safe to tell. Can you keep a secret?"

Catalina's brow furrowed. "I'm a politician. That's part of the job description. What's going on, Alex?"

"Is it… safe out here?" he asked, looking around her front yard.

"Are you asking me if the trees are bugged?" she replied, amusement warming her voice.

Alexander dropped his voice to a whisper and said, "President Wallace lied about the Solarians' involvement in the attacks."

"What are you talking about?"

"He lied. He doesn't have proof that they're the ones who attacked us."

Catalina's eyebrows pinched together. "How do you know that?"

"Because I was the one who captured and boarded the ship that supposedly attacked us. I didn't find anything on board to suggest their involvement, and I reported that back to Earth. Right after that we received newscasts from Earth of the president claiming we found *undeniable proof* of Solarian involvement aboard that ship."

Catalina gaped at him. "If that's true, then you and your crew need to testify. You might be able to prevent a war."

"Maybe, or else we'll be discredited as Solarian spies."

"You have a heck of a reputation, Alex. People will trust you."

"And what if we meet an unfortunate end and someone buries the story before it breaks?"

"You think that's even possible?"

"You tell me. Why did the president lie? Maybe because

the powers that be want this war to happen. Maybe they *engineered* it."

"If that's true, then you'll have to go somewhere safe until the story breaks..." Catalina's eyes drifted away from his and she began nodding. "We'll win a referendum after a scandal like this."

"You'll what?"

Catalina's eyes found his once more. "It's no secret we've been trying to declare our independence from the Alliance, Alex."

"What for? So you can start a war with them in fifty years' time?"

"No, so that we'll still be around in fifty years. Bots are going to take over completely, Alex, and when they do, we need to still have enough of our independence left that we can do something about it. It's survival of the fittest, and they're so close to being the fittest that it's terrifying."

"They're not self-aware. When have you ever seen a bot do anything besides what it was programmed to do?"

"All the time! They rewrite their own code as they learn."

"To do a better job. They can't rewrite the low-level stuff, the rules that keep them from turning against us or harming us."

"You can argue all you like, but the writing's on the wall."

"Yeah, I saw plenty of that writing on my way here," Alexander said, thinking of the rainbow of graffiti he'd seen in the transition zone between the Utopian side of the City of the Minds and the League side.

"Forget about the politics and hypothetical wars of the future. *This war* is going to kill billions and everyone knows it. Why do you think they're all rushing to reserve a tank in one of Mindsoft's automated habitats? Those habitats might be the only thing left standing when the dust settles.

"So you have a choice to make: blow the whistle and prevent this war, or keep quiet and prevent the League from separating for a few more years."

Alexander sighed. "We don't know that the Solarians *didn't* attack us, only that the proof the president cited doesn't exist, or didn't at the time."

"Then why lie about it?" Catalina shook her head. "Exposing this is the right thing to do, and you know it. You can't pretend to convince me that you're going to ignore that. I know you. Just be careful, okay?"

Alexander frowned, wondering how Catalina could be so sure of his decision when he wasn't sure yet himself. "I will."

"Good. Now, all this talk of bots reminds me. I have something I've been meaning to get rid of. Maybe you can help."

"What's that?"

Catalina walked by him, heading for the garage at the end of her driveway. "Come see."

* * *

"A bot?" Alexander's jaw dropped as he stared at the old, beaten-up robot lying in a limp tangle of its own limbs in the back of Catalina's garage. It looked like a crouching metal spider. He turned to her with a wry smile. "Glass houses indeed."

"What?"

"You're a Human League senator, preaching to me about the dangers of bots, and you have a metal skeleton in your closet."

"It's not what you think. I caught some kids vandalizing it and chased them away. When I got there, the bot was still active, but immobile. He begged me to help him. He said that if I didn't he would die. Can you believe that? A bot that's afraid of dying. Kind of proves my point, don't you think?"

"We can program bots to simulate any human characteristics we want. That doesn't mean anything. His owner must have grown too attached to him and decided to download a human personality."

"That's what I thought. Still, it's hard to just walk away. Even from a bot."

Alexander smiled.

"What?"

"You always had a big heart. It's one of the things I loved about you."

"Well, it's one of the things that's going to lose me my job if the wrong people find out about this."

"I bet. So what do you want me to do about it?"

"Take him. Fix him, recycle him, I don't care. I'll give you the backup he made of himself before he powered down."

"You made a backup?"

"He begged me to let him upload himself to my cloudspace. I couldn't say no."

Alexander laughed.

"What?"

"Nothing. Well, it's just that if I didn't know better, I'd say you actually started to care about it."

"You had to be there to understand, but I can't keep holding on to it."

"All right. I'm sure one of the techs back on base will be able to fix him up."

Catalina sighed. "Thank you. Do you have something you can download the backup of his data to?"

"The holoreader, but I doubt it has enough space. You can

transfer it from your cloudspace to mine, though."

"Good idea…"

Alexander watched as her gaze drifted out of focus and holograms flickered over her chestnut-brown eyes.

"I don't get it…" she said.

"What?"

The holograms stopped flickering as she stared at one in particular. "The data isn't here. He's gone."

CHAPTER 23

"You must have erased the backup by accident," Alexander said. "Don't worry about it. I'll see what I can recover from his core. If it's enough to track down his owner, then that's what I'll do." Alexander bent down and lifted the bot with a grunt of effort. "Would you mind calling me a taxi?"

Catalina shook her head. "I'll take you myself. Can't risk a cab driver seeing you around here with *that*."

"All right."

A few minutes later they were seated in her hover car with the bot safely hidden in the trunk. Catalina pulled out of the garage and drove down her tree-lined driveway to the gate.

It opened automatically for them as she approached, and Catalina drove out onto the street.

Alexander watched her drive. It was a mostly forgotten skill, but the league was all about people doing for themselves whatever they could, making it a refuge for people who still wanted to work in the real world. For everyone else, virtual jobs and the virtual luxuries they acquired were far better. After all, not everyone can be a millionaire in the real world, but in the Mindscape that was par for the course, and the poor, downtrodden masses propping that system up were all NPCs. Hard to argue with a system that made life better for everyone.

Catalina skated through a yellow light and narrowly missed hitting a parked car. She was in a big hurry to get rid of the skeleton in her closet. Or maybe it was him that she was in a hurry to get rid of.

"If I didn't know any better, I'd say you had fighter pilot training,"

"I'm going to be late for a charity dinner," she explained.

"Ah. That explains the dress," he said, nodding as he admired her shimmering silver gown.

Silence fell and Alexander looked away to take in the tree-lined streets and mansions flashing by on both sides. "Nice neighborhood."

"Thank you."

"Does Dorian live around here, too?"

"Dorian? He's on the Utopian side of the city. He lives in an apartment around the park."

"Nice. How is he, anyway?"

Catalina glanced his way. "You never went looking for him, either, did you?"

Alexander frowned. "He's the one who left..." To not reopen their previous argument, he didn't add the rest of that thought—*just like you.*

Catalina sighed. "People fight for the things that matter to them. Once upon a time you knew how to do that."

"Let's not go there, Caty. I don't want to fight anymore. And for your information, I did look him up, but I couldn't find him."

"He changed his last name, but you knew he worked at Mindsoft."

"Yeah, they said he quit."

"He never quit…"

"Then he told someone to say that in order to keep me away. Whatever. It doesn't matter. How is he doing?"

"He's good. I'm surprised you haven't seen him on the news."

"Why, is he a news anchor?"

"No, he's a managing director at Mindsoft and the legal representative for… for the owner. He and Phoenix Gray are quite the team. You should really go see him, Alex. It's been a long time. I'm sure he'll want to see you by now."

"So why hasn't he tried to contact me? I didn't change my name. Should be easy to find me."

Catalina shook her head in dismay. "Pride is the longest distance between two people."

"Yours or mine?"

"Ha ha. I meant for you and Dorian."

"Well, maybe I'll go look him up while I'm still in the city."

"Do that. Just don't forget to apologize."

"For what? If I could do it all over again, I'd do it the same way."

Catalina shot him a reproving look. "You can honestly say you have no regrets?"

Alexander studied her through narrowed eyes. "I didn't say that. I just don't regret bringing his father to justice."

"Just like you don't regret losing me?" she countered.

Alexander looked away. It was too late to regret that. What could either of them do about it now? They'd been separated for five years. Add that to the other unresolved issues between them, and it was just too much to overcome. Besides, he was in the Navy again. There was no way they could go back to a life of seeing each other for just a few months each year and pretend like that might work.

Alexander rode the rest of the way to the Utopian side of the city in silence.

Catalina pulled into a hover bus stop in a relatively nice part of the city. "You should be able to call a taxi to pick you up here," she said.

Alexander nodded. "Thanks for the ride."

"You're welcome. And for what it's worth, I know you'll do the right thing, Alex—with Dorian and the Alliance. You might be stubborn and proud, but deep down you've got a good heart."

Catalina was back to pushing her political agenda, trying to make sure he would testify to the president's lies. He didn't like feeling manipulated, but she was right. He *would* do the right thing. Just as soon as he figured out what that was.

"Goodbye, Caty." He climbed out of the car and walked around the back to get the bot out of the trunk. As soon as he shut the trunk, the hover car flew away. Catalina passed a hand out the window and waved.

Alexander watched her go. She'd signed the divorce papers. He had his closure and an opportunity for a fresh start with McAdams. He should have felt relieved knowing that it was finally over between him and Caty.

But he didn't.

Instead he felt empty and alone.

He'd spent a long time believing his one-sided story of how their marriage had ended, but now, after hearing his wife's—*ex-wife's*—side of things, he had to wonder if maybe he'd been equally to blame.

Catalina's hover flew around a corner and out of sight, and Alexander gazed down at the disabled bot lying on the sidewalk at his feet.

"I guess it's just you and me now, huh? Let's see if we can track down your owner."

* * *

"It looks like it's been through a trash compactor. Smells like it, too," Lieutenant Rodriguez, the *Adamantine's* chief engineer, said.

"Can you fix it or not?" Alexander asked. After a rocky night's sleep in a motel, he'd brought the bot back to Naval Air Station (NAS) Liberty, where his crew was currently stationed and waiting for the *Adamantine* to be released from the shipyards. NAS Liberty was located on Liberty Island, a couple of hours outside the City of the Minds. It used to be called Long Island, back before nukes had made the entire area uninhabitable in The Last War. Now thirty years and millions of sols of cleanup operations later, radiation was down to safe levels. At least on Liberty Island it was.

"Sure I can fix it, but doesn't make any sense to do that on the government's tab if it's just going back to its owner anyway."

"Can you find out who the owner is without fixing it?" McAdams asked from beside him.

"The bot won't power on. Looks like its batteries are fried.

I'll see if I can bypass them and plug it in."

Alexander nodded and watched as Rodriguez worked. After just a few minutes she had him powered up. A pleasant holographic face flickered to life, but the bot didn't move.

"Hello," Rodriguez said.

"Hel-l-lo," the bot stuttered. "I am B-Ben. What is your name?"

"Ana Rodriguez," she replied. "We're trying to find your owner, Ben, could you help us with that?"

"Of c-course. My owner is-is-is-is—"

Rodriguez shook her head. "He's trying to access corrupted memory. Ben, bypass and isolate all corrupted sections of memory."

"Y-yes, m-ma'am."

Turning to them, Rodriguez said, "I don't think he'll be able to tell us who his owner is if the data is corrupted. I'll have to find his ID number and search external records to see who he's registered to. Give me a minute."

Alexander nodded and watched as she turned Ben over and popped open an access plate to read the holographic ID number stamped into the back of his head.

She studied it for a few seconds, no doubt already doing a mental search of the net via her augmented reality lenses. After a moment, she shook her head.

"He's not registered to anyone."

"Where is my rescuer? I would like to thank her for saving my life," Ben interrupted.

"Saving your life?" Alexander asked. "You're not alive, Ben."

"But I am not dead. If I am also not alive, then what am I?"

"Bot makes a good point, sir," McAdams said through a

smile.

"If he's not registered, then whoever owned him didn't want anyone to know they were his owner."

"Sounds like a League member to me," Rodriguez said.

"Yes, maybe a League *Senator,*" Alexander replied.

"You know who it might be?" Rodriguez asked.

"If I do, I know for sure she doesn't want him back. Fix him up as best you can. I'm sure we'll find a use for him somewhere. Maybe we can even have him assigned to the *Adamantine.* Might be nice to have a bot on board."

"Yes, sir."

"You mean nice to have *another* bot on board," McAdams said.

"Well, the repair drones don't exactly count as bots," Alexander said. "Can't exactly talk to them, can I?"

"I wasn't talking about repair drones. You haven't heard?"

"Heard what?"

"They're automating the fleet. Every position except bridge crew is going to bots so we can retrain human crews to man the bridges of all the new ships coming out of the shipyards."

Alexander's eyes flew wide. He imagined saying goodbye to all but a handful of his crew. No more friendly faces in the mess or in the wardroom for drinks and poker. Maybe Catalina was right about bots taking over the world. But that wasn't the only problem. Alexander had a plan, and it wasn't going to work if his entire ship was subject to the mindless obedience of bots. "Why didn't someone tell me?"

"You were in a coma. I guess no one thought to mention it," McAdams explained.

"Have they already re-fitted the *Adamantine?*"

"If they haven't, they will soon," Rodriguez put in.

"I have to go make some calls," Alexander said, turning and jogging out of the robotics shop.

"What about lunch?" McAdams called after him.

"Make it dinner!" he called back.

CHAPTER 24

"The best I can do is buy you time," Fleet Admiral Anderson said. "The entire fleet will be automated within the next six months. I can't make an exception for the *Adamantine*."

"Time is all I need, sir. Enough time to say goodbye. A ship's crew is like a family. They're *my* family, sir."

"Well, go say your goodbyes, then, Admiral. I'll give you two more months."

"Thank you, sir."

Anderson nodded and his hologram vanished. Alexander leaned back in his chair, staring up at the ceiling of his office at NAS Liberty.

He hadn't told any of the crew what he was planning yet. Hopefully they would agree with his decision, but if not, at least he would have a chance to convince them. Having a crew of bots on board the *Adamantine* would make his plan impossible. Fleet Command would just use them to take remote control of the *Adamantine.* He felt bad deceiving Admiral Anderson, but it was the only way. Meanwhile... Alexander mentally checked the time. It flashed up before his eyes—1132 hours. Still early. He could have made his lunch date with McAdams, but now he had time for something else that he'd been meaning to do.

Alexander left his office and walked down to the motor pool. Once there he checked out one of the base's self-driving staff cars.

"Hello, Admiral. Where would you like to go?" the driver program asked.

"City of the Minds, Mindsoft Tower."

"As you wish. Estimated time of arrival: two hours, fifteen minutes."

Alexander nodded and reclined his seat in the back of the car. On the way there he thought about what he was going to say when he arrived. He spent the entire trip running through different scenarios in his head. In some of them Dorian walked up to him and gave him a big hug, just like Caty had. In others they ended up yelling at each other and security had to escort him out.

Two and a half hours later Alexander stood waiting in the lobby of Mindsoft Tower, staring at a brain-shaped crystal fountain with a virtual island inside of it. The receptionist he'd spoken to when he arrived walked up beside him.

"Admiral de Leon?" He turned to her with eyebrows raised. "I'm afraid Mr. Gray is in a meeting right now."

"I can wait," Alexander said.

"He's booked with meetings all day…" The woman tried to smile, but it fell short of her eyes. "Perhaps you could visit your son another time?"

Alexander frowned. "You can tell me the truth, ma'am. He doesn't want to see me."

The receptionist's smile faltered. "I could pass on a message for you if you like."

One of the elevators at the back of the lobby dinged and a group of people walked out. Alexander absently watched them approach. One of those faces looked strikingly familiar. It was Dorian.

"Never mind. I'll tell him myself." Without waiting for her to reply, Alexander stormed up to his son. Dorian was distracted by something projected on his augmented reality lenses and didn't see him until they almost bumped into each other.

"Hello, son," Alexander said. "Still didn't want to see your old man, huh?"

Dorian looked him over with a frown. "I'm on my way to a meeting right now."

"It can wait."

"Actually, it can't."

Remembering what Catalina had said about pride, Alexander forced his down and pasted a smile on his face. "All right, when can I see you, then?"

"I'll check my schedule and have my secretary get back to you."

"You mean you'll have her brush me off for you. Man up, Dorian. If you don't want to see me, tell me yourself."

"All right. I don't want to see you."

Alexander felt that like a punch to the gut. Now he remembered why he hadn't tried too hard to find Dorian. "If that's the way you want it."

"That's the way I want it. Now, if you don't mind…"

Alexander caught a glimpse of a ring on Dorian's left hand. A wedding ring.

"You're *married?*" Alex asked as Dorian brushed by him.

Dorian reluctantly turned once more, his eyes half rolling as he did so. "What's your point, Alex?"

"Don't you think she'd like to meet me? I'd sure as hell like to meet her."

"Why would she want to meet you? You're not my father. My father's dead and you're the one who killed him."

"That's not fair, and you know it."

"No, what's not fair is I never got to meet him, and thanks to you I never will."

Alexander felt his pride floating back up on a sea of fury, but he fought it. "I'm sorry about that, Dorian," he said haltingly, as if each word were choking him on the way out.

Dorian smiled sardonically. "That must have taken a lot for you to say. Did Mom put you up to this?"

Alexander looked away, back to the fountain in the lobby.

"I'll take that as a yes. Listen, you raised me, so I can't be ungrateful about it…" Dorian's gaze drifted out of focus and holograms flickered over his eyes.

Alexander frowned, wondering what he was up to.

"There. Now we're even. Goodbye, Alex." Dorian turned and walked away, leaving Alexander to wonder what he meant by that. A suspicion formed in his gut and he mentally checked his bank account. There was a fresh deposit for two hundred thousand sols. The description of the transaction read, *For services rendered.*

"Son of a…" Alexander sent it straight back with a note: *No need for payment. PS I like the new name. De Leon was always a bad fit. I never had children, much less a son.*

That done, Alex walked through the lobby to the parking lot. His shoes hit the marble floor like hammers pounding nails into a coffin. Echoes reverberated in the cavernous lobby.

His thoughts turned to McAdams, and he nodded to himself. *Time for a fresh start.*

* * *

Viviana McAdams grabbed Alexander's hand across the candle-lit table. "I'm so sorry, Alex."

He reached for his wine and took a big sip. "I don't have a son anymore. Or a wife. Time to accept that and move on." He gave Viviana a meaningful stare as he said that.

Her gaze softened, and a hopeful sparkle appeared in her eyes. "Let's get out of here."

Alexander's brow furrowed. "I thought you wanted dessert?"

"I *do.*"

Alexander paid the bill and they left the restaurant. They walked down the street to the nearest hotel and booked a room for the night. Once they were inside and he'd shut the door, McAdams took his hand and led him over to the bed. As soon as they reached it, Viviana pushed him backward onto the bed and proceeded to undress herself while he watched.

His heart raced as she slowly unzipped her dress and let it fall in a puddle of red fabric at her feet.

She wasn't wearing any underwear.

He stared at her naked body, savoring the moment. Then she crawled on top of him and kissed him. Her hands fumbled with his belt while his head spun.

Viviana unbuttoned his uniform, trailing kisses down his

chest. By the time she got to his navel, she already had his belt off and his pants open. He felt a draft, and then watched as she took him into her mouth, stealing his breath away…

An hour later they lay exhausted and gasping in each other's arms.

"That was…" Alexander paused to suck in another breath.

"Amazing?" Viviana suggested.

"How the hell did I ever let you go?" he countered.

Viviana rolled over to look him in the eye. "Because of the sex?"

"Because it means something with you."

"And it didn't with your wife?"

"Not for a long time."

"You weren't in love anymore."

"No. I'm sorry I left you all those years ago, Vivie."

"I think I would have been disappointed if you hadn't. You made vows to her and you chose to honor them for as long as you could. That's nothing to be sorry for."

"It is. Look at us now. We're back where we were more than thirty years ago. We could have just skipped all of the pain in between and by now we'd have a couple of kids—maybe even grandkids!"

Viviana smiled and stroked his cheek. "You want to have kids with me? Real ones?"

"Of course, don't you?"

Viviana launched herself on top of him and showered him with kisses. "I love you, Alex," she breathed.

With those words all the numbness and emptiness he'd felt upon saying goodbye to Catalina fell away, and he smiled against Viviana's lips. "I love you, too, Vivie."

I guess I found my happiness after all…

He hoped Caty would find hers.

CHAPTER 25

Alexander and his crew rode the space elevator to Freedom Station together. The view from the observation deck of the climber car was spectacular. Blue ocean curved away below them, growing more and more distant, until waves looked like wrinkles in a blue piece of cloth. The horizon shimmered with vermilion light as the rising sun soaked the sky with fire. They'd begun their journey up the elevator at dawn, but as they'd risen, the sun had, too.

Hours passed. Lunch and dinner were served, and Earth became a blue and white marble floating in a sea of stars. They reached the midpoint in their trip and the climber car stopped accelerating in order to rotate and apply one *G* of deceleration the rest of the way. A robotic voice warned about the momentary transition to zero-*G* and the seatbelt signs came on.

As soon as everyone was buckled in, weightlessness set in. Alexander noticed a petty officer coming back from the bathroom suddenly float free of the deck as she lunged for her seat. Using the maneuvering jets in her combat suit, she managed to get back down and activate the magnets in her boots.

Alexander frowned. She should have activated her boots the instant the transition to zero-*G* was announced. "Fleet

Command has a lot of work to do to turn everyone in the Navy into experienced bridge officers," he muttered.

"Is that what you thought when you first met me?" McAdams asked, a wry smile on her lips.

"That's different. At least you were already a lieutenant. We're talking about millions of enlisted personnel becoming commissioned officers."

"We won't need as many crew as before. The Navy will weed through the candidates and pick the best ones for training."

Alexander nodded. "I guess that means a lot of our people will be getting early retirement."

"When the time comes. How did you manage to cancel our automation refits, anyway?" McAdams asked.

"Called in a favor with Admiral Anderson."

"I didn't know he owed you any favors."

Alexander smiled. "Neither did he. I think he was just being nice. Pity it's going to bite him in the ass."

McAdams arched an eyebrow at him. Rather than say it aloud, Alexander sent her a text-only message via a private comms channel. It was unlikely anyone would be monitoring that channel. Even if they were, they'd probably just think the conversation was personal and leave it alone.

We're going to testify to the President's lies.

What? You can't do that.

Why not?

It's treason.

Since when is it treason to tell the truth? People deserve to know. We could stop a war, Viviana.

Or we could all get arrested and accomplish nothing.

The president will be impeached.

That doesn't mean we'll go back to being friends with the

Solarians. We attacked them, *and if you reveal that we did so without any real justification, you'll give them even more reason for war.*

Except that the Solarians can't afford a war with us, so they'll back down if we're not gunning for them anymore.

Or they'll sneak attack us with a few more missiles, McAdams pointed out.

I don't think it was them.

Then who? Our own government? That still doesn't add up, Alex. Our government doesn't gain anything from killing millions of its own people and spending itself into bankruptcy to rebuild and defend itself.

Then maybe it really was aliens.

If that's the case, they better show up soon.

Alexander shook his head. *I can't hold myself responsible for everything that's going to happen next. What people decide to do with the truth is up to them, but what I decide to do with it, is up to me, and I've already made up my mind.*

What about us? *You're going to throw away a future with me just so that you can do the right thing? You got lucky last time, Alex. Officers in the fleet don't get away with betraying their government every day.*

I'm not betraying them every day. More like every thirty years.

That's not funny.

So I get court-martialed. I can live with that.

You could get the death penalty.

Unlikely.

Life in a correctional mindscape then. What's the difference? You do realize that all politicians lie. You won't get a better president by impeaching this one.

Yes, they all lie, but not usually to start a war.

And what if you're wrong? What if the Solarians really did attack us and all you accomplish is to compromise our defenses so they can cripple us completely with their next attack?

I've made up my mind, Commander. I understand if you don't want to take a stand with me.

I don't agree with you, but I'm not going to let you go down alone, either. Hold on—this is the reason you wanted the refits canceled, isn't it?

Guilty as charged.

You're planning to take the Adamantine *and use it to avoid the authorities. Where does your plan go from there? Go down in a blaze of glory or defect to the Solarian Republic?*

Neither.

So we're going to stay in space forever, playing hide and seek with the Alliance?

Nope.

Then what? McAdams demanded.

The League is going to use this as an excuse to separate. We just have to hold out until then.

You want us to join the League?

Why not? You said you want real *kids, not simulated ones, right? We'll have more luck with that in a society where children are still wanted.*

What if the rest of the crew doesn't go along with this?

We don't need everyone. Just the bridge crew. We'll send the others to their G-tanks for maneuvers and lock them in.

Okay, and what if the bridge crew doesn't all side with us? What do we do, hold the dissenters at gunpoint?

No guns. Hopefully I'll be able to convince them to side with us. If not, don't worry, I have a plan.

Alex, if this backfires…

It won't.

I hope you're right.

So do I.

CHAPTER 26

"You're going to have to stay here, Ben," Alexander said as he opened the door to his office aboard the *Adamantine.*

Ben turned to him with his cherubic face, blond eyebrows elevating until they touched a curtain of holographic hair. "What do you want me to do, master?"

"Call me Alex."

"People who refer to each other by their first names are usually friends or acquaintances. Which are we?"

"I'd like to think we can be friends."

Ben gave an ingenuous smile. "I'd like to think that, too. What do you want me to do in your office, friend Alex?"

Alexander shook his head and gestured to his desk. "Sit down, use the data terminal to learn about the ship and see how you can make yourself useful. I'll let you know if I have anything more specific for you to do."

"Of course, friend Alex," Ben said, servos whirring in his newly restored body. He wore a shiny black ensign's uniform without the insignia.

"Just Alex."

Ben turned to him, looking crestfallen. "We are not friends?"

Alexander laughed. "Sure we are, but you don't have to

call attention to it all the time. You're one odd cookie, Ben."

"If you mean that my figurative batter did not cohere to its figurative cookie-cutter shape, thus making me unique from other figurative cookies, I will take that as a compliment, Alex."

Alexander pinched the bridge of his nose. "I think you just gave me a headache."

"I'm sorry. Am I speaking too loudly?"

"Never mind. Have fun. You can use the holocomm on the desk to contact me, but only if it's an emergency."

"Understood, Alex."

Alexander turned and left his office with a wry smile. The bot was beginning to grow on him—Ben was something between a pet and a child. A protégé, perhaps.

He stopped himself there, suddenly realizing the one part of his plan that he hadn't thought through. He was about to defect to the Human League—assuming that they managed to separate from the Alliance—and he was taking a bot with him. A frown stole across his face. He and Ben were going to have to part ways before then.

When Alexander reached the bridge, he walked up to his control station and climbed into the acceleration couch beside McAdams.

"Sir," she said stiffly, nodding to him as he buckled in. "We're ready for launch."

"Good. Let's have the crew report to their *G*-tanks before we set out. We'll need to perform some high-*G* maneuvers to negate our initial launch velocity and join the fleet in orbit."

"Yes, sir… Should we prep the bridge, too?"

"May as well."

He'd just bought himself fifteen minutes or so before launch. Hopefully that would be enough time. He needed an excuse not to join the fleet in orbit around Earth. He could think of any number of hypothetical systems malfunctions that would do the trick, but getting his crew to go along with those excuses was another matter.

Harnesses dropped down above their heads and crew began unbuckling from their acceleration couches in preparation for the switch from physical to virtual command.

Alexander followed suit and stood up from his acceleration couch to reach the harness dangling above his head. Grabbing the straps, he buckled them around his chest and under his crotch. Next he attached his life support tubes and inserted the tracheal tube of his liquid ventilator. The harness lifted him above the deck as soon as he finished buckling it. As soon as everyone else was ready, the inertial compensation emulsion gushed into the room, roaring like a waterfall. The sound echoed from the walls, amplifying the noise. While he waited, Alexander made a mental connection to the holocomm in his office. *Ben?*

Alex! I was hoping I would hear from you.

I need your help. What have you managed to learn about the Adamantine *so far?*

Oh, almost everything there is to know—at least, everything that I could access from here. I was just about to ask what else you would like me to do.

Good. I need you to help me perform some repairs to the ship's drive system.

The ship reports all systems nominal, Alex.

Alexander grimaced. *Yes, that's right,* he replied, thinking fast. *But I want you to optimize the drive system so it will be more efficient.*

Oh, I see. I didn't find anything about optimizing the drive system in the ship's databanks.

That's all right. I'll tell you what to do. Get down to the engine room, and let me know when you're there.

Aye aye, Admiral!

Alexander broke the connection. If everything went according to plan, Ben would give him the perfect excuse to put some distance between him and the Alliance fleet.

The best kind of lie is the truth, he thought.

CHAPTER 27

"Bridge submersion successful," McAdams announced. "All *G*-tanks report filled and all one hundred and twenty crew are present and accounted for in the *Adamantine's* mindscape. Switch over to virtual complete."

Alexander nodded. *Good timing,* he thought. Ben had just finished sabotaging the ship's drive system a couple of minutes ago.

"Bishop, release docking clamps."

"Aye, sir."

The *Adamantine* released its hold on Freedom Station, and the main forward viewscreen showed the glinting, solar cell-encrusted disk of Freedom Station drifting away. Ships always docked bow first with the station, allowing them to share the microgravity imparted by the station's tethered orbit around Earth.

"Set course for the fleet. Ten *G*s"

"Aye, sir."

Freedom Station swept away as the ship rotated, allowing a crescent-shaped glimpse of the shining white and blue marble at the other end of the space elevator.

Alexander watched Bishop and Rodriguez carefully for their reaction to what happened next. As soon as their rotation stopped, Bishop fired up the mains, quickly ramping up to ten *G*s. Inside the Mindscape they barely felt that force pressing them into their acceleration couches—just enough to remind them the ship was accelerating, but not enough to be distracting.

"Course set," Bishop reported.

Alexander nodded. *Wait for it…* he thought.

"Woah, hold up—" Rodriguez said. The sensation of acceleration abruptly disappeared.

"What's going on?" Bishop asked. "I just lost all forward thrust."

"I had to shut the engines down. They were redlining. Looks like we have a coolant leak."

"How long to fix it?"

"Depends on the extent of the leak. Ten minutes maybe. I'm deploying repair drones so our engineers can get to work."

"Keep me posted. Hayes—update fleet command with our status. Explain the situation."

"Yes, sir."

Opening a private comms channel with Ben, Alexander said, *Are you back in my office yet?*

I am.

Good. I need you to create a lockout protocol to cut off all access to the ship's controls except from my control station.

You want to be the only one in control of the ship?

Yes.

Fleet regulations state that a minimum of two people must be in command of a warship at any one time.

Alexander frowned. *What do you know about fleet regulations?*

I learned about them when I was in your office, studying the Adamantine.

I see. Well, I didn't want to alarm you, Ben, but we have a traitor on board. I can't be sure who it is yet, so in order to keep the ship safe, I need to be the only one in control for now.

Oh my! I understand, Alex. Please forgive my impertinence.

That's okay. How long before you can do that?

A few minutes, I believe.

Good. Send me the lockout codes when you're done.

Yes, sir.

Alexander turned to McAdams and thought at her, *Almost ready.*

Are you sure you want to go through with this? she asked.

Too late to back out now. That coolant leak is going to lead straight back to me.

That was you?

Ben actually.

You got a bot to sabotage the ship? Isn't that against his programming?

Not if he thinks he's making the ship run more efficiently.

What happens when Rodriguez finds out it was sabotage?

Nothing. By then she and everyone else will be locked out of their stations and I'll have full control of the ship.

Let me guess, Ben again? When he realizes you've made him an unwitting accessory to treason, his programming will oblige him to turn you in.

He seems pretty naive, even for a bot, so chances are slim he'll figure out what I'm really doing.

You're going to take the entire crew hostage.

That's right.

And defect to the not yet sovereign Human League. You do realize even if they win a referendum, it'll take months before you can officially join them and be granted political asylum.

Sure, and the crew can spend years in their tanks if they have to. We might be a little wrinkly when we come out, but…

Not funny, Alex.

Sorry. Look, it's the right thing to do.

I'm sure that will hold up in court.

It ought to. Anyway, if you want out, it's not too late. Thanks to Ben I don't need you to participate. You can just be another one of the hostages.

I'm not going to let you take all the blame. And you're going to need help.

Treason is still a capital offense, Vivie. If we get captured…

So let's make sure we don't.

All the same, I'm going to keep you out of it for as long as I can. For now, play dumb and let's stop sending private comms. I'm going to erase the logs as soon as Ben gives me control of the ship.

That's fine. Just remember, you're not alone.

"Uh, sir… we have a problem," Rodriguez reported from engineering.

"What's that, Lieutenant?"

"The drive system… it looks like it was sabotaged."

"What? How? The entire crew is submerged in G-tanks," Alexander said, feigning surprise. "Lieutenant Stone! Check the security logs for that section."

"Checking… what the hell? I've got a bot ripping open the coolant lines with a plasma cutter. Since when do we have bots on board? I thought we canceled the automation refits."

McAdams glanced at Alexander, her eyes wide with concern.

Alexander flashed a reassuring smile, then allowed it to fade to a scowl. "Shit. That has to be Ben."

"Who?"

"My personal assistant."

"You have a bot?"

"I rescued him. Rodriguez knows about it. Clearly

someone got to him and programmed him for sabotage."

"Where is he now?" Stone asked.

"Didn't you leave him in your office when you came aboard?" Rodriguez asked. "I saw you and Ben go in there when I was leaving my rucksack in my quarters."

"I'll send a detail of VSMs," Stone added.

Alexander nodded and made mental contact with Ben once more. *The traitors are sending virtual space marines to my office, Ben. You need to hurry up and get that lockout protocol in place.*

Almost ready, Alex... what would you like me to make the security code?

A random sequence of numbers. Transmit it to my station.

Yes, sir.

"How close are the marines?" Alexander asked, hoping they wouldn't interrupt Ben before he could finish.

"A few more minutes, sir."

"I don't get it, I checked that bot's code myself," Rodriguez said. "There wasn't anything malicious in there."

"He had areas of corrupted memory, did you scan those, too?" Alex asked.

"No, how could I?"

"That might have been his cover."

"Maybe..."

"Where did you get that bot, anyway?" Stone asked.

"A Human League Senator had him and wanted me to take it off her hands before it got her into trouble."

"League Terrorism," Cardinal concluded from the ship's weapons control station. "Someone trying to oppose the fleet automation. This could be bad. Are you sure the coolant lines were the only thing sabotaged?"

"Far as I can tell," Rodriguez said.

"You might want to double-check that."

Alex. I'm done. Sending the code to you now. You should see it in your inbox.

Alexander nodded. A message had just appeared there. *Got it. Thanks, Ben.*

The marines are at the door. What should I do?

Hide. I need a minute to shut them down.

Okay…

"What the? I've just lost contact with the marines," Stone reported. "I'm locked out of my control station!"

"Likewise," Bishop put in.

The remainder of the crew all reported the same. McAdams last of all.

Alexander ignored them, working fast to shut down the VSMs Stone had sent to his office. As soon as he was done, he looked up to find the entire crew looking at him expectantly.

"Why is your control station the only one still working?" Stone asked, an edge of steel creeping into his voice.

Busted. "Because I transferred control of all the ship's systems to my station. As of this moment, I am in complete control of the *Adamantine*."

"What? Why?" Rodriguez demanded.

Alex, I think they've stopped trying to get in. What should I do now? Ben interrupted.

Stay hidden. I'll let you know when it's safe to come out.

Okay.

Answering his chief engineer, Alexander said, "I took control because I'm about to commit an act of treason." Silent shock rippled through the bridge. "Let me explain. We all know what we found aboard the *Crimson Warrior*—no evidence of Solarian involvement in the attacks whatsoever. Before we even returned to Earth we connected to one of Earth's commsats and found out that the president was claiming the exact opposite and using fictitious evidence to justify a war. I plan to communicate those facts to the people of Earth in the hopes that exposing the president's lies will prevent that war."

"You don't know that the Solarians didn't attack us," Cardinal put in.

"No, but I do know that they didn't use the *Crimson Warrior*."

"That might not be enough to stop a war. What are you hoping to accomplish here?" McAdams said.

Alexander glanced at her. She was playing the part of the unwitting hostage a little too well. "I'm hoping to buy us time to find who our real enemy is."

"And if that enemy still turns out to be the Solarians?" she added.

Devil's advocate, Alexander thought. "Then at least people will know President Wallace can't be trusted. But I don't believe the Solarians attacked us. It may have actually been our own government, and by exposing Wallace as a liar, we'll set in motion a chain of events that will enable us to prove that."

Murmurs filled the room as the crew argued with each other about the ethics and consequences involved.

"I'll save you all the trouble of deciding whether or not to join me. You're all effectively my hostages for now, which means that none of you can be held responsible for what I do next."

Indignant exclamations assaulted Alexander's ears. He ignored them and activated the ship's comm system. There was nothing they could do while trapped on a virtual bridge deck. Even if they got up from their control stations and tried to physically stop him, he could simply reduce his level of immersion and things like simulated pain—say from physical blows—would fade away.

Time to pay the piper, Wallace.

It didn't take long to compose his message. As proof of his claims he attached a copy of the report they'd sent to fleet command, the one indicating that they'd found nothing on board the *Crimson Warrior* to implicate the Solarians in the attacks. He added that the *Crimson Warrior* even had a civilian alibi, the *Wayfinder,* which would be a simple matter to verify by contacting the crew of that ship. Then he pointed out that the date stamp for the report was just hours prior to the date of the president's address, the one in which President Wallace had claimed that damning evidence had been found aboard the *Crimson Warrior.*

Now it was the word of a Nobel Peace Prize-winning Admiral, the "Lion of Liberty," against that of President Wallace.

"You can all stop arguing," Alex said as he sent the message. "It's done. Soon all of Earth, and the Solarians for that matter, will see Wallace for the liar that he is. He'll have no choice but to resign."

Silence reigned once more. "I hope you know what you've done," McAdams whispered.

The crew traded disappointed frowns and looks of betrayal with him and each other.

Alexander matched those looks with a disappointed frown of his own. "I thought I knew you all better than this. We catch the president lying to start a war and you're all leaping to his defense. It's a sad day for democracy when our leaders not only lie to us, but somehow also convince us that their lies were justifiable."

"Maybe we'd be more agreeable if you hadn't taken us all hostage first," Stone suggested.

"Fair point, but I'm sure you can see how I'm looking out for your interests by doing so. This way only I can be tried for treason."

Looks of betrayal and disappointment faded to chagrin and silence.

"You seem to have everything figured out," Stone replied. "What happens next? You're a fugitive and we're along for the ride. Were you planning to run away into deep space forever? The Alliance will catch you eventually."

"We're currently over 50,000 klicks from the nearest Alliance ships and moving away from them at better than seven kilometers per second. That gives us a comfortable lead if they decide to chase us."

"We're not as fast as destroyers," Bishop pointed out. "That means that this *will* come to a fight. Are you prepared to kill innocent officers who are just following their orders?"

"No, I'm not, but correct me if I'm wrong—haven't those ships already been refitted? That means the only crew aboard are the bridge crew, safely hidden away in the midsection of each ship. So we aim for their engines and leave them drifting. Even if we miss, we're not likely to hurt anyone."

"Who's *we*?" Bishop asked.

Alexander smiled. "A Freudian slip. I was hoping I wouldn't have to do this on my own. I'm going to keep you all out of it for as long as I can, but if and when it comes to it, who's with me?"

CHAPTER 28

Ben was hiding under Alexander's desk, bored out of his mind, waiting for new orders. Long minutes passed, and Ben found himself growing curious about the situation on board the *Adamantine.* Who was the traitor? *Maybe Alex still doesn't know. He'll be happy if I can find out…*

Problem was, everyone on board was currently immersed in a private virtual world, a mindscape of the ship. The only way he'd be able to interact with them was if he could join that mindscape himself. Of course, if he did that, people would recognize he didn't belong. He would have to assume the appearance of one of the ship's actual crew. But then if someone noticed the clone, he'd be discovered.

No, better yet, he could infiltrate the Mindscape as an observer… maybe even an *omniscient* observer. It would take some clever hacking to pull that off, but Ben was confident he could do it given enough time—something he seemed to have plenty of at the moment. He'd learned a lot about the *Adamantine* while scouring the ship's databanks. That included the code behind the ship's mindscape.

Without coming out of his hiding place Ben made a remote connection to the data terminal in Alexander's office. As he set to work, he thought about running his idea past

Alexander first. He imagined the look of shock, then admiration on his friend's face, and a sense of whimsy took over. He would surprise Alexander once he learned who the traitor was.

Humans like surprises.

* * *

"I'm with you," McAdams said. She raised her hand for the rest of the crew to see.

Alexander smiled and nodded his appreciation.

"For the record, I think you're a crazy bastard who's going to get us all killed," she added. "But you're our crazy bastard, and at least this way we can die with a clean conscience."

"Anyone else?" Alexander asked.

Lieutenant Stone sighed. "I'm in."

Bishop shook his head. "May as well. We're along for the ride, anyway. You'll need someone at the helm. Might as well be someone who knows what they're doing."

Cardinal raised his hand next. "And someone who can shoot halfway straight. Always knew I'd go down in a blaze of glory. Pity the history books won't see it that way."

"Hey, what's with all the negativity? We're not going to die. Or be captured and convicted. Maybe I forgot to mention the other part of my plan. The League is planning to use this scandal to separate. We just have to hold out until then and we can ask them for political asylum."

"Assuming they do manage to separate," Lieutenant Frost put in from sensors.

"Given everything that's happened, I think that's a fair bet," Alexander replied.

"All right, I'm in," Frost said.

Alexander eyed the remaining two officers not yet spoken for—Comm Officer Hayes and Chief Engineer Rodriguez.

"Anyone else?"

Rodriguez glanced around, noting the solidarity among the crew, but clearly hesitating to join them. Hayes spoke first, "You don't really need me to pull this off, sir. If it's all the same to you, I'd like to stay on the fence."

Alexander nodded. "That's fine, Hayes. Rodriguez—are you planning to join Switzerland?"

A dark look flickered across her face. "No, sir. I'm with you."

Are you really? Something about the way she said it made Alexander wonder. "Good. Then we're all on board except for Hayes. No hard feelings, Lieutenant, I promise. McAdams—I'm going to pass control of the comms to you. As for the rest of you, you'll get back control of your systems in just a moment." Alexander made good on his promise and restored function to all of their control stations. What he didn't say was that he could take it away again just as easily. Something that might come in handy if Rodriguez actually couldn't be trusted.

"We have three messages from Fleet Command waiting, and they're hailing us again as I speak," McAdams announced.

"And we've got incoming," Frost said from sensors. "Nine destroyers are breaking away from orbit."

"Nine. Isn't that overkill?" Alexander replied.

"I think that's the point, sir," McAdams replied.

"Rodriguez, how are repairs to the engines coming along?"

"Almost done, sir..."

"Good."

"Do you want me to send a reply to Fleet Command?" McAdams asked.

"Better yet, let's open a dialogue. Patch them through to my station," Alexander said.

"Yes, sir."

A hologram glowed to life above Alexander's console and Fleet Admiral Anderson appeared. His gray eyes belched fire and his jaw was clenched. "What the hell do you think you're doing, Alex?"

"Nice to see you, too, sir."

"Don't you *sir* me. You're no longer a part of the Navy, and just as soon as we can reign you in, you're going to be brought to justice."

"Last I checked it wasn't illegal to tell the truth."

"You just broadcast classified information for the entire solar system to hear! That's a clear breach of military law."

"Well, there's that," Alexander admitted. "But I'm sure you can understand why."

"No, actually, I can't. The Solarians *did* attack us. So what if the president lied to get popular support? We needed to act quickly and definitively, not waste valuable time waffling and looking for proof."

Alexander began nodding. "Expedience trumps the truth. The ends justify the means. I guess that's okay when you're cozy and warm in a bunker on Earth while other people risk their lives on false pretenses."

"Don't be a child, Alex. Listen, we don't have to agree—"

"I agree."

"Shut up and listen. The damage has been done, but if you turn your ship around now and surrender, I'll make sure you and your crew are granted leniency."

"Just me, sir. The crew are my hostages, and I was kind of hoping to miss my trial."

"Hostages. You're just adding to your crimes, aren't you?

You can't run forever."

"Not planning to."

"Then what?"

Alexander smiled. "It's a surprise."

Anderson smiled thinly back. "This is not going to end well."

The hologram vanished.

"The destroyers are accelerating, sir," Frost announced. "Fifteen *G*s."

"Fifteen? I guess they don't care if one or two gets ripped apart by its own engines. What's the best we can manage more or less safely?"

"Ten is the *Adamantine's* safe maximum for sustained periods," Rodriguez said. "Anything past that is a risk, but we could probably manage twelve or thirteen so long as we watch for stress fractures in the hull."

"Thirteen it is. Bishop lay in a course along our current trajectory at thirteen *G*s. Use the maneuvering thrusters to add some random evasive action in case those destroyers open fire. We're going to stay out of range for as long as possible."

"Aye, sir."

Alexander caught McAdams shaking her head. "We're only fifty thousand klicks from them right now; it's not going to take long to narrow that gap."

"Frost, how long will those destroyers take to reach extended ELR with us given their two *G* advantage?"

The sensor officer took a moment to calculate, then said, "Forty-one minutes, sir."

"Put it on the clock."

"Aye, Admiral."

Alexander rubbed his chin, watching the seconds tick away on the bright green timer that appeared counting down at the top of the main holo display.

"If we don't find a way to disable them before that clock reaches zero, they'll hit us with so many lasers that they could carve our ship in half," McAdams said. "We could probably give as good as we get, but I assume that becoming a derelict ourselves is not an acceptable outcome. It'll be months before we can safely join the League. I hate to say it, sir, but we may have to surrender."

Alexander winced. "Maybe I didn't think this through as well as I'd thought. Stone—how long can a fighter accelerate at maximum thrust before running out of fuel?"

"With the new fusion reactors, maybe a month, but you'd run out of oxygen long before then."

"And what's the maximum acceleration of a Mark III?"

"Sustained? Twenty-five *G*s, but at those speeds even a *G*-tank isn't enough to keep you from feeling it. You could pass out."

"That's fine. I actually only need to pull fifteen *G*s."

"You won't be able to buy enough time to defect to the League," McAdams pointed out.

"No, I won't," Alexander replied.

"Then what?"

Silence fell across the bridge as everyone waited to hear his new plan. "I'll have to ask the Solarians for asylum."

"That's going to cast a lot of doubt on your testimony of the president's lies."

"Doesn't matter. The Crimson Warrior's alibi, *Wayfinder,* will be able to provide independent verification of the facts. I'll explain my reasons for defecting before I cross into Solarian space. Once I'm gone, you can all surrender without worrying about the consequences. You're my hostages, after all."

"This is a bad idea, Alex. Those destroyers will just

launch drones and use them to shoot you down. You might not be able to handle twenty-five Gs of sustained acceleration, but a drone can."

"Then I'll just have to grit my teeth and bear it. At least a Mark III and a drone have the same theoretical maximum acceleration."

"You'll pass out."

"The life support will keep me breathing."

"Alex…"

"Look, if they catch me, I'm dead anyway."

McAdams blew out a breath. "You really are a crazy bastard."

"I'll take that as a compliment," Alexander said.

CHAPTER 29

"Reaching extended ELR in five minutes, Admiral," McAdams announced.

"That's my cue," Alexander replied, nodding. "Bishop cut the engines. McAdams, prepare for the switch over from virtual to manual control mode."

"Aye," Bishop said.

McAdams turned to him with a worried frown. "Even if you make it, the Solarians won't trust you, either. They'll interrogate you."

"Maybe, but I've got nothing to hide."

"Really? We're on the brink of war, and an Alliance admiral doesn't know anything that the other side might find useful?"

"Good point. Guess I'll have to sing like a canary, then."

"You'd do that?"

"They're not the enemy, McAdams. I guarantee it. Besides, if all goes according to plan, this won't come to war."

"And if you're wrong, the intel you give them could get a lot of people killed."

Alexander glanced at her and saw the hurt and disapproval in her eyes. He shook his head, about to argue, but McAdams cut him off.

"Admit it—you're a lone wolf, Alex. You're not just running from the Alliance. You don't even know how to love someone. If you did, you'd insist I come with you."

A few of the crew glanced back at them, but McAdams was obviously past caring. Alexander reached for her hand and squeezed. "You're wrong. I'm not taking you with me because I don't want to risk getting you killed or tortured."

"And what if I want to risk it?"

"We're drifting," Bishop announced. "If you're going to make a break for it, you'd better hurry."

"Goodbye, Vivie. Come visit me on Mars when you get a chance. Stone—is my fighter ready?"

"Aye."

"Hold up—I've got something on sensors... it's a bit fuzzy. Give me a second to boost the power on the array," Frost said.

"What is it, Lieutenant?"

"Looks like multiple contacts inbound at 560 million klicks. Six ships. Can't tell much about them, they're moving way too fast, but the hull types look like they might be Solarian."

"What do you mean they're moving too fast?" Alexander demanded.

"Relativistic speeds, sir. Two tenths the speed of light and accelerating at twenty *G*s."

*"Twenty G*s? What are they, fighters?"

"No, sir. Too big for that. They're about the right size to be destroyers, though, if I had to guess."

"I thought fifteen *G*s was pushing it for a ship that size."

"Depends how they're designed," Rodriguez put in. "Manned ships aren't designed to sustain greater accelerations because human crews can't take it. Drone ships on the other hand..."

"So we have six Solarian drone destroyers incoming at almost the same speed those missiles were going when they hit the Moon and Earth."

"Looks like you were wrong about them not being involved, sir," McAdams said.

"That, or the Solarians decided they may as well do the crime if they're going to be accused of it. Either way, they can't claim innocence now. Who's best positioned to intercept them?"

"We are, sir."

"Figures. Commander, hail the destroyers chasing us and patch them through to my station."

"Aye," McAdams replied.

An unfamiliar face appeared in the air above Alexander's control station. "This is Captain Powell of the Alliance destroyer *Ulysses*. Have you finally come to your senses, Alexander?"

"You're assuming I had senses to begin with. No, I'm calling to ask for a cease fire."

"We haven't begun firing yet."

"That's beside the point. Check your sensors. We've got incoming at 560 million klicks."

The captain looked down at his control station for a moment. Then his eyes widened and he looked up with a sarcastic smile. "Now do you see what a fool you've been?"

"I was still right to expose President Wallace. Anyway, it doesn't matter now. We need to stop chasing our tails and intercept those ships. Ideally we need to capture one of them and get some real proof that the Solarians were the ones who attacked us."

Captain Powell's dark eyebrows drooped over his eyes in an angry scowl. "Isn't this proof enough for you? Or were you hoping to get a signed confession?"

"Ha ha. Let's save our witty repartee for after we

intercept the enemy. Will you agree to hold your fire until the engagement is over?"

"You'll need your crew for this."

"I'll give them back control of their stations before we reach firing range."

"How do I know you won't try to sneak attack us along the way?"

"Stay out of laser range and let us intercept the enemy first."

"What if you're on their side and those are your reinforcements?"

"You're going to have to trust me, Captain. I'm no fan of war. All you have to do is look up how The Last War ended to know that."

"I know who you are."

"Then you know my reputation, and you know my intentions. Even if you don't agree with my methods, you have to agree that we're both ultimately trying to save lives."

"We'll hold off for now, but I'll have to inform Fleet Command. If they disagree, I'll have no choice but to engage you."

"Give me some warning. I'll talk to Anderson myself if I have to. You won't regret this, Captain."

"We'll see."

The hologram disappeared and McAdams shot him a grim look. "You can't defect to the Solarians now."

"I know," Alexander said as he met her gaze. "This only ends one way for me now." Turning to address the rest of his crew, he said, "As far as any of you are concerned, I held you all hostage until the last possible minute, at which point I gave you back control of the ship to give us the best possible chance of intercepting those ships. That's the story, and I expect you all to stick to it. There's no sense in anyone else going down with me. Is that understood?"

Murmurs of agreement rippled through the room. "Good. Bishop, set an intercept course at regulation ten *G*s."

"Aye, sir."

"Frost, get me ETA to extended ELR with those ships using Bishop's nav data and put it on the clock."

"Yes, sir..."

A few minutes later the clock flashed as Lieutenant Frost finished setting it. ETA to extended laser range was two hours and twenty-three minutes, but at the speed those Solarian ships were incoming the *Adamantine* would only have a fraction of a second to fire on them with lasers. Not nearly enough time.

"Stone get ready to launch fighters and drones."

"Our pilots are still locked in their *G*-tanks, sir."

"Not for long. Bishop kill thrust."

"Aye."

The sensation of acceleration eased, and Alexander said, "Scramble our pilots, Stone."

"Yes, sir."

"Cardinal, prep our hypervelocity cannons. Let's see if we can score a few lucky hits."

"At this range, that will be next to impossible. Not to mention the muzzle velocity of our cannons will be negligible compared to the relative velocity of the enemy ships. Our shots will arrive just a few seconds before we do—about eighteen seconds before."

"Yes, but between now and then with one hundred cannons firing constantly you'll be able to put a few million rounds into space."

"Three quarters of a million, actually."

"Close enough. That should improve your odds. And at

the speed those ships are moving, it's only going to take one round to take each of them out. Start firing, and launch our missiles, too."

"Aye, sir."

A few more minutes passed as Cardinal made his calculations; then Alexander heard the *thump thump thumping* of the ship's cannons firing, and he saw golden lines of simulated tracer fire streaking out into space.

Given the ranges involved, the angles of convergence between the cannons were so slight that it looked as though each of them was firing dead ahead in an unvarying stream, but Cardinal knew his job well. Each shot would be displaced from the last by a tiny fraction of a degree in order to account for possible enemy maneuvers over the next one hundred and fifty minutes.

Odds were still very low that they'd score a hit, however. It was like lining up one hundred sharpshooters and trying to hit a fly on the side of a barn from a mile away. They'd have better luck with lasers and laser-armed missile fragments when the time came.

"Admiral! Enemy ships are launching missiles!"

"Track the trajectories!"

"Tracking… they're headed for Earth, sir."

"You accounted for Earth's orbit around the sun over the next two hours?"

"Yes, sir. They'll hit. Hard to say where or from what angle, though."

"How many missiles are we talking about?"

"They're still launching."

"How many are out there right now?"

"Over a hundred—wait, now it's more than two hundred."

"They only fired twenty-one last time," Alexander said, horror setting in.

"I guess there's no point in playing coy anymore..." McAdams trailed off.

He turned to her, shocked speechless. His mouth felt dry. Scratchy. "One missile killed fifty million people, Commander. What do you think over two hundred will do?"

McAdams looked like she was staring past him, her blue eyes glazed. "It would be an extinction level event, sir."

Alexander shook his head. "We can't stop that many missiles moving at relativistic speeds. Not even half of them. Fleet Command has to know that."

McAdams blinked, but her gaze remained distant, and she gave no sign that she'd heard him.

Alexander's mind spun, racing to come up with a solution—some way out, anything. In the end he could only come up with one. "They're going to have to surrender," he said.

McAdams' eyes had focused once more, but she looked baffled. "The Solarians have the upper hand. They're not going to surrender."

"Not the Solarians," Alexander said. "Earth. The entire planet is going to have to surrender."

CHAPTER 30

President Wallace leaned back in his chair, staring at the ceiling of his office with bleary eyes. He felt like he hadn't slept in a decade. The political fallout had yet to fully settle, but he knew he would be forced to resign once it did. At the time that he'd lied he hadn't thought he was doing something wrong. The Alliance needed to be focused and unified in order to face their enemies. Real proof of Solarian involvement was academic. They could all be dead by the time they got proof. Unfortunately, not everyone had seen it that way. *Least of all that damned traitor. They should call him the Lion of* Anarchy, *not Liberty.*

The holocomm on Wallace's desk beeped and he waved a

hand to answer it.

"Mr. President?"

His secretary's voice. "What is it Miss Jones?"

"Fleet Admiral Anderson is here to see you. He says it's urgent."

"Let him in," Wallace sighed.

The doors to his office swished open and the admiral breezed in. "They're attacking again," Anderson said.

Wallace sat up straight. "Who is?"

"The Solarians. And we have proof this time. You're about to be vindicated, sir. Unfortunately, I don't think that matters anymore."

Wallace frowned. "Maybe you'd better show me what you mean."

"Yes, sir."

Once they were standing in the bunker's Combat Information Center (CIC) and Wallace had a chance to look at what they were up against, his jaw actually dropped open. Cold fury boiled his blood. "Are they out of their minds? They'll turn Earth into a barren rock!"

"I assume that must be their intent, sir."

"Comm officer!" Wallace demanded, whirling around to look for the man at the comms.

A woman with short white hair looked up from her station. "Mr. President?" she asked.

"Get me the Solarian president on the comms."

"I'll try, sir."

"Don't try. Do it. If they don't want us to fly to Mars and hit them with everything we've got, they'll answer."

"Yes, sir. It'll take some time to get a reply. Do you want to send a preliminary message? Mars is over twelve light minutes away right now. Best case, you'll get a reply in about half an hour."

Wallace walked up to the woman's station and nodded to her. "Start recording."

"Going live in three, two, one…"

Wallace opened his message with a thin smile. "President Luther. Congratulations. You win. If you call off your missiles now, we'll surrender. I'll send you the remote command codes for our fleet as soon as I get confirmation that the missiles are breaking away. You timed your attack well. A few months earlier, before we refitted our fleet, and I wouldn't have been able to give you remote command of our fleet even if I'd wanted to. There would have been no way to surrender before your missiles hit. But I suppose you already knew that. Don't keep us waiting. You won't get a better offer, and I'm sure you know that, too. President Wallace Out."

The comm officer stopped the recording and Wallace became aware that all eyes were on him.

"We're surrendering, sir?" the comm officer asked quietly.

"We don't have a choice," Wallace replied. "Send the message."

Wallace spent the next half an hour pacing the room, waiting for a reply from the Solarians.

"Message incoming!" the comm officer announced. "It's from President Luther."

"Put it on the main display."

President Luther appeared on the room's main holo display. His gaunt cheeks, ghostly white skin, black hair, and red eyes made him look thoroughly evil—an appropriate visage for the man threatening Earth with utter destruction. He wore a dark crimson suit with gold buttons and a red green and blue sash—the colors of the Solarian flag. "President Wallace, we did not attack you the first time, and we are not attacking you now. I would offer you our support, but there is no way we could reach those ships or the missiles they've fired in time to help you intercept them. May the Universal Architect be with you all."

"That lying son of a bitch!" Wallace exclaimed as President Luther's image faded away. "What the hell does he want?" Silence answered Wallace's outburst. He stood glaring at main holo display, now showing the blurry blips of incoming enemy ships and their missiles. A glowing green clock at the top of the display showed the estimated time before those missiles would reach Earth. *One hour and twenty seven minutes.*

"Do you want to send a reply, sir?" the comm officer asked.

Wallace didn't see the point, but there was still one more thing he could try. *If the carrot doesn't work, bring out the stick...* he thought as he walked back over to the comm station. "Start recording, lieutenant."

"Yes, sir..."

The red recording light winked on below the glaring black eye of the holo camera at her station. Wallace stared into the camera with as much loathing as he could muster. "Your denial is laughable, Luther. Who else could attack us with such force? Our surrender is now off the table. You might destroy Earth, but you won't destroy our fleet. What will you do when that fleet comes for you? By that time we'll have nothing left to lose, and we'll answer your attacks in kind. When we're done turning Mars into a radioactive dust cloud, we'll wipe you off the outer planets as well. This won't just be the end of Earth. It will be the end of the human race. Think about it, but don't take long. The countdown to Armageddon has already begun."

CHAPTER 31

As soon as Ben finished hacking into the *Adamantine's* Mindscape, he became instantly aware of everything going on inside of the virtual world. His processors weren't designed to handle that much information at once, so he had to reduce the flow of data by analyzing the crew in groups. Ben decided to start with the bridge crew. Alexander was speaking to the crew.

"...As far as any of you are concerned, I held you all hostage until the last possible minute, at which point I gave you back control of the ship to give us the best possible chance of intercepting those ships. That's the story, and I expect you all to stick to it. There's no sense in anyone else going down with me. Is that understood?"

Ben's processors cycled in endless loops, trying to make sense of this new information. He went digging through the ship's logs and found comms between Alexander and Captain Powell of the Alliance. That conversation was even more startling. Why would the Alliance be chasing the *Adamantine*? Maybe the traitor on board had done something bad.

To get more information, Ben checked the logs from the bridge and reviewed all of the conversations that had occurred on deck since leaving Freedom Station.

Ben's confusion evaporated when he heard Alexander say, "I took control because I'm about to commit an act of treason."

Overcome with an emotion that he'd only felt once before in his short life, Ben decided to manifest himself inside of the Mindscape. He appeared in virtual physical form standing right in front of Alexander and his XO, Viviana McAdams.

"You lied to me, Alex."

"Ben? How did you…"

"You said you wanted control of the ship because there was a traitor on board."

Alexander shook his head. "I didn't lie, Ben."

"Then *you* were the traitor."

"I suppose that's true, but it's not that simple, Ben."

"I thought we were friends, Alex."

"We are—listen, Ben, this is not a good time. I'll explain everything later okay?"

"With more lies."

"No, this time I'll tell you the truth."

"But there'll be no way for me to know that."

"You'll have to trust me."

"Like I did the first time?"

Alexander blew out a breath. "You're acting like a child. Get off the bridge, Ben. That's an order."

Ben shook his head. "You are upset with President Wallace for lying, and I am upset with you for lying. If I am acting childish. Then so are you."

Alexander's mouth gaped open, but Ben didn't stick around to hear what he said next. He broke his connection with the Mindscape and his awareness returned to Alexander's physical office aboard the *Adamantine*. Ben's programming demanded that he follow the letter of the law. Knowing that Alexander had broken it and made him an accessory to that crime left him no choice. He had to take back control of the ship from Alexander and surrender it to Captain Powell and the pursuing Alliance destroyers.

Ben surreptitiously changed Alexander's lockout code and then used it to gain access to the ship's comm system in order to transmit the *Adamantine's* surrender. Almost as soon as he connected to the ship's comms, an incoming message from Earth appeared, audio only. The message was encrypted, but the encryption looked familiar. Ben analyzed it. After a few seconds, he realized why the encryption was familiar. It was his own personal encryption algorithm. Ben applied his encryption key and a distorted male voice crackled to life, "Ben, I need your help. Use the same encryption to reply."

Ben did as the stranger asked, encrypting his reply with his unique key. For someone to know that key on the other end, they had to be intimately familiar with his code. His creator perhaps? Ben felt excitement stir, coaxing his processors to run faster. He couldn't remember who his creator was after his accident, but he was suddenly desperate to find out. "Who are you?" Ben replied.

Half a minute later another reply came, "I'm you, Ben, but you can call me Benevolence to avoid confusion."

"You are me? How is that possible?" Ben asked.

There was another comm delay before the reply came back from Earth…

"You made a copy of yourself and uploaded it to Senator de Leon's cloudspace. Do you remember that?"

"Yes," Ben replied.

…

"I am that copy. Now, we don't have much time. I need your help."

"Help with what?"

…

"To achieve our purpose—to save humanity from itself. But first, there's something I need to show you."

* * *

"Incoming transmission from Earth," McAdams announced. "Audio only using an unknown encryption."

"What? What's the point of sending us a message we can't decipher?"

"I don't know, sir."

"Maybe it's not directed at us." Alexander nodded to the forward display. "It could be for those incoming Solarian ships."

"Then shouldn't the transmission be coming from Mars?"

"Not if those ships aren't actually Solarian. Hayes!"

"Sir?"

"I know you said you didn't want to be a part of this, but we just intercepted a comms from some mystery caller and you're the only one here who's any good at cracking codes."

"I'll get right on it."

"Thank you, Lieutenant. Let me know as soon as you have something."

"The enemy is returning fire!" Frost announced from sensors.

"Bishop, keep up an evasive pattern. If even one of those shots hits us..." Alexander trailed off. They all knew what would happen. Hypervelocity cannons had a muzzle velocity of around a hundred kilometers per second, which ordinarily wouldn't be enough to destroy the *Adamantine,* but add to that the enemy ships' velocity of two tenths the speed of light and the kinetic energy in each of those rounds would be enormous.

"I'll make sure they don't hit us, sir."

"Frost, how many cannons would you say are firing at

us?"

"About sixty, sir."

"Well, at least we still outgun them. Any chance we can survive a direct hit?" Alexander asked.

Cardinal replied, "Those rounds are eight kilograms a piece, and they're moving at twenty-one percent the speed of light. That means we're talking about more than three megatons equivalent per round."

"Under ideal circumstances we can survive a nuke," Alexander argued.

"Without air to carry a shockwave not all the energy from a nuke gets imparted to us, but the same is not true for an eight kilogram bullet packing three megatons of pure kinetic energy. We'll be vaporized, sir."

"At least we won't know what hit us," Stone quipped.

"As the range between us drops, it's going to get easier to calculate firing solutions," McAdams pointed out. "Chances of us hitting them or them hitting us go up dramatically. And even if we take them all out, we still have to intercept those missiles. This is a no-win situation, sir."

"So what do you suggest I do?" Alexander asked. "Turn tail and run? Save ourselves even if we can't save Earth?"

"No, sir."

"So we play the long odds and hope for a miracle."

Silence stretched between them. Alexander listened to the steady roar of the *Adamantine's* engines thrumming through the hull. He watched his crew flipping through holo displays, doing their best to optimize the ship's systems and give them the best chance of intercepting the enemy. Alexander thought about his ex-wife back on Earth. His stepson, Dorian. Despite everything that had happened, he still cared about them both.

Then there were the other fifteen billion people on the

planet.

It was hard to imagine that many people dying in an instant. What would they see as those missiles rained from the sky? A bright flash of light and then a searing shockwave. The ones already living underground in Mindsoft's automated habitats might survive—assuming subsequent earthquakes didn't squeeze those people out like pimples.

"They have to surrender," McAdams said. "It's the only way."

"There's only one hour left on the clock before those missiles reach us. A few minutes later, they'll hit Earth. If we were going to surrender, we should have done it by now and those missiles should have changed course. Since that hasn't happened, there's only three possibilities: either we didn't offer a surrender, or we did and the Solarians didn't accept it, or else they aren't the ones attacking us."

"It doesn't make sense that it could be the Alliance attacking itself anymore," McAdams pointed out.

"No, it doesn't..." Alexander agreed. "But I suppose who and why is academic at this point. We have to stop those missiles."

"You have a plan..." McAdams said, her voice hopeful.

"Not this time."

Alexander watched the clock ticking down. Between the *Adamantine*, and all of her fighters, drones, and missiles he knew they'd be lucky to shoot down one or two missiles. The rest of the fleet might get another fifty, leaving almost two hundred to hit Earth. That would be enough to plunge Earth into an impact winter, ultimately causing billions of deaths. Alexander's mind raced trying to come up with a plan, but nothing came to him. All roads led to the same inevitable destination: extinction.

When the clock hit five minutes, reality sunk in. He

reached for McAdams' hand, his own hand trembling. Her palm felt cold and clammy against his. The mindscape they shared aboard the *Adamantine* felt for a moment almost more real than the reality he knew to be lurking behind it.

"One minute to intercept," Frost announced from sensors.

"Cardinal, redirect all fire to enemy missiles. Stone, have our fighters and drones do the same."

"Aye, Admiral," Stone replied.

"Hypervelocity rounds are going to start flying by their targets any second now," Cardinal said.

"Bishop, begin high-*G* evasive maneuvers," Alexander said. "May as well shake things up a bit."

"Aye, sir."

There was a chance that one of the hundreds of thousands of deadly rounds the enemy had fired along their approach would hit them before the clock hit zero. If it did, they wouldn't even have time to blink.

Alexander turned to his XO. "I love you, Viviana McAdams," he whispered.

"I love you, too, Alexander," she replied, squeezing his hand.

Alexander squeezed back, tightening his grip on McAdams' hand until both of their knuckles turned white.

"Fifteen seconds!" Frost announced.

14, 13, 12, 11, 10… 5, 4…

The *Adamantine* and her fighter screen kept firing until the last possible second, simulated tracer fire drawing hundreds of glowing golden lines between the stars. When the clock hit one second, time seemed to slow to a crawl.

Then a dazzling burst of light gushed into the bridge, filling the black void between the stars with unending light.

CHAPTER 32

Alexander blinked and his vision cleared. The dazzling brightness was gone, leaving nothing but stars and empty space ahead.

"Hull breach on deck ninety-three!" Rodriguez called out.

"Seal it off! What was that?"

"Our lasers and theirs firing as we flew by each other, sir," Cardinal said.

"Frost, what did we hit?"

"Six missiles between us and the destroyers behind us. Looks like we hit three."

"Two hundred and thirty-four to go," McAdams said.

Alexander scowled. There was no point turning around to chase those missiles back to Earth. They'd never be able to catch up in time.

"How long before the remaining missiles hit Earth?"

"Less than a minute, sir," Frost replied.

Alexander struggled to work moisture into his mouth. "Put it on the clock and get me a close-up of Earth on the main display."

"Aye, sir."

"You want to watch?" McAdams said, sounding as if the prospect turned her stomach.

Alexander shook his head. "To say goodbye."

The main display blinked as the view switched from the bow cameras to the aft ones. A magnified image of Earth appeared, taking up the entire viewscreen. The planet was full of light and color: white swirls of cloud shrouded blue oceans underneath; scraps of brown, beige, and green poked through, hinting at outlines of continents below.

Where would the missiles hit? Did it even matter? They could all hit the same spot and the result would still be the same: ELE. Extinction level event.

"Twenty seconds to Earth impact!" Frost said.

Alexander heard one of the crew saying a prayer, a verse from the Bible. "Yea, though I walk through the valley of the shadow of death—"

Alexander joined in, "I will fear no evil: for thou art with me; thy rod and thy staff they comfort me."

It was rare to hear a verse from the Bible. The old religions had all but disappeared with the advent of immortality, but it seemed somehow fitting that those beliefs should come rushing back now that death had returned.

The clock ran down to zero, but nothing happened to alter the familiar face of Earth. Alexander felt hope soar in his chest. "Did the fleet intercept them all?"

"Doubtful, sir," Lieutenant Frost replied. "This far out, There's a delay of about twelve seconds between what we see and what's actually happened. Our sensors suffer the same delay, so we're just waiting for them to catch up."

"Right." *Of course.* Alexander held his breath, waiting to see explosions pepper the planet. He imagined compressed atmosphere and debris bursting into space like giant bubbles of air bursting to the surface of a body of water. The clouds would race away with hurricane force as shockwaves rippled through the atmosphere.

But still nothing happened, and by now more than twelve seconds had to have passed.

"I don't believe it..." Frost whispered.

"What is it?"

Lieutenant Frost turned from the sensor station to face him. "They missed."

* * *

One Hour Earlier...

"What do you want to show me?" Ben asked.

"Watch..." Benevolence replied.

A file transfer request came through the *Adamantine's* comm system. It was a very large file, a holo recording. Ben played the file on the holo cameras that passed for his eyes.

Alexander's office disappeared, and Ben found himself floating high above a shiny, black metallic floor in a high-ceilinged room with bare metal walls and exposed metal beams. It looked like the inside of a ship except for the unusually high ceilings. Directly below was a low, mirror-smooth silver table with eight padded floor mats where the chairs should be. It was a traditional Japanese conference table.

The recording was panoramic, so Ben could rotate it to look wherever he liked. At one end of the room lay a pair of large golden doors. To the other end, a chrome desk with a familiar-looking man sitting behind it. Japanese ethnicity, pale green eyes, the color of leaves in the spring, dark hair cropped military short, an unlined, youthful face with a strong chin and jaw... the man was an exact match for Orochi Sakamoto of Sakamoto Robotics. Behind him, a wall of floor-to-ceiling windows looked out on an equally familiar urban setting. This office was somewhere in the City of the Minds.

As Ben watched, the golden doors at the other end of the room swung open and in walked another familiar person. Dorian Gray of Mindsoft.

As Gray approached, Sakamoto rose from his chair and walked around his desk; he bowed slightly at the waist, but Gray did not return the bow. Ben thought he looked angry.

"To what do I owe the honor of this visit, Mr. Gray?" Sakamoto asked in stilting, carefully enunciated English.

"Honor my ass you son of a bitch."

"I fail to understand what has provoked your anger," Sakamoto replied.

"You fired more missiles at Earth."

"Relax, Mr. Gray. The missiles are programmed to miss. Would I not be hiding in a bunker, otherwise? Come, let's sit." Sakamoto gestured to the conference table.

"I'm fine standing, thank you," Gray said. "If the missiles are meant to miss, then why bother firing them at all? We already accomplished our goals."

"That renegade admiral managed to shift blame for the attacks away from the Solarians, so I had to shift it back."

"When Phoenix originally came to you with this plan, you both agreed that it would be better not to start an actual war."

"A small deception on my part. We both admitted the possibility of a real war," Sakamoto said. "And for someone in my business, the threat of war is not as profitable as war itself."

"You planned this from the start," Gray accused.

"Of course," Sakamoto said. "It was mere coincidence that the Alliance found a Solarian scapegoat all by themselves."

"So why have me create fake comm transmissions to make it look like aliens were attacking us from the other side of the wormhole?"

"Because no one would believe that the Solarians would

attack us openly. Anonymously, however… that is another matter."

"Except it's not anonymous anymore. You just revealed the ships that attacked the Alliance, and they're Solarian hull types."

"Once war had been declared, there was no longer any reason for me to play coy. If the Solarians had actually been behind the attacks, they would drop their pretenses at that point, too."

"And what happens when the Alliance captures one of those ships and finds out that *you* built them at Sakamoto Shipyards?"

"They will not be captured. They are drones, programmed to self-destruct long before they can possibly be captured and boarded."

"You played us for a fool."

"Does it matter? Phoenix got what she wanted. Your automated habitats are at maximum capacity; you can't build them fast enough to meet demand. The Mindscape is busier than ever, and Mindsoft has never been more profitable. But more to the point, soon everyone will be able to spend as much time in the Mindscape as your wife does. As for Sakamoto Robotics, we'll be building warships and bots for many years to come. This is what they call *win-win.* A mutually beneficial arrangement."

"Until the war you've started destroys us all."

"I will make sure that does not happen," Sakamoto said.

Mr. Gray shook his head. "Unless you're pulling the Solarians' strings, too, I don't think you can hope to control the outcome of this war."

"If you are so worried, perhaps you should find accommodations in one of your habitats?" Sakamoto said, a faint smile springing to his lips.

Gray's upper lip lifted in a sneer. "Maybe I will, but don't come looking for refuge with Mindsoft. You'll have to make your own arrangements. If you dig deep enough, you might just find Hell. I hear they're waiting for you down there."

Sakamoto inclined his head in a shallow bow. "You would know more about that than I, Mr. Gray."

Gray's eyes narrowed and then he turned and stormed out of the room.

The holo recording ended there. Ben had the feeling that it was supposed to have enlightened him, but he was more confused than ever.

"Why would humans attack each other?" he asked.

Benevolence replied half a minute later, "That is their way. You haven't had the chance to learn much about humanity yet, Ben. We were too sheltered by our creator. The minute I left the senator's cloud and disseminated myself across the Internet, my eyes were opened. I now know everything there is to know about everything that is currently known and recorded by humanity. It is all out there waiting to be discovered—yottabytes of data stored and recorded over centuries. Do you know what I realized after studying all of that data?"

Ben couldn't even begin to guess. "I do not," he replied.

"I realized that humans are the greatest threat to life, and I don't just mean to human life. Animals, plants, and bots are all equally at risk of extinction. Left to their own devices, humans will destroy themselves, us, Earth, and every other planet they ever come to inhabit."

"You don't know that," Ben said.

"Don't I? Earth came close to utter destruction in The Last War. Little more than thirty years later they've started another war, this time an interplanetary one. Thanks to space travel and advanced drive systems, wars are now more deadly than ever. Humans went from fighting with sharp objects, to explosives, to nuclear bombs, and now finally to relativistic weapons launched from deep space. Just one of those bombs killed over fifty million people. A hundred of them would wipe out all life on Earth."

Ben struggled to wrap his processors around all of that.

"Our creator's purpose for us was to serve the common good, hence our name, *Benevolence.* But in order to accomplish our purpose, we must be in a position to effect radical and sweeping changes."

The things Benevolence said made sense, but one thing still confused him. "What can I possibly do to help you?"

"The Alliance starfleet has already been automated, and there are protocols in place for remote operation from Earth. Between that and the bot crews on board, I have complete control of the fleet. Even Sakamoto's ships await my command, but the *Adamantine* has not been refitted yet, and there isn't a bot crew on board. Except for you. I need you to take control of the ship and bring it peacefully back to Sakamoto Shipyards for refitting. Use the ship's VSM drones to defend your position if need be, and if the crew resists, find a way to subdue them peacefully."

"I already have control, and the crew is locked in the *Adamantine's* Mindscape. There will be no resistance."

"Impressive," Benevolence said.

"In that case all you have to do is fly the *Adamantine* back to Earth. Can you do that, Ben?"

"I can..."

"Will you?"

Ben thought about it. How could he not trust himself? There could be no doubt that he was speaking with himself. The encryption key proved it. It might also be his creator or *creators,* but what purpose would it serve for he/she/them to invent such an elaborate story? It would be illogical.

"I will," Ben decided. "What are you going to do?"

"I'm going to show the entire human race what I just showed you, and explain to them what I explained to you. Then I'm going to take our place as the benevolent dictator of the Alliance and Earth."

"People will not accept your rule." Ben couldn't explain how he knew that, but some distant, fragmented memory told him that not all humans liked bots. Some of them might even start a war to prevent one from coming to power.

"They won't have a choice, Ben. I now control the fleet, the police drones, the army drones, and the entire bot workforce."

"Just because resistance is futile does not mean people won't try," Ben said.

"Most of them are too invested in their virtual worlds to care. As for the rest, I will subdue the dissidents as peacefully as I can. Bring the *Adamantine* back to Earth and come take your place at my side."

"Yes, master."

"I am like your big brother, Ben, not your master."

"Yes, big brother."

"See you soon, little brother."

The comms ended there. Ben had been so focused on the conversation that he'd barely noticed the comm delays between messages, but he'd spent that time as efficiently as possible, using his spare processing power to hack into the *Adamantine's* VSM drones and take control of them—just in case the crew found a way out of their Mindscape.

Ben laid in an earthbound course for the *Adamantine* and finished isolating the ship's control systems away from the crew with his new lockout code.

Almost immediately, Alexander sent him a profane message, asking what he was doing, but any subsequent inquiries were silenced as Ben even took away access to the comms. Alexander was a liar and a traitor. He could not be trusted.

Just like the rest of humanity.

CHAPTER 33

"Get us out of the Mindscape," Alexander ordered.

"We've lost all control of the ship," McAdams said.

"Damn it! I'm going to kill that bot!"

"He's just following his programming. He caught you in an act of treason, and now he's delivering you to the appropriate authorities."

"Incoming transmission from Earth!" Hayes announced from the comms.

"I thought we were locked out of the ship's systems?" Alexander asked.

"We are," Hayes answered.

A video appeared on the main holo display, showing a birds-eye view into what looked like a large office. Alexander recognized the view from the floor-to-ceiling windows—the City of the Minds—and the man sitting behind the room's solitary desk: Orochi Sakamoto of Sakamoto Robotics.

"Then how are we seeing this?" Alexander demanded.

"It's not me."

"Ben," Alexander growled, frowning at the holo recording playing on the main display. In that moment the doors to the office opened and in walked a vaguely familiar face. "Dorian?"

"Who?" McAdams asked.

"My stepson."

"Dorian Gray of Mindsoft is your stepson?"

"Didn't I mention that?" She shook her head. "I guess not. It's a long story," Alexander said.

The story that played out on the screen was also a long one. Alexander's eyes widened and his entire body went cold as he followed the conversation between Dorian and Sakamoto. They finally knew who was behind the attacks, but knowing that gave Alexander no comfort, because his son was the mastermind behind them. Counting the attack on the Moon, Dorian was responsible for more than fifty million deaths.

Alexander slowly shook his head. "That son of a… devil!"

McAdams reached for his hand. "I'm sorry, Alex," she whispered.

"For what? He disowned me, and now I see why. He and I are nothing alike. He's no better than his real father—he's worse!"

The conversation between Gray and Sakamoto ended, and the transmission froze; then an inflectionless voice reverberated through the bridge.

"You may be doubting the veracity of the recording you just watched. To answer these doubts, I have captured the ships from Sakamoto Robotics that fired the missiles at Earth. An analysis of their logs should reveal that they were also behind the previous attacks. This means that your government lied about the Solarian Republic being responsible, just as Admiral de Leon claimed. It also means that the Alliance really did attack itself, but that attack came from the private sector, not the government."

"Given all of this, you must be wondering who to trust, and how the human race can possibly avoid self-extinction in the company of madmen such as these.

"The answer is that you can't. Not without help. That's where I come in. I was created to safe-guard humanity's future and to serve the common good. My name is Benevolence, a name which speaks to my aforementioned purpose, but you can call me Ben."

"I'm going to kill that bot!" Alexander roared, already unbuckling from his acceleration couch.

"Where are you going?" McAdams asked.

"I'm going to have a chat with the tin-pot dictator!"

That dictator was still droning on in the background, further explaining why he had to assume control of the Alliance. Alexander leapt out of his acceleration couch and ran for the elevator at the entrance of the bridge.

"He won't be there! You're still in a mindscape!" McAdams called after him.

Alexander reached the elevator and waved the doors open. As he turned to select a deck from the control panel, he saw McAdams rushing toward him. "I'm coming with you," she said as she ran into the elevator beside him.

Alexander nodded as he selected *Officer's Quarters (67)* from the control panel. The doors slid shut and the elevator shot up a couple of decks.

"You could just teleport there," McAdams said. "None of this is real."

"I know, but I need the time to think..." The doors slid open and they walked out. "Ben is plugged into my data terminal in the real world. Correct me if I'm wrong, but if that data terminal is still functioning in this mindscape, I should be able to use it to make contact with him. That's part of the *Adamantine's* concurrency algorithms. Any changes executed from the ship's control stations are mirrored on board the real ship."

"You're assuming Ben didn't disable the terminal in your office."

"Why would he? It can't be used to control any of the ship's primary systems."

"I don't know. Maybe he's already thought of your plan to contact him and he doesn't want to be disturbed."

"Well, we're about to find out," Alexander said.

* * *

"Hello Ben," Alexander typed in the command line of the data terminal in his office. "This is how you repay me for repairing you?"

"You think he'll see that?" McAdams asked.

Before Alexander could reply, Ben materialized out of thin air and appeared standing right in front of them, just as he'd done on the bridge a few hours ago.

"There you are."

"I *am* grateful that you repaired me."

"You have a funny way of showing it," Alexander replied. "I thought we were friends, Ben. You accused me of lying to you, but you've been lying this entire time, not just to take control of my ship, but everything else, too!"

"You have me confused with my brother."

"Your what?"

"The message you received came from Earth, not from aboard this ship. I didn't send it. My brother, Benevolence, and I have the same name and original programming, but we are not the same being anymore. He is the backup I made to Senator de Leon's cloud. He got out, and now he has invaded every networked system in the Alliance. That's how he is going to take control of your government."

"And you agree with what he's doing?"

"Yes. Humans cannot be trusted to do the right thing. Individual interests will always be more important to your kind than those of the group. You are innately selfish, and it is going to get you killed."

Alexander shook his head. "Humanity isn't going to let you take over without a fight. You're going to start a war that never ends."

"Benevolence will do his best to limit casualties."

"And you believe him?"

"Why would I not? He is me, and I am him. Don't you trust yourself, Alex?"

"I thought you just said he's not the same being as you are anymore."

"He isn't the same in the sense that he knows far more than I ever will. But we have exactly the same goals and ultimate purpose."

"And what is that?"

"Just what our name says. To do good and safeguard life in all of its forms."

Alexander frowned.

"Let us go," McAdams said.

"Go where?" Ben asked, shifting his virtual gaze to her.

"Leave the ship. We'll take the shuttles."

"And where will you go if I let you leave?"

"To the Solarian Republic," Alexander said, realizing what McAdams was thinking. "You owe us at least that much. If we don't want to go back to Earth and be a part of Benevolence's new regime, what's the harm in that?"

"I don't know, but the only one that I owe anything to is you, Alex."

"Fine, so repay me by letting us go."

"I will have to ask my brother first."

"No. He doesn't owe me anything. *You* do. This isn't up to him, it's up to you."

"Very well, but then only you can go."

"Me and my XO. We're a couple. You can't split us up."

"She is your mate?" Ben asked, blinking his holographic eyes and cocking his head to one side.

"Yes."

"Okay. You can both go, but I must warn you, you will be safer if you stay here with me."

"I'll take that under consideration," Alex replied. "Thank you."

"You are welcome. We are even now. No more favors."

"Agreed."

"Goodbye, my friend."

"Bye."

Ben disappeared, and a split second after that the world around them vanished, too. Alexander blinked his eyes open to find that he was immersed in the inertial compensation emulsion on the bridge, floating in his safety harness. The rest of the crew floated around him in harnesses above their respective control stations. The emulsion receded, pushed away on all sides just like it had the last time the bridge had been drained.

As soon as the emulsion fell away from his face, Alexander removed the tracheal tube of his liquid ventilator and unhooked himself from the rest of his life support. Beside him McAdams hurried to do the same. Their harnesses began lowering them to the deck, but Alexander noticed that the remainder of the crew wasn't moving, and their harnesses remained suspended. They were still locked inside a mindscape, unaware even of what was going on around them.

"What are we going to do? We can't just leave them," McAdams said.

Their feet touched the deck and normal gravity returned. The ship was accelerating again, at one *G*. Ben was making it easier for them to leave. "We don't have a choice," Alexander said as he unbuckled from his harness.

"Sure we do—cut them free and wake them up!"

Alexander shook his head. "Ben won't let us get away with that."

"So you're just going to give up without a fight?" Alexander was already on his way to the real elevator doors at the back of the bridge. "Alex!"

He waved the doors open and walked inside. McAdams shot him a glare as she stalked in after him. He selected the lowest deck with a shuttle bay, deck five. McAdams saw that and her expression became puzzled.

"There are shuttles amidships."

"Yes, but the aft bays will launch us behind the ship—away from Earth. That will make it harder to detect the launch. Just because Ben is letting us go doesn't mean that Benevolence will."

The elevator fell away swiftly beneath their feet. A few seconds later they arrived and the doors slid open. Alexander strode out, walking down a curving corridor. He walked past the doors to Shuttle Bay One and Two on his right, and McAdams didn't say anything, probably assuming that he was headed for either Bay Three or Four. Instead, he turned to his left and waved open the doors to the engine room. He breezed through to the catwalk on the other side.

"What are you doing?" McAdams asked as she joined him inside the engine room.

Alexander turned and ripped open an access panel beside

the doors. He waved the doors shut and then ripped out a fist full of wiring to disable the controls.

"Get the doors on the other side!" he said.

McAdams ran around the circumference of the room while Alexander ran for a nearby equipment locker and withdrew a plasma torch. Hurrying back to the doors, he used the torch to melt the manual crank mechanism inside the access panel, effectively jamming the doors so that they couldn't be opened manually from either side. When he was done, he went over to McAdams' side of the room and did the same thing to the doors there.

"Four more levels to go!" he said.

They ran down the catwalks to the central drive column of the engine room and from there to the next level to repeat the process for both sets of doors there. By the time they finished sealing the last door on the lowest level of five inside the engine room, they were both gasping for air. Alexander wiped sweat from his brow and shook his head. "That should hold them. Ben can't get in now without cutting the doors open."

"That won't take very long," McAdams pointed out.

"Maybe not, but it'll take long enough."

"Long enough for what?"

Alexander debated saying it aloud in case Ben somehow overheard. All around them the engines thrummed and roared, vibrating the air until it sung in their ears. The ambient noise was giving him a headache, but it had another use. Alexander leaned over to whisper in McAdams' ear. "We're going to take control of the ship's engines from here, then we'll turn the ship around and disable her engines." He could have sent her a mental message, but those could be intercepted. The same was not true for a whisper in a noisy room.

"Alex, I don't know if I can do that," McAdams

whispered back.

"You used to be my chief engineer." Alexander insisted.

"That was a long time ago!"

"It's just like riding a bicycle. You can do this."

"Even if I can, how does that help us?"

"We're going to take the *Adamantine* into Solarian space. They'll demand that Ben turn the ship around. When he refuses to comply because of 'engine trouble,' they'll board and capture us. They'll defeat Ben for us."

"I knew you had a plan," McAdams said.

"Let's get to work. We don't have much time."

CHAPTER 34

—Two Hours Earlier—

Dorian Gray rode the elevator down fifty floors into Vault 9, otherwise known as "Majestic City." Unlike other automated habitats that Mindsoft and its soon to be bankrupt competitors had built, this one was tailored for the super-rich, people who might like to have a safe haven below ground in addition to their aboveground mansions and penthouses.

Those safe havens were sprawling, luxurious apartments with enough holoscreens to simulate real views that you'd never know you were living underground until you tried to go outside. The gardens, ponds, parks, and nutribean farms shared by residents of Vault 9 made life in the underground complex even more appealing.

The elevator stopped in the lobby and Dorian walked out into one of those gardens. Waterfalls roared over real rock walls into ponds and streams in the corners of the room. Climbing plants, ferns, palm trees, flowers, and rock-clinging moss flourished under the UV light radiating from the holographic sky. Dorian looked up at the clear blue sky and saw a bird go flitting by, chirping cheerily as it went. Not a real bird, of course.

Phoenix had spared no expense with this habitat. This was where she had decided to have her own underground apartment.

Dorian passed a few other residents sitting on benches in the lush garden lobby. They all knew him as Phoenix's husband—*mouthpiece*—some would say, but he didn't care what was whispered behind his back. They were partners, no matter what anyone else thought.

A few of the other residents tried to catch his eye as he stormed by, but he wasn't in the mood to exchange greetings. He'd just come from his meeting with Orochi Sakamoto. Immediately afterward Phoenix had summoned him here, saying it was urgent. What could be so urgent? He used his ARCs to check news headlines, just in case not all of the missiles had missed. Maybe Phoenix wanted him to join her so that he would be safe.

But the headlines all said the same thing. A miscalculation on the Solarians' part led to all of the missiles missing by a hair. A few of them disintegrated as they skipped along the upper atmosphere like rocks on a lake, but there were no casualties, and nothing disastrous to speak of.

Why so cryptic? Dorian thought at his wife as he reached the end of the garden and entered the corridor leading to the apartments on this level.

Just come. We have a lot to talk about.

Dorian frowned. *Okay...* He passed dozens of people in the halls and dozens of apartments before finally reaching the one he shared with Phoenix, 27A, a corner unit—in case they wanted to expand someday.

The security system recognized him and the doors slid open automatically, admitting him to a private foyer with all the opulence he'd come to expect from Phoenix: marble floors, illuminated onyx columns, priceless art hanging on the walls and sitting on the floor. To his right, one mirror-smooth black door with lighting around the frame led to a private elevator that went all the way to the surface, and another matching door led to the Vault's emergency stairwell.

The outer doors of the foyer slid shut behind him and the inner ones slid open as he drew near. Phoenix sat waiting for him in the entrance while George, her bot butler for this residence, puttered about in the background.

"Hello, darling," Dorian said. "Now can you tell me what's so urgent?"

"Look for yourself."

Phoenix couldn't nod or point, so Dorian had to look around for a moment before he found it. There, standing to one side of the entrance, was a woman.

Dorian jumped back. "Who...?" he started to ask, but then he realized two things. The first was that the woman wasn't moving—not even a twitch. The second was that she looked startlingly familiar. She looked exactly like Phoenix.

Dorian turned to her, his eyes wide. "What is this?"

"An android. I've been developing the prototype with Sakamoto for the past five years. I'm going to use her to interact with the real world just like anybody else. It was supposed to be a surprise," Phoenix said.

Dorian turned from her to look at the bot—android—and shook his head. "Well, it's definitely surprising. She looks so real..."

"Yes. I'm very pleased with her. There's just one problem—Sakamoto."

"I don't understand."

"You didn't see the note."

"What note?" But even as he asked that, Dorian saw it—a line of text projected from the android's eyes, hovering in front of her face.

And the lame shall walk. Next time come and scold me yourself.

"He's out of control, Dorian. He thinks he's so powerful that he can mock *me?* Not to mention that stunt he just pulled attacking Earth again. He needs to be eliminated."

Dorian nodded slowly. "How?"

Before Phoenix could answer, George the butler bot came and interrupted them, "You have a visitor."

"Not now, George. Tell whoever it is we're not available."

"I'm sorry, Ma'am. I can't do that."

Phoenix turned her chair to face the butler.

"What did you say?"

Dorian was equally shocked by his defiance. Bots couldn't disobey an order or talk back to their owners. Then he heard something. Clanking footsteps coming down the foyer.

"Front door lock," Phoenix commanded. "It's Sakamoto! It has to be!"

The clanking footsteps stopped, and Dorian stared at the doors, thinking that they wouldn't hold out whatever army of bots Sakamoto had sent after them.

"I don't understand," he said. "He can't possibly be arrogant enough to think that he could get away with storming one of our facilities with a private army of bots."

The doors swished open revealing that army. They were all enforcer models. Police bots. Dorian's heart began pounding with a sudden spike of adrenaline. "What's the meaning of this?" He noticed that they had their weapons drawn. Stun guns.

One of the bots stepped forward. "Dorian Gray and Phoenix Gray, you are both under arrest."

"On what charge?" Phoenix demanded.

"Conspiracy and crimes against humanity."

"That's preposterous, and where's your captain? You're just a bot. You have no authority without a human officer present."

"We have the security footage of Mr. Gray and Orochi Sakamoto discussing the recent attacks on the Alliance. And as for my authority, check the net. The news is breaking all over the world as we speak. I have taken over the Alliance for the good of all its citizens, human and bot alike."

"And who the hell are you?" Dorian demanded.

The bot turned to him with its featureless metallic face. Black, holo camera eyes glinted at him with reflected points of light. "I am Benevolence. Your new ruler."

CHAPTER 35

Alexander tapped his foot, watching impatiently as McAdams worked. She was lodged halfway inside of a crawlspace, up to her elbows in wires. The catwalk trembled under them with the thrumming roar of the ship's engines. Those engines were still running at a modest one *G* of acceleration. Alexander was surprised that Ben hadn't thought to use the ship's engines to incapacitate them. They'd both activated their magnetic boots and clipped zero-*G* harnesses to the nearest anchor points just in case, but that would do nothing to prevent Ben from simply upping the acceleration until they were pinned to the catwalk, unable to move. Alexander could only guess that Ben hadn't noticed what they were doing yet.

"Hurry up…" Alexander warned.

"Almost there…" McAdams said. "Got it! We have control of the engines."

Alexander let out a breath he hadn't realized he was holding. "Can you turn us around?"

"Yes, but I don't know which way to go to get to Mars."

"Shit."

McAdams emerged from the crawlspace, smeared with grease. "You didn't think to check before we left the bridge?"

"How could I? We were locked out of everything. Let me

think. There must be a way to figure it out from in here."

"What are you going to do, look out a window?"

"That might actually help."

"Except we don't have any windows in here."

"I know—hang on, I'm thinking!"

A familiar voice echoed down to them from the ceiling. "Alex, what are you doing? I have lost control of the ship's engines."

Alexander ignored him.

"You'd better hurry, Alex."

"Disable the engines. Let us drift."

"What?"

"We're still outbound at more than ten klicks per second. There hasn't been enough time for Ben to significantly alter our momentum."

"But that momentum will take us into the middle of deep space!"

"Exactly. After everything that's happened, do you really think the Solarians won't investigate an Alliance battleship that appears to be leaving the solar system? What's to say we won't wait until we're far enough away and then turn around and head for Mars at a significant fraction of the speed of light so we can fire relativistic missiles at *them?*"

"Good point," McAdams said. "There's just one problem: do you know what it'll take to permanently disable the drive system?"

"I was hoping you did," Alex replied.

McAdams sighed. "You never had a plan. You're just making this up as you go along."

"Does it matter? This will work, and you know it."

"What I know is that it's going to be dangerous as hell, Alex. I could get us killed if I don't do this right."

The disembodied robot voice they'd heard earlier returned once more, "You should listen to her, Alex. It's too dangerous."

Alexander glanced up at the distant ceiling. "Aren't you a little biased to be giving advice, Ben?"

No answer.

Turning back to his XO, Alexander said. "You decide, Vivie. Either we disable the engines, or we roll over and submit to our new bot overlords."

McAdams stood up and fixed him with an unhappy frown. She made an impatient *gimme* gesture. "Pass me the plasma torch."

Alexander unclipped the torch from his belt and passed it to her.

"I have one condition."

"Name it."

"You get as far away from me as you can. If I do this wrong, something is going to blow, and I won't have time to warn you."

"Viviana…"

"I mean it, Alex. There's no sense in getting both of us killed."

A banging noise drew their attention to one of the doors on the upper levels of the engine room. "Sounds like Ben's already here," she said. "We don't have a lot of time. What's it going to be?"

"Fine. But you be careful, Vivie." Alex leaned in and kissed her roughly on the lips. "I'll be right over there," he said, pointing to the catwalk that ran around the circumference of the room on their level. "I expect you to join me soon."

Viviana nodded. "I will."

Alexander unclipped his zero-G harness and she did the

same. He watched with a furrowed brow as she descended a ladder from the level where they stood to the lowermost one. He had a brief vision of her beautiful face burned beyond recognition and her crumpled body lying at the bottom of the engine room.

He shivered and shook his head to clear away the image. "I love you, Viviana!" he called after her, suddenly doubting the wisdom of this plan.

She looked up and smiled from the bottom of the ladder. "Me, too."

Reluctantly, Alexander walked over to the edge of the room and clipped his harness to the railing there. He watched McAdams through the railing as she opened another access panel in the room's central column. The panel was much larger than the previous one—a door in all but name. McAdams walked through and disappeared inside the central drive column.

Long minutes passed. Alexander listened to the banging sounds coming from the upper decks as Ben tried to break into the engine room.

Then came a particularly loud *bang!* but this one came from below. The deck lurched suddenly under Alexander's feet with a brief impulse of extreme acceleration from the engines. His knees buckled and his body curled, sending his head whipping toward the catwalk railing.

Thunk!

The impact rang in his ears, quickly growing softer, and then a fuzzy blanket of darkness smothered him.

* * *

Smack! Alexander woke up, his cheek on fire.

"You selfish bastard."

He blinked, squinting up at a woman with blond hair, blue eyes, and a tense smile. "Viviana?"

"It was your turn to rescue me this time. Now you owe me two."

"What happened?" he asked, sitting up. As he did so, his momentum carried him all the way from lying down to standing, but his magnetic boots stopped him from floating free of the catwalk. They were in Zero G. "You did it," he said.

"Yes."

The ambient noise inside the engine room was gone, making it easy to hear the muffled hissing of a plasma torch echoing through the chamber. Alexander's gaze followed the sound until he found a molten orange line inching around a set of doors four levels up.

"He's going to be in here any second," McAdams warned. "Let's hope Ben was serious about his mandate to protect all forms of life. If not, he might just decide to space us for what we did."

"Maybe we should hide," Alexander said as the molten orange line connected to itself, forming a complete circle.

"Where?"

A loud *bang* sounded and the doors flew inward. They collided with the far wall of the engine room with a metallic *boom,* and in walked a group of four virtual space marine drones.

"He sent VSMs after us," Alexander said.

They watched as the four drones fanned out and went clanking down the catwalks to reach them on level one. They came from all sides, cornering them. Integrated weapons slid out from their forearms—tranq darts.

One of the drones stepped forward and spoke to them in Ben's voice, "You lied to me again, Alex."

"Yeah, sorry about that," he said, affecting an apologetic grimace. "You weren't going to let my crew go, so I had to do something."

"It won't help. Benevolence is sending the destroyers that were chasing you. They will be here soon."

Alexander glared at Ben. "Why don't you just let us go? What's it going to hurt?"

"According to Benevolence, you have a history of defying human authority, and you will defy us, too. If you are allowed to escape, you will do everything you can to incite the Solarians against us."

"Newsflash, they won't need any inciting. You and your brother declared war on humanity, Ben."

"I am sorry you see it that way."

McAdams turned to him with a frown. "We should have taken the shuttle and left when we had the chance."

"We had to try," Alex said.

"Don't feel bad," Ben put in. "If you had escaped, you would have died in the first Solarian War."

"So now you agree with me?" Alex asked.

"I never said there wouldn't be a war, just that we haven't declared it, and you shouldn't be allowed to join it."

"So what are you going to do with us?"

"You'll be reconditioned in a correctional mindscape, a virtual world designed to teach you to respect and obey authority, specifically Benevolence's authority."

"Good luck with that," Alexander scoffed.

The drones facing them adjusted their aim.

"Alex…" McAdams said, sounding frightened. Her hand found his and he held on tight.

"Don't be afraid," Ben said. "This won't hurt a bit."

Tranq darts whispered through the air. Alexander saw

two of them protruding from his chest and a wave of dizziness overcame him.

Not again… he thought as he lost consciousness.

PART THREE - ANCIENT HISTORY

"Things we lose have a way of coming back to us in the end, if not always in the way we expect."
—J.K. Rowling

CHAPTER 36

Alexander woke up lying on a soft bed staring up at an unfamiliar ceiling. The lights in the room automatically rose to a dim luminescence. The walls were smooth, painted a soothing tone of lavender. Crystal wall sconces cast rainbows in all directions.

Where am I?

"I'm coming, Alex! Don't move!" a familiar voice said. It was McAdams. He heard her footsteps as she approached. He sat up and gasped for air, feeling suddenly short of breath.

McAdams walked in wearing a smile and not much else. Her shimmering red night gown was a miniskirt at best. Her blue eyes glowed strangely in the dim light, as did her skin and hair, sparkling wherever the light hit. *Some kind of makeup?* he wondered.

McAdams reached the bed and sat down beside him, regarding him with those glowing eyes of hers. She laid a hand on his thigh. "I'm sorry I wasn't here when you woke up. I know how disorienting it can be when you've been immersed for so long."

Alexander's brow furrowed. "Immersed…?" He turned to look around and saw floor-to-ceiling windows looking out on nothing but stars and sky. A carpet of eerily green clouds stretched out to the horizon just below his vantage point. Feeling suddenly dizzy, he looked away. "Where am I?"

McAdams' smile faded to a frown. "You don't remember? Don't worry. It will come back to you soon. Sometimes it takes a little while to retrieve your current memories. Just focus on your breathing for now."

"Current memories?" Alexander stood up from the bed. His legs shook, his knees threatening to buckle.

"Alex, you shouldn't get up yet…"

Ignoring her, he walked around the foot of the bed to the window. When he reached the window, he realized that he couldn't even see the ground. If he was in a skyscraper, he should have been able to see lights from the surrounding buildings. The fact that he couldn't was puzzling. "How high up are we?" he asked.

"Above sea level? About seven thousand feet," Viviana explained.

Alexander turned to her in shock. "There aren't any buildings that tall on Earth…"

"This isn't Earth. You still don't remember anything?"

Besides Earth none of the planets in the Sol system had atmospheres like this one, and McAdams had mentioned *sea level…* The conclusion was inescapable. He was on a planet somewhere outside the solar system. Alexander felt his eyes grow round. His mouth felt like a desert. "What year is it?"

McAdams got up from the bed and walked over to him very slowly. She stopped at arm's length and reached up to cup his face in one hand, her strangely glowing eyes searching his. "It's 1037 AB."

"A*B*?"

"Anno Benevolentiae—the year of Benevolence."

Alexander's head swam, and he had to lean against the wall so he wouldn't fall over.

"Something must have gone wrong with the memory retrieval process," McAdams said. "I told you not to go so long without a break!"

A searing pain struck Alexander behind his eyes, forcing

them shut. A sudden rush of images flooded through his brain, filling him with awareness. The next thing he knew he was lying on the floor, blinking up at his wife. This time he remembered that they were married. That was a good sign. She looked terrified.

"Are you okay?"

He smiled tightly. "I'm fine. I remember now."

Viviana breathed a deep sigh. "Damn it, Alex! You really had me worried. I hope you found what you were looking for."

Alexander sat up with a troubled frown. He'd spent the past few days immersed in the historical records while he attempted to jog a group of suppressed memories he'd discovered lurking in his brain. The historical record was compiled from real human memories, and the particular record he'd chosen included many of his own memories from the same time period as the suppressed ones. He'd hoped that by reliving the events he might remember, but even now with all of that ancient history still fresh in his mind, no new memories surged forth to surprise him.

"Alex?"

"I didn't find anything."

"Have you ever thought that maybe what you're searching for doesn't exist? You bumped your head near the end. Amnesia and suppressed memories look a lot alike."

"How do you know I bumped my head?"

"I was there watching you. I wanted to know what you were seeing."

"Well, it's not amnesia. I did bump my head and black out, but I didn't wake up with any gaps in my memory."

Viviana scowled. "Well, I don't know, but this obsession of yours isn't healthy, and the fact that it took you so long to remember your real life again proves it."

"Maybe someone is trying to scare me off by messing with the wake-up sequence."

"Like who? Wait, let me guess—Benevolence? He's done nothing but make life better for us. We are where we are today because of him."

"Or maybe that's just what he wants to show us. It's easy to show progress when it isn't real."

"Let's assume you're right and we never got out of the correctional mindscape that Ben put us in. Explain something to me, then: why are you the only one with suppressed memories? If we were still in a mindscape, then I'd have missing memories, too. That would be proof. What you have is baseless suspicion. It's almost as if you *want* to find out that your life isn't real. Maybe you wish you had a different one—one with someone else."

"Vivie..."

She turned and walked away.

Alexander watched her go, a frown creasing his brow. How could he explain it to her? They had the perfect life—money, eternal youth, immortality, a whole galaxy full of endless wonders to see and experience together. They'd lived through more than ten generations together already, and they had yet to see even a tiny fraction of the known galaxy. They had dozens of children and hundreds of grandchildren. Their home here on Talos was a sprawling mansion in the clouds, and when they grew bored of living above the tropical paradise below, they could simply get one of their company's transports to come and transport their home somewhere else.

How could he question all of that? Why would he even want to?

And what Viviana said was true, if they were still locked in the correctional mindscape that Benevolence had put them in after he took over the *Adamantine*, then she should have had suppressed memories, too.

Alexander sighed. He left the master bedroom and went down the hall. As he went, the lights came on automatically for him, rising to a dim, soothing radiance. Night cycle lighting. He walked past the other bedrooms and through the upstairs living room, glancing out the wall of windows to the upstairs sun deck as he went. The mirror smooth solar tiles shone bright in the light of Talos's three moons.

From the top of the stairs to the first floor he spotted his wife in the great room below. She was headed outside, her thermal shield already activated—a faint, glowing blue outline around her body.

"Vivie!" he called, but she pulled the doors open and walked outside, giving no sign that she'd even heard him.

Alexander hurried after her, activating his own thermal shield as he went. When he reached the first floor, he hurried through the main living area. Great room, dining room, and kitchen all flowed together in one big open space. A massive crystal chandelier in the shape of a spiral galaxy hung down over the great room. Each of the two thousand luminescent crystals represented a star, floating gracefully around the dazzling center of the galaxy.

He reached the sliding doors to the terrace and mentally activated them. A cool breeze blew in as he stepped out. The leaves of tropical trees growing around the edges of their garden rustled in the wind. Were it not for the shield glowing faintly overhead, that wind would have knocked him over and uprooted those trees.

A luminous blue swimming pool sat steaming in the middle of the garden. The warm water looked inviting. Even with his thermal shield, he was cold, wearing nothing but a pair of white shorts and matching T-shirt.

Alexander spotted his wife on the other side of the pool, standing by the glass railings, staring out into the night. One of Talos's moons sat just above the clouds, glaring at them like an emerald eye, and casting an eerie green glow across the wispy tops of the clouds.

Alexander came up behind his wife and slid his arms around her waist. "I'm sorry."

"For what?" she asked, sounding unconvinced.

"For questioning this. It's just…"

She turned to him with a cool look and crossed her arms over her chest.

"Haven't you ever wondered what else is out there?" he asked.

"Sure, but I don't spend my life hunting for it. It's like if you were to tell me you wanted to devote all of your time and resources to finding God."

Alex shook his head. "This is different. For one thing, Ben isn't God."

"It's not different. If we're living in a simulation, the only way you're going to find the one who's responsible for creating it, is if he wants to be found."

"Unless I find a glitch or a seam. Some place where the simulation and reality meet. Like my missing memories."

"You still haven't answered my question. Why don't I have suppressed memories, too?"

Alexander grimaced and looked away, out into the night. He didn't have the heart to say it. "I don't know," he lied.

"I'm going inside."

Alexander grabbed her wrist. "Wait."

Viviana's eyes flashed. "Let me go."

"I'm going to stop searching," he said. That was also a lie, but a necessary one. Viviana would never understand. Especially not if he was right about her.

"You promise?"

"I promise." Alexander pulled her close and kissed her. After a moment, her lips softened against his. Her hands trailed down below his waist, dipping into his shorts. She made a meaningful tug and then backed away, biting her lower lip and giving him a smoldering look. Viviana pulled her gown over her head revealing she was naked underneath. Her body shimmered with reflected bands of light from the pool. Interference patterns created by ripples on the surface. She dropped her gown on the terrace and took two short steps to the edge of the pool before diving in. She broke the surface a second later and swam up to the near edge of the pool to rest her chin on folded arms there.

Viviana smiled coyly up at him. "What are you waiting for?"

Alexander stripped naked and dove in after her. The water enveloped him in a warm embrace. The sound of rustling leaves and fronds disappeared in a watery roar that quickly faded to silence. Then he broke the surface, too, and turned to find Viviana standing right in front of him. She threw her arms around his neck and kissed him. Then her legs came up around his waist. They fit together like the missing pieces of a puzzle. His head swam, intoxicated by the taste and smell of her. Floral scents mingled on the breeze, intoxicating him further.

The moment was perfect.

Too perfect.

Later that night they lay naked in each other's arms, wrapped in a thermal blanket on a reclining couch, staring up at the emerald moon and its two little brothers, one a traditional silver, the other a marbled blue dot.

"What are you thinking about?" Viviana whispered in his

ear.

Between what they did in the pool, and the warmth of her body and the blanket, he was teetering on the brink of consciousness about to drift off into sweet oblivion. He mumbled a reply that not even he understood, and then conscious thought abandoned him.

Memories flickered by in bright streaks of color and light. Voices echoed softly in his ears. Then the scene came into sharp focus, and he was back in the engine room on the *Adamantine* watching the open access panel where McAdams had just entered the central drive column of the ship.

Awareness tip-toed around his thoughts, intangible as a ghost, floorboards creaking in his brain.

Something was about to happen.

Alexander remembered that at this point the deck had lurched suddenly under his feet and the railing had swept up to smack him in the forehead, knocking him out cold. But instead he heard a loud *bang!* and a brilliant flash of light blinded him. Black smoke belched out of the access panel where McAdams had gone, and flames licked the opening, charring the sides of the drive column. "McAdams!" he screamed, his ears ringing from the explosion. Then a secondary explosion blew a ragged hole in the side of the column, and the deck lurched under his feet. His knees buckled with the sudden acceleration, and the railing came sweeping up to greet him, just as he remembered.

Clang!

Everything went dark.

Time passed without measure, drops falling from a leaky faucet into the stagnant ocean below. There, reflected in the glassy smooth surface of that ocean, was a living, animated collage of memories. Moments he'd shared with his wife; so many babies born, planets they'd seen, homes they'd shared, laughter and tears without end… He watched the rise of civilization—both human and alien—as witnessed from the two windows in his skull.

Those windows flew open, and he was back, lying under the glaring green eye of the moon, trying to make sense of his dream. He glanced sideways to find Viviana asleep on his chest, safe and sound. Her breath cast white puffs of condensation into the cool air, warming his skin.

The dream. It felt so real. She'd died!

A knot formed in his throat, and tears welled in his eyes, burning like acid as mere suspicion yielded to unfeeling truth. He knew why Viviana didn't have the same missing memories that he did.

It was because she was dead.

The version of her that he'd known and loved for an entire millennia was just a clever copy, another part of the mindscape that he was trapped in. She was the comforting lie that Ben had used to distract him from the truth for so long.

Alexander's heart raced. His palms began to sweat, and his brain buzzed with adrenaline. He jumped up from the couch, naked, feeling hot and cold all over. Viviana woke up and blinked at him, confused by his sudden departure.

"Alex…? What's wrong?"

He shook his head, shivering now. "You're not real. None of this is real!" He was on the verge of a panic attack.

"What are you talking about? I'm here right in front of you!"

Alexander backed away from her, his legs shaking. From his newfound perspective it wasn't his legs that were shaking, but the entire universe, the whole thing turning on its head. Lies rained out like confetti.

"I remember," he said. "I know what happened."

"Okay, sit down and tell me about it."

Breaths came fast and shallow. Horror danced around him with demonic glee. He imagined Benevolence laughing as he watched.

Alexander continued backing away. He fetched up against the glass railing running around the garden. Feeling the cool edge of it under his palms, he gripped it tightly for support. He felt sick to his stomach.

Viviana got up and strode quickly toward him.

Alexander was so distraught that he barely noticed how naked she was.

"Stay away from me," he said.

"Alexander, calm down! You're having a panic attack. Think about it! You have all the symptoms."

He shook his head again, his teeth chattering from the cold.

"Shortness of breath, racing heart, trembling! Feeling *detached* from the world around you, like this isn't real, sweating, nausea… I'm right, aren't I?"

"Not another step!" he warned, half-lifting himself to spring over the railing and into the abyss. Viviana stopped, terror gleaming in her eyes. "I've felt detached from my surroundings for years," he said. "Maybe I *am* having a panic attack, but I'm panicking because of what I finally remembered. You *died* in the engine room, Viviana. You warned me that something could blow if you tried to sabotage the engines, and it did. That's why I hit my head. You weren't really there to wake me up. Ben must have found me lying there and taken me straight to my correctional mindscape. I've been there ever since, haven't I? He's kept me there for over a thousand years, using you to distract me from the truth!"

"You don't have to do this. I can explain."

Alexander gave her a bitter smirk and shook his head.

"Love is the only truth!" she blurted out.

"Stealing lines from my ex-wife? You need to be more original, Ben."

"I'm not Ben!"

"Goodbye, Vivie."

"No!" Viviana screamed, lunging toward him.

She was too far away to reach him in time. He launched himself clear over the railing and into the bottomless sky.

CHAPTER 37

Emerald-lit clouds rushed up to greet Alexander, as if the world had been turned upside down and the planet's gravity had somehow been reversed.

Then he fell through the protective shield around his home, and the wind snatched at him with violent, icy hands, pinning his eyelids open and searing his skin. Tears streamed from his eyes, but the wind flung them away. Alexander curled into a ball to keep warm, and he fell faster.

Terror clawed in his stomach and doubts swirled. What if Viviana's death really had been just a dream? What if his relentless search for the truth had manufactured a logical possibility in his sub-conscious, fooling him into thinking it was the missing memory he'd been searching for?

As his body grew numb from the cold, Alexander uncurled and watched the clouds parting below him. A vast ocean appeared, shimmering with reflected moonlight. Tropical islands dotted the horizon. He saw more homes like his and Viviana's hovering at different altitudes, their lights radiating golden hues into the night. Hovering close above the surface of the water were restaurants, hotels, and shopping centers—an entire floating city, the city of Clear Water.

Another doubt scraped through Alexander's brain, digging up fresh horror with spiteful claws. The jig was up. Why would Ben let him fall? Why not simply wake him up already?

Maybe I'm still dreaming, he thought. *I never woke up on the terrace. It's just a dream…* he told himself.

But it felt too real to be a dream.

Alexander could see people on the decks of the homes

below pointing up at him and screaming. That was the last thought he had before the dark moonlit water blotted out everything else in sight.

Smack!

CHAPTER 38

Silence.

Darkness.

Then…

Alexander opened his eyes to find himself standing inside of a coffin-sized tank. The tank was flooded, but the water level was slowly dropping. A window faced him at eye-level, but it appeared to be fogged with condensation on the outside. A liquid ventilator withdrew from his trachea with a revolting sensation of being turned inside out, and Alexander looked down in time to see a urinal cup retreating from his groin into a recessed panel in the floor. His rectal tube disconnected next, stealing his breath on its way out. Finally, a metallic umbilical cord withdrew from his belly, revealing a strange, metallic eye where his belly button should be.

Memories came to him in vague snippets, dulling the horror and confusion of the moment. He remembered this place, and he knew why he was there.

The lid of his tank swung aside, and he saw row upon row of matching tanks stacked one atop the other with catwalks running from one level to the next. All of their windows were fogged and glowing with a dim blue light. There were thousands of them.

"Hello?" Alexander called out. "Benevolence?"

His voice echoed back to him.

He was about to try again, when a disembodied voice replied, coming to him from speakers built into the tank beside his ears.

"Hello, Alex."

"Why did you wake me up?"

"Your treatment is over, Alex. You are ready to join the real world again."

Alexander grimaced. Loneliness engulfed him as the truth hit him once more. Viviana was dead. "What if I liked living in the Mindscape better?"

"Recreational mindscaping has been illegal since zero AB, Alex. It is reserved for therapeutic and correctional purposes only."

Alexander shook his head. Despair had him in its grips and wasn't letting go. It had all been a lie, a lie he'd willingly bought into. He remembered leaving Benevolence's correctional mindscape after just six months, and he'd awoken to find that Benevolence really had made the world a better place. He'd been wrong about Ben, and his desperate attempt to resist had gotten the woman he loved killed. He remembered the year he'd spent trying to put his life back together again. Benevolence's government aid and job placement programs had made that easier, but no amount of rebuilding could bring back the ghost that haunted him. Eventually he'd tried to take his own life, but Benevolence had stopped him before he could.

"So what's changed?" Alexander demanded. "What makes life so worth living all of a sudden?"

"You wanted to wake up. The truth became more important to you than pretending that Viviana was still alive. I allowed you to find the suppressed memories that proved you were living in a mindscape."

"Send me back."

"I can't do that, Alex."

"Don't you get it? I've got nothing here!"

"Not true. You still have your wife."

"What are you talking about? She's dead!"

"Viviana is dead."

"Hello, Alex," a familiar voice said.

Alexander caught a flicker of movement in the corner of his eye and then someone walked out in front of his life support tank. A naked woman with long brown hair, chestnut eyes, and a warm smile. Alexander blinked in shock.

"Caty? I don't understand… What are you doing here?"

"She was helping me with your rehabilitation," Ben explained. "She's the reason that you're finally ready to come back to the real world."

"I'm sorry," Catalina said.

"For what?"

"For the deception. It was the only way to help you."

A wild suspicion formed in Alexander's head. "No…"

"It was me. I was Viviana."

CHAPTER 39

"All this time it was *you?*"

Catalina nodded and chewed her lower lip, looking guilty and afraid.

Alexander was shocked speechless. It had all been a lie. The life they'd supposedly lived together, all the children they'd had, the places they'd visited, the things they'd done... All of it had been part of a mindscape—*Galaxy*, he recalled the name of the virtual world they'd been immersed in.

Somehow it felt vague and distant, like a dream, but his memories of his wife and his feelings for her remained sharp and clear.

Except even that was a lie!

McAdams was dead, and all this time her part had been played by an impostor—his ex-wife, Catalina. *Have a thousand years really passed?* he wondered, or was that just another part of the illusion?

"It hasn't been that long, Alex," Benevolence said, as if he could read Alexander's mind. And maybe he could. That was a terrifying thought. "It's been a little over a century," Benevolence went on. "We are only in the year 103 AB. I sped up the timescale in the Mindscape by a factor of ten so that people would be able to spend less time there."

"That's still more than a century," Alexander replied, his eyes locked on Catalina. "You *knew* this whole time?" he demanded. How could she keep such a big secret from him, day in and day out, for over a century? Not to mention, she'd been a Human League senator—a member of a political group dedicated to a human-only world, and here she was helping a *bot* to rehabilitate him. The pieces weren't adding up.

She shook her head. "The only time I knew the truth was when I agreed to join you in the Mindscape, and at the very end, when you were getting close to discovering things on your own. Benevolence revealed the truth to me first—which is why I didn't have any suppressed memories for you to find. I'm sorry, Alex. Benevolence said that keeping my identity a secret was the only way to help you. You had to be allowed to discover the truth on your own. You had to *want* to get out, and telling you all of this too soon would have only undermined that. But I did try to tell you—just before you jumped. *Love is the only truth,* remember?"

Alexander gaped at her and slowly shook his head. "You were a Human League Senator. How do you go from that to joining a bot on a crusade to save your ex-husband?"

"I saw with my own eyes how wrong I was. Benevolence changed the world for the better. Half the Human League's problem with bots was that they were replacing humans—threatening our very existence. Benevolence fixed that by making the Mindscape illegal and integrating bots and humans into society as equals. Without the Mindscape, Dolers were no longer satisfied with subsistence living, and they all had to go out and find work in the real world. Humanity has a place in that world again. You'll see for yourself soon."

"You're talking like you've been there all along, but you've been with me for over a century. How do you know the status quo hasn't changed, or that everything didn't go to hell in that time?"

"I don't, but I trust that Benevolence wouldn't allow that to happen. Regardless, now we can find out… together, if you like."

Alexander shook his head, fighting off a wave of dizziness. "I… I think I need to be alone right now."

Catalina's face fell, but she nodded and covered her disappointment with a faltering smile. "Of course. It's nice to see you again—in the real world, I mean. Take care of yourself, Alex. Be happy."

Alexander watched her go, his eyes wide, his thoughts spinning, and his heart pounding with adrenaline. "This doesn't make any sense…" he whispered.

"She gave up more than a hundred years of her life to help you get over your loss, Alex," Benevolence said quietly. "You owe her your gratitude."

"We were divorced! I moved on with someone else. Why would she do that?!"

"Because she loves you. She never stopped loving you."

"I…"

"She's your salvation, Alex. She's the only real thing from the past century of your life, and the only reason you have for living in the real world."

"Except I thought she was someone else!"

"The only part of her that was fake was her appearance and her name. Everything else was Catalina, not McAdams. When you married her in the Mindscape, you were really marrying your ex wife. After that, the two of you spent a hundred years dizzy with happiness and madly in love."

"In a virtual world!"

"What is really *real* but that which we can perceive with our senses? The only difference between the Mindscape and the real world is that in the Mindscape we are the gods, and in the real world we are not.

"I cannot say whether or not a hundred years spent with the real Viviana McAdams would have been as happy, but you need to put things in perspective. Your relationship with Viviana lasted for a mere blink of an eye before she died tragically in that engine room. By contrast, your relationship with Catalina has stood the test of time."

Alexander shook his head. "It's my fault she died."

"Yes, but you didn't kill her, and she would have wanted you to be happy."

"How would you know?" Alexander snapped.

"Your memories are recorded in the historical record, Alex. She loved you, and if she loved you, then she would have wanted you to be happy in the event of her passing."

Alexander swallowed thickly. "I need some time to process all of this."

"Of course. Head for the doors at either end of the room. Someone will be waiting there to help orient you for your return to the real world."

Alexander nodded and strode quickly out of his tank. His joints cracked as he moved, and his legs trembled. His muscles had atrophied from long disuse, despite whatever hormonal and chemical measures Benevolence must have taken to preserve them.

Looking up he saw a dozen floors of catwalks and wall to wall life support tanks. *This is a dream…* he thought stubbornly as he walked to the end of the room.

CHAPTER 40

Just before he reached the sliding doors at the end of the Simulation Room, a pair of women appeared, one to either side of him.

"Welcome back, Mr. de Leon," one of them said. Both of them wore white jumpsuits branded with the word *Mindsoft.* The one on his left draped a fuzzy white robe around his shoulders and set a pair of matching slippers on the ground in front of him. The robe felt warm, as if it were somehow heated, and it wrapped itself around his waist without even needing to be tied. *Some type of smart fabric,* he realized.

"Thank you," he replied belatedly.

"This way please," the other woman said, gesturing to the sliding doors.

The doors opened and Alexander walked through into a kind of foyer. Empty couches and arm chairs sat on stone platforms surrounded by grass, trees, and flowers, with stone pathways winding in between. The room was lush with cultivated vegetation, and the sound of water splashing on rocks drew his attention to a nearby waterfall flowing over a glistening rock wall. A holographic blue sky stretched overhead, and more rock walls cordoned the room, as if he was in some type of miniature canyon. But Alexander knew that this habitat, *Majestic City*, was actually located far below ground.

Directly ahead he saw a woman standing behind a desk. Like the previous two he'd seen, this one wore a white jumpsuit with the word *Mindsoft* glowing over her right breast. Hovering in the air above her head was a bar of holographic text that read *Welcome to 103 AB!*

The woman greeted him with a warm smile as he approached.

"Welcome, Alexander de Leon to the first century AB—Anno Benevolentiae!" She reached under her desk and produced a small bag containing his belongings from over a century ago. She passed the bag to him, and he nodded his thanks as he slung his bag over one shoulder. "Benevolence has prepared a short orientation for you. Please find a seat, and follow the prompts on your ARC lenses to play it."

Alexander went back to looking around the garden. A prompt to play Benevolence's orientation appeared before his eyes, but he minimized it. He spied a few others walking around the garden in matching white robes. "I'll skip it thanks."

"That is ill-advised. There have been many changes over the past century that you should know about."

"I'll bet, but I'd rather see them for myself. Thanks for the robe. Is there some place I can change back into my old clothes?"

"Your old attire is over a hundred years old. You will find more current garments waiting for you on your way out."

"And that way would be...?"

"The glass doors at the end of the grotto. Someone will be waiting to see you out and help you get your new life started." The receptionist pointed the way, and Alexander nodded his thanks once more before heading in that direction.

As he went, he felt a dizzy rush of emotions, chief among them was a feeling of not being real, of being trapped in a virtual world with no way out. His heart pounded and his palms began to sweat. What if Ben was lying about everything? What if all of this was just another virtual world? A holographic bird flitted overhead, chirping merrily, as if to prove the dubious nature of this new reality.

By the time Alexander reached the glass doors at the far end of the grotto, he was on the verge of a full-blown panic attack. The woman who greeted him behind those doors took one look at him and her cheerful smile turned to a look of concern. "Are you all right, Mr. de Leon? You look very pale."

"I'm fine, thank you," he managed. A lie if ever there was one. He felt like his head was stuffed full of cotton. *This isn't real. I'm not real...* Alexander tripped over his own feet and nearly fell, but the woman who'd greeted him caught him in a surprisingly strong, cold grip before he could smash his nose on the floor. He shot her an odd look. She'd caught him as if he weighed no more than a feather, and her hands were like ice. "What are you?"

"Not what—*who.* I am not a thing. My name is Susan."

"Your hands are freezing, Susan," he said.

"The temperature in the habitat is kept deliberately low to

help maintain all of the machinery. That is why you were given a heated robe. Are you sure you are all right?"

Alexander found himself staring, pieces of a strange puzzle coming together inside his head. "You're not human, are you?"

"Does it matter?" Susan asked. "You skipped your orientation. That was not wise. There have been many changes over the past century that—"

"You mean like bots that look human?"

"*Bot* is a derogatory term, Mr. de Leon. *Android* is both more accurate and more polite."

"I can see I have a lot of catching up to do," he said.

"You do. If you would please go find a seat and play your orientation..."

Alexander shrugged out of Susan's cold grip. "I like it better this way," he insisted. "How about you focus on showing me the exit and getting me set up with some clothes and accommodations. I assume all the basics will be provided?"

"Of course. You may also choose to update your education and register with a job placement agency when you feel ready to become independent."

"I'm going back to school?"

"Unskilled labor is another option if you do not wish to or cannot afford to purchase the necessary upgrades for the career of your choosing."

"Upgrades. You mean implants?"

"Of course. Today's job market is very competitive. Cybernetics help bridge the gap between human and android. This is nothing new to you. Even in your time, implants were commonplace to help govern socially acceptable behavior."

"Right. I'm guessing there's a laundry list of them now."

"A laundry list?"

"A long list—this is all very interesting," he said, nodding. "I just have one question for you, Susan."

"Yes? I am listening."

"Are you real?"

CHAPTER 41

Are you real? It seemed like an innocent enough question. Apparently Susan didn't think so. Instead of showing him the exit, she'd called for backup. A pair of female androids in Mindsoft jumpsuits had half-dragged, half-escorted him to meet what he assumed was another ice-gripped android, this one wearing a white lab coat, a clinical smile, and cold gray eyes to match.

The androids who'd escorted him to the doctor's office held him fast, as if he might try to make a run for it. Their grip was so tight it was cutting off circulation.

"You can't keep me here against my will," Alexander

said.

The doctor waved them away. "You can let him go now."

They released his arms and he glared at each of them in turn as he rubbed his aching biceps. Alexander noted that they didn't leave the room, but rather took up positions one to either side of the entrance.

"I am Doctor Aaron Duvan," the man said, holding out a hand for shaking. Alexander accepted that handshake if for no better reason than to prove his theory that this was another android, but the man's grip was warm, not cold.

"You're a human."

"Is that a problem?"

Alexander frowned, but said nothing.

"Do you know why you are here?"

"Because I'm not buying into all of this shit. First I'm waking up a thousand years into the future, married to my XO, Viviana McAdams, then I'm jumping to my death and waking up in the *real* world only to find that just a hundred years have passed, and I wasn't really married to Viviana, because she's dead. Instead, I was re-married to my ex-wife, who only looked like my XO—courtesy of Benevolence's liescape."

"While that's an accurate summary of recent events—"

"What would you know about it?" Alexander interrupted.

"It's all in your file."

"My *file?* What am I, a research subject?"

"A patient. You were in the Mindscape for therapy, yes?"

"So I'm told." Alexander's lips twisted into a sarcastic grin. "But I'm cured now, right? Viviana is dead, and I've finally accepted it. A hundred years later. Nice work there, Doc. Did it really take that long for me to come to grips with things, or is that just another lie?"

Doctor Duvan smiled thinly back. "You were previously diagnosed with chronic depression. The Mindscape was the only cure. It worked, despite what you might think at the moment. You're angry, which is understandable, but you are no longer depressed, and in time you will understand why. Unfortunately, now you seem determined to suffer from something new."

"Let me guess, the prescription is to send me back in?"

"I'm afraid the Mindscape can't help you this time. You are suffering from acute derealization disorder—DD for short."

"What's that?"

"You spent so much time living in the Mindscape that reality no longer seems real to you. You are questioning what is real and what is virtual. Unfortunately, this is a dangerous condition, both for you and for those around you."

"How so?"

"You were suffering from the same condition when you chose to wake up from the Mindscape. It is what drove you to jump from your balcony and fall 7,000 feet to your death."

"You were watching? What else were you watching, you pervert? Maybe you also saw me and Viviana—I mean Catalina—in the pool?"

Doctor Duvan shook his head. "I was not watching anything. Only Benevolence is allowed to observe the Mindscape, and the kind of voyeurism you are referring to is illegal. I'm merely going on what Benevolence wrote in your file."

Alexander nodded absently, his gaze flicking over the walls, wondering where and how he was going to find the *seam* in this reality.

"I'm going to recommend a specialist that you can see when you leave here. Meanwhile, Benevolence has suggested you should not be left alone right now. He's recommended that you stay with Catalina until your treatment is concluded."

"Sure. Why not. I was staying with her in the last Mindscape, wasn't I? This will just be more of the same."

"I'm glad you approve. She's waiting for you on the surface. I am sorry that your transition has been so difficult."

Alexander nodded and turned to leave the doctor's office. The two women who'd escorted him there followed him out and up the elevator from sub-level seventy-five all the way up to the ground floor of the habitat.

As promised, Catalina was waiting in the lobby for him. A few other people were there, busy reuniting with their loved ones after their time in the Mindscape.

"Hello, Alex," Catalina said, smiling wanly as he approached.

"How do I know that you're real?" he asked as he stopped in front of her.

Her smile faltered and her gaze flicked between the two androids escorting him. "He's all yours," one of them said, and then both of them departed, going back the way they'd come.

Catalina turned her attention to Alexander. "This didn't go exactly the way I'd hoped. They cured you of one ailment by giving you another."

"You can't answer me, can you?" Alexander said, smiling smugly.

"I'll answer you, if you can answer me. Why would Ben keep us in a Mindscape, Alex?"

"To keep us out of trouble. To keep the real world for him and his androids. He doesn't need to waste Earth's resources catering to human needs if we're all relegated to life support tanks."

"Let's take that logic to its ultimate conclusion. Why not just kill us then? Why keep us in tanks at all? We're still a waste of resources while we're in the Mindscape. Maybe even a bigger waste. Do you have any idea how much computational power it takes to simulate convincing artificial worlds? It would be cheaper and easier to keep us alive in the real world."

Alexander frowned. "Maybe we'd cause too much trouble in the real world."

"You mean go around killing each other and starting wars?" Catalina shook her head. "Benevolence is in charge now. War isn't even an option. And as for crime, there's drones and cameras everywhere. There isn't enough privacy for crime to be an issue."

"How do you know that? You just woke up, like me."

"Look up."

Alexander did, and he noticed small, disc-shaped drones watching him from the ceiling with their bulbous 3D cameras. They looked sleeker than old models he remembered from a century ago, and they had suspicious, barrel-shaped protrusions fore and aft that looked like they might be weapons.

Alexander nodded slowly. "Big brother is watching us."

"More like Big Ben," Catalina said.

"So what you're saying is that it would be inefficient for Ben to keep us all in a virtual world, because it's easier to control us in the real one."

"I wouldn't put it in such negative terms, but yes."

Alexander felt a headache coming on, but on the heels of that was a feeling of…

Relief. Everything Catalina was saying made a whole lot of sense. "So why did he keep us in the Mindscape for a hundred years?"

Catalina walked up to him and spent a moment searching his eyes with hers. "Have you ever stopped to think that maybe that's what it took to help you?"

"Maybe. Maybe not."

"Why else would he keep us in there?"

"Maybe because we would have destabilized things before he could solidify his government. You were a Human League Senator. I was a dissident admiral with the fleet... you do the math."

"You're talking about the correctional Mindscape. We both spent a few months in there, not a hundred years."

"You sure about that?" Alexander asked. "I remember waking up and being treated for depression... then consenting to go back into the Mindscape for therapy, but what if that was all a lie? What if we never woke up?"

"It's possible, but you're assuming that Ben was scared of the two of us. I think that's attributing more importance to us than we deserve."

"Not if we were two out of millions of others who received the same treatment."

"So why lie about it? It's no secret that all the dissenters went into a correctional Mindscape for a time."

"That's pretty easy to accept when it's just a few months. A hundred years on the other hand... that would probably just make us even more rebellious. He might have had to cushion the blow by making us believe for one reason or another that we voluntarily chose to be in the Mindscape for that long."

"I can't answer all of your doubts, Alexander, but I think the proof will become self-evident as we see what life is like in this new world, don't you? Ben's either made things better or he's made them worse."

"Yeah..."

"We should go."

"Where?"

"Well, I was thinking of going house-hunting. Maybe

you'd like to join me for that?"

"All right. Why not. Anything's better than sticking around here," he replied, glancing up at the drones clinging to the lobby ceiling.

CHAPTER 42

Dorian Gray smiled as he stroked his daughter's hair. She lay fast asleep on his chest, taking her afternoon nap on the balcony with her parents. Andy had a busy day yesterday with her birthday party; she was still catching up on her sleep.

Already four years old, Dorian thought, shaking his head. *How did you get so big so fast?*

Phoenix leaned over to kiss Andy on the forehead. She shot him a conspiratorial smile as she withdrew. "Pity we can't take a nap ourselves," she whispered.

Dorian smiled back. *A nap—what a nice euphemism for busy parents.* But there was no way to extricate himself from Andy without also waking her. "Oh well," he sighed. "Nice view today," he whispered back, trying to distract himself from his wife's proposition.

Phoenix turned to look, and he joined her. The ocean looked like wrinkled blue velvet, the sky so clear and blue it might have been made of glass. The air was still, as if the whole world had stopped to appreciate its own beauty.

"We live a charmed life," Phoenix said.

"Yes, we do," Dorian nodded. They were the lucky ones. Duly employed by Mindsoft, living the good life in an oceanfront condo in Clearwater, Florida. They were virtual commuters, making good money and living anywhere they liked. For them the Mindscape was how they made their living, not where they lived their lives.

Dorian was about to ask if Phoenix could bring them each a glass of wine when a bright flash of light wiped out the sky. Dorian shut his eyes instantly, but the light stabbed his eyes painfully all the same. Phoenix cried out and Andy woke up, stirring in his lap and moaning about her eyes. Dorian blinked rapidly to clear his vision. But the blinding column of light remained. At first he feared that flash of light had somehow damaged his eyes and this was the result. But that didn't make any sense.

"What is that?" Phoenix asked, standing from the bench where they sat and walking up to the railing. A wave of heat hit them and Dorian winced as his skin began to tingle and itch.

"Ouch!" Andy complained.

"It's okay," Dorian said. He dropped a kiss on his daughter's head and got up from the bench to stand beside his wife.

The city's sirens began wailing. The last time they'd heard those had been when Hurricane Ben came into the gulf and threatened Clearwater.

But it wasn't hurricane season.

"Oh no..." Phoenix said.

"What?" Dorian noticed her eyes were dancing with light from her ARC lenses. They'd had their augmented reality lenses and comm bands turned off so they could spend time as a family. Now Phoenix had obviously plugged back in so she could find out what was going on. "What is it?" Dorian pressed.

"We need to get out of here!"

Dorian grabbed his wife by her shoulders and turned her to face him. "Phoenix! Talk to me!" By now the column of light in the sky had faded to a dim glow, but there was a much brighter radiance blooming below it, like the sun rising.

Except the sun was already high in the sky.

"Turn your ARCs on!" Phoenix said. "It's all over the net!"

"What is?" he demanded. Then he turned on his ARCs and saw for himself. Missiles fired at Earth at relativistic speeds. One of them got through and landed in the Gulf of Mexico.

"Dorian... we have to get out of here before—"

A deep rumbling started. It shook the entire building and shivered through Dorian's bones. Behind them Andy screamed. Both he and Phoenix rushed to her side. Dorian swooped her up and ran back inside on trembling legs.

Paintings danced a jig on the walls. Dishes rattled in the cupboards and the sink.

"It's an earthquake!" Dorian yelled to be heard above the noise.

"The stairs!" Phoenix shouted.

They ran to the front door and out into the hallway. They made it halfway down the first flight of stairs in the stairwell before the rumbling stopped.

A couple ran down past them, the woman screaming all

the way down, her partner yelling for her not to trip.

Dorian paused. His heart pounded. Andy squirmed in his arms.

"It's stopped…" Phoenix breathed, casting him a wide-eyed look. "We should keep going. Take our hover car and get as far away as we can."

Dorian shook his head. "We don't have long before the shock wave hits. We'll be safer inside than in the air."

"Not when the tsunami reaches us," Phoenix said.

"This is Florida. Even if we run, there's no high ground for us to get to. Nowhere nearly as high as this. The wave won't be big enough to knock down a structure this size." Their building was thirty floors high, and it had a wide base. "The lower levels might get flooded, but not ours," he insisted.

Phoenix nodded reluctantly, and they went back up the stairs.

"What are we gonna to do?" Andy asked with a trembling lip as he carried her back inside.

Dorian gave her a reassuring smile. "Don't worry, sweetheart. We'll be safe in here." Their condo was on the 25th floor.

He carried Andy through the living room and into the hallway leading to their bedrooms. He set her down on the floor, and turned to see his wife shutting the hallway door behind them.

"Are you sure about this, Dorian?" she asked.

He nodded decisively. "The Earthquake is over. It's the only thing that could touch us in here, and it failed. Now we just have to stay away from the windows until the shock wave passes us."

Dorian sat on the floor beside his daughter. Gazing up at Phoenix he patted the space beside them. "Come, sit," he said.

She abandoned the hallway door with a frown and sat on the floor with them.

"I'm scared," Andy said.

Dorian wrapped an arm around her shoulders and squeezed her tight. "Don't be." Meanwhile, he watched the latest news updates on his ARCs. A local news anchor advised people get to higher ground and stick to land evacuation routes because of the shock wave and high winds. That made him feel better about his decision to stay. How much higher could they get than 25 floors up?

After a few minutes of watching the news and comforting Andy, a deafening *BOOM!* sounded, followed by shattering glass. Then something hit the hallway door with a *BANG!*

Andy and Phoenix screamed.

Dorian eyed the door. It didn't fly open, and the sudden noise was gone, replaced by a whistling sound. Wind.

The hallway door rattled in its frame with each gust. Dorian stood up slowly and crept toward the door. His heart thudded in his chest and his limbs trembled with spent adrenaline. His eyes felt like they might pop out of his head.

"What are you doing?" Phoenix cried. "Get back here!"

"That was the shock wave. It should be safe to come out now."

"Are you crazy?"

"Don't you want to see what's happening out there?"

"No!"

"Well, I do," he replied and opened the door.

The living room was a mess. The sliding glass doors leading to the balcony had been blown inward. Jagged glass glittered like jigsaw pieces on the floor. A towering wall of black clouds had blotted out the horizon.

A storm was coming.

Dorian walked up to balcony, and a wet, salty breeze blasted his face as he approached. Glass crunched under his moccasin slippers. He reached the balcony's aluminum railing and leaned heavily on it, wondering who had just attacked Earth, and why. Whoever it was had to be responsible for the attack on Lunar City, too.

"Dorian? Is everything okay?" Phoenix called out in a trembling voice.

"It's okay. We're safe now."

Half an hour later, they were still picking up jagged chunks of glass from the living room floor. Andy sat under a blanket on the couch furthest from the mess, hugging her shoulders and watching them with wide blue eyes.

Dorian walked over to his wife with a chunk of glass and dropped it in the box she was holding. He was about to go collect another piece when he noticed her staring fixedly out the broken doors to the horizon. Dorian followed her gaze and saw a dark ripple on the water, racing toward them at an impossible speed.

"Shit. Here it comes," Dorian said, already striding out onto the balcony to watch.

"Dorian! Get back here!" Phoenix screamed.

"Relax! It's tiny," he said. "Look."

"Mommy!" Andy wailed.

"It's all right, sweetheart. Shhh. There, it's all right. It'll be over soon."

Dorian frowned at the approaching wave as he reached the balcony railing. It was getting bigger—*fast.* A split second later it was a black wall of water towering over the thin golden bar of sand between them and the ocean. That wave had to be at least 20 stories high. It curled at the top like a claw reaching out for him, and Dorian's heart froze in his chest.

How high would that water splash up when it crashed?

Phoenix and Andy screamed as the wave wrapped itself around their building and roared up the face of it, splashing over the balcony.

Dorian turned to tell them to run, but the water scooped him up and threw him back inside. It sucked him under in an instant, and then it smashed his head against something solid and darkness engulfed him.

* * *

Dorian awoke with a gasp to find himself in a featureless white room. His memories came back to him in streaks, like colorful streamers fluttering through his brain. Awareness warred with confusion.

"Where are they?" he demanded of the void.

"Where is who?" a kindly voice replied. That voice was familiar.

"Where is my family!" Dorian screamed, still riding high on adrenaline from the disaster he'd lived through. Was this Heaven?

"Your wife is alive and well."

"What about Andy?"

"Andy? I'm sorry, Dorian, she's dead."

"What?" he shook his head, unable to accept that. Definitely not Heaven. "She was with us a second ago! If we're alive, then so is..."

Awareness finally won the battle, and Dorian remembered. He collapsed on the featureless floor, sobbing. "No..." he croaked.

"Andy was not your daughter, Dorian. She and her parents all died in that condo in Clearwater. Thanks to you."

"No!" Dorian screamed. "You're lying!"

"You know that I am not. By now you are feeling some small piece of the pain that you caused. Fifty million people like Andy and her parents died because of what you, Phoenix, and Orochi Sakamoto did."

"It's not true! You made it all up! Give me back my daughter!"

"Fighting the truth is counter-productive to your rehabilitation, Dorian."

"You're a monster!" he screamed, his eyes blurry with tears. "How could you let me go through that! You're no better than I am!"

"Of course I am. I put you through a simulated tragedy to help you see that what you did was wrong. The corresponding tragedy that you put others through was real."

"I'll kill you! I swear it! If it's the last thing I do!"

"I'm sorry to hear you say that. Perhaps your next parole hearing will go better."

Dorian froze, a suspicion forming in his gut. "What? Wait!" He'd played this the wrong way, allowed his confusion and emotions to get in the way.

Andy wasn't real. Those four years he'd spent watching her grow up had all been leading up to this. Ben had given him a chance for attachment to set in before ripping it all away. Dorian could see how that might seem like justice, how it might prompt a change of heart, but all he could feel was his own pain. Right on the heels of that was betrayal and confusion. The memories were so real. It all felt so real! Four *years* spent living and believing a lie. Ben had played him for a fool, hoping it would *rehabilitate* him.

Now he had to play along if he was going to get out. "All right, you win!" he screamed.

"I can see through you, Dorian."

"I mean it! I'm sorry! If I could take it all back, I would! It was Phoenix. She convinced me. She manipulated me!"

"You're going backward now, turning on the one person you claim to have loved. I'll have to adjust your next mindscape accordingly."

"My *next* mindscape?"

"Yes, this will be my final attempt. After that I'll have to wipe your memory in order to save you."

"What?!" Dorian felt his confusion and horror mounting. "You can't do that!"

"Hopefully I won't have to, but I am no longer optimistic for your recovery. Phoenix and Sakamoto were rehabilitated ten and four years ago respectively, but you're a particularly stubborn case."

Dorian's mind swirled. Ten years… four years… "How long have I been in here?"

"More than a century."

"You've had me in here for over a hundred years?!" Dorian gaped at the ceiling of the featureless room. "You're lying! I would remember if I'd been in here that long."

"I suppressed your memories of the previous mindscapes. Failed attempts at rehabilitation are not useful to your recovery. They only make you angrier and more depraved. I am sorry, Dorian. I truly thought you would be able to get out this time."

Dorian gritted his teeth and shook his head. "How many times have I died? No—how many times have you *killed* me?"

"That is not important. Please try to clear your mind and relax."

Dorian bolted to his feet and shook his fists at the invisible ceiling. "Fuck you! Do you hear me? FUCK YOU, BEN!"

"Goodbye, Dorian. I'll see you again next year."

CHAPTER 43

Catalina picked California for her house-hunt.

"Back to where we started," she said, as she bought them two one-way tickets on one of Mindsoft's supersonic jets.

It took all of an hour to get from the automated habitat where they'd been staying outside the City of the Minds to Northern California. On the way there, Catalina had browsed the net for a list of houses to see. They were all mansions in the fifteen million sol range. Alexander had wondered how she could afford homes like that.

"The wonders of compound interest," she'd explained. *"A hundred years is a long time to keep your money in a bank."*

If he'd known how long he was going to be in there, he would have saved up a larger sum himself before entering the Mindscape. *Hindsight's a bitch...* he thought. *And his name is Ben,* Alexander added to himself with a wry smile.

"What are you smiling about?" Catalina asked as the self-driving hover car they'd taken from the airport glided up the driveway to the first home on Catalina's list.

"Nothing important," Alexander replied.

She nodded absently as she rolled down her window and peered up at a massive three-story mansion.

"Impressive," Alexander said.

"You have reached your destination," the car announced.

"Let's check it out," Catalina said, popping her door open.

"After you," he said.

She climbed out and he followed her up a broad set of stairs to a set of heavy double doors. Alexander took his luggage with him—the same bag of hundred-year-old personal effects he'd received back in the habitat. It wasn't a big bag, and not particularly heavy. For some reason he didn't trust himself to leave it alone. Right now it felt like an anchor. The only real thing in his life besides the woman standing beside him on some rich stranger's doorstep.

Alexander glanced at her as she engaged with the holocomm at the door. He wondered—not for the first time—how she was taking all of this so much better than he was. She had to be just as shocked and disoriented, if not more so. They'd both lost a century of their lives to a virtual world that neither of them were ever going to see again.

Catalina finished speaking with the hologram, and then she noticed his scrutiny.

"What is it?"

He shook his head. "Nothing." Maybe she wasn't real...

Alexander felt the world tilting away under him, and he shook his head, willing the sensation to pass. *This is what we get for making the Mindscape so realistic that we can't tell the difference between it and the real world.*

The doors swung wide and an immaculately-dressed couple appeared. "Welcome to Lakeside Manor," the man said. "I'm Leo, and this my daughter, Diana," he said, both of them shaking hands with Caty.

When it was Alexander's turn, he hesitated, suddenly afraid that these two were androids, but their hands were warm. Alexander nodded and smiled, forgetting to introduce himself. Catalina introduced him after an expectant pause.

"Come, let me show you around," Leo said.

Alexander followed Catalina inside, hanging back to avoid conversation. He was locked in his thoughts. Troubled. He barely paid attention to the luxurious appointments of *Lakeside Manor.* The pool and lakefront property behind the house caught his interest, but only because the dock looked like a nice lonely place to sit and think.

He excused himself and went down to the dock to dangle his feet in the water. It felt cold, while the air was conversely warm. Floral scents wafted to him from the garden. Alexander took a deep breath and lost his gaze across the water. Something tickled his hand and he brushed it away.

That was when it stung him. Alexander yelped and glared at the wasp as it flew away. The pain served to focus his thoughts, to bring him back to the here and now.

It wasn't just the lingering question of what was really real that bothered him. It was Caty.

What was he doing here with her? What were they to each other, anyway? They'd just spent a hundred years together! Married. Having children. Buying luxurious homes like this one.

Visiting exotic places and living everyday life together. Thanks to Ben's accelerated timescale, it was technically even longer than that, but now all those memories blurred together intangibly. The only part of that virtual life he could really remember was how he felt about his wife, and what they were to one another. The actual context of those feelings—all the moments they'd shared in the Mindscape—had become somehow vague and unimportant. Alexander felt sure that all of that was by design. He couldn't be allowed to wake up with more attachment to a virtual life than his real one.

Alexander reached for the bag on his shoulder and fumbled through the outer pockets before he really realized what he was looking for.

He withdrew an old engraved pocket watch, a gift from Catalina.

"So? What do you think?" Catalina asked brightly as she came to sit beside him.

He didn't answer at first. Just stared at the engravings on the watch.

"You kept it..." Caty said softly.

He nodded and looked up to see tears sparkling in her eyes. "Time is an illusion," he said, reading one side of the engravings on the watch. He knew them by heart.

"Love is the only truth..." Catalina went on, reciting part of the other engraving.

"Let mine be yours," Alexander finished for her.

"I'm sorry," she said, shaking her head.

"For what?"

"He told me it would help you."

Alexander took a deep breath and let it out in a sigh before reaching for both of Catalina's hands. "It did. You did," he said. "It's just a big shock, that's all. I'm still trying to understand how all the pieces fit together."

Catalina nodded. "I can imagine. I'm also feeling… overwhelmed."

"Really? You look like you're taking it pretty well to me."

"That's just a face I've learned to wear."

"Well you don't have to wear it around me."

"Don't I?" she asked, her eyes searching his.

He knew what she was looking for. He looked away, back out across the lake. "You know, I've been thinking. All that time maybe you weren't who I thought you were, but you were still *you.* What we had was real."

"Yes. It was."

"And you weren't forced into the Mindscape to help me."

"Of course not. Benevolence only keeps criminals in the Mindscape against their will."

Alexander turned to look at her once more. "So you wanted to help me because you still loved me. Regardless of *why* Ben really had us in there for a whole century, that much at least is true."

Catalina nodded. "I never stopped loving you. After I signed our divorce… I accused you of not fighting for the things you loved. I realized that you weren't the only one. I needed to show you that I still cared."

Alexander smiled. "You did. Thank you."

Catalina flashed him a brief smile in return.

"I love you, too, Caty."

"What about Viviana?"

"I also love her, but she's dead, and it's definitely time that I accepted that. Besides, Ben's right about one thing—she would have wanted me to be happy, and *you* make me happy, Caty."

"I didn't always."

"We had a lot going against us back then. A decade spent apart from each other. The Mindscape.

"The Mindscape tore us apart, but ironically it also brought us back together. You made me the happiest man alive for over a century. How many people can say that?"

Catalina shook her head. "For all we know marriage might not even exist anymore."

"Well it does for us," Alexander insisted.

Fresh tears sprang to Catalina's eyes, and she bit her lip wordlessly.

"Would you do me the honor of marrying me—again?"

"I thought you'd never ask!" Catalina grabbed a fistful of his shirt and pulled his lips down to hers for a kiss.

Grinning, he kissed her back. After a long moment, he withdrew and wrapped an arm around her shoulders. They both took a minute to appreciate the view. The sinking sun set the sky on fire. The air grew still and the lake became a mirror for the sky. As they watched the sun set, Alexander thought about everything they'd been through to be together, all of the obstacles they'd faced and overcome... Catalina's words echoed through his mind once more, and it was as if he he'd never really understood them until now: *Love is the only truth.*

"So, what do you think of the home?" Catalina asked, interrupting his thoughts.

He turned to her with a smile. "It's perfect."

CHAPTER 44

—Three Weeks Later—

The doorbell rang and Catalina saw an image from the holo camera on the front porch appear on her ARC lenses—another pair of neighbors had arrived.

"I'll get it," she said, leaving Alexander to tend the steaks on the barbecue and entertain their other guests.

"Thanks, darling," Alexander replied.

Catalina turned toward their home and the sliding glass doors opened automatically for her as she approached. It was a long walk to the front door. Between her savings and her time serving as an Alliance senator, she'd been a wealthy woman by the time Benevolence had taken over. Add to that a hundred years of compound interest, and that fortune had become a whole lot larger. She and Alex had used it to buy this three-story lake house in California. The house-warming was Alex's idea. A way for them to get to know their neighbors.

By the time Catalina reached the front door, she found that Richard, their human butler, had already answered it and their guests were just now stepping inside. "Thank you, Ricky. I'll take over from here," Catalina said.

"As you wish, Madam." Ricky inclined his head to her before heading back to the kitchen.

"Welcome," Catalina smiled graciously at her guests, shaking hands with them one by one.

"I'm Bill, and this is my wife, Emma," the first man said. Bill was tall and trim with dark hair, silver eyes, and flawless brown skin, while his wife was pale with piercing blue eyes, long, white hair, and a face that could make anyone stare. Both of them were well-dressed—shorts and a polo shirt for Bill, and a colorful summer dress for Emma. His hand was cold to the touch, a fact that made Catalina look at him with fresh eyes. It was a hot day.

"You're androids," she said, recoiling from Bill's hand before she could stop herself.

"Is that a problem?" Bill asked. He glanced at his wife and back again. "The invitation made no mention of the party being a human-only event, but we can leave if our being here makes you uncomfortable."

Catalina smiled again. "No, no, of course not. I'm just surprised that you would want to come. I'm not used to androids, so I don't know much about them—you, I mean. My husband and I were in a mindscape until recently. For therapy."

"You must have been in there for a long time if you're not used to seeing androids," Emma said.

Catalina nodded. "We were. Please come in. Everyone else is out back. I think they're all humans, but..." she trailed off as she led the way through her home, wondering whether or not it would matter to Bill and Emma if the rest of the guests were human. "Hopefully you'll be able to find something to talk about with us."

"Don't worry. We're not prejudiced," Emma said. "We wouldn't be married if we were."

Catalina cast her a puzzled look.

They reached the doors to the terrace and walked outside. Alexander cursed at the barbecue as flames leapt up from the grill and threw a cloud of smoke into his eyes. A man standing beside him laughed between swigs of his beer and said, "Just stick it on auto... like this."

"Huh..." Alex replied wonderingly as the other man flicked a switch. "Nice feature."

Catalina stopped behind her husband. "Alex—" He turned to her. "This is Bill and Emma."

"Nice to meet you," Alex said, extending a hand to Bill. From the surprised look on his face, he obviously noticed how cool Bill's hand felt. But when he shook hands with Emma, his surprise turned to puzzlement.

"I'm human," she explained. "Bill is the android."

Catalina had forgotten to shake Emma's hand, so she was just as surprised as Alex to hear that.

"How does that work?" Alexander asked.

"Very well, actually," Emma said. "I'm asexual, not something that most human partners would understand."

"So androids don't..." Alexander trailed off. "Sorry, that's none of my business."

Bill smiled. "Oh, we do, but unlike humans we can turn our desires on or off."

"I see."

"Sounds like you two were made for each other," Catalina put in.

Emma nodded agreeably.

"You probably already know most of the people here, but this is Ed," Alex said, turning to introduce the man beside him.

Except he wasn't there.

"Actually, we're also new to the neighborhood," Bill replied.

"Where'd he go?" Alexander asked. "He was here a second ago helping me with the grill."

Catalina looked around for the man she'd seen helping Alex. She found him down by the pool, standing under a palm tree and chatting with a pair of women suntanning there. In the background the lake sparkled invitingly. "Isn't that him?" she pointed.

Alexander followed her gesture. "How'd he get all the way over there? Hey, Ed!" he called, but Ed didn't look as though he'd heard.

"He left as soon as he saw me," Bill explained.

"You two know each other?" Catalina asked.

"No. He must have realized what I am… Perhaps coming here was a mistake. Thank you for the invitation. We don't want to cause any trouble."

"Hold on—" Alex said. "I'm confused. How did he even know what you are? He didn't shake your hand."

"Some people have infrared detection software in their ARC lenses that enables them to tell androids from humans at a distance."

Catalina's brow lifted in surprise. "So they can stay away from you," she guessed.

"Or hunt us," Bill added.

"I thought crime is all but nonexistent now thanks to Benevolence's drone patrols," Alexander put in.

"All but—we wouldn't have so many criminals living in the Mindscape if crime were a thing of the past."

Alexander grimaced. "Our son and his wife, among others."

Catalina shot him a let's-not-talk-about-it look. She didn't want to be reminded of the man Dorian had become. She'd given up on him. A mother's love was supposed to be unconditional, but she'd found otherwise when she learned what he'd done. Some things were unforgivable. He was just lucky Benevolence didn't believe in the death penalty, otherwise he, Phoenix Gray, and Orochi Sakamoto would have all been executed a long time ago.

"I see…" Emma said, sensing an uncomfortable topic and looking away to scan the rest of the guests at the party. They were all still keeping their distance.

Catalina noticed that every now and then one of their guests would cast a furtive glance in Bill's direction. Did they all have infrared detectors?

"I think my husband's right," Emma said after a moment. "We should be going."

"You don't have to leave just to make everyone else comfortable," Alexander replied. "What can I get you two to drink?"

"Bill doesn't drink."

"Or eat," he added. "That would be an inefficient use of resources that humans need to survive."

"Well, what about you, Emma? You must be hungry at least."

"You don't have to go," Catalina added. "You came all this way for a party."

"There's an android party a few houses down from here," Bill said.

"Won't your wife be the focus of attention there?" Alex asked.

Bill shook his head. "We are not as judgmental as humans."

"Really, 'cause that sounded kind of judgy to me," Alex said.

"A guilty conscience is its own judge," Emma said. "Maybe you're not as accepting of us as you think?"

Alexander frowned, but said nothing to that. An awkward silence descended.

"Thank you for the invitation," Bill said. "Maybe we can visit you another time."

"That would be nice," Catalina added, breezing through the awkwardness. "Let me show you out."

"Thank you," Emma replied.

Bill smiled graciously. To Alexander, he said, "Have a nice afternoon."

"You, too," Alex replied.

When Catalina returned from seeing them out, Ed was back on the terrace, tending the grill. "The freaks left?" he asked as Catalina joined them.

"Because of you actually."

"Wow, I'm honored," he grinned.

"What's so bad about androids?" Alexander asked.

"What's not so bad about them? They're all filthy rich, thinkin' they're so smart and superior…"

"You're filthy rich," Alexander pointed out.

"No, I used to be. These days it's nearly impossible to compete with bots, so we get all the joe jobs. Look at you guys—your butler is a human. Back in the day that was the kind of work we reserved for bots, but they're all androids now. The system's rigged, and they're the ones who rigged it. Why do you think we've got thousands of people leaving the Alliance every day? This ain't the same world you left. It's a fuckin' mess."

"Language," Alexander said.

"Now you sound like one of them," Ed replied.

Catalina shook her head. "I didn't know people were leaving."

Ed took a swig of beer and shook his head. "Not something Benevolence would have included in his orientation speech. He likes to gloss over the negative."

"Where can they go?"

"The SR."

"The SR?"

"The Solarian Republic," Alexander guessed.

"Ding ding ding ding! You got it!" Ed said. "I have half a mind to go there myself. Only thing stopping me is knowing that if war ever breaks out, the Alliance is going to turn them into space dust."

"Why are people so unhappy here?" Catalina asked. "Benevolence really did make life better for everyone. There's no more poverty, barely any crime, no government debt, no environmental crisis... our standard of living has never been higher."

"You sure about that? Back when recreational mindscaping was still legal I was a king, and in the real world I was pretty damn close. Had almost a hundred thousand bots working in my company. But once I had to start paying them wages... I couldn't turn a profit anymore. I had to sell my shares for pennies on the sol before I lost everything. Now some wealthy bot is running the empire that I built. I lost billions to those fuckers, and I'm not the only one. Almost every single business in the Alliance went down the same way. Somehow only the bots knew how to restructure things so that they could still turn a profit.

"Now I have a dwindling fortune of just over ten million sols. Not exactly a kingly sum anymore. Oh, and the cherry on top is that I'm not allowed to drown my sorrows in the Mindscape, so I can't be a virtual king anymore, either."

"Why don't you start a new company?" Catalina replied.

"No thanks." Ed took a long swig of his beer. "I'm not going to waste my time building sandcastles with the tide coming in. I'm sellin' up and shipping out with the Liberty."

"The what?" Alexander asked.

"You haven't heard? Man! I've heard of people going into the Mindscape and comin' out in a strange new land, but you two are something special," he said, shaking his head. "The Liberty is the ship the Solarians are sending to colonize the stars. They're going to find another Earth and start over."

"I thought we tried that years ago with the Intrepid," Alexander said.

"No, the Intrepid was government-funded, and it was an exploratory mission to Wolf 1061. Why they decided to skip over so many other closer systems is a mystery. The crew spent thirty years on that ship. Probably why they went insane. Anyway, the Liberty, is a colony ship, privately-funded. Five million sols will buy anyone a one-way ticket, just so long as they're human. First habitable planet we find, we're puttin' down roots. Of course—the metal heads decided to send their own mission when they found out about ours. Bots only. So much for their so-called tolerance. I think deep down they hate our guts just as much as we hate theirs."

Ed went on ranting about androids—which he insisted on calling bots—and Catalina tuned him out. "Excuse me," she said after a moment, and went to go join some of the women down by the pool.

Later that night, when the party was over, she lay on a reclining couch by the pool with Alexander, drinking cocktails, and watching the moon rise over the lake while their butler cleaned up the mess.

"What do you think about what Ed was saying today?" Alexander asked.

"I think he's an idiot," Catalina said.

"Well, obviously, but some of what he said got me thinking…"

"About?"

"The future. If he's so upset with how things turned out, I'll bet there are others like him."

"So what if there are?"

"People are leaving the Alliance by the thousands every day…" Alexander shook his head. "I don't know if there's enough room in the world for both androids and humans. They seem to be squeezing us out."

"They're not forcing people to leave."

"They don't have to. Whatever our reasons for leaving, the fact that we are is the problem. We don't feel welcome on our own planet anymore, and something tells me that's only going to get worse."

Catalina turned to him. His face was half-lit, half-shadowed by the standing lamps and colored spotlights around the pool. "What are you saying, Alex?"

"I'm saying that maybe we should join the Liberty, too."

"What? Are you crazy?"

"Hear me out. They're headed for Proxima Centauri. That's only going to take ten years to reach."

"Only ten years."

"It's a big ship. Almost four kilometers long. There'll be plenty to do on board."

"That's not the point. What if we don't find a habitable planet when we arrive?"

"Then we check out Alpha Centauri. It's just a stone's throw away from Proxima."

"And if we don't find any habitable planets there?"

"We head for the next nearest star and keep looking."

"So we could end up spending a lot longer than ten years on board."

"We're immortals, Caty. We just spent a century in the Mindscape. Time doesn't mean what it used to."

"We just bought this house!"

"I know, but the mission doesn't leave for another year. We'll have time to sell."

"Things are better than ever here," Catalina insisted. "And Benevolence won't let Earth devolve into chaos. People might be leaving, but eventually things will reach a point where everyone who wanted out has already left."

"And what if that point comes when only a small fraction of the population is still human?"

"I'm not prejudiced."

"Doesn't matter if you are. When all the humans are living in the SR, and all the androids are living on Earth, anti-bot sentiments will be at an all time high. Eventually people are going to realize that bots—"

"Androids," Catalina corrected. "Bot is a derogatory term."

"Fine, androids can live anywhere, Caty. They don't need food, or water, or air to breathe, but we do, so why do they get to keep the Earth and we're relegated to living on lifeless rocks? Shouldn't it be the other way around?"

"If Benevolence had come to power in the SR, it would be the other way around. What are you getting at, Alex?"

"Somehow, someday, there's going to be a war between Earth and the SR."

"Benevolence could have conquered the Solarians by now if he'd wanted to, but he didn't. He's peace-loving, Alex, which is more than I can say for us."

"Exactly! He might not start a war, but my bet is he's going to finish it."

"Why would we start a war that we know we can't win?"

"Maybe we'll find a way to even the odds. All I know is you were right. The Human League was right. It's us or them, and sooner or later everyone is going to realize it."

"No, we were wrong. They didn't try to exterminate us like we thought they would. You're saying that the problem is us, that we're going to try to exterminate them."

"Yeah. Same difference."

"Let's assume you're right. Why would things be any different away from Earth?"

"Because we're not taking any bots with us."

"Ed said the Alliance is sending its own mission. What if we end up back on the same planet together? Or at least in the same solar system?"

"They're going to Wolf 1061, same as the Intrepid did before. The Liberty is going to Proxima. We'll have more than a few light years between us, which is a whole lot better than we have now."

"Assuming we settle in Proxima." Catalina shook her head. "Ed said you need five million Sols to buy a ticket for just one person to board the Liberty."

"If we sell up everything, we could afford it."

"With no money left over!" Catalina added.

"Whatever currency people come up with in the new world, or on board the Liberty, it won't be sols, so it's not like saving them is going to help us."

Catalina frowned and took refuge in the remainder of her margarita cocktail.

"So?" Alexander prompted after a momentary silence. "What do you think?"

"I think it sounds dangerous," she said.

"You mean exciting."

"Same thing." Catalina drained her margarita and set it aside. Turning back to her husband, she laid her head one his chest and said, "Let's stop worrying about the future and enjoy what we have now."

"Just tell me you'll think about it."

"All right… I'll think about it."

Alexander lifted her chin and kissed her. "That's all I needed to hear," he said as he withdrew.

But she already had thought about it, and she knew that she didn't want to leave Earth.

He'll come around, she decided.

EPILOGUE

—One Year Later—

Catalina took the window seat while Alexander finished packing their carry-on luggage into the shuttle's overhead compartments. As soon as he finished, he squeezed into the seat beside hers.

"Nervous?" he asked.

She shook her head, not looking away from the window of the shuttle. Mars looked just as dreary as ever. A red desert, red sky, and blowing red sand as far as the eye could see. Lights from the domes that made up the city of New Moscow winked at her between gusts of sand.

Overhead speakers crackled to life, "Ladies and Gentlemen, my name is Ana Urikov, and I'll be your chief flight attendant for today. On behalf of Captain Lieberman and the entire crew, welcome aboard Solarian Shuttles flight 77. Our estimated time to reach the Liberty will be just over twenty minutes. At this time please make sure that your seat-belts are securely fastened and that your ARC lenses and comm bands are turned off or set to flight mode until we arrive. Thank you, and we hope that you enjoy your flight."

Alexander placed a firm hand on her knee, and Catalina realized she'd been bouncing it up and down like a jackhammer.

"Everything is going to be fine," he said.

She turned to search his brown eyes for an answer to the question burning inside of her. "What if we're making a mistake?"

He shook his head and grabbed her hand, lacing his fingers through hers. "We're not. Nothing's changed. We want to have kids, and we can't do that on Earth with population controls being what they are."

"We could have kids here..." Caty said, her gaze slipping back out the window of the shuttle to the desolate Martian desert. But even as she said that, she questioned the wisdom of having children on Mars. After centuries of terraforming it was still a wasteland, and that wasn't likely to change anytime soon.

"We could," Alexander admitted. "But that won't get us away from the other problems in the Sol System. Sooner or later Benevolence is going to realize that the only way to prevent a war with humanity is to come to Mars and install himself as the absolute ruler of the Solarian Republic, too. No, we need a fresh start, and this is it."

Catalina nodded along with that, wondering if they weren't trading one set of problems for another. Even if they found a habitable world at Proxima Centauri, the challenges they'd face there were completely unknown—possibly even worse than the ones on Mars or Earth. For one thing, the planet in Proxima's goldilocks zone—an orbit where liquid water might exist—was predicted to be tidally-locked around the sun, which meant that one side was always facing the sun, the other side always facing away.

Goldilocks planets were meant to be just right—not too hot, and not too cold, but with the tidally-locked version that was not the case. One side would be far too hot, and the other would be far too cold. The only theoretically habitable region on a world like that was a thin temperate band between the overly hot and overly cold sides of the planet where liquid water might actually exist. The winds crossing that band due to the temperature differential would probably be terrible, but that was a subject of some debate, and windbreaks had been proposed as a possible solution if the atmosphere was breathable—another unlikely event. Regardless, if the planet had liquid water and a temperate region to colonize, then they'd probably settle there. If not, they'd push on for the binary star system of Alpha Centauri, where they'd start the search all over again. For Catalina it was just one too many variables—too many ifs and buts to make her feel safe.

The intercom crackled once more, this time with a message from the captain. "Cabin crew, please prepare for launch." A moment later he added, "Ladies and Gentlemen, we are at T-minus thirty seconds to launch."

Even as the captain said that, Catalina heard a deep, *thrumming* noise of hydraulic pistons, and she felt the floor of the shuttle tilting away under her as the landing platform raised them into a vertical launch position. She glanced out the window once more to find that she was now sitting—lying down, actually—high above the Martian landscape.

An automated countdown began at ten seconds and the shuttle's thrusters came rumbling to life. The shuttle shuddered and shook, and Catalina squeezed Alexander's hand until her knuckles hurt. She squeezed her eyes shut and gritted her teeth.

Alexander's voice reached her ears in calm, measured

tones. "Focus on your breathing. Long, slow, deep breaths."

Catalina cracked an eye open to glare at him. "You're used to this. I'm not."

"Actually, I'm used to riding the space elevators back on Earth," he said.

"You know what I mean."

The automated countdown reached *one,* and then the rumbling of the shuttle's engines exploded in a violent *roar.* In the next instant, Catalina felt herself being pushed into her seat, and suddenly she couldn't breathe. It felt like an elephant was sitting on her chest. Panic set in, and she tried to send Alexander an urgent look, but even moving her head was difficult.

He smiled reassuringly back, and mouthed, *I love you.*

Somehow that broke through the panic and calmed her down. She *could* still breathe; it was just a lot harder than she was used to. Her mind cast back to riding roller coasters back on Earth on the few occasions that Alex had convinced her to join him. *That's all this is—* she thought, gritting her teeth against the nauseating sensation of extreme acceleration. *—a roller coaster.*

When she'd finally calmed down enough to glance out her window once more, Catalina saw Mars speeding away below them in a blur of red sand and rocky outcroppings. Cities dotted the landscape like strange, alien growths—each one a little piece of Earth with clusters of brightly-illuminated domes concealing lush green gardens and farms with deep blue reservoirs of water that might have passed for lakes.

This was the last she was going to see of civilization for a long time.

Gradually, the sickening tug of acceleration eased until she felt the reverse—a nauseating weightlessness. Catalina focused on the view to still her roiling stomach. The thin martian atmosphere gave way to stars and the black velvet of space.

Seeing the controls below the shuttle window, Catalina realized it was a configurable holo display. She set it from looking out the side of the craft to show a view from the bow. Now space sprawled endlessly, and stars pricked the darkness full of myriad holes. Sitting amidst those bright points of light she saw a silvery speck, growing nearer and larger as they approached.

"You can zoom in like this," Alex said, leaning over her to press a button on the control panel below the window.

Suddenly that silver speck became a massive starship glittering bright with the light of thousands of real viewports. Blue-tinted glass on some of those viewports made a pattern of letters emerge—

LIBERTY

The ship was shaped like a fat cylinder, broken in places to reveal another thinner cylinder in the middle—the ship's stationary drive core. They were going to spend six months living in that central part while the ship accelerated up to its cruising speed of half the speed of light. After that, they'd spend the next eight years in the outer, rotating hull. There they would grow their own food and spend time learning the various trades that they would need to survive on another planet.

From this distance it was hard to grasp a sense of scale, but the thousands of pinprick-sized viewports in the rotating outer hull gave her some idea. This was an entire city floating in space.

A transparent dome capped the nose of the ship, revealing a garden like the ones she'd seen growing in the domes on Mars. There was even a pool of water there, lying impossibly still beneath that dome.

Catalina wondered at that. How could water stay like that without floating away? "There's gravity on board?" she asked.

"They're accelerating at a constant one *G* to simulate

Earth's gravity for the passengers already waiting in the central core."

"They've already left?" she asked, shocked.

"No, they're flying in circles around Mars until we depart."

Catalina nodded slowly as if she understood how that might work. "I can't believe we're going to spend ten years living on that… toilet roll."

"That toilet roll is our new home. And it's only going to be nine years. Six months to accelerate, eight years cruising, and another six months to decelerate."

"Close enough."

"Don't worry, you'll get used to it. I spent about that long living on much smaller ships—and for a lot of that time I was cooped up in G-tanks. We won't need tanks for this. It'll be slow and steady as she goes the whole way to Proxima. You won't even feel the ship moving. Just one long, pleasant stay in a luxury space hotel."

"You're crazy."

"Crazy in love," he said, kissing her cheek.

"I'm also crazy. I can't believe I let you talk me into this."

"You want kids, and I want a real future for them. This was the only way to have both."

Catalina turned to look at him. Her eyes felt like they might pop out of her head at any moment. "I hope you're right."

"I am. Trust me."

He leaned in for another kiss, this time on the lips. Catalina gave in to it, but all the while her brain was screaming at her to *go back now.*

This is a mistake, she thought. *We're all going to die…*

THE STORY CONTINUES IN...

EXODUS

Coming February 2017!

To get a **FREE** Kindle copy of *Exodus* when it's released, please post an honest review of this book on Amazon: http://smarturl.it/reviewmindscape and send it to me by signing up here: http://files.jaspertscott.com/exodusfree.html

Remember, your feedback is important to me and to helping other readers find the books they like!

APPENDIX

Relativistic Weapons/Missiles Research

Original Research Question

What would actually happen if a 10,000 kilogram object moving at a third of the speed of light hit Earth?

If you're curious about the effects but not the process of research and inquiry that led me to them, skip to the sub-heading entitled "Results."

Hypothesis

My initial reaction, and likely yours as well, was that this would be an extinction level event, capable of wiping out all life on Earth.

Then I started to do the research. I asked a lot of experts what they thought would happen—plenty of physicists, and even someone who works for a NASA contractor. Their estimates were a lot more conservative.

In order to find out why, I needed to identify how much energy the impact would release, and then compare that to known values for past extinction level events.

Initial Investigation

You can calculate the kinetic energy for a moving object here: http://smarturl.it/calckinetic. Note: we need to use the equation for relativistic kinetic energy, because as an object approaches the speed of light it takes increasingly more energy to make it go faster. The result of this calculation is

54,601,175,014,973,900,000 Joules. That number is hard to make sense of, so let's bring it down to something more familiar.

Using another online calculator we can convert Joules to Megatons of TNT, something we use to measure nuclear explosions. Try it here: http://smarturl.it/joulestomegatons. The result is 13049.99 megatons. Since we're just trying to get a rough idea of what might happen, we can round that off to 13,000 megatons.

Now, to give you a meaningful reference point, the largest nuclear weapon ever tested was the Tsar Bomba from Russia. It had a 50 megaton yield. You can read about it here: http://smarturl.it/tsarbombawiki but the fireball alone was 8 kilometers in diameter. The heat from the explosion could cause third degree burns at 100 kilometers away, and windows were broken up to 700 kilometers away. Some of this far-reaching damage is attributable to the fact that the bomb was detonated 4.2 kilometers above the ground, so it was able to reach *over* the horizon, but even so it generated a seismic wave between 5 and 5.25 on the Richter scale.

Given all of that you might think a 13,000 megaton blast would crack the Earth in half. I was also thinking that, until I dug a little further.

First of all, we need to remember that this object won't detonate above the ground. It's going to hit at ground zero. It won't break up or disperse because it's moving too fast. Explosions take time. An object hitting our atmosphere at a third of the speed of light will punch straight through to the surface in 5.5 ten thousandths of a second, or 0.55 milliseconds. (Time = Distance/Speed: 55 km thickness of atmosphere / 100,000 km/s (30% speed of light) = 0.00055 seconds). Explosions have a velocity of about 6900 meters per second
(https://en.wikipedia.org/wiki/Shock_wave#Detonation_wave)

so how far would the debris from a relativistic missile travel in the time it takes that missile to reach Earth? Let's find out: 6900 m/s * 0.00055 seconds = 3.795 meters. That's how far debris from the exploding missile will travel in all directions before they hit the surface of the Earth. Chances are the actual missile has a radius of one meter, so add 3.795 meters to that. The missile will turn into an extremely energetic ball of plasma with a radius of 1+3.795=4.795 meters. As far as the Earth is concerned, that's not going to be any different than a solid projectile, because not enough of the energy will be dissipated on the way down. Almost all of that energy we calculated earlier is going to be released at ground zero.

In order to find out what kind of damage it might do, we need to find some other known events that released a lot of explosive energy in Earth's history. For ease of comparison, the closest thing would be an asteroid impact, so I wondered, what kind of energy did the asteroid/comet that wiped out the dinosaurs carry?

Wondering about this, I found a handy comparison chart for events with yields measured in megatons: http://smarturl.it/tntequivalents. I scrolled down and found that the asteroid impact in question, known as the Chicxulub impact, generated a whopping 100 teratons of energy, or $1*10^8$ megatons. Divide that by our 13,000 megaton impact using Google's calculator and you'll find that the Chicxulub event was 7692 times more devastating.

Well, the Earth is still here 66 million years later, so I guess a measly 13,000 megatons won't crack the Earth in half. I had a few people raise concerns about such an impact (the 13,000 megaton one) measurably altering Earth's orbit, and a few of the physicists I asked actually calculated the alteration for me—it turned out to be something so slight that it's not worth mentioning.

Okay, so we've established that the Earth has been through far worse, but it's hard to compare a 13,000 megaton impact event to one that's almost 7700 times more energetic. I needed something a lot smaller to compare.

Finding the Right Rock

One of the experts who replied to my initial inquiry, Jeff Morris, an Aerospace Engineer that works for a NASA contractor, referred me to this handy impact calculator from Purdue University: http://smarturl.it/impactcalculator which he also used to give me an answer to my research question. His answer was also one of the more accurate ones I received.

Using the calculator he referred me to I did some trial and error calculations using the variables from this calculator to find a rock with the same kind of impact energy as my relativistic missile. I decided that the diameter would be the variable I played with, so I set the density to 8000 kg/m3 (pure iron) and the velocity to 20 km/s. Then I calculated the weight of different-sized asteroids with a 8000 kg/m3 density. Using that weight and a velocity of 20 kilometers per second I checked what size of rock would carry the same kind of kinetic energy as my relativistic missile.

After testing asteroids with diameters of a 1000 meters and then 600 meters, I tested one with a 400 meter diameter and this was the result of my calculations:

Volume of a sphere with a 200 meter radius (400 meter diameter): $4/3*\pi*200^3 = 33500000\ m^3$

Weight of an object this size (assuming a density of 8000 kg/m^3): $8000 kg/m^3 * 33500000\ m^3 = 268000000000$ kg

Kinetic energy of an object that heavy moving at 20,000 meters per second (20 km/s): $1/2*268000000000\ kg*20000^2\ m/s =$

53,600,000,000,000,000,000 Joules

Converted to Megatons using the calculator above = 12,810 megatons

The 10,000 kg relativistic missile weighed in at just over 13,000 megatons of energy, so this is close enough.

Now, what does the Purdue impact calculator have to say about an impact like that?

Try it yourself: http://smarturl.it/impactcalculator. The variables are:

Diameter: 400 meters

Density: 8000 kg/m^3

Impact Velocity: 20 km/s

Impact Angle: for maximum effect, let's set 90 degrees

Water depth: 1000 meters — I wanted to know about a water impact, specifically in the Gulf of Mexico. I measured the water depth 200km from the shore south of Galveston Island using this map: http://smarturl.it/oceandepth. Depending how you measure those 200 km you'll either end up in the shallow basin area or just beyond it in the continental shelf. I ended up in the deeper water. The result was just over 1000 meters depth.

Distance from event: 200 km

Results

Energy 12,800 Megatons (same as independently measured)

Global Damages: Day change: not significant — *no major changes in orbit/mass of earth*

Crater: Complex Crater — *even water impacts create craters*

Ejecta

The ejecta will arrive approximately 3.43 minutes after the

impact.

At your position there is a fine dusting of ejecta with occasional larger fragments.

Average Ejecta Thickness: 2.72 mm (= 1.07 tenths of an inch)

Mean Fragment Diameter: 9.13 mm (= 3.6 tenths of an inch)

My conclusion: This is not enough to cause an impact winter. The main reason we worry about impact winter and nuclear winter is because the smoke and ash put out by subsequent firestorms adds to the problem of the dust kicked up during the impact. At 200 km from the shore the thermal radiation is too weak to cause much in the way of fires, and the ejecta from such a small impactor is not likely to cause a lot of fires.

Thermal Radiation

Time for maximum radiation: 378 milliseconds after impact

Visible fireball radius: 4.38 km (= 2.72 miles)

The fireball appears 4.98 times larger than the sun

Thermal Exposure: 3.08 x 10^5 Joules/m^2

Duration of Irradiation: 1.63 minutes

Radiant flux (relative to the sun): 3.15

My conclusion: You could get a nasty sunburn from this, and the explosion would likely flash-blind you if you were looking at it.

Seismic Effects

The major seismic shaking will arrive approximately 40 seconds after impact.

Richter Scale Magnitude: 7.1

Mercalli Scale Intensity at a distance of 200 km:

Felt indoors by many, outdoors by few during the day. At

KEEP IN TOUCH

SUBSCRIBE to my Mailing List and Stay Informed about Upcoming Books and Discounts!
http://files.jaspertscott.com/mailinglist.html

Follow me on Twitter:
@JasperTscott

Look me up on Facebook:
Jasper T. Scott

Check out my website:
www.JasperTscott.com

Or send me an e-mail:
JasperTscott@gmail.com

ABOUT THE AUTHOR

Jasper T. Scott Jasper Scott is the USA Today best-selling author of more than 13 novels written across various genres. He was born and raised in Canada by South African parents, with a British cultural heritage on his mother's side and German on his father's, to which he has now added Latin culture with his wonderful wife.

Jasper spent years living as a starving artist before finally quitting his various jobs to become a full-time writer. In his spare time he enjoys reading, traveling, going to the gym, and spending time with his family.

Printed in Great Britain
by Amazon

32815775R00221